W9-AMB-921

Counting Stars

a novel

Michele Paige Holmes

Covenant Communications, Inc.

Cover Image © iStock Photo. www.istockphoto.com

Cover design copyrighted 2007 by Covenant Communications, Inc.

Published by Covenant Communications, Inc.
American Fork, Utah

Copyright © 2007 by Michele Paige Holmes
All rights reserved. No part of this book may be reproduced in any format or in any medium without the written permission of the publisher, Covenant Communications, Inc., P.O. Box 416, American Fork, UT 84003. This work is not an official publication of The Church of Jesus Christ of Latter-day Saints.

This is a work of fiction. The characters, names, incidents, places, and dialogue are products of the author's imagination, and are not to be construed as real.

Printed in United States of America
First Printing: June 2007

13 12 11 10 09 08 07   10 9 8 7 6 5 4 3 2 1

ISBN 978-1-59811-357-0

Acknowledgements

My critique group will naturally expect that I wax long here, and I cannot disappoint as they and so many others have helped with this manuscript.

Many thanks to Shauna Andreason for introducing me to Annette, and for a long-ago conversation about your degree in landscape design. Little did either of us know how pertinent that would be to Jane's story!

Many thanks to Heather Henrie for years of friendship and for sharing your knowledge and experiences as a newborn-nursery nurse. I am also grateful to my sister-in-law Danna for her willingness to read manuscripts and for supplying Jane's psychology jargon. Great appreciation goes to Leland and Hilda Gamette for filling their suitcases with all manner of Seattle memorabilia and toting it back to me. In addition, I'm ever so grateful to DJ Johnson for the hours spent keeping our computer limping along. Kerry Blair was extremely kind and helpful in getting me firsthand (from her son) information about life in Iraq. And finally, Angela Eschler has been the epitome of patience in guiding me through the editing process.

A simple acknowledgement will never be enough to express the gratitude I feel for my critique group—seven of the most talented, generous people I've ever had the privilege to associate with. Annette, Stephanni, LuAnn, Heather, Lynda, Jeff, and James, thank you for your patience with me. Thank you for sharing your talent, skills, and inspiration and teaching me how to get the stories in my head down on paper. I owe all of you so much.

I am also grateful for an amazing family. My parents have supplied me with a wealth of experiences to draw from (gotta love remembering those Tin Man tights, Dad!), and my mother especially has been a great example of developing talent and reaching for the stars—no matter how far away they may seem.

My children will likely say they suffered long while their mother pursued publication, and I am thankful for their sacrifices. Even moms have dreams, and Spencer, Carissa, Alyssa, and Hannah have helped me to reach mine.

But certainly that never would have happened without my wonderful husband Dixon. Thank you first, dear, for not rolling your eyes out of your head all those years ago when I announced I was going to write a book. Instead, you were my instant champion, and then my hero—taking our children to dozens of Saturday movies by yourself so I would have time to write, using your vacation days so I could finish a manuscript, understanding that printer ink has a place in our budget somewhere between tithing and groceries, and arranging a romantic week in Seattle for the two of us. The list could go on and on. How fortunate I feel to have your love and support. I thank my Father in Heaven daily for the life we share and for the imagination with which He has blessed me.

To Dixon.
For more romance than I could ever begin to write about.

Prologue

Seventeen minutes.

Paul pulled his eyes from the dashboard clock and swung into the nearest parking stall. His seatbelt already unfastened, he leapt from the Jeep and ran toward Swedish Medical Center's emergency entrance. His mind raced. Seventeen minutes had passed since he'd seen Northwest Airlift flashing across the screen of his cell phone.

Seventeen minutes since they'd life-flighted Tami.

He ran through the automatic double doors, just clearing the glass as they slid sideways. Ironic, he thought as he scanned the signs, that in all of his hospital visits over the past year and a half, he'd never been here. Following the arrows, Paul turned left and found himself in front of a stout woman seated at the central desk of the ER. She was on the phone, but he made eye contact.

"I—"

She pursed her lips and used the end of a pencil to point to the sign on the counter.

Please be seated. We will be with you in a few moments. Seated? A few moments? What if he didn't have that long?

"My wife was life-flighted here," he blurted and glanced at his watch again. "About twenty minutes ago. She was in a car accident. She's pregnant."

The woman's expression softened. "Mr. Bryant?"

Her tone was not as stern as he'd expected.

"Yes." He nodded.

"Please hold," she said into the phone, then dropped the receiver on the desk.

Something told him that wasn't a good sign.

She spun her chair around and stood.

Paul met her at the other end of the U-shaped desk. She glanced at him once as they marched briskly toward the stainless steel doors at the end of the hall.

The pity he saw in her eyes terrified him. "My wife's carrying twins. Do you know if—?"

"I'm sorry, but you'll have to talk to the doctor."

"Hey lady," called a youth with spiked hair and multiple piercings. He sprawled across two of the waiting room chairs. "Glo–ri–a," he said, grossly exaggerating as he read her name tag. "I got a busted arm and I been here two hours. How come this guy gets right in?"

Gloria turned her head as she marched past the young man, her earlier matron-like discipline returning. "If you had been hit by a truck, Mr. Stone, I would be glad to see that you're next."

Truck? Paul's heart lurched. The medic hadn't told him that. He reached the doors, his hands cold on the metal as he pushed them open.

* * *

Jane Warner shoved her purse in a cubby and walked over to the sink. Stepping on the foot pedal, she activated the spray of warm water across her hands. A couple of squirts of the gritty soap and she began scrubbing up, remembering to wash all the way to her elbows and in between her fingers as the nurses had instructed.

Last time here, Jane thought as the warm water ran over her hands. She was not surprised at the accompanying pang of sorrow. Beginning tomorrow, she would have free time again. Time for really important things, like working late, ordering takeout, reading books, and renting movies.

To watch alone.

Jane sighed as she pulled a paper towel from the dispenser. A glance at her watch prompted her to hurry. It was 2:20—nearly Andrew's feeding time, and like all infants, he didn't like to be kept waiting. Grabbing a smock from the pile on the counter, Jane pulled it over her arms, reaching behind to fasten the Velcro closures. Taking a mask from the box, she picked up the cylindrical container of breast milk, her sister Caroline's, and walked to the door and pressed the buzzer.

Less than a minute later, Amy, one of the nurses often working Tuesday and Thursday afternoons, opened the door to the Neonatal Intensive Care Unit—or NICU, as those who frequented it called it.

A cacophony of sickly cries came with the open door. Jane felt another pang of sympathy for the infants. Maybe she should have been a nurse. Was twenty-nine too late to start yet another career?

"Here you go," Jane said, handing Amy the container of milk.

"Great. He's ready for it," Amy said. "I think Lisa's just about finished doing his hourly. I'll be back in a second." She carried the milk off toward the prep counter, and Jane headed toward Andrew's bassinet.

"Hey little guy," she said, smiling down at her nephew.

"So he's going home tomorrow?" Lisa asked as she held the stethoscope to Andrew's chest.

"Yep." Jane nodded. "All healthy now, aren't you, buddy?"

In answer to her question, Andrew hiccuped, his slight body lurching against Lisa's hands.

"There," she proclaimed a minute later. "All done. Now you can have your lunch." She stepped aside, and Jane reached down to pick up Andrew. Carefully cradling his head, she crossed the room and settled into one of several rockers while she waited for Amy to bring his bottle.

As she rocked, Jane discreetly watched the woman at the end of the row struggling to hold her daughter despite all the tubes and wires attached to the child. Jane ran her finger across Andrew's cheek, grateful his lungs were better, that his illness had not been nearly as serious as those of so many babies here.

Lisa brought a pillow for her arm. "So are his parents going to come and get him—or are you going to continue as substitute mom awhile longer?"

"No," Jane said sadly. "My job's about finished. Caroline is taking the other kids to the doctor today to get the all clear."

"Mmm. I imagine that'll be a relief," Amy said as she walked toward them, bottle in hand. "What a nightmare—delivering your fourth child and three others at home with the chicken pox."

Jane nodded. "Yeah, but the worst of it was Caroline getting it too."

"She'll never forget this," Amy said with a laugh as she handed Jane the bottle.

"No," Jane agreed as she nudged the nipple into Andrew's mouth. "It's definitely been a month to remember."

"I'd say your sister owes you big-time," Lisa said.

"I suppose she does," Jane agreed quietly.

The nurses went to tend the other babies in the NICU while Jane rocked Andrew contentedly, wondering for the thousandth time what it would be like if he was her son and would be coming home with her. She was going to miss being here, caring for him every day. She loved all of her fourteen nieces and nephews, but she and Andrew already had a special bond, one she hoped wouldn't change when she didn't see him every day.

"Hey, Lisa," another nurse called as she stepped into the NICU.

"Over here." Lisa waved her hand from behind a monitor and the tangle of cords attached to it.

"Who's charge with you today?" The nurse moved quickly toward a row of empty bassinets.

"Heather, but she's with a mom right now," Lisa answered.

"Page her." There was tension in her voice.

Lisa walked toward the phone. "If you need someone, I've got eleven nurses on this side and only nine babies. We've sent four home today."

The nurse shook her head. "I need Heather. We've got new patients."

"Patient*s?*" Lisa asked, emphasizing the *s* as she punched in Heather's number.

"Twins," the nurse confirmed as she rushed through loading up the bassinets. "Probably about thirty weeks. Their mother arrested on the way—lung punctured—a car accident."

"Did they get her back?" Lisa asked.

"No. They were headed to Harborview, but . . ."

Lisa nodded somberly. "Now the babies are priority."

The nurse rolled the first bassinet out and returned for the second. "They're delivering right now. Respiratory's already down there. Tell Heather I'm—"

Heather ran through the door, a frantic look on her face. "Who's coding? Is it Patrick?"

"Everyone here is fine," Lisa quickly assured her.

"But we've got twins," the other nurse explained as she ran past, grabbing Heather's arm. "Been without oxygen approximately—" The door swung shut behind them, and Jane forced her attention back to Andrew. She felt the sting of tears as she hoisted him gently to her shoulder and began patting his back.

"Poor babies," she whispered.

* * *

Patricia Neilson paced the emergency waiting room. It was after eleven, and her back and shoulders ached. There was no logical reason for her to continue waiting and yet . . . She stuck her hand in her jacket pocket, fingers closing automatically around the paper there. She had to stay. Perhaps it was just morbid curiosity, perhaps it was the need to keep the promise she'd made to a dying woman.

Or was it because she worried the car wreck she'd responded to earlier was not simply an accident?

Whatever the case, she determined to wait it out and watch Paul Bryant's face as she handed him the note from his wife.

What kind of a creep leaves his wife when she's seven months pregnant with his children? she wondered again. *A pretty average one,* came the answer. She'd known her share of low-life guys, but today was the first time she'd felt the urge to do something about it.

Patricia sank into a nearby chair and closed her eyes, remembering Tami Bryant's gasping breaths and her last words. *God must have known I couldn't live without you.* What could that mean except that her husband was abandoning her in her time of greatest need? And *Find our babies a mother.* How heartbreaking. Patricia clenched her fists, thinking that she couldn't wait to give Paul Bryant a piece of her mind—at least. And if there was *any* indication her hunch about the accident was correct, any at all . . .

She looked up as a man stepped off the elevator. His head was downcast and he looked extremely tired. He adjusted his Mariners baseball cap, and in that second she glimpsed a completely bald head. The man came nearer, heading for the exit. As he walked by she noticed the pallor of his skin—a sickly yellow. Immediately, her years as a nurse on the oncology floor came to mind. This man looked sick. A patient maybe? Leaving this late at night? Possible in the ER, but—

Patricia's heart lurched as she watched him bend over the drinking fountain and she saw the unmistakable bulge of a port-a-catheter beneath his shirt. This man *was* sick. Her heart sank, and her previous judgments fled as a new possibility entered her mind.

* * *

Paul stopped at the water fountain and drank for a long time, trying to soothe his raw throat. He straightened and felt for the candy bar in his pocket. A kind nurse had handed it to him hours before, but until now he hadn't been able to think about eating. Now he knew if he didn't, he'd never make it home.

Does it matter? The thought came to him as he tore the wrapper and bit into the chocolate. What reason did he have to make it safely home?

Two of them, upstairs.

With difficulty Paul swallowed and started walking again. He'd almost reached the exit when a woman called to him.

"Mr. Bryant?" Her voice was tentative.

"Yes?" Turning, he glanced back in the direction he'd just come. His eyes flicked to the double doors. "Has something—?"

"No." The woman shook her head quickly, then walked toward him. "I'm not a nurse here. I'm a paramedic. I work for Airlift." Her hand went automatically to the symbol emblazoned on her jacket.

"Oh, I see." Paul shoved one shaking hand in his pocket and tightened his grip on the candy bar.

"I came to—I waited to—I was with your wife," the woman said. Taking a deep breath, she continued. "She was alive when we got to the accident. She asked me to tell you something."

Paul felt like he'd been punched. He exhaled sharply. "You spoke with Tami?"

The woman nodded and took another step toward him. "I'm so sorry." She held out an unopened sterile bandage. "I didn't have anything else to write on, and I wanted to remember what she said. I knew it was important."

Paul blinked twice and looked up at the ceiling, but he pulled his hand from his pocket and his shaking fingers took the bandage. "Thank you," he said when he trusted himself to speak again. He clutched the bandage in his hand, knowing he didn't dare look at it until he was alone.

"I'm so sorry," the woman repeated.

Paul shifted uncomfortably. "Me too." He met her eyes briefly and saw pity there. "Thank you again—for waiting so long. It was very kind." He turned toward the exit. As he left, he felt the woman's eyes on him.

He stepped into the cool night air, his fingers still trembling around the bandage in his hand. *Tami's last thoughts. Her last words.* A wave of nausea washed over him, and he willed his body to make it to the car. He needed to get home—needed to shower, get something to eat, get some measure of control back. Then he would read Tami's note.

He unlocked the door as a tear slipped down his cheek. He opened the door and slid into the driver's seat, leaning forward, his hands and face over the steering wheel.

He wasn't going anywhere.

After several anguished minutes, his tears and shaking stopped and he found the willpower to sit back. Slowly, he opened his fingers and smoothed the bandage flat. He flipped on the dome light and began to read:

> *God must have known I couldn't live without you, Paul. Find our babies a mother. You know who their father should be. I'll be waiting.*
>
> *I love you.*
> *Tami*

Part One

Then Come the Babies in the Baby Carriage

Chapter One

Jane turned into the ferry parking lot. *Unbelievable.*

"Does that guy camp here or what?" she mumbled to herself as she nudged her Corolla into lane three behind a green Ford Taurus. Never mind that they were the only two cars in the lot. She wanted lane three, and Green Taurus had beat her. Again.

"Oh well," Jane said aloud, then stuck a straw through the lid of her University of Washington mug. She picked it up and enjoyed a taste of her First Friday breakfast special—a homemade smoothie replete with strawberries, raspberries, bananas, sherbet, vanilla ice cream and *real* whipping cream. Not exactly a dieter's delight, but it *was* the first Friday of the month, her ritual time for indulgence.

Setting the drink aside, Jane eyed the rolled newspaper on the seat, figuring that it wouldn't hurt to get an early start on the personals. She opened the paper and had just read the first ad when Mr. Green Taurus opened his door and stepped out, facing the bay, away from her. Jane's hand froze.

This was revolutionary. In nine months the guy had never set so much as a toe out of his car. Not here in the parking lot when there were twenty minutes to spare, and not even on the ferry.

She glanced at her door locks and then around the lot, relieved to see a truck in lane one and two more cars pulling in. Lowering the paper, Jane nonchalantly returned her attention to the man standing a dozen feet away. Still thinking of the personals, she sized him up. *Single White Male?* Maybe. She was too far away to see the ring finger of his left hand. Or perhaps he was a DWM, his fixation for arriving early having driven a sane wife away.

He stood still, looking out toward Seattle. Jane continued her perusal.

Approximately six feet. Hair—sandy blond, over the collar, a little shaggy. Eyes? Maybe blue. Always went well with blond hair. Athletic? Not particularly, Jane thought, noting the slight build of his shoulders. Yet there was something alluring there. Something familiar . . .

"Got it." She grinned. He looked like Westley from *The Princess Bride*—currently number thirty-seven on her list of favorite romantic movies.

Okay, so the white shirt and navy slacks didn't exactly fit the bill, but that hair told the whole story. Jane leaned back in her seat, imagining.

Westley looked across the shimmering lake, his heart breaking as he watched his beloved Buttercup drift away, a captive of evil Prince Humperdinck. Pity Westley didn't realize that the real love of his life, Jane, was ever-so close— parked behind him in the '94 Corolla, a 700-calorie shake in her hand . . .

Green Taurus/Westley turned sideways, watching the ferry approach Bainbridge. He glanced back toward her car for a moment, and Jane gave him a hesitant smile, which he did not return. Embarrassed, she quickly looked down at her paper. Picking up her mug, she took a long drink of smoothie, nearly choking as a chunk of berry came through the straw.

Apparently it wasn't a morning for fairy tales.

* * *

Being second in lane three pretty much guaranteed she'd get her favorite seat on the ferry. Nevertheless, as soon as she'd parked, Jane got out of her car and hurried toward the nearest stairwell. She took the stairs two at a time—not only because it was faster, but she'd read somewhere it was good for your thighs too, kind of like those lunges on her Tae Bo video.

Her favorite seat by the window was waiting. In fact, the entire row was empty. Jane sat down and put her purse and mug on the seat beside her. Chances were the ferry wouldn't be full, and if no one sat next to her she wouldn't have to feel embarrassed about reading the personals.

It wasn't as if it was something she did every day. It was a first-Friday-of-the-month-only indulgence, one she looked forward to with hope and anticipation. After all, it was her mother who'd said one never knew where true love might be found. Though at the time, she'd been referring to the singles' conference she'd signed Jane up for.

Remembering that conference, Jane grimaced. The speakers were good and the activities enjoyable, but that was as far as it went. Dancing with men twice her age or twice divorced hadn't made for a stellar weekend. It was shortly after that she'd decided it was time to broaden her scope and start thinking about meeting and dating guys who weren't LDS. Of course her parents didn't approve, but they also didn't understand what it was like to be single in a church of families.

Jane pulled a red pen from her purse and tucked it behind her ear— prepared just in case today yielded more than the usual. Starting at the top of the page, she read carefully, her finger moving down the first column.

DWM, mid forties seeks . . .

Too old.

SWM seeks SWF for a great time, a few laughs, nothing permanent . . .

Nothing new.

SWM looking for fit SWF, preferably blonde, 5'7" . . .

"Yeah, I'd prefer it too," Jane muttered as she toyed with a strand of her brown hair. She frowned as she finished reading the first several, shallow ads. Wasn't there anyone out there interested in a real relationship? With a sigh she set the paper down.

"Hey, Jane."

She froze at the sound of the familiar male voice.

"Been a long time." A guitar case swung into view followed by telltale black boots.

Without looking up, Jane snatched her purse and turned toward the window as she felt the jostle of the connected seats. *It can't be.* Heart racing, she watched the whitecaps on the water, the nightmare she'd lived two and half years earlier replaying in her mind.

"Aren't you even going to say hi to an old friend?"

"*Friend?*" Jane turned to face Jay Kendrich. "I have a restraining order against you."

"*Had,* actually." Jay grinned boyishly. "It expired six months ago."

"Then I'll just have to see the judge about another one."

"I love it when you're angry." Jay reclined in his seat, his arm extended casually over the back of the chair between them.

Jane's eyes blazed in anger as she took in his appearance. Same long dark hair, though at least it looked better clean and tied in a ponytail. He wore a long-sleeved shirt—no doubt to hide his needle marks.

She pinched her lips together as she grabbed her mug and stood. With her purse in one hand and her drink in the other, the newspaper slid to the floor. Jay bent over to pick it up.

"You've taken to reading the personals, I see." He stared pointedly at her left hand.

Jane skirted his guitar and made for the aisle. He reached out and caught her wrist, tipping her drink precariously.

"Let go," Jane whispered, furious. She didn't want to make a scene, but she was not going to be pulled into Jay's lair again.

He loosened his grip but leaned forward. "Do you ever answer them?"

"*What?*"

"Do you ever respond to any of the personals? You know, go on a date with one of those poor saps who advertise?"

"That's none of your business."

"It could be." He released her so suddenly she stumbled backward. Jane felt a slow burn creeping up her face.

To her surprise, Jay didn't laugh. "Have a good life, Jane," he said quietly. "Oh, and happy thirtieth next month."

Just leave, a voice inside her head warned, but she stood rooted to the spot. "How did you know—?"

"Lifted your wallet at the center one day—you were on the phone."

"How dare you." Her eyes blazed again.

"Yeah," Jay said, completely serious now. "I was a real jerk then, and I'm sorry."

For a brief moment their eyes met, and Jane was shaken by what she saw there. His gaze was even more intense than she remembered. She knew she could still lose herself in those eyes, honest-to-goodness blue eyes that, today at least, didn't appear to be glazed over or bloodshot from drug use.

"Let me see your arms," she demanded.

Jay raised an eyebrow. "I thought you quit counseling."

"I did. Your fault too. Now roll up your sleeves." She lowered herself into the chair across from him and waited expectantly.

Jay sighed and began to unbutton his cuffs. "All right."

Jane watched with trepidation as he neatly rolled first the right and then the left sleeve up. Her eyes widened. His arms were clean.

She wasn't fooled for a minute.

"Are you snorting, or is it pills now?" she asked caustically.

Jay pushed his sleeves down and took his time buttoning them. When he was done, he leaned back in his chair and looked up at her. "Nothing. I'm clean. *Your* fault."

Jane wasn't sure what to say. She just stared at him, wishing she had polygraph abilities.

How many times before had he fed her that lie? *Don't fall for it,* her inner voice warned.

Jay raised his eyebrows. "What would it take for you to believe me?"

"I don't know," she answered truthfully.

"How about seventy-two-hour surveillance? You could hang out at my place for a weekend and—"

"You haven't changed," Jane snapped as she rose from her chair. "Everything is still a big joke."

"Nah, Jane. This isn't a joke. I'm sorry." He raked his fingers through his hair and stood just a foot away, facing her. "I wanted to see you today to show you I *have* changed—got my life in order. I stayed away longer than I had to, but I thought of you every day, biding my time till I thought you might be able to forget how I was and . . . Forgive me?"

She took a deep breath. "You're forgiven. And I'm glad you've turned your life around—really I am. But I'm leaving."

"I wish you wouldn't, because—" He took a step closer and spoke quietly. "I also came to ask you out."

Jane shook her head as she looked up at him. "No. Don't start that again."

"Nothing ever got started. I wasn't good enough for you then."

"You weren't *old* enough for me. And you're not now. You're only what—twenty-five?"

"Twenty-six—today."

She frowned. "It's your birthday?" This complicated things. She knew Jay had no family and would likely spend the day alone. How could she turn him down on his birthday? Yet how could she *not* turn him down?

"I came to ask the prettiest girl I know to have lunch with me." He shoved his hands in his pockets and gave her a half-smile, as if he sensed her dilemma and a possible victory.

"I have a lunch appointment," she said curtly.

"Dinner then?"

"No," Jane said louder than she'd intended. Two rows away a little boy stared, but his mother was engrossed in a book. The only other person nearby was a suit, his eyes riveted to his laptop. She let out a relieved sigh as she looked at Jay again and spoke quieter this time.

"Listen, Jay. Before, you weren't sober, so maybe you don't remember what a wreck you made me. But *I* remember it well. Because of you, I left a very difficult, prestigious program in my last semester of a master's degree. Instead of being able to treat—"

"Fruitcakes, you became a fruitcake yourself," Jay finished.

Jane found it maddening that she had to fight back a smile. "Well that's not really the scientific term, but yeah. I was a mess. You were too. But now we're both doing great, so let's just part ways and be happy for each other."

"I'd rather be happy *with* each other." He winked at her.

Instead of smiling, she stepped over his guitar case and into the aisle.

"Wait," he pled, moving in front of her.

She took a step backward. "Jay, this would never work. Not now, not in a year—"

"Great idea," he said. "I'll take no for an answer today if you'll promise to think about going to lunch with me on my birthday next year."

She shook her head.

"Just listen to my terms. A year from today you meet me on the morning ferry. If you've got a guy by then—from your personals or whatever—I'll leave you alone, just walk away for good. *But,* if you're still single I get to treat you to lunch at a restaurant of your choice. You can even bring someone with you—your parents, a bodyguard, your sister's kids. Say yes and you've got nothing to lose."

"Except my sanity," Jane muttered.

He gave her a look filled with hope.

"You're a good-looking guy, Jay. And if you're clean now, why not find some nice girl your age?"

"Because I owe you."

Not this again. "You don't."

He shrugged. "Easy for you to say, but from this vantage point, I'd have been six feet under a long time ago except for a nice girl with pretty brown eyes." He tried to look into those eyes now, but Jane kept her gaze fixed on the toe of her shoe. "A really wonderful girl who didn't give up on me."

She looked at him. "But I did give up on you."

His eyes met hers. "You gave up on yourself."

Awkward silence followed this comment. Jane gripped the shoulder strap of her purse, aware that an exit was only a few feet behind her. She closed her eyes, feeling a monstrous headache coming on. What a day this was going to be, and she wasn't even at work yet.

Jay stepped forward, took the smoothie from her numb hand, and set it on the seat. He rubbed her cold fingers in his own. "Ever hear of hand-fasting?" he asked in a quirky Scottish accent.

Jane's eyebrows shot up. "As in a year and a day—that medieval marriage thing?"

Jay nodded, the serious look in his eyes giving her sudden chills.

She tried to pull her hand away. Both the boy and his mother were staring at them. "I've heard of it. I read romance novels."

"I remember that," Jay teased and held her hand firm. "But it's not just in stories. I had an ancestor—a long time ago—actually get married that way. It's quite a story."

"The ferry's nearly docking," Jane said. "And my car's up front."

"So handfast with me then—for lunch only," he added quickly, seeing her eyes grow large. "Agree that one year from today you'll meet me on this same ferry, and *if* prince charming hasn't swept you away by then, we'll do lunch. Nothing more. I promise."

"You *promise?* You swear that after one lunch, you'll leave me alone forever?"

"Ouch. But if that's what you want . . ."

She looked at him skeptically. "And I won't see you until then? Not even once?"

"I'll disappear completely."

"All right," Jane said, feeling her hand pumped up and down, then finally released. "Bye," she called, grabbing her mug and the paper as she headed for the door.

* * *

Jay picked up his guitar and walked the opposite direction. *Best to start right away,* he thought, keeping his promise to disappear. He climbed the stairs to the top deck and walked to the back of the ferry. A quick look around told him that he was alone—most everyone else was preparing to dock. Lucky for him, he'd sold his car last week.

He set his guitar case down and knelt next to it, undoing the clips. Reaching inside, he ran his fingers down the inside of the case lid until he came to a slight swell in the fabric. His fingers located a transparent thread, and he pulled until the velvet puckered, then fell away. A clear plastic bag dropped into his hand. Jay closed his fingers around it, then shut the case and stood.

A slow stroll along the deck convinced him he was still alone. Standing beside the rail, he opened his hand and stared at the tiny pouch in his palm. The white granules inside shimmered in the sunlight, and Jay could already feel their texture on his tongue and taste their bitter tang.

His private heaven—and hell.

He'd saved this bag for a year and a half—hadn't even known he had it until a few months after rehab. And then one day there it was, his manna, stuffed in the toe of a pair of shoes he hadn't worn in years. He'd told himself that he would save it. It would be his reward, his comfort to fall back on if things didn't work out. Countless times he'd taken the bag out, looked at it, rubbed it between his palms. Once he'd even brought the plastic to his face, pressing it against his nostrils. But he had never opened it. He kept promises now—especially those he made to himself.

So here he was this morning, having finally reached the designated day of his reward. And here was his comfort waiting for him because things hadn't worked out. There would be no birthday lunch with Jane. But he deserved a present, didn't he? No one else would be giving him one. But then, come to think of it, he couldn't recall a birthday where he had received any gifts.

Nothing had changed, and it wouldn't do to feel sorry for himself now. He'd learned that was the first step on the path to self-destruction.

Jay rubbed the baggie between his fingers one last time and then, with a flick of his wrist, watched as it sailed out into the bay. Withdrawing his wallet from his back pocket, he thumbed through it quickly, searching for the paper amid the bills.

It was real. He stared at it—this ticketless travel voucher that was about to drastically alter the course of his life. The confirmation number stood out in bold, along with the flight number and times:

American Airlines 1263
Departure: SEA 1:05 P.M.
Arrival: BOS 9:23 P.M.
One way.

Jay closed his wallet and turned, facing Seattle in the glory of the morning sun.

Because of Jane, another day was his to live. And if that was all the reward he ever got, it was enough.

Chapter Two

The Emerald Realty downtown office was quiet when, at exactly 12:00, Tara Mollagen opened her purse and took out a compact and lipstick. Squinting in the small mirror, she applied a fresh coat of *Pink Pout* and practiced doing just that as she slid her feet into silver pumps beneath her desk.

Shoes in place, she left her chair and strode purposefully down the row of cubicles. Stopping at Jane's nook, she poked her head inside.

"You up for lunch today?"

"Can't," Jane said without taking her eyes off the computer screen. She rolled the mouse, moving the cursor to the PRINT icon. "I've got an appointment with the Sweviecs."

"You *still* haven't found those poor people a house?" Tara drummed her polished nails on top of the divider.

Jane rolled her eyes. "The only thing poor about them is their attitude. And I've found them *thirty-seven* houses."

"Ah," Tara said, understanding. "Shown them everything between here and Canada, have you?"

Jane nodded. "And then some."

"Well perhaps, as Zack would say, it's 'time to cut bait.'"

Jane spun around in her chair. "And just how is Zack these days?" She looked Tara straight in the eye. "He cut your bait yet?"

"Nooo," Tara said slowly. "We had a fight last night, but—"

"About?" Jane crossed her arms. "Spill it."

"My cat. He doesn't like cats, and when I moved in I brought Taffy. Zack said it'd be okay, but now it's not." Tara sniffed loudly.

"Come here," Jane said, opening her arms as she stood. She gave Tara a hug, then reached behind her to retrieve the box of tissues from the desk.

"Sorry," Tara mumbled, blowing her nose. "I always blubber."

"It's good to cry," Jane assured her, making a mental note to buy more tissue. She'd just given her fourth and last box to Tara. Poor soul. This boyfriend had her up to a box a week. "Talk about cutting bait . . ."

"I know, I know. I'll have to get rid of the cat."

"Tara!" Jane said sharply. "Don't you dare. Just think about this. First he threw out your plants. Then he talked you out of your art class, and now he wants to get rid of your pet. Next thing you know, he'll want to put your parents in an old folks home."

"Do you really think so?" Tara asked anxiously. Fresh tears appeared in her eyes before she'd pulled another tissue out. "Oh Jane."

Jane looked at her watch. She had twenty-five minutes before she was due to meet the Sweviecs. She only had three new properties to show them, but . . . Tara needed her. "All right. I've got a few minutes to spare."

Tara's face brightened. "Great. That's enough time to forget our sorrows in one of those fabulous orange rolls at the bakery."

"I really shouldn't," Jane said, grabbing her purse. "My breakfast was already three days worth of Weight Watchers points."

"So," Tara said, leading the way. "Today's your First Friday thing, isn't it?"

* * *

"You know you can stay at my place." Jane repeated the offer she had made many times before when trying to convince Tara that living with her boyfriend wasn't a good idea.

"Thanks, but no." Tara licked the frosting from her fingers, then tried changing the subject. "So why don't you just dump the Sweviecs?"

"Because if I can hang in there and make a sale, the commission will cover my mortgage for months." Jane glanced at her watch again.

"Is it worth it?"

Jane chewed her roll and considered. A smile crossed her face as she thought of the new white picket fence surrounding her yard. It was definitely worth it. She looked at Tara. "Is *Zack* worth it?"

"It's better than being alone."

"Hmm." Jane slid off her stool and headed for the door. "That's a matter of opinion."

Tara followed her. "That's not fair. I mean—you've never taken the relationship plunge, so how would you know whether it's better or not?"

Jane rolled her eyes. "I know."

"You don't," Tara insisted. "How could you? You won't even get your feet wet. I bet you haven't been on a date in weeks."

Months, Jane amended silently as she walked toward the office, trying to pretend Tara's remark hadn't stung.

"If I don't take the plunge, it's because the water's shallow." She thought of Tara's previous boyfriend, Stan, who'd been about as intellectually deep as her toilet bowl. "And I refuse to stick my feet—or even my little toe—in water that's murky." She looked sideways at Tara. "And I'm telling you, Zack is murky. *Manipulative* and murky."

Tara's shoulders slumped, and she stopped as they reached the office door. "I know. I'm not so blind I don't see it too. But it's just that sometimes you've got to settle a bit, and I *swear,* even settling is better than being alone."

Jane stared at her, unconvinced.

"Think of it this way," Tara said. "This world's full of pollution. You can't escape it anywhere. There are no pristine, sparkling lakes left—or if there are they're sure hidden well, and getting to them involves far more hiking than I'm ready to do. Anyway—" She waved her hand in the air. "Here in the city, you gotta settle for the best water you can get. And once you're used to the taste, it really isn't too bad."

Jane pushed open the door and held it while Tara, her shoulders square again, walked inside. *Is she right?* Jane wondered and thought again of her morning encounter with Jay. Should she have gotten her feet wet? What would one lunch date have hurt? Jay had a past, and he certainly wasn't LDS, but what had years of singles dances and activities yielded her?

Nothing.

It was too late for that lunch date now, though it wasn't too late to do something else. A determined look in her eyes, Jane walked through the door and headed toward her cubicle. The want ads were calling her. *Ever answer one?* Jay had asked. *Ever go out with one of those poor saps?* They couldn't all be poor saps. Somewhere out there, there had to be a normal, decent guy with no defects—other than that he was suffering from the same malady she was.

An acute case of loneliness.

Chapter Three

Caroline surveyed the contents of the freezer. *What to fix for dinner?* Nothing sounded good—or worth the effort of cooking, anyway. It was Friday, and she needed to get out of the house. She closed the freezer as a plan formed. She'd arrange a sitter, feed the kids macaroni and cheese, then she and Ryan could grab a burger and maybe catch a movie. It would be heaven to sit in a dark theater together, watching something that wasn't animated, and without the threat of spilled soda or the interruption of having to take a child to the bathroom. She walked to the sink and stared out the kitchen window, thinking dreamily of the possibility.

It was almost five o'clock. She would have to find a babysitter fast.

She picked up the phone, hitting 2 on the speed dial for her parents. Her mom would understand her sudden need for escape. But the phone rang and rang until finally, discouraged, Caroline set the receiver down. If only her parents would quit living in the dark ages and get an answering machine or a cell phone.

She glanced at the fridge calendar. It was September fifth, the first Friday of the month—Jane's romance night. Well, maybe if she was just reading a book she could read it over here. Caroline picked up the cordless again, this time hitting 1 on the speed dial. She smiled when Jane picked up after the second ring.

"So who's your hot date for tonight?" Caroline asked as she dug through the laundry for a pair of socks. "Or should I ask which romance author has a new book out this week?"

"No date and no book," Jane said. "And hi to you too, sis."

Caroline heard the familiar sound of chocolate chips being dumped into a mixer.

"No guy real *or* imaginary?" she asked, stumped both by the lack of socks in the pile of clean laundry and her sister's answer.

"Actually, I read two romance novels already this week," Jane admitted.

"You *cheated*," Caroline said. "Tsk. Tsk. You know that's breaking your commitment with Hopeless Romantics Anonymous."

"Yeah, well it was a rough couple of days."

"Excuses, excuses," Caroline muttered, holding up a pair of Jessica's socks. "So what *are* you doing, then?"

"Not babysitting, if that's what you're getting at," Jane said. "I've got a batch of double chocolate chip cookies going in the oven and a pint of Häagen Dazs Macadamia Nut Brittle in the freezer."

Strike two. "And the man?" Caroline asked, squeezing her foot into her daughter's sock.

"I'm thinking it's a Darcy night."

"Must've been some week if you're holing up with *Pride and Prejudice* again."

Jane laughed. "You know me so well."

Caroline frowned. "I thought Christopher dropped one of those tapes in the bathtub last summer."

"Yeah," Jane groaned. "He dropped the video in the tub, my brush in the toilet, and an expensive library book in the sink. That kid has some serious water issues." She sighed. "But I bought the DVD set today, the A&E edition."

Caroline gave up on the sock. "What time you starting?" Getting out without Ryan wouldn't be as much fun, but chocolate chip cookies and Jane Austen was a pretty good offer too.

"I'm already on the second hour. You're not thinking of coming, are you?"

"Absolutely," Caroline said, her mind suddenly made up.

"You'd have to spend the night," Jane said. "The last ferry—"

"And I'd have to bring Andrew and put him to bed at your place."

"Great." Jane said, meaning it. "I'd love to see my favorite nephew, and this house could do with some testosterone." She tried to laugh. "Can you leave Ryan by himself with the rest of the kids?" she mumbled through a mouthful of cookie dough.

"He'll be fine," Caroline assured her. "Don't watch any more until I get there, okay?"

"All right, but bring your own ice cream."

* * *

"This is the best part. Watch how he looks at her when they dance."

"You've pointed out half a dozen *best parts* already. Quit narrating the movie," Caroline complained.

Jane ignored her. "You can see it in Darcy's eyes. He's lost in her, *hungering* for her." She sighed. "I wish someone would look at me like that."

"You don't," Caroline said. "Trust me."

"Yes. I do," Jane insisted. She stabbed her spoon into the ice cream again as she stared at the television.

Caroline reached for another cookie, then kicked her slippered feet up on the old trunk that served as Jane's coffee table. "That's the only way anyone ever looks at me—with hunger in their eyes. At three in the morning it's Andrew howling for a bottle. Then at six thirty it's 'what's for breakfast, Mom, and did I get a Twinkie in my lunch box?' When they walk in the door after school it's 'I'm st-aaar-ving Mom. Got any cookies?' Even the dog only looks at me when he wants to eat."

Jane elbowed Caroline. "You know what I mean."

"I know *exactly* what you mean, and let me tell you, by the time Ryan looks at me with that kind of hunger, it's ten thirty at night, and I just want to slug him."

Jane rolled her eyes. "You're real romantic."

"Just wait. Someday you'll be there, and I'll remind you."

Jane turned to her. "Will I be there? I mean, honestly? One more month and I'll be thirty. I haven't had a date in—in I don't know how long, and I haven't got any prospects for one either. So how am I ever going to be *there*—with a husband and a house full of kids?" She looked back at the movie just in time to see Elizabeth walk away. "Wake up. He loves you." Irritated, Jane grabbed the remote and snapped the television off. She put the lid back on her ice cream and slammed it onto the table.

"I'm sorry, Jane. I didn't mean to—"

"I know," Jane muttered. "It's okay." She leaned her head back against the couch and closed her eyes.

"Was this part of your rough week?" Caroline asked.

"No—yes. I don't know." Jane sighed, then opened her eyes and turned to Caroline. "I ran into Jay Kendrich on the ferry this morning."

Caroline leaned closer. "Jay? As in restraining-order Jay?"

"Yep." Jane nodded. "Apparently after a few years those things aren't good anymore."

"Well, are you going to get another one?"

"No. I don't think I'll have to. Jay was actually pretty—agreeable."

"*Agreeable?*" Caroline asked, bewildered. "Jane, this is the guy who made you so nuts that you dropped out of life for a year. This is the guy who was one beat away from a stalker."

"I know. I know." Jane picked at a fuzz on the arm of the sofa. "He seemed different today. People can change."

"Maybe." Caroline bit her lip. "You're not going to see him again are you? Please tell me you didn't agree to a date or anything."

Jane rolled her eyes. "I'm not stupid. I was actually quite curt with him."

"Good," Caroline said, relief in her voice. "You had me worried."

"I promised to meet him on the ferry one year from today. And if I'm still unattached, then he can take me out to lunch."

"So you did agree to a date!" Caroline exclaimed.

Jane frowned at her. "Thanks for the vote of confidence."

"I didn't mean it that way." Caroline touched Jane's arm. "It's just that the guy is trouble. You can do better than that."

"Can I?" Jane looked at her." I don't see how, Caroline. I'm getting old. It's getting real lonely."

"Come here," Caroline put her arm around Jane and pulled her against her shoulder.

Jane sighed as she leaned into her sister. "I know Jay was messed up, but if he's not now—if there is even a chance . . ." Her voice trailed off.

"I don't think—" Caroline began.

Jane continued. "Whenever we were in the same room together, there was this feeling, we were just drawn to each other. I tried to avoid it. I gave all the other patients in my class more attention than him, but it was like he had some kind of magnetic pull I couldn't resist. And that one time he kissed me—" She closed her eyes, remembering the bittersweet moment when Jay had stopped her in the hall, taken her face in his hands, and kissed her as she'd never been kissed before. There was simply no way to describe it. Fireworks was an understatement. It was *Gone with the Wind, Casablanca,* and *Ever After* all rolled into one. It left her breathless, head spinning, heart pounding. It became the moment she knew the stuff written in romance novels could be true.

Jane opened her eyes and looked up at Caroline. "I'd do it again. It was stupid to send him away today."

Caroline sat up straight, faced Jane, and gripped her shoulders. "Listen to me. All that was between you and Jay was *chemistry.* And while I'll be the first to admit that physical attraction *is* very nice, I also know there *has* to be more. There has to be friendship and faith and love—*life-altering love,* Jane. That's what you're holding out for."

"What Jay and I had was life altering." Jane smiled sadly. "I lost my internship and couldn't graduate, remember?"

"Oh Jane." Caroline pulled her close again. "You are going to meet the right guy. And he's going to be worth every moment, every hour, every day that you had to wait for him. And all your sisters will be insanely jealous because this guy is so great. And then we're all going to clobber him for waiting so long to find you."

Jane gave a halfhearted attempt at laughter. "When is all this going to happen?"

"That, I don't know," Caroline admitted.

"And how will I meet this guy? Where will I find him?"

"I don't know specifics, but I am serious. It's a gut feeling I have. Mother's instinct." Caroline brought her palm to her chest.

"You're not my mother."

"Might as well have been for as often as I got stuck watching you."

"All right then." Jane sat up and reached for her portfolio next to the couch. "Tell me your mother's instinct on this." She held out the newspaper with the circled personal.

"A single's ad?" Caroline took it, reading quickly.

```
Seeking kind, loving woman to be the
        mother of my children.

           Call 555-3288
```

She raised an eyebrow. "Different and definitely to the point."

Jane nodded. "I'm thinking of answering it."

"Bad idea. Probably some psychopath."

Jane shrugged. "Could be. If I get a date, I figure I'll have you and the kids tail me for safety."

It was Caroline's turn to laugh. "That'd be enough to change anyone's mind about being a father. But I'm serious, Jane. That ad is scary."

"Not compared to all the others." Jane took the paper from Caroline and unfolded it. "Look at these—bust size, hair color, age requirements. They're all terrible. But *this* guy just wants someone kind and loving. He wants what I want . . . a family."

"An *eternal* family?" Caroline looked skeptical. "Come on, Jane. Odds are highly unlikely this guy is LDS."

"I know," Jane admitted. "But I'm not having any luck with guys that are in the Church. And I'm tired of being alone."

Caroline looked at her sadly. "So . . . what? You've just decided that's it. You're going to lower your expectations that much?"

"I haven't lowered anything," Jane insisted. "It's just this one ad. I can't explain—I'm just drawn to it."

"This whole meet-a-complete-stranger business makes me very nervous." Caroline sighed. "You'd have to meet in a public place in the middle of the day, and I'd want to be there—"

Jane shook her head.

"Right outside then," Caroline reluctantly conceded. "Mom will kill me when she hears about this. Are you sure you want to—?" Caroline broke off as Jane turned to her, conviction in her eyes.

"I am." Jane took a deep breath. "Maybe it's *my* mother's intuition starting to kick in."

Chapter Four

"You don't have anything for breakfast," Caroline complained as she riffled through Jane's kitchen cupboards the next morning.

"Grapefruit—right crisper," Jane said as she peeled off her gardening gloves. She bent to unlace her muddy shoes. "It's the only acceptable breakfast after last night's chocolate and ice cream rampage."

Caroline wrinkled her nose. "Ugh."

"What, were you hoping for Lucky Charms?" Jane teased. She pulled off her shoes and left them on the mat by the back door.

"No, but Belgian waffles, crisp bacon, and fresh-squeezed orange juice would be nice."

"Ah," Jane said, grabbing a grapefruit from the fridge. "Mom's classic Saturday sleepover breakfast." She looked at Caroline. "Sorry. Guess I didn't plan well." Jane grabbed two knives and spoons from the silverware caddy on the counter. She sat across the table from Caroline, put the grapefruit on a paper plate and began cutting. "Where's Andrew?"

"Asleep again. I just nursed him." Caroline reluctantly accepted the grapefruit half Jane held out to her. "Did you call yet?"

Jane glanced at the newspaper on the table. "It's too early."

"You've been up for hours."

"So?" Jane began sectioning her grapefruit. "Not everyone feels the need to fertilize while the dew is still on."

"Calling early will let you know right away if this guy is a morning person like yourself." Caroline reached behind her and took the cordless phone from its charger on the counter.

"I don't want to know if he gets up early. In fact, I don't want to know anything about him." Jane took the phone from Caroline and set it aside. "The whole thing was a bad idea, born of an acute case of late-night loneliness."

"Oh no you don't," Caroline said, snatching the phone and paper. "Last night you convinced me this was a good idea, and now you're going through with it. If, for no other reason, so I can prove to you that the want ads aren't the way to go about finding a husband."

Jane jumped up from her chair and slapped her hand over her sister's. "*Don't*, Caroline—*please?*" She maneuvered both phone and paper back to her side of the table.

"Why not?" Caroline asked, rubbing the hand Jane had smacked. "I don't get you. You're always saying you want to date, but you won't take the steps to do it. You doom yourself from the start."

"Doomed—*exactly,*" Jane said through her first juicy bite. "I'm cursed, so why even bother?"

Caroline rolled her eyes. "You are not."

"Am too," Jane insisted. "My whole life it's been that way. It's okay. I'm used to it."

"That is so *not* true." Caroline's lips puckered as she tasted the grapefruit. "You've known lots of nice guys—had some great dates, too."

Jane's spoon stopped halfway to her mouth. "Are you kidding? The only nice guys I know are the ones I'm related to, and I've *never* had any luck dating."

"Sure you have. It seems like you were always off doing something—even in high school."

"Off doing something and dating are two different things." Jane pushed back her chair, went to the fridge, and removed two water bottles. "I was involved in clubs and stuff, but I didn't *date.*"

Caroline made a face as she took another bite. "This grapefruit is sour. You sure you don't have any cereal—or a cup of sugar?"

Jane shook her head as she sat down. "I don't think so, but feel free to look."

Caroline rose from the table and began searching through Jane's cupboards. Jane continued eating, her gaze straying to the circled ad in the paper beside her.

"Ah ha," Caroline exclaimed a few minutes later. She held up a dusty box of Cheerios. "You were holding out on me."

"I forgot. Those have been there for months—probably left over from when I babysat Christopher."

Caroline searched the box for an expiration date. "They're still good. See, it was all a matter of my willingness to put forth the effort to find a box of cereal. If *you'd* put forth the effort to find a nice, *LDS* man, you'd also get what you're after."

Jane scowled at her sister as Caroline sat down again.

"That's easy for you to say when you met your husband at the tender age of nineteen. Love practically dropped itself in your lap, but I've never had that experience before. I've never even had what I would call a decent date."

Caroline waved her spoon. "You've just forgotten, that's all. Think back to high school. I remember you going out with—let's see it was . . . Evan Thatcher." She pointed her spoon at Jane and flashed her an *I told you so* look. "I *know* he asked you out once. I remember helping you get ready."

"*Once* being the key word," Jane said. "And it was a disaster."

Caroline poured milk into her cereal. "What happened?"

"Nothing."

"C'mon. Tell me," Caroline coaxed.

Jane pushed her finished grapefruit aside and looked at Caroline. "All right, but don't you *dare* laugh."

"I won't. Pinky promise," Caroline said, linking her little fingers together.

"I think you're supposed to do that with the other person," Jane said.

"Oh, right. Well, I still promise."

Jane took a long drink from her water bottle and leaned back in her chair. "We'd been to a movie and ice cream and were sitting in the parking lot of Swensons when Evan asked me if I wanted a French kiss. I said yes, and he told me to close my eyes and open my mouth. At this point I was thinking along the lines of french fries, French bread, French mousse—I don't know, some special chocolate like a Hershey's Kiss, but made in France."

"*No!*" Caroline said, nearly choking on her cereal.

"You *promised*," Jane warned. "I haven't even gotten to the awful part yet."

Caroline clamped a hand over her mouth. "I'm not laughing," she said in a muffled voice. "Go on."

"So . . . he stuck his tongue in my mouth and . . . I bit it."

Caroline choked. *"Hard?"*

"Mmm-hmm." Jane nodded. "Really hard. We ended up at the emergency room. He got five stitches."

"*No way,*" Caroline exclaimed. "They stitch tongues?"

"They stitched his. It was nearly cut through." Jane stuck out her tongue and made a cutting motion with her fingers.

Caroline let out a horrified shriek. "I never knew."

"We made a pact, Evan and I, that we'd never tell anyone what happened."

"Wasn't he angry with you?"

"Probably." Jane smiled wickedly. "But it wasn't like he could yell at me right then."

"How old were you—*sixteen*? I can't believe you didn't know what French kissing was."

"Me either. Especially with *you* for a sister."

"Yeah really—*hey.*" Caroline looked properly offended. "What's that supposed to mean?"

Jane shrugged. "You know. You dated everyone. Wasn't it your senior-year goal to kiss the entire football team?"

"Of course not," Caroline said, indignant. She wrinkled her nose. "Football players are gross. They're always grunting and butting heads." She sighed. "*I* was trying for the basketball team."

"See," Jane smirked. "You had all the men."

The teasing look on Caroline's face was suddenly gone, replaced by sadness. "Please don't say that."

Jane looked at her in surprise. "Sorry. I was only stating the obvious. You dated tons. You—"

"Came very close to ruining my life and a few others'," Caroline finished. "I probably single-handedly caused every gray hair on Mom's head."

"I wouldn't say that," Jane argued. "Michael gave her at least a few of them."

"Maybe," Caroline said. "But I was the awful one. And because of that, my life—and Mom and Dad's—*was* awful. I'd give a lot to be able to go back and change the person I was then." She sighed wistfully. "Jane, be so glad you weren't like me. Be glad you didn't kiss everyone—that you've waited this long for—"

"For what?" Jane asked. "For my own little run-down house? For the opportunity to be the family babysitter? For the privilege of being the subject of Mom and Dad's fast every month?"

"No." Caroline reached across the table and squeezed Jane's hands. "For a heavenly mansion, children of your own, and a sacred love—like Mom and Dad's. I know you've waited a long time, but don't ruin it now." Caroline's voice grew quiet. "Don't make the mistakes I made."

* * *

"Bye, sweet boy." Jane bent over Andrew's car seat and gave him a quick kiss. She ducked out of the van, and Caroline slid the door closed.

"Thanks," Jane said, giving her sister a hug. "This was a lot of fun—like the old days."

"I needed it as much as you," Caroline said as she climbed into the driver's seat of her minivan. "Remember your promise."

"I will." Jane patted the pocket of her jeans where the ad lay. "I'm going to search for my cereal," she quipped.

Caroline started the car and rolled down her window. "Just remember that the sugary stuff may taste good, and it's fun to find a prize in the box, but it's the fiber and whole grain that sustain you over time."

"That's what I'm going for," Jane assured her. "And I'm betting that someone looking for a mother for his children has got to be a Wheaties kind of guy."

Caroline shook her head. "Not Wheaties—*Life*." She smiled as she backed out of the driveway. "It's eternal life you're after, and don't settle for anything less."

Chapter Five

Paul stifled a yawn and forced his bloodshot eyes to focus on the email on his computer screen. *Just send it*, he thought, his hand hovering over the mouse. It was after midnight and he'd been sitting here for two hours, trying to write an impossible letter, a ludicrous request to someone unlikely to respond anyway. It had been too long, and it wasn't as if he were about to apologize—even now. If anything, Pete owed *him* an apology. With that thought, pride demanded that he pull his hand away, but the arrow remained poised over the SEND icon.

I shouldn't have to do this.

A sudden, unexpected surge of anger coursed through him as he looked at his wedding photo on the desk. He was furious with Tami, though he knew it was wrong—terrible of him. How dare she leave him to do this alone. How dare she abandon him and their children—two helpless infants, barely hanging onto the brink of life themselves. And what kind of wife dictated who should raise them when she was gone?

When he was gone too.

It was a terrible thing Tami had asked of him, and for a moment Paul hated her for it and refused to feel guilty. Guilt would come later, he was certain. The therapist they'd hooked him up with at the hospital had tried to tell him as much.

Paul took a sip from the soda on his desk and again recalled that awful day—the first of many he'd endured without Tami.

The counselor had started with, "My name's Collin. I work here at Swedish, and I'll be available to help you through the difficulties of the coming weeks."

Paul shook Collin's extended hand and read the words *grief counselor* below his name on his hospital badge.

"Here's a pamphlet I recommend you read." With his free hand, Collin pulled a paper from his coat pocket. "It lists the stages of grief a person goes through after a traumatic event in his life. As long as you're moving continuously through these emotions we don't tend to worry, but if you feel like you've become stuck on any one stage, it might be best to come in and talk to someone on a regular basis." Seeing Paul's dumbfounded look, he added, "I can give you some names . . ."

Paul stared numbly at the words on the paper. A *pamphlet?* That was the best they could do for him? That was all they had to offer a man with terminal cancer, premature twins, and a dead wife? He glared angrily at the list.

Denial. Complete denial. It was the only way to cope at first.

Sorrow. So overwhelming that it leads to . . .

Depression. Which was really bad when you had to force yourself to get up and get to the doctor every week. And, of course, the all-consuming . . .

Anger. Misdirected as it was and followed quickly by . . .

Guilt. Yeah. Been there, done that one too.

He could have written the list himself. A year and a half of hellish treatments and death at his doorstep practically made him an expert.

"You ever have a terminal illness?" Paul asked as he folded the pamphlet and stuffed it in his pocket.

Collin shook his head. "Uh, no. I had an aunt with—"

"Ever have a child in the intensive care unit?"

Again Collin shook his head.

"You married?" Paul asked.

"Four years." The therapist seemed relieved that he could give a positive answer.

"I don't suppose your wife's ever been hit by a drunk driver on the way home from her baby shower."

"Uh, no," Collin said quietly. "Listen, I know what you're getting at, but just because I haven't experienced the things you are going through right now doesn't mean I—"

But Paul had turned and walked away, unwilling to let the *grief counselor* see stage four in action.

He knew well enough that every sort of emotion was to be expected right now. And he thought he'd just about had them all. He'd imagined conversations with Tami, where together they discussed the major decisions that lay before them. It wasn't until the woman who delivered his mail had asked if his wife was in the hospital having their babies and he had said "yes" that Paul began to face reality. That reality being his acknowledgment that Tami was actually gone and he was going it alone. After that, he hadn't been able to get out of bed for three days.

Then there was the day when he'd actually cried with *joy.* It was after Mark's surgery, and the doctor said for the first time that Mark looked like he was going to pull through. Paul had cried like a baby himself. His son was going to live.

But right now he was just mad, and justifiably so, at Tami. The one thing he'd said he'd never do, she'd asked of him. He picked up the crumpled note beside the computer and reread the familiar lines without really looking at them. *You know who their father should be.* She hadn't said his name. He could find someone else—some nice young couple longing for children.

Paul set the note down again. Trouble was, Tami was right. He *did* know who should raise their twins. Pete. Funny thing, how a person could nearly hate a family member yet have incredible respect for him at the same time.

Paul drummed his fingers on the bottom of the keyboard. It was 12:17 now. Doctor Kline would tell him off for sure if he found out the hours he'd been keeping. And the twins weren't even home yet. Soon he'd be up at night with babies. *His* babies.

He thought of two-and-a-half-pound Madison and two-pound Mark lying in their side-by-side isolettes in the NICU, ventilators whooshing congruently. He thought of the unassembled cribs, the car seats still in boxes, and the piles of unopened baby paraphernalia in the other room. He thought of his chemo treatments and the dire predictions of time allotted to him that had already passed.

Paul swallowed a lump in his throat along with the last of his pride. His eyes scanned the screen again, rereading the email one last time.

> Date: Sat, 6 September 2003 12:43 AM
> From: "Paul Warner" <pbryantarchitect@hotmail.com>
> To: "Peter Bryant" <petesdragon2@hotmail.com>
> Subject: Still there for me?
>
> Pete,
>
> Remember when we were nine or ten—fourth grade I think—and I took your baseball signed by Bruce Bochte to school, and it got stolen? It happened on a Monday, and by Friday afternoon you still hadn't spoken to me. That was the day Josh Harper decided to get me good because you weren't around. I was walking home, about half a block behind you, when Josh jumped out of a bush and started whaling on me. When he was finished, I had a bloody nose, two black eyes, and a loose tooth. Later, when I walked into the house and you saw me, you got right up and came to help, getting me an ice pack and Band-Aids. When I told you what happened, you said, "Man, why didn't you yell for me? I woulda come."
>
> I was astounded. After all, I'd lost your only signed ball. You must have sensed my doubt because you put your hand on my shoulder and looked me straight in the eyes.

I still remember what you said.

"You're my brother. No matter what, I'll always be there for you. You just gotta ask."

Pete, I don't know if "no matter what" still applies. But I'm asking.

Paul

It took every ounce of Paul's willpower to hit SEND.

Chapter Six

Jane turned sideways in the mirror. "*Nice,*" she muttered under her breath as she noted a three-inch run down the back of her nylons. It must have happened after work last week when she'd babysat her two year-old niece, Megan. Megan had a way of clinging to people's legs, her chubby, sticky hands grasping clothes, skin or—in this case—nylons.

Jane sighed. So much for wearing the sexy black suit for her first date with the man of her dreams—the only man alive who, like her, longed so much for a family of his own that he was willing to advertise for it.

She reached for the zipper in the back of her skirt. There wasn't time to run to the store before she left. She'd just have to find something else to wear for her first meeting with *Paul.* His name rolled around in her mind in a dreamy sort of way. It was the same dreamy state she'd been in since she'd picked up the phone Saturday morning and dialed the number from Friday's most unique personal. The man who answered said his name was Paul, and in his deep voice he had readily agreed to a date. A date! She, Jane Warner, had an honest-to-goodness date, and she had arranged it herself. It was an exhilarating feeling.

Reluctantly, Jane took off the suit and hung it in her closet. *Too bad,* she thought. The suit was the best thing in her wardrobe. It made her look ten pounds slimmer, and men noticed her when she wore it. Today, she wanted to be noticed. She wanted this date to go well. She wanted to get her feet wet . . . in pristine water. And a man willing to put his heart on the line—like Paul had in that ad—was surely as pure as they came.

Jane peeled off the black nylons and kicked them aside to be thrown away later. Sliding the closet door open, she brought a hand to her chin as she critically examined her wardrobe.

Jeans? Too casual, though they were only meeting at a Starbucks. Still, it was a midday meeting and she couldn't wear jeans to work anyway.

Slacks? No. She was a skirt person, and for a date, no matter how casual, it was probably better to err on the feminine side. Jane shoved the pants out of the way and grabbed the cluster of skirt hangers. Laying her choices on the bed, she pulled several shirts from the closet for possible matches. White cotton blouse with long denim skirt? Too country-western. White linen with the khaki? Not when the khaki was missing a button and the linen would be wrinkled by noon.

She looked in the mirror as she held up another possibility. Dark top with light skirt? Nope, after Friday's serious chocolate overdose, she wasn't feeling slim enough for that combo. Navy cotton with . . . Jane gasped as the DJ on the radio announced the time—7:45. How could it be so late? Not only would Green Taurus beat her today, but the ferry might very well leave without her. Jane grabbed the closest skirt—a floral she'd worn to her mom's for Sunday dinner two days ago. Pulling a short-sleeve sweater over her head, she ran into the bathroom, hoping the circuits wouldn't short out before she was finished blow-drying her hair.

* * *

Paul waited impatiently for his computer to connect with the Internet. He'd just checked his email an hour ago, but with the time difference overseas and all, he reasoned it wouldn't hurt to look once more before he left for the hospital. He closed his eyes, practicing the breathing exercises he and Tami had learned at their Lamaze classes. This morning he wasn't trying to get past the pain—he'd all but given up trying to be valiant on that front. Knowing what was ahead of him today, he'd taken painkillers before he even rolled out of bed. It was the anxiety that had him feeling ill right now. What man in his shoes wouldn't be nervous?

Six weeks ago he'd been married. Today, he was meeting fourteen different women, because he *had* to find a mother—whether he wanted to or not. It would be far better for the twins to go to someone he knew for a short while than to some caseworker from the Department of Child Welfare Services.

Paul reclined in his chair. For a moment he went back in time, the image of a Vietnamese orphan flashing before his closed eyes. He hadn't thought about Mary for years. And then it had still been with animosity for the upheaval she'd caused in their lives—especially his mother's. Now, for the first time, Paul thought of Mary differently. He saw her as a child in a strange land, abandoned to a system that was ill equipped to handle misplaced children. He remembered her thin dress and worn sandals. How long had it taken them to get her new clothes and shoes? And when they did, were they cast-offs from someone else? He shuddered, thinking of his own children abandoned to such a fate.

Where was Mary now? Had she stayed in America or been sent back to . . . What? Or *who* was probably the better question. Guilt nagged at him, but he pushed it away. Pete would know what became of her. He had made sure she was taken care of. Just like he would make sure Madison and Mark were taken care of.

Paul opened his eyes and stared at the computer screen.

You have new mail.

"C'mon, Pete," Paul said as he opened his inbox.

Monthly statement from Wells Fargo, he read somberly. No other new messages.

"Just take your sweet time, brother," Paul grumbled. Discouraged, he shut down his computer and mentally prepared for the day ahead. He told himself it was okay if he didn't hear from Pete today, this week—or even this month. After all, what could he really do from the other side of the world? What was really important now, *today,* was finding a woman, a kind, caring woman who would be there for his children when he would not. Everything else, his brother included, could wait until later.

* * *

Jane self-consciously smoothed the left side of her hair as she walked. The ponytail helped but did not completely hide that she'd only been able to blow-dry half of her hair straight this morning. The circuits had over-loaded again before she'd been able to get the other half of her natural curl under control. She was going to have to get the wiring fixed—soon. Nothing like going on a first date looking like half her head had suffered an electric shock. And if her hair wasn't bad enough . . . Jane frowned as she looked down at the wet spot on her skirt. It wasn't until she'd gotten to work that she'd realized her skirt had a purple stain right in front. She'd been holding her two year-old niece Sunday evening while they ate dessert—blueberry pie. Copious amounts of water and soap from the office bathroom had only made the spot more obvious. Tara had offered to trade her outfits for the afternoon, but Jane had declined, preferring one purple stain to the fuchsia miniskirt her friend sported. Tara had looked hurt at first, until Jane hastily explained that the outfit would clash with her toenails—currently striped glitter orange and silver, thanks to her eleven-year-old niece, Jessica.

Jane looked down at her toes now. Too bad—in her haste this morning, she'd grabbed sandals. Maybe, with a little luck, she'd be able to slide her feet under the table before Paul noticed the hideous combination of color. Of course, she wouldn't be as fortunate with her hands. Her fingernails were typically short, and no matter how much scrubbing she did, it seemed green plant stains and potting soil remnants always lingered. Jane held her hands out it front of her. It seemed the term "green thumb" had some truth to it.

It looked like she was going to need her family's prayers after all, if there was going to be a second date. Jane felt her confidence slip another notch as she remembered the episode at dinner Sunday evening.

It was tradition—even more entrenched than her First Friday rituals—that the whole family gather at her parents' home the first Sunday of the month for family dinner. With seven brothers and sisters—and all but her married and producing grandchildren—it was quite the occasion. Her parents' table, refinished in recent years, stretched to ten feet, and an odd assortment of chairs and benches squeezed around it to fit all but the youngest grandchildren. Mom always cooked a roast—or *three* these days—and her famous potato rolls. Caroline baked pies, and the other siblings all pitched in with their favorite side dishes.

Jane always brought salad. Her mother was still afraid she was going to electrocute herself in "that old house with faulty wiring," so she wouldn't allow Jane to bring anything that had to be cooked. And afterward, Mom always sent her home with enough food so she wouldn't have to turn her oven on for a week—so long as she could stomach leftover roast again.

It was normally a happy, enjoyable sort of chaos that Jane really looked forward to. But last Sunday, just as everyone had taken their seats, and right before her father offered prayer, Caroline had announced, "Jane has a date this week."

Reaction was instantaneous. Her father's head snapped up, and he beamed at her. Her mother froze, the basket of rolls tipping precariously in her hands.

"Oh Jane, dear, how wonderful."

Jane couldn't be certain, but she thought she saw tears in her mother's eyes.

"Who is he? Who is he, Aunt Jane?" her nieces Amber and Jessica clamored.

"Way to go, Jane," from Scott, her brother-in-law.

Jane glared at Caroline. "Thanks," she muttered. "Remind me to announce to everyone the next time you think you're pregnant, or you mess up your hair color or—"

"You're coloring your hair *already*?" Mindy, their eldest sister, asked, staring closely at Caroline. "Wow. I didn't have to start until—"

"Food's getting cold," their father boomed. All eyes turned toward the head of the table. Mom slid into her seat, and their father continued. "Let's give thanks to our Father in Heaven for our family and this wonderful meal."

"And Jane's date," Jessica piped up.

And so they had. After blessing their food, her father had petitioned God that this man would finally be the right one for Jane, and that she would find happiness. *Who ever said she wasn't happy?* Then all twenty-eight voices chimed in a vehement amen. Even two-year-old Megan got the word right. It seemed everyone believed Jane would never succeed on her own.

Well, she would.

Jane forced her hand away from her uneven hair and slung her purse over her shoulder, away from the stain she'd been hoping to cover. If Paul was truly a man looking for a woman who wanted to be a mother, then messy hair and a skirt stained by a *child* wouldn't matter to him.

It wouldn't matter at all.

Chapter Seven

Paul took a sip of cold coffee and grimaced. Having his appointments at Starbucks had originally seemed like a good idea—something like that eight-minute dating café in New York he'd seen featured on TV. But now, three hours and forty-seven minutes into the ordeal, overloaded with coffee and sufficiently frightened by the scary women he'd met, he realized what a mistake Starbucks had been—what a mistake this whole thing was.

He should never have advertised in the personals. At the very least, he should have specified that *he* wasn't part of the deal. Who would have thought his simple ad would unleash a torrent of women on the ultimate manhunt.

Unfortunately, it was a little late for revisions, and he still had . . . Paul glanced at his laptop. Nine more interviews to go. He groaned, then seriously contemplated getting up and walking away, pretending he'd never had such a stupid idea. Of course, then there would be a slew of angry women calling him. He'd have to change his phone number, and his address was listed in the phone book as well. He stared out the window, eyes darting from one woman to the next as he recalled a scene from *Fatal Attraction.*

Deciding it wasn't worth the effort of relocating, Paul closed his laptop and rested his head in his hands. At least he had ten minutes to recuperate before the next attack.

* * *

Remembering that her *How to Catch a Guy and Keep Him* manual said never to appear over eager, Jane slowed her hurried walk to a casual stroll as she crossed in front of the large glass window fronting Starbucks. She opened the door and stepped inside, her eyes searching for the corner table opposite the counter, where Paul had said he would be.

Someone was there all right, but Jane frowned as she moved closer. A man wearing a baseball cap sat at the table, facing away from her, his head leaning against the window. Could this be Paul? *Asleep?* She looked at her watch and saw she was barely two minutes late. Maybe he was one of those stickler-for-being-on-time type guys, and feigning sleep was his way of showing he was annoyed she was late.

Disappointment surged through Jane as she walked toward the table. She hoped this wasn't Paul. With his head to the side and the baseball cap hiding his face, she couldn't tell much about his features, except that he didn't have any hair. Too bad she couldn't give him some of hers. She ran her hand over her own frizzy mass again.

And why the Mariners cap? Was he just a really casual guy? Probably— after all, they were meeting at a coffee shop. That should have been her first clue. Maybe he was trying to tell her right off that sports came first in his life, and if she didn't like it, then she should just move on right now. She *would* move right along if that was the case. Her brother-in-law Scott—aka Sportsmaniac—was like that, and she'd seen what it had done to her sister Karen. In the fifteen years they'd been married, the poor woman hadn't had her husband beside her at Thanksgiving dinner once that Jane could remember. And Scott's idea of a perfect date always involved playoffs of some sort—never, heaven forbid, tickets to *Phantom,* or an overnight at a bed and breakfast, or anything remotely romantic.

Nope. If this guy was Paul and he was an impatient sports maniac, then this wouldn't work at all. She could live with his baldness—she'd dealt with her own hair problems her whole life—but romance she could not live without. She needed it the way everyone else needed air. She'd been overcompensating for the lack of romance with chocolate, movies, and novels for a long while now, and while those things were nice, it was a miracle she'd survived this long.

A step away from the table, Jane hesitated. She could just keep walking right on past, and Paul—if that was him—would never even know she'd been here. It was a tempting thought. After all, what were the odds that anything was going to develop between two people whose hairstyles were polar opposites?

You ever answer them? Do you ever go out with any of those poor saps who advertise? Jay's voice rang in her head. Poor saps indeed, she thought, looking down at the sleeping man. Still, she'd promised herself that she would take the plunge—or get her toes wet, anyway. Gathering her courage, she stepped forward. She'd never know until she tried.

Jane slid into the chair opposite the sleeping man, careful to jostle the table just a little as she did so. It had the desired effect. His head snapped up and he looked at her, surprised.

Jane smiled. Score one. He hadn't seen her hideous toes *or* the stain on her skirt.

"Hello." She offered her hand.

He took it, though his look was panicked.

"Are you Paul?" she asked hesitantly, looking around. Maybe this *was* the wrong guy. He looked exhausted—like he'd never have the energy to chase after all the children she'd imagined having. Maybe she was at the wrong table, or the wrong Starbucks, or—

"Yes, I'm Paul. And you're . . ." He released her hand and flipped open his laptop. His panicked look intensified as he stared at the blank screen.

"Jane," she offered. He couldn't remember her *name*?

"Oh, yes. Sorry." He smiled faintly, revealing nice cheekbones. "I'm really sorry. I had a late night, and I guess I must have fallen asleep for a few minutes."

And you woke up, saw me, and were momentarily befuddled by the bizarre hairstyle. That would be enough to cause anyone temporary memory loss. "Don't worry about it," Jane said.

"So, is Jane short for anything—Janice or—"

"No, it's just Jane. I'm the youngest of seven children, and I think my parents were all out of creativity by the time they got to me."

"Wow, seven." Paul leaned back in his chair. "That's quite a family. But you're the youngest?"

Jane nodded.

"Oh," he said, unable to keep the disappointment out of his voice. "Then I don't suppose you've spent a lot of time around children."

"Actually, I'm around them all the time. I have fourteen nieces and nephews, and their parents leave them at my place as much as they can." She laughed lightly, but quickly stopped when Paul didn't join in.

"So, can I get you something?" He gestured to the menu over the counter.

"A cranapple juice would be great."

"I'll be right back." Paul rose from his chair and headed toward the short line by the register.

Jane closed her eyes for a moment and offered a prayer of her own. *Please, God, let this get better or let it be over quick.*

* * *

A few minutes later, Paul returned from the counter with two drinks in his hand. Reaching the table, he placed the juice in front of Jane and sat opposite her. *Don't stare at her hair anymore,* he commanded himself. They each sipped their drinks for a minute, then began speaking at the same time.

"So what do you—? What do—?" They broke off, smiling. She did have a nice smile.

"Go ahead," Jane said.

He did. This same awkwardness had happened too many times already for him to gallantly say, "Ladies first." If he'd learned one thing today, it was that ladies didn't want to go first—at least not in this particular situation. It was better if he asked them the questions. Women could talk for hours, so while he might not have found what he was looking for, at least they'd be past the uncomfortable silences.

"So what do you do for a living?" he asked.

Jane took another sip of her juice before answering. "Currently, I'm a realtor."

"Oh." What more could he say? He would have been more impressed if she'd told him she drove a garbage truck. Right now he wasn't overly fond of real-estate agents. The one he'd been unfortunate enough to list his property with had about as much compassion for his situation as—

"Is that bad?" Jane asked. "Because you're looking at me like I'm a vulture or something."

Paul nearly choked on his coffee. *Vulture.* He couldn't have said it better himself.

"One step above a crooked lawyer, maybe?" Jane asked, sarcasm lacing her words.

A lawyer. Now that was good. It would serve Pete right too, and who knows? Maybe it would be a match made in heaven. A vulturous realtor and a conniving attorney. Paul thought perhaps he ought to consider it.

"Sorry," he apologized again. How many apologies was that now? He'd forgotten how much a man said "sorry" around women. "It's just that I'm in the process of selling some property, and I *have* had the misfortune to work with some rather carnivorous realtors."

"I'm sorry then." Jane nodded, understanding. "We have a few like that in our office—anything-for-the-sale types. But I'm only in real estate until my business takes off. I'm actually terrible at selling—my biggest accomplishment is keeping my checking account in the black for nearly six months now. But hopefully that will change when I get my business going."

"Business?" Paul asked, leaning forward over the table.

"In college I ended up majoring in landscape architecture," Jane said, warming to the topic. "I've been trying to get my own landscape design company going. Real estate is actually a great way to find clients. After work and on weekends I spend my time designing and running a small crew on the jobs I've landed."

"Not to be rude—" Paul cleared his throat. "But did you read my ad?"

"Yes," Jane said, giving him a perplexed look. She sat up straighter, folding her arms across her chest. "What are you getting at?"

"Well, I don't see how you'll have time to be a mother. I mean, how would you take care of children and be a real estate agent *and* run your own business?"

"Women do it all the time," Jane countered. "However, I would love to be able to stay—"

"I'm sorry, Miss—" Paul glanced down at his laptop. "Miss Warner. But I don't think this is going to work out. I do appreciate you coming today."

Jane forced her mouth shut. But she continued to stare at the man across from her. *Paul.* How could she ever have thought that was a nice name? Now she'd have to add it to her list—at the very top—of names she could never possibly give her children.

She bent down to pick up her purse and saw the stain on her skirt. And to think she'd been worried about how she looked. She stood, feeling hurt and angry all at once. This hadn't been a date, it had been an interview, which she had grossly failed because this man in all his shallow-mindedness hadn't been able to see past her job title. If he'd only been willing to look just a smidgen deeper, he'd have seen that she would gladly give up her paycheck, her clients, her yard, just about everything, for the privilege of having a child—of being a mother. Tears smarted in her eyes. Appalled, she walked briskly past Paul, murmuring a hasty thanks for the juice he'd bought.

As she walked out the door, the thought struck her that her prayer had been answered—it had indeed ended quickly.

Chapter Eight

"It was *terrible*." Jane's voice trembled as she spoke into her cell phone. "No, Caroline. I'll be fine. Thanks." Jane disconnected the call, walked around the corner from Starbucks, and took a moment to sit on a bench and compose herself. She'd no sooner opened her purse to find a tissue than a woman sat down beside her.

"Don't take it so hard. I knew right away you weren't his type."

Jane looked at the woman. "Excuse me?"

"Paul." The woman said his name in the same dreamy voice Jane had used just this morning.

"You're not what he's—" the woman inclined her head toward the entrance to Starbucks, "—looking for."

"And I suppose *you* are?" Jane found a tissue and snapped her purse shut.

"Exactly. Only he doesn't know it yet. But after a day of meeting the wrong women, I'll be here waiting for him, to make it *all* better."

"Wait a minute," Jane said. "Are you telling me that *he—Paul—*is meeting with different women all day long?"

"Every forty minutes, honey."

Jane frowned at this information. It *had* been a job interview.

"That poor, *poor* man. Can you imagine how hard this must be for him?"

"No, I can't," Jane muttered sarcastically. She dabbed at her eyes with the tissue.

The woman nodded. "It's enough to make anyone cry. Imagine losing your spouse and having a baby in the ICU. Just terrible, isn't it?"

Jane's eyes widened. A *baby?* In the *ICU?* "Yes," she said quietly. He already had a baby. A wife . . .

Jane rose from the bench and looked down at the woman. "Well, good luck then."

The woman's collagen-filled lips turned up in a smile. She flipped her long, blonde hair over her shoulder and stood, revealing more cleavage than Jane and all her sisters had collectively. *This* woman thought she was the right one. *This* woman had managed to learn that Paul had been married, lost a wife, had a baby . . . Whereas she, Jane, had learned . . . nothing about him.

She *was* a terrible date and a terrible interview. Sobered, Jane turned and continued down the street.

* * *

Jane sat in her car with the door open, listening to voices echo through the hospital parking garage. Her mind had been so preoccupied since her failure of a date and the revelations that followed, she'd hardly recognized where she was going until she'd gotten here. It seemed that through a will of its own, her subconscious had guided her through lunch traffic to Swedish Medical Center.

What are the odds his baby is here? she wondered as she finally got out of her car and started toward the entrance. There were several Seattle hospitals that treated children. But the woman outside Starbucks had said Paul had a *baby.* Still, infants were treated at Children's Hospital too. She remembered her brother's little boy having surgery there when he was about three months old.

She supposed she could go there next.

At this thought, Jane stopped walking and sat down on a shaded bench outside the main entrance. What was she doing? Was she so desperate that she'd taken to stalking men and their children? She folded her arms and sat thinking as her cell rang—again.

"Three guesses," Jane muttered as she opened her purse. A quick glance at the phone confirmed her suspicions. It was the Sweviecs, calling for the third time in half an hour. Jane let the call go to voice mail before dialing Tara's number to see if she knew what was up.

"Emerald Realty downtown," Tara answered with her usual lilting casualness. "*This* is Tara."

"May I help you?" Jane finished for her. It was a wonder Tara kept her job.

"Jane!" Tara exclaimed. "How was your date? Did he turn out to be a nutcase looking to lull innocent women into his lair?"

"Yes," Jane said, absently. "I'm in his convertible right now, on my way to his apartment."

Tara gasped. "You have *all* the luck."

Jane rolled her eyes. "I'm joking, Tara."

"Oh," Tara said.

Jane heard the pout in her voice. "Listen, I need you to cover my phone awhile longer, and by chance have the Sweviecs called?"

"They did. Where are you? What's going on? *Are* you at Paul's apartment?"

"Not hardly. The date—*interview*—was a disaster."

"Told you. You should have gone and got your hair fixed."

"I didn't have time. *Some* of us actually work for a living. Now tell me what's going on with my clients."

"Not much. Mrs. Sweviec just called to say they've changed their mind about wanting a corner Jacuzzi with glass block. Now she wants an oval— still a minimum of eight jets—with travertine surround."

"Three calls for *that?*" Jane grumbled.

"Oh, I don't doubt they've been calling," Tara said. "I knew my idea would work. I knew it!"

"What idea? *Tara.* What have you done?" Jane rose from the bench and began pacing. "I've hung in there with these people for *eleven weeks,* biding my time, using every ounce of patience I have to please them so I can make a sale—a sale that will pay my bills for a good, long time."

"Precisely," Tara said. "And I imagine now, if you call them back, you may just have that sale."

"What?" Jane stopped pacing and ran a hand through her tousled hair.

"I told them it was a good thing they didn't want that old corner tub after all, because you were, at that very moment, with another couple who were writing up an offer for the same house."

"You didn't," Jane said, appalled.

Tara laughed. "I did. And I must say, Mrs. Sweviec seemed a little concerned that she had competition."

"Imaginary competition. What you did was dishonest and—and probably illegal too."

"I was just prompting them a little."

"It was *wrong,* Tara."

"Hmmph," Tara snorted into the phone. "Some people are so unappreciative."

"We could get in trouble, you know."

"We?" Tara asked. "They're *your* clients."

"Thanks," Jane muttered.

"No problem. I'm happy to help anytime." Jane heard the snap of Tara's gum.

"Then help me now. What do I say when they call back?"

"Don't know," Tara said. "But I'm sure you'll think of something good."

Jane heard a click, and a second later the phone went dead. Frustrated, she stared at it, then jumped when it rang again.

She pushed the button without looking at the caller ID. "Hello."

"Jane dear, this is Martha Sweviec. I've been trying to reach you all morning."

"I'm sorry. I had an appointment." Jane clenched her teeth.

"Your assistant told us all about it. And frankly, that's the reason I'm calling. We've had a change of heart about the bathroom at the house you showed us last Thursday."

"I just got my messages," Jane said hastily. "Tara told me you'd prefer an oval with—"

"No, no, dear. We've decided the corner Jacuzzi will do fine, that is, if it's still available."

"It's—"

"And if there's an offer, let me just say that Wallace and I might be willing to go higher. The master bedroom and sitting room *are* exactly what we've been looking for."

Jane rubbed her ear to make sure she was hearing correctly. This sweet person could *not* be Mrs. Sweviec.

"So, how high was the offer?" Mrs. Sweviec demanded.

Jane smiled, now *that* voice she knew.

"I'm afraid I'm not at liberty to discuss other clients, Mrs. Sweviec, but if you'd like to come in tomorrow morning, I'm sure we can write up an acceptable offer." Jane cringed. *Not at liberty?* Where had that come from? Next thing she knew, she'd be running for office.

"That would be fine, dear. Shall we say, nine?"

"Nine is great, but Mrs. Sweviec, I feel I need to explain—"

"No need. I understand perfectly. You're loyal to all of your clients. Just remember that we're counting on you to be loyal to *us* tomorrow. Goodbye, dear."

Jane heard the disconnecting click but continued to hold her phone a minute longer, wondering if she should call Mrs. Sweviec back and explain that there was no other offer. Deciding that would be best done tomorrow—after she'd had time to think about *how* she would explain Tara's deception—Jane slipped the phone into her purse. Feeling guilty but grateful, she followed her instincts to the hospital entrance and then took the elevator up to the NICU.

Once inside the viewing area, Jane peered through the large glass window and wondered what to do next. She watched as the nurses on duty moved from one isolette to another, monitoring and caring for their tiny patients. There was no way to know which, if any, of the infants belonged to Paul.

Behind her the door swung open, and Jane turned to see who it was, then smiled as she recognized Mrs. Howard, the grandmother of a little boy who'd been in the NICU when Andrew was there.

"Mrs. Howard. It's so good to see you again."

"Please, call me Marion," the elderly woman said. "It's Jane, isn't it?"

Jane nodded, and Marion took her hands in a friendly squeeze.

"How is that little boy of yours?"

"Andrew is fine. He's at home with his mother—my sister—right now. Remember, I was just filling in for her when she had chicken pox?"

"Yes, yes. That's right." Marion nodded. "Baking soda paste. Best thing in the world for those, you know. No need to buy any of that expensive pink stuff."

Jane smile widened. "Is that how you treated your children?"

"Every one of them. Common sense and extra loving got them through the pox and much worse. Same thing applies today. All these babies need—" She inclined her head toward the nursery window, "is a little extra loving and they'll be just fine."

"I'm sure you're right," Jane said. "Is your grandson still here?"

"Yes, though he's so much better. He's a fighter, that one, got all the spunk of his granddad."

"And I see you're still coming to see him. He's lucky to have you." Jane didn't doubt for a minute that time spent in this woman's arms would be a powerful healer for anyone. With a pang of sorrow, she thought of her own grandmother who had passed away three years earlier, and she suddenly wished Mrs. Howard would take her hands again.

"*I'm* the lucky one," Marion insisted. "I'm so fortunate to come here while my Penny is at work. In fact, I've enjoyed it so much, I'm even thinking of volunteering here after Jesse is better and goes home. Though—" She leaned in closer to Jane and lowered her voice to a whisper. "My friend Carol says I should work with her down in geriatrics. She thinks *her* job is the best because of all the widowers there to flirt with. Says it reminds her of nursing during the war."

Jane laughed. "I can see it would be hard to choose."

"Oh no, not for me. These babies are the best. There's something special about them."

"I agree," Jane said, turning back toward the nursery window.

Marion patted Jane's arm. "So if your nephew is at home, what brings you here today?"

"My um . . ." Jane realized that she was staring at the answer to her dilemma. Mrs. Howard knew about *every* baby in the NICU. Not only was she Jesse's grandmother, but she had been dubbed the NICU grandmother by several families—at least when Andrew was here. Jane doubted much had changed. There was something about Marion's sweet countenance that made people open up to her. She was a great listener and a genuinely compassionate person. Of course she would know about Paul's baby.

"My friend, Paul—Bryant—has a baby here, and I was hoping to see . . ." *Him? Her?* Jane didn't even know that much.

"You're friends with Mr. Bryant," Marion exclaimed, looking at Jane differently. "How wonderful. That poor man needs some friends. Losing his wife and no other family to help him . . ." She shook her head sadly. "But which baby did you come to see?"

Jane gave Marion a puzzled look.

"After all," Marion continued, "he has two."

* * *

Depressed at how tired he was, Paul stepped off the elevator and wearily made his way toward the NICU. It was one thing to get winded taking the stairs, but quite another when just getting on and off an elevator took every ounce of energy he had left. Ignoring the nagging worry that his cancer was spreading again, he reasoned it was the painkillers he'd swallowed this morning that were making him so tired. His health couldn't be declining *that* fast. Not now. More likely it was those women who had taken it out of him, leaving him physically and emotionally drained.

He'd hardly been able to stand that last appointment. *Sharlene* had spent an agonizing thirty-eight minutes on her Grande Mocha Frappuccino. He'd never seen anyone drink so slowly. He glanced over his shoulder again, worried he was being followed by her or that blonde bombshell. *What a nightmare.* He could still hear her shouting, "But I'm right for you! And I absolutely love children."

About now, the Department of Child Welfare didn't look so bad.

And to think he'd only met half the women he was supposed to today. He hated to imagine an afternoon to match this morning. Skipping out on his later interviews was worth getting an unlisted number—and a bodyguard if necessary.

Paul knew he was being picky, but who wouldn't in his situation? Had meeting women been so stressful or downright scary before? He thought back to his college days, trying to form a mental image of some of the girls he'd gone out with. His mind drew a blank. He had dated, hadn't he? There'd been that one homecoming dance . . . Paul groaned. He hadn't *meant* to shut his date's dress in the car door and drive like that the whole ten miles to the restaurant. But she *had* meant it when she told him off at the dance and called her roommate to come get her.

No wonder he was so bad at this. If it hadn't been for Pete introducing him to Tami, who knows what might have happened.

Or *not* happened. If it hadn't been for Pete . . .

Trying to shake off his misery and exhaustion, Paul went to the sink and began scrubbing up. Across the room, he saw two women standing by the NICU door. He hoped nothing bad had happened today. He wasn't worried that it might have been Mark or Madison—the hospital would have called him. But he hated it when *any* baby had a particularly bad day. He somehow felt like they—he and the other parents here—were all in this together. They made up a club of sorts whose membership required being a parent of a critically ill infant. When one of those infants suffered, all the parents felt it, because they knew it could have just as easily been their child.

It could be his next.

Dreading any more bad news, Paul pulled a mask from the box and turned toward the door.

Several steps away he stopped, shock registering on his tired face as he recognized the woman standing beside Marion. He was used to seeing Marion here, but the woman with her . . . He catalogued her features— just to make certain.

Sandals, fluorescent toes—he could see them even from across the room—flowered skirt, wild hair. It was her all right. One of his many appointments that had gone terribly wrong from the beginning. Paul tried to remember why this one had been so awful. After a moment he had it.

She was the *realtor*. He moved closer. She was looking at Madison through the glass like a . . . *vulture*. Wasn't that the word she'd used? Paul moved closer.

"Poor woman," Marion said. "Died right after the paramedics got there. It's really a miracle the twins survived."

Jane, a look of revelation on her face, turned away from the window and looked at Marion. "I think I was here that day, taking care of Andrew when a nurse came in and . . . How old are they? About seven weeks?"

Marion nodded.

"Then I'm sure of it. I remember." Jane looked through the window again, straining to see the infant in the isolette Marion had pointed out.

Paul watched, both fascinated and worried, as Jane leaned her forehead against the glass. *Who is she?* he wondered. If she was a realtor, then what was she doing in the NICU the day his babies were born? Was she a volunteer? Who was Andrew?

Marion stepped closer to the window and to Jane. "The little girl, Madison—Maddie I like to call her—she's had spunk from the get-go. But her brother Mark, he's got a problem with his heart. I'm not quite sure what it is exactly. I hear he's better though, since his surgery awhile back."

"Surgery," Jane murmured. "On a preemie. That must have been so— so terrifying for his father—for Paul."

Marion pursed her lips together and nodded, looking at Jane thoughtfully. "I imagine fear is a feeling he's become well acquainted with. Having cancer does that to a person," she finished meaningfully.

"What?" Jane gasped, her gaze pulled from the window to Marion.

Paul froze, hoping she hadn't seen him.

Marion misinterpreted Jane's exclamation. "Yes, dear. I had cancer too—breast cancer. I was only forty-two when I had a mastectomy. It was quite terrifying—and I don't just mean the surgery. It's the uncertainty of it all—not knowing how long you'll be around." She shook her head. "What Mr. Bryant must be going through . . . I count my blessings each and every day that I'm here with my grandchildren." She gave Jane a final squeeze. "And now I'd better get in to see that grandson of mine." She turned and headed for the sink, nearly running into Paul. She smiled at him. "Good afternoon, Mr. Bryant. Eavesdropping were you?" she asked with a knowing wink. Then, before Paul could reply, she added, "She's a keeper, that one."

Unaware of the drama unfolding around her, Marion continued across the room. Adrenaline surged through Paul as he walked toward Jane.

She stared at him, her eyes wide.

"What are you doing—?" Paul broke off, studying her face for the first time. Her eyes glistened with unshed tears, but it was her intense look of longing that stopped him.

She's the one.

Paul looked around, wondering who had spoken. But there was no one near them. The only sound to be heard was the water running on the far side of the room.

"I'm sorry," Jane began. "I had no right, I only wanted . . ." She glanced back at the window as her voice trailed off.

She wants to be a mother. The voice again.

Paul didn't bother looking around this time but instead watched Jane as she folded her arms across her chest, hugging herself as if she were cold.

Another awkward moment passed, and she spoke again. "I'd better be going." She brushed past him, heading for the elevator.

"No—wait." He heard himself speak before he realized what he was doing.

Jane turned around slowly, a questioning look on her face.

He took a step toward her and his eyes locked with hers. She wasn't what he'd planned on, what he'd expected. How could he even be considering a woman who sold real estate, wanted to have her own business, and had fluorescent toes? And yet . . . She was looking past him again, toward the nursery. Paul turned around, following her gaze. The nurse stood at the window, carefully holding Mark.

Paul heard Jane's breath catch.

"He's so tiny. So perfect."

Perfect? Paul looked at the mess of tubes and wires coming out of his son. Perfect?

Yes. She is perfect.

Suddenly it felt as if a portion of the weight lifted from his shoulders. A bit of his tiredness faded away as he turned back to Jane. He walked toward her, his lips curving in a half-smile.

"I think, maybe . . . Can we start again?" he asked, stopping in front of her. He didn't wait for a reply. "Hi. I'm Paul. I have terminal cancer. My wife was killed in a car accident, and I'm looking for a woman to raise my children." He extended his hand.

Jane hesitated for the merest second before a smile broke out over her face and she put her hand in his.

"I'm Jane."

Chapter Nine

Paul held up a limp french fry. "I've eaten way too many of these lately."

Across the table from him, Jane moved her fork slowly around her own plate. The macaroni and cheese and wilted salad weren't doing much for her. "Kind of makes you wonder if the hospital has some sort of contract with the cafeteria. You know, they supply so many new patients per day from food poisoning cases, and the hospital gives them a deal on rent or something."

Paul grinned. "That's a good theory, though I haven't succumbed yet . . ." His smile faded, and he looked up at Jane, his face grave.

"Will you tell me about your cancer?" she asked.

"There's not much to tell." Paul pushed his plate aside and leaned back in his chair. "It'll be two years this December that I was diagnosed. Liver cancer." He grimaced. "Made a lousy Christmas present. They tell you right off that it's fatal. Although *actually dying* can take years sometimes."

"That's good, isn't it?" Jane asked. "I mean the *years* part."

He shrugged. "It can be, but . . ."

"What?" Jane prodded.

"Though in my case, the doctor originally predicted months, not years."

"It would seem you've proved them wrong." Jane put her fork down and picked up her water glass, swirling the ice cubes around as she waited for Paul to continue.

He nodded. "At first Tami and I were aggressive with my treatments. When you're told something is going to kill you, I think your feelings can go two ways. You either accept it—give up in essence and succumb to depression, that sort of thing, or you get really mad and decide that no, this is not going to get you. In spite of the terrible odds I was given, Tami and I felt certain we could beat the cancer." He smiled faintly. "I guess we hadn't quite outgrown the immortal feeling of youth."

"I would think that's a pretty healthy attitude to have."

"It's great—until your first letdown. When that first CT scan comes back showing no improvement, then you're hit harder than if you'd just accepted reality at first."

Jane leaned forward across the table. "What do you mean?"

Paul took a drink, then set his glass down and rubbed his eyes. "You said it best yourself."

Not understanding, Jane looked at him.

He inclined his head toward the elevator doors. "How heartbreaking to have to leave them."

"But you haven't. You're still here," she said, her voice subdued.

For how long? he wanted to ask. More than that, he found himself wanting to tell her how long the doctors thought he had this time. Instead, he rose from the table.

"You're right. I am here, and I haven't held my children yet today."

"I've kept you. I'm sorry." Jane bent to pick up her purse, then stood. "Thank you for lunch." She held out her hand.

Paul took it, holding on a second longer than necessary. "Thank *you*. It was a nice break. I wasn't feeling well—needed something to eat." He put his hands in his pockets and shrugged. "Too much coffee on an empty stomach . . ."

Jane smiled. "I can imagine." She turned toward the door.

Don't let her get away.

"Jane, wait."

"Yes?" She paused midstride and looked back.

Paul shifted awkwardly from one foot to the other. "I think I'll feel even better if I apologize."

"Oh?" Jane asked, her eyebrows raised.

"I went about this whole thing all wrong today. I was a real jerk."

She folded her arms across her chest. "Now that you mention it, yes you did, and you were. However—" Her face softened. "Given the circumstances, I think it's entirely understandable. Forgiveness granted." She smiled again. "You're off my list."

"*List?*" he asked, confused.

"The never-going-to-give-my-children-that-name list. After this morning, *Paul* was right at the top."

He grimaced.

Jane continued. "Now your name has been officially removed. Feel better?"

"Not really," Paul said. "You see, the thing is . . ." He stopped, wondering how on earth to even begin to ask what he had to. Agitated, he rubbed the back of his neck. "The thing is I feel guilty every time I go upstairs. I only spend about fifteen minutes holding Madison, then I head to the other side of the NICU and spend an hour or more with Mark." He took a breath and rambled on. "It's not that I favor him or anything, it just seems like he needs me more right now. And a lot of the time, I can't even hold him. He's in this isolette—all these tubes and monitors. I just hold his tiny hand and talk to him—tell him about his mom—tell him to hang in there." Paul looked up, pleading in his voice. "So you can see how it would really help me out if I knew someone was spending time with my daughter while I'm with my son. It would only be about an hour or two a day. And you *have* experience. I heard you talking to Mrs. Howard—" Paul stopped, noticing Jane's sudden frown.

"Is this a paid position?" she asked, her voice strained.

"*What?*—no," he said, perplexed at her sudden change of attitude.

"Then quit making it sound like a *job*. Back at Starbucks I felt like I'd been through a horrible job interview, and now you're doing it again. Just pretend I'm your friend—that I've been your friend for longer than—" She glanced at her watch. "Longer than an hour, and you're asking me for a favor."

"I—I—"

"Yes, I know." Jane waved her hand. "You're bad at this sort of thing. Most men are. All the more reason to practice." She clasped her hands in front of her and smiled at him expectantly. "Go on."

Paul looked at her a moment more, then took a step closer. "Jane," he began, doing his best to look sincere. "Would you, knowing there is nothing in it for you—no dating, no relationship—would you, as my *friend*, be willing to come to the hospital sometimes to help me care for my children?"

He waited a heartbeat, then watched as Jane's smile reached her eyes.

"I'd love to."

Chapter Ten

Reeling with déjà vu, Jane walked through the door to the nursery.

Paul followed right behind. "If you want to grab a rocker, I'll tell Amy what we're going to do."

"I'll be over there, then," Jane said, heading for her favorite rocker— the glider type with a comfy blue cushion. It was the same one she'd sat in when she'd come to feed Andrew. Jane sank into the chair and looked around. Not much had changed in a month and a half. It was nice to be here, helping someone again. Maybe, like Marion, she should consider volunteering on a permanent basis.

A few moments later, Paul walked over, his daughter cradled in his arms.

"Ready?" he asked.

Jane nodded enthusiastically. "Yes."

Paul bent over, carefully placing Madison in her outstretched arms.

Jane looked down at the little girl's tiny, perfect face, and suddenly being here felt *very* different.

With Andrew, Jane had always felt the intruder—certain her nephew recognized her as a mere substitute for his real mother. But Madison had never been held by her mother, and it had been nearly two months since Madison had felt the ties of the womb. Jane knew the nurses' schedules were hectic, and if Paul only spent fifteen minutes with his daughter each time he came . . .

This little girl was likely as starved for affection as Jane was.

Jane placed her finger in Madison's palm and watched as her tiny hand curved around it. Jane's heart constricted, and she felt a rush of something that was much more than longing. But it was too soon, and she didn't dare let herself put a name to it. Pasting a bright smile on her face and looking up at Paul with what she hoped were not too moist of eyes, she said merely, "She's beautiful."

* * *

Two hours later, Paul held the elevator door open as Jane squeezed on amid a group of clipboard-holding interns. With bloodshot eyes and constant yawns, they all looked exhausted. Jane smiled at them anyway. She couldn't help it. She felt happier than she'd been in—in as long as she could remember.

Paul looked happy too. "You want to get a bite to eat or something?" he asked as they stepped into the lobby.

Jane looked warily in the direction of the cafeteria.

"I didn't mean there," Paul said, chuckling. "I wouldn't try to poison you, not after all your help today."

"In that case, yes," Jane said.

He followed her to her car in the parking garage, then she drove him to his car and followed him to get fast food—not a big date—but definitely better than the hospital cafeteria. They lingered over shakes and bacon cheeseburgers, talking about Paul's adorable children for a good hour until Jane realized she needed to hurry to catch her ferry.

"I'm sorry, but I've got to go."

"Now *I've* kept you," Paul said, walking ahead of her to hold the door open.

"I had a terrific afternoon," Jane reassured him. "It's just that I live on Bainbridge and my ferry leaves at 6:30. If I miss it, I'll be home after dark, and my power doesn't always work, so it's best I get there before sunset. That way I can fiddle with the fuse box if there's a problem."

Paul was giving her a peculiar look. "You're an island-dweller and an electrician too?"

"No to the electrician part." Jane rummaged through her purse, searching for her keys. "But I've found that if I speak very kindly to my fuse box, it will often do what I ask it to."

"And when it doesn't?" Paul asked, a smile playing at the corners of his mouth.

"Pounding on it is sometimes equally effective." Jane pulled her keys out and held them up. "Success. And as for the island-dweller part—don't think you've met a rich girl. Last year our agency listed a cottage that had been *severely* fire damaged. The owner just wanted to dump the place, and I *loved* the property, so I lucked out and got it. The cottage is still a mess—it passed inspection, *barely*—but that's about it. The whole inside needs to be redone, but the yard is gorgeous, and the view . . ." Jane paused. "Well, you have to climb up on the roof to see anything. Someday I'll build a deck up there, but the view is breathtaking. On clear nights I can see across the bay to the Seattle skyline."

"You don't happen to have a telescope do you?" Paul asked, hopeful.

She shook her head. "No."

"I mean, with that great view, it would seem the logical thing."

"I don't even have a deck yet—just a rickety old ladder I climb for occasional roof-sitting. It's enough to let me count the stars."

Jane stopped at her car, parked next to his in the small lot. "Thank you for a lovely afternoon—evening," she amended, looking up at the sky. "I'll meet you at the hospital anytime. Just let me know when."

"I'll call you," Paul said.

"Great." Jane opened her door and got in.

Paul waved as she drove away, then stood, hands in his pockets, staring after her until she'd turned the corner out of sight.

Something about her had changed over the course of their afternoon together. She'd lost the ponytail hours ago, and in the damp Seattle evening, her hair had curled naturally around her face, perfectly framing luminescent brown eyes. He realized, quite suddenly and happily, that she wasn't bad-looking at all. In fact, apart from her striped toenails, she was really very pretty. That was good. Pete liked pretty. Paul wondered what else there was about Jane that his brother might find appealing. He imagined there were quite a few things. Maybe this whole idea wasn't so crazy after all.

Counting stars. It's not astronomy, Pete, but it's a start.

* * *

"I'll call you," Jane grumbled under her breath as she grabbed a shovel from her garden shed. "Famous *last* words." She slammed the shed door shut and marched around to the front of the house. It had been four—nearly five—days since the strange and delightful afternoon she'd spent with Paul.

Four days without a single phone call.

"Men," she fumed as she thrust her shovel into the ground. Levering the blade with her weight, she pulled back, scooping a generous amount of dirt over her shoulder.

"Noncommittal, emotionally draining, selfish, insecure, egotistical, shallow-minded, oppositionally defiant—" The litany of psychology terms continued as she dug. She may not have graduated, but it was times like these that she recalled with clarity the many case studies she'd written papers about. She jumped on the shovel again. "Narcissistic, antisocial, delusional, anxiety-producing, *developmentally delayed.* So delayed they don't know how to use a phone," she muttered. "Why are they *never* any different?" Certain she would never know the answer, she threw her anger and energy into twenty minutes of vigorous digging.

Finished with the task but still agitated, Jane finally tossed her shovel aside and stormed up the front steps and into her house. She headed for the kitchen, pushing the play button on her answering machine as she walked by the phone. But, of course, there were no new messages. She'd had the phone outside with her all morning.

After pouring herself a glass of lemonade, Jane returned to the front yard. The two holes were dug now—at least her frustration had amounted to something—and she could plant the rose topiaries she'd purchased in celebration of the Sweviecs' offer being accepted.

But even the thought of the two new trees flanking her walkway didn't have the brightening effect on her mood it should have. Tired and dejected, Jane sat down on the crumbling steps and wondered for the hundredth time what had gone wrong.

She rested her elbows on her knees, head bent forward as she threaded her fingers through her hair, removing dirt. In her mind, she went over the afternoon with Paul, but nothing had changed since she'd replayed it the previous twenty times. She'd think it was all some bizarre dream except . . . Except she'd never forget what it felt like holding little Madison. It was all she'd thought of for the last five days. It was all she could think of now.

So why hadn't he called?

Surely he'd been back to the hospital at least once since Tuesday. He'd told her he went almost every day.

The hospital.

A sick feeling erupted in her stomach. What if—while she'd been fretting and then ranting and raving that Paul hadn't called—what if that whole time he hadn't *been able* to call? The man had cancer, for heaven's sake. Jane rose from the step and went into the house.

How bad was his cancer? She didn't really know. He'd seemed okay—except for his obvious fatigue, and she'd chalked that up to worry about his children more than anything else.

Jane grabbed her purse off the table and headed outside, convinced that something terrible had happened. Something she should have tuned into *much* sooner.

Chapter Eleven

Jane sat in her car, waiting for the ferry to dock. She dialed Paul's number again and was not surprised when his answering machine picked up after the fourth ring. This time she decided to leave a message.

"Paul, this is Jane—from the hospital the other day. Tuesday, actually. And since that was four days ago, and you told me you go to the hospital *every* day, and you haven't called me . . . Well, I just got worried that maybe something happened to you or your babies. So even if you don't want to see me again, could you please call and let me know everyone is okay? And if you ever need any help—well, I just wanted to let you know that I really enjoyed holding Madison. It was the best thing I've done in a long time."

The machine beeped, signaling the end of her message. Jane grimaced, certain that if Paul *was* okay, hearing her needy voice would have the reverse effect she wanted, and he would never call her. Oh well, at least she had tried.

An hour later, Jane stood in front of the NICU window, unable to believe what she was seeing. Next to the rockers, Paul stood—looking as well as he had the other day—talking to a *woman* who was holding Madison. Jane moved to the side and squinted, looking closer to make sure it really was Paul's daughter. As the woman lifted the baby to her shoulder, Jane's suspicions were confirmed. Her heart sank; there was no mistaking Madison's tuft of brown hair or her dainty little nose. Jane started to turn away from the window just as Paul looked over.

He did a double take and Jane was sure he muttered an expletive as he spotted her. He said something to the woman, then started toward the door.

Jane turned and fled. Practically running from the room, she left the nursery and walked briskly down the hall. She pressed the elevator button, then thought the better of bawling on an elevator full of people. She headed for the stairs. Entering the deserted stairwell, she ran down two flights, then stopped, sitting on the landing just as the tears started to flow.

How stupid could she be—trusting a guy the very day he'd been a complete jerk to her? Why had she believed he was any different? His whole story—the cancer and *everything* was probably just some ploy for—for what? What had he gained from their meeting? Nothing. Unless he had some strange penchant for taking a variety of women out for fast food.

Jane pulled a tissue from her purse and dabbed at her eyes. She tried to get a grip. *Look at me,* she thought. Pretty soon she'd be just like Tara—and then there would be *no* tissue boxes left in the office.

Jane blew her nose and hugged her knees to her chest. So this was what it felt like getting your feet wet. She'd been right all along. It wasn't worth it.

"Thanks for nothing, Jay," she muttered, thinking again of his taunt that had led her to answer Paul's ad in the first place.

Above her, Jane heard a door open and footsteps on the stairs. Taking a shaky breath, she stood and started down. When she reached the lobby, she headed for the exit, searching for her keys in her purse as she walked.

"You know, you really ought to clean out that purse," Paul said as he stepped up beside her.

Jane glared at him and walked faster. "You ought to try honesty."

"I did—I *was.* Listen, Jane," He put his hand on her sleeve. "It's not what you think."

She shrugged his hand away. "You have *no* idea what I think." Lengthening her stride, she walked through the door.

Paul kept right up beside her.

"I'm not having a bunch of different women to the hospital each day to hold my daughter."

"Why not?" Jane snapped. "You met several different women for coffee, why not follow with a heart-breaking cancer story and an hour in the NICU? I'm sure it will get you all the sympathy or whatever it is you want."

"What I *want* is to find someone to take care of my children when I'm not around. *You* know that."

"Do I?" Jane asked sarcastically. She'd reached her car and turned the key in the lock. Tossing her purse inside, she turned and looked at Paul. "I *thought* I'd met a really nice guy who had about the worst set of circumstances I could imagine. I *thought* we were going to be friends. I *thought* he was going to call me." Jane sat in the driver's seat and jammed the key into the ignition, but when she went to close the door, Paul held it fast.

"The woman you saw holding Madison is Beth Meyers. Her *husband,* Nick, is with Mark right now." Paul sighed. "Yesterday I had an appointment with an adoption agency. They had this profile book . . . I had to select three couples. The Meyers are the first of those couples. I get a chance to see each of them interact with Mark and Madison before I make a final decision."

Jane's hand dropped to her lap. "Adoption agency?" She looked up at Paul. "I thought . . ."

"I didn't tell you this Tuesday." Paul began. "I thought I'd probably overwhelmed you enough—but I'm taking the last combination of drugs that are known to shrink the kind of tumors I have." He looked away as he continued. "I've tried three others. One of them worked for a while, then nothing."

"I'm so sorry," Jane whispered.

"Me too," Paul said. "I'd like to have more hope, but as I told you the other day, it's worse that way. Eventually, there will be a letdown with this drug too, and when that happens there's nothing to do but try *experimental* treatments—basically be a human laboratory—or just wait to die." He looked down at her again. "I *have* to be realistic, Jane. I *have* to make sure my kids are taken care of. I've emailed my brother in Iraq, and he hasn't responded. We were sort of at odds the last time we met. It's been a couple of years, but I'd hoped . . ." Paul shrugged. "He's the only family I've got. So you see . . ."

"Were you ever going to call me?" Jane asked quietly.

"I was," Paul insisted. "I just wasn't sure what to say. I never expected to see you here though. I guess I should have known—since you were curious enough to come the last time." He gave her a half-smile.

Jane swallowed the lump in her throat and reached for a bag in the backseat.

"It's better this way," Paul said. "The twins will be with a couple who really want kids. They'll be loved and provided for. And I won't have to burden you or anyone else."

"I wouldn't have felt burdened," Jane said, looking up at him again.

"Maybe not at first," Paul agreed. "But I could see already, just after the other night, that it would have been really hard for you to help as much as I'd hoped."

"How so?" Jane asked, a note of irritation returning to her voice.

"Well . . ." Paul faltered. "I could just tell. For instance, you live on Bainbridge. It would be a major inconvenience for you to come to Seattle every day to see my kids."

"I *work* in Seattle," Jane pointed out. "And I'm here quite often on weekends too—my entire family lives here. Remember? I'm the youngest of seven."

"Being with Mark and Madison would take time away from your nieces and nephews."

"My nieces and nephews get plenty of attention," Jane said, her ire rising.

"Okay, well, what about your house and your business? Your whole face lit up the other evening when you were telling me about your home, your garden, your view. There's no way I could ask you to give that up to help me. It wouldn't be fair, and you wouldn't do it."

Jane pursed her lips, trying to keep her temper under control. "So basically, you're telling me you decided adoption was the right solution based on your *eventual* death and our meeting the other night."

"More or less." Paul shifted uncomfortably. "I just assumed . . ."

"Exactly." Jane swung her legs out of the car and stood, facing him. "Haven't you ever learned what happens when you *assume?*" She didn't wait for him to answer. "It's one of the many valuable things my seminary teacher taught me."

"Seminary?" Paul asked, confused.

"Never mind." Jane waved her hand in the air. "If my face was *all lit up* the other night it was because—" Her eyes clouded and she looked up at the concrete beams of the parking garage, trying to get control of her emotions. She continued in a quieter voice. "It was because in the space of about an hour, I fell totally, completely in love with your daughter." She looked at him again, not caring that tears were sliding down her cheeks. "How *dare* you assume I'd care more about my house than a baby." She thrust the bag she held into his hands. "These are for Mark and Madison. In case you haven't noticed, they're practically the only children in the nursery still wearing those stupid hospital shirts."

Jane got back in her car and pulled the door shut. She started the engine and backed out, driving away from any hope she'd had that her life was going to change.

Chapter Twelve

Paul carried the plate with his tuna fish sandwich over to the coffee table. He sat down in his favorite chair, took a drink of water, and reached for the remote. Instead, his hand bumped the bag Jane had left him. Scowling, he pushed it away, still not having looked inside. He'd give it to the nurses at the hospital tomorrow, and they could dress his children—since apparently he was incapable of the task. Jane's last remark still stung. *They're practically the only children still wearing those stupid hospital shirts.*

Paul had to admit she was right about the shirts. They were kind of a pain the way they crossed over in front. But he hadn't noticed, he *honestly* had not noticed that his children were the only ones wearing them. It had never occurred to him that he ought to bring other clothes to the hospital. He wondered how many other things he'd missed.

Things Tami would have noticed and taken care of.

It was a good thing he was getting the twins a real set of parents soon—a father *and* a mother. Mark and Madison deserved a good, stable home, with parents who knew what they were doing.

It was the right thing to do.

Paul took a bite of his sandwich and leaned back in his chair. He reached for the remote again, but this time was stopped by the framed picture of him and Tami at the beach. For some reason the picture seemed different than it had before. He looked at it closer, then rubbed his eyes. Instead of her usual smile, it appeared Tami was frowning at him. Unnerved, Paul turned the picture away and grabbed the remote.

He pointed it toward the TV in the corner of the apartment but did not push POWER. Instead, he rose from his chair and was headed to the kitchen when his wedding picture caught his eye. The eleven-by-seventeen was in the same location it had always been, but the tone seemed different. He was still in his tux, sitting. Tami stood behind him, her hand on his shoulder. He looked excessively happy. She looked . . . *mad.*

Shaken, Paul stepped back from the wall. He was losing it. Maybe it was the drugs, or maybe he was nearer the end than he thought and was getting delusional. The doctors had warned him about strange side effects. He just hadn't expected this. His sandwich and the news forgotten, he walked down the hall to the spare bedroom—where there were no pictures hung at all.

* * *

Paul woke with a start and pressed the Indiglo button on his watch—
3:13 A.M. He'd only been asleep for an hour, and now the pain was worse.
He felt—as he had so many times before—like he'd just been stabbed on
the right side, just below his ribs. He rolled to the side of the bed, careful
not to disturb the rolls of blueprints stacked beside him. His feet touched
the ground, but he found he couldn't stand straight. Bent over and
clutching his abdomen, he made his way to the bathroom.

Switching on the light, he fumbled with the bottles on the counter,
seeking relief for at least *some* of the pain. Popping the pills in his mouth,
he took a drink of water and swallowed. He'd probably just doomed
himself to more hallucinations, but at the moment he didn't care. Pain had
a funny way of doing that to you—driving you to the point where it didn't
matter what happened, so long as the pain went away. It was like that just
now, and Paul braced his hands on the counter, head bent as he tried to
focus on something—*anything*—to keep from falling to the floor and
crying like a baby.

Make a to do list.

"Thanks, Tam," he whispered, certain he'd just heard her voice again.
Sometimes he swore she was still here with him. All through his sickness
she'd coaxed him to keep going, to keep making plans for the future—the
next day, week, month, even years ahead. And Tami had been right. If he
had a list for tomorrow, then he would have to be around to do it.

He closed his eyes and thought. The first thing to do in the morning
was call the adoption agency and tell them he'd chosen the Meyers.

No!

"Come on, Tami. You can't—can't expect me to do this—alone." Paul
looked around the small bathroom, half expecting to see her frowning at
him. "Left me with—quite a—mess." He gasped as a wave of nausea rolled
over him.

Paul leaned over the sink and stared at the drain. From the corner of
his eye, he noticed for the first time the dust covering Tami's makeup tray.
He hadn't even had time to think what to do with her belongings. He realized he would have to soon. In less than a month, his lease was up, and he
hadn't bothered to renew because he needed to find someplace cheaper and
closer to the hospital. Paul closed his eyes and groaned, this time not from
pain, but from the thought of all that lay ahead. He had a *major* to do list,
and somehow he knew he'd be around long enough to see it all done.

Just the thought of packing was enough to make him exhausted. And
he had no idea what to do with all of Tami's things. How was he supposed

to decide what to keep and what to give away? He didn't want to get rid of anything. Though he'd seen her casket lowered into the ground, somehow he knew that getting rid of her belongings was what would really make his loss permanent. As long as he came home and saw her mug in the kitchen, her bathrobe on the back of the door, her makeup on the counter . . . she was still here—still real to him.

Paul picked up one of Tami's lipsticks, pulled off the top, and slowly turned it. A wistful smile crossed his face as he looked at the mirror, remembering the first time Tami had surprised him with a message there.

It was Christmas 2001—their first Christmas. They'd been married only three weeks. He'd awoken in the middle of the night with what he thought was the pain of a burst appendix. After making his way to the bathroom, he'd turned on the light to find the mirror ablaze with red lip prints, and across the middle Tami had written, *Thanks for the best Christmas ever. I love you so much.*

And she did. She'd stuck by him when, less than twenty-four hours later, they'd learned he had terminal cancer. It was a bad start to a long year.

Haunted by memories, Paul left the bathroom and went to lie down on his own bed. It didn't matter where he was. Tamara's presence was every-where in the apartment, and he both loved and hated it.

The sheets on their bed hadn't been changed in the nearly two months since her death. He couldn't bear the thought of washing anything she had touched. In his darkest hour, he could lay his head on her pillow and know Tamara was somehow with him. He remembered her hair spread across the pillowcase. He could imagine that the faint scent of her perfume still lingered on the sheets.

Choosing Tami's side of the bed instead of his own, Paul lay down. The pain in his stomach was a little better now, and he closed his eyes as he let his mind drift—hopeful the memories would ease the pain in his heart.

* * *

5:23 . . . 5:24 . . . 5:25. Paul watched the numbers on the digital clock change. He'd dozed for a while but now lay wide awake again.

Get up, lazy bones.

Paul smiled into the dark. Of course, that's what Tami would say to him if she were here. She'd tell him to quit wasting time wishing he could sleep when he could be doing something productive. As if sleep wasn't productive.

But then, Tami had never let him wallow in self-pity or anything else. *Kind of like Jane.*

Paul pushed the thought aside and rolled away from the clock. Tami had been tough with him because she had to be, because that's what had kept his spirits up, had kept him alive. He thought back to that first terrifying day in the hospital, while they'd waited for his biopsy results.

Tami, a serious look on her face, had sat on the chair beside his bed. "Paul?"

He gave her a wan smile.

"You're in big trouble, you know. That property you gave me for Christmas was all well and fine, but I was expecting a house on it by Valentine's. That gives you . . ." She opened her purse and consulted the calendar on the back of her checkbook. "Forty-eight days." She sighed. "I imagine this little stay in the hospital will set us back a bit."

"Needed a break from my demanding wife." His voice was raspy as he reached for the pitcher on the nightstand. Tami walked around the bed and poured him some water, then held it to his lips as he drank.

"Well," she said, once he had finished. "I was warned to let you get your rest, so I think I'll go talk with the doctor." She bent over and kissed Paul's lips. "I think I'll offer him your new golf clubs—maybe that'll bring his price down."

"Love you too," Paul whispered.

"Don't you forget it," Tami called over her shoulder, then blew him another kiss and left.

Paul looked at the ceiling now, coming out of the memory. He touched a finger to his lips, then raised his hand to the ceiling and blew.

"Help me, Tam," he pled as tears welled in his eyes. "Help me get through this. I miss you so much."

Chapter Thirteen

When Paul woke at 8:40 the next morning, the pain in his liver had subsided to a dull ache, though his heart felt much the same. The intense sorrows of the night had given way to the ever-present loneliness of daytime, and he felt grateful to be somewhat in control of both mind and body again.

These days, that was as good as it got.

Knowing this, Paul decided to get something done while he had both physical and mental stamina. After his shower, he went to the kitchen and poured himself a glass of orange juice. As he stood at the sink drinking, he looked around the messy room. The espresso maker was never put away anymore—nor was the basket containing individual flavor packets. Empty bread bags, paper plates, and butter knives littered the counter beside the toaster. Dishes were stacked in the sink. Two bags of trash leaned against the wall beside the full trash can. Bills and junk mail were piled next to the phone. Clutter had taken over in Tami's absence. She'd been the organized one, whereas he was . . . the slob.

Chagrined at how bad he'd let things get, Paul set his glass down and went to the trash. He tied up the bag, pulled it out of the can and took all three bags out to the garbage. When he returned, he looked under the sink for another liner. That there were none did not surprise him. Over the past seven weeks, he'd been slowly running out of everything. Sooner or later he'd have to make a list and do some real shopping, but for now he grabbed a paper grocery bag from the stack beneath the sink and stuffed it down into the plastic can. He'd just make do—as he did with every other aspect of his life.

Feeling queasy, Paul sat down at the kitchen table. He was tired again, and as much as he suddenly wanted to clean the kitchen, he knew he didn't have the energy to stand at the sink and wash so much as one dish.

But he had to do *something*. Paul looked at the calendar on the wall and saw that it was still on July—the date of Tami's baby shower marked with a teddy-bear sticker. He got up and flipped it to September, where the twins' due date was circled and starred. It seemed just yesterday that he and Tami had sat at this table, counting the days until their babies would be born. Now he started counting days until his lease was up. Unless he did something soon, he was going to be homeless. As he considered this, Paul looked around the crowded room, his eyes again straying to the now-empty garbage. Seeing the paper grocery bag, he formed a plan.

Grabbing a marker from the cup on the table, he took three more paper bags from beneath the sink. He looked at the bags a moment, then wrote one word on each of them. The first said "keep," the second "charity," and the third "trash." He remembered watching Tami do this when she moved from her apartment to his just before they were married. Paul gathered the bags up and returned to his room. Deciding to start small, he sat down on Tami's side of the bed. He'd clean out her nightstand today and pat himself on the back if he made it through.

Paul pulled open the drawer and reached inside. The first item was easy. Her reading glasses would go to charity. Because of Tami, someone in need would be able to read a book, like the one he put in the bag next to the glasses. Two more paperbacks followed.

The next item stopped him cold.

A baby pacifier lay untouched in a small gold box. Paul picked it up as another poignant memory came to him.

Valentine's Day—their second. Their last, he thought sadly as he stared at the pacifier and remembered.

"You said *no* presents until tonight," Paul protested, handing the small box back to Tami. "That's cheating."

"I don't care. I can't wait that long." She dropped the package back in his lap and sat, cross-legged, on the bed beside him. "Open it."

"Women," Paul grumbled. "Always changing the rules." He picked up the present and shook it. "Did you get me that titanium golf ball I saw at—?"

"Open it. *Now*."

"All right, all right. Take all the fun out of it." He untied the ribbon. "You've spoiled the whole romantic thing, you know. We're supposed to be at dinner, all dressed up . . . I haven't even shaved."

"It doesn't matter." She scooted closer on the bed.

Paul tore the paper away and took the lid off the box.

A baby pacifier lay nestled on a bed of cotton. He looked at it a moment, then looked up at Tami.

Her eyes were shining.

"You're sure?" he asked, his own eyes suddenly moist.

"Positive." Reaching over, she pulled a pregnancy test from her night-stand drawer. "See the pink line?"

Paul looked at it and nodded, swallowing the lump in his throat. *Thank you, God.* The Christmas before last they'd talked about starting a family, and his present to Tami had been the deed to the property where they were going to build their dream home. But instead of spending the year building that home, they'd been through a nightmare just trying to keep him alive.

It was July before the doctors had finally found the right combination of chemo drugs to shrink his tumors. He'd started getting better, but by then he hadn't worked in six months, and the medical bills were piling up. So he and Tami had made the agonizing decision to take a loan against his life insurance so they could get out of debt. Then—in an even bigger risk—they'd spent not ten, but twenty thousand dollars of that precious money on two tries at artificial insemination. He looked at how happy Tami was and suddenly felt very grateful they'd spent the money.

Paul wrapped his arms around her, pulling them both to the pillows. His face mere inches from hers, he whispered, "I love you."

Tears in his eyes again, Paul searched the drawer for the box lid, ribbon, and pregnancy test. He found all three and carefully placed them in the "keep" bag. Someday, he thought, his children should know their parents had wanted them very much.

* * *

Twenty minutes later, Tami's nightstand stood empty, but instead of feeling good that he'd accomplished something, Paul simply felt drained. The bag for charity was nearly full. The trash bag was completely empty. The bag of things he wanted to keep for Mark and Madison had spilled over onto a pile on the floor. Paul never would have thought of himself as sentimental, but he'd been unable to part with things like Tami's marked-up copy of *What to Expect When You're Expecting,* or the half-finished baby booties she'd been working on. They were her first attempt at crocheting, and Paul couldn't help but smile as he remembered the nights she'd worked on them, or the times she'd flung them across the room in frustration.

He picked up his empty juice glass and stood, wincing when he felt the familiar stab of pain. *Not a good sign, buddy.* He'd have to call Dr. Kline and schedule another MRI. Somehow he just knew this new combination of drugs was not doing what it was supposed to. What was surprising was that the thought of the cancer spreading didn't terrify him as it used to. It was an inevitable fact that it was going to get him, and so long as he had arrangements made for his children before it happened, then it really didn't matter. After facing Tami's death, his own no longer seemed so terrible.

Paul walked down the hall to the spare bedroom—also his home office. He looked around the crowded room, searching for the thick folder that held all of his medical information. He supposed he ought to have Dr. Kline's number memorized now, and a dozen times he'd told himself to put the hospital on speed dial, but he always forgot to get around to it. His memory wasn't what it used to be. Paul rubbed the top of his head absently, knowing the chemo had robbed him of much more than his hair.

He found the folder on top of the dresser, but he continued to scan the room, thinking of what would have to be packed and eventually moved. Two unassembled cribs were stacked against the far wall. Another corner held a double stroller. On top of the dresser and next to the bed were bags and boxes he'd yet to look into. A couple of days after the accident they'd been returned to him—the gifts from Tamara's baby shower. He couldn't bring himself to look at them. He'd never have to now. He'd just have the Meyers—or whichever couple took the twins—take it all away.

That would only leave him the furniture and his files and blueprints to go through. And a garbage can would take care of most of that. He hadn't worked in months, nor was he likely to again, he thought, looking fondly at his drafting table. That could go too, he realized. There was no point in keeping anything except . . . His eyes were again drawn to the plans piled on the bed. Well, maybe there was one set he ought to keep. It would be nice for Mark and Madison to know their parents had hoped for a future together.

Paul carried the file into the living room, purposely avoiding looking at his wedding picture on the wall. He hadn't taken any painkillers since the middle of the night, but he still didn't trust himself to see things clearly. If Tami was mad at him—and somehow haunting him—well he just couldn't handle that and everything else right now.

He was doing the best he could without help from anyone else.

Jane wanted to help you.

Paul pushed the thought away and went to retrieve the newspaper. He placed it on the counter and poured himself a bowl of cereal. A picture on the front of the paper showed a group of reservists sleeping in the shade of their armored vehicles, and the headline read "Life in Iraq."

It's a sign.

"No it isn't," Paul grumbled. Great. Now he was talking to himself. He poured milk in his cereal, then sat at his desk and switched on the computer. He would prove it wasn't a sign. Pete hadn't responded to his email in the last nine days, and he wouldn't respond now.

Paul logged on the Internet and waited for his inbox to open. There was one new message.

Paul nearly knocked his cereal off the desk as he read the sender—petesdragon2.

"You always *were* full of hot air," Paul mumbled, but he felt his heart pounding as he opened the email. His eyes quickly scanned the message.

I'm here for you, brother.

Pete

Told you so.

"I know, I know," Paul said as he leaned forward, head in his hands. So he was back to where he'd been a few weeks ago—imagined conversations with Tami. The hospital counselor had told him to worry if he got stuck in any one stage; the counselor hadn't said what to do if he started to regress. Maybe it was time to look at the phone numbers on that grief pamphlet. Maybe he should see someone about it on a regular basis. Maybe . . .

Out of the corner of his eye, Paul saw the red light flashing on his answering machine. His head snapped up and his finger pushed the play button as fear for Mark and Madison flooded him. But instead of the hospital, he heard Jane's worried voice.

Paul listened to the entire message, but it was her last words on the tape and from the parking garage yesterday that stuck in his mind.

Holding Madison was the best thing I've done in a long time . . . In the space of an hour, I fell totally, completely in love with your daughter . . . How dare you assume I'd care more about my house than a baby . . .

Paul looked back at the computer screen.

I'm here for you, brother.

He glanced at the crumpled paper that held Tami's last words.

Find our babies a mother. You know who their father should be.

Pushing his cereal aside, Paul looked at the open phone book, the name of the adoption agency circled in red. He'd chosen that agency—The Children's Hearts—based on the picture in their ad. It took up half a page and showed a family—mom, dad, boy, and girl running in a circle and holding hands as if playing ring-around-the-rosy. It was a nice picture. One he could imagine he and Tami, Mark and Madison in. Or if not he and Tami, then at least Mark and Madison.

Still, he acknowledged, a picture wasn't much basis for the most critical decision he'd ever make. Yet he'd felt good about it—sort of.

How could *anyone* ever feel entirely good about giving their children away? But what choice did he have?

Pete wasn't really *here*. He was in Iraq—for who knew how long. Before that he'd been in Afghanistan, and after Iraq he'd probably feel compelled to go fly his helicopter in some other dangerous, foreign place.

There was no way he could do that *and* be a father here. Pete, of all people, would understand that.

Pete will *understand.*

Of course. The thought stunned Paul. Why hadn't he realized that before? Pete knew what it was to grow up without a father, and he would never let his children suffer the same fate he had. Nor would he let his brother's children suffer that way. Paul leaned back in his chair, his worry suddenly alleviated at such an obvious conclusion. He moved the cursor to reply, anxious to share his burden with his brother. But his fingers hesitated on the keyboard, and after a moment Paul opened the drawer and removed a piece of paper. An email was certainly more efficient, but *this* letter he needed to write.

Chapter Fourteen

Dear Peter,

It is with much sorrow I share with you the news that Tami was killed in a car accident . . .

* * *

Jane was on the phone going over listings with a prospective client when a potted, miniature yellow rosebush was delivered to her desk.

Tara arrived two seconds later.

"Who's it from?" she demanded.

Jane shrugged and pointed to the phone, swiveling back to face her computer screen.

Tara helped herself to the white envelope tied to the pot. Jane reached her free hand around to try to snatch it from her, but Tara had already moved down the row of cubicles, sashaying away with her treasure.

Jane sighed to herself, then continued her phone conversation for another five minutes. Finally free, she spun her chair around, got up, and marched toward Tara's desk.

She could have walked there blindfolded. The heavy scent of perfume grew stronger the closer she got, until her nostrils were burning.

Tara was waiting for her.

"Any man who begins with an apology . . . might actually be okay," she said, grinning.

Jane held out her hand. "Give it to me."

Tara obliged. "I thought you said your date with Paul was a disaster. Now he's sending you roses. So what gives? And who's Madison?"

"Thank you," Jane said sharply and walked back to her cubicle, reading the note as she went.

Once there, she bent over to inhale the sweet smell of the roses—and to clear her head of Tara's perfume. She stuck the card in her purse and went back to work, but her eyes kept straying to the clock on her desk all morning.

* * *

Jane paced in front of the nursery window, trying to ward off the sick feeling in her stomach. Paul was fifteen minutes late. She hadn't misunderstood his note, had she? Was she a fool for even being here? *Who cares?* she thought. The chance to hold Madison again was worth the risk. After the other day, it didn't really matter what Paul thought.

But Jane cared about his daughter. That was why she'd come.

She wasn't certain, but Paul's brief note implied that he might have changed his mind about adoption. She pulled the paper out of her pocket, rereading it just to make certain she hadn't imagined the whole thing.

> *I was wrong. Forgive me?*
>
> *Madison is hoping you'll come this week. She needs you. I'll be at the hospital at one.*
>
> *Paul*

Madison needed her father too, so where was he? Jane decided to ask the nurses if they knew anything. She pressed the buzzer next to the door and waited until Amy made her way over.

"Hi Jane. You all washed?"

Jane nodded.

"Come in then," Amy said. "We've been expecting you."

"You have?" Jane asked. "I thought I was supposed to meet Paul outside—"

"He's already here." Amy walked past Jane and held the door open to the critical side of the Newborn Intensive Care Unit. "It's been a good day," Amy whispered as she motioned Jane into the room.

Unsure what to expect, Jane walked through the double doors that had previously been off limits to her. This was the side of the NICU where the most critical infants were kept, where the sounds of the machines keeping those infants alive replaced the sickly cries heard on the other side.

Paul was standing by an isolette. He smiled and beckoned to her.

"I'd like you to meet my son," he said proudly when Jane was closer. "Mark is breathing on his own right now, and he's doing great."

Jane looked down at the baby, smaller than his sister but just as adorable. She noticed he wore the blue hat and matching booties she'd purchased.

"I have to wait on the sleeper," Paul explained. "Mark's had open-heart surgery, and there's still quite a bit of equipment he needs." Paul pointed to the monitors and wires connected to his son's tiny chest.

"What's wrong with his heart?" Jane asked.

"A lot, unfortunately," Paul said. "The technical name is Hypoplastic Left Heart Syndrome—basically the left side of his heart is underdeveloped and can't pump enough oxygenated blood to the rest of the body. It's a pretty serious thing but fixable." He pointed to the scar on Mark's chest.

"Poor little guy," Jane murmured.

"There are a series of three surgeries," Paul said. "One down—two to go."

"*Two* more?" Jane asked, appalled. "He seems so fragile . . ."

"He is. But he would have died a few days after birth if they hadn't operated. And he *has* been getting better since the surgery."

Jane looked at Mark and felt overwhelmed with worry for him. "Wow," she said, looking at Paul with new appreciation. "You're amazing, you know that?"

He shook his head. "Actually, I think I'm kind of dense sometimes."

"No." Jane looked away, her face coloring as she recalled the harsh words she'd said to him. "May I?" she asked, holding her finger above Mark's arm.

Paul nodded. "It's good for him to be touched."

Jane lightly placed her finger on Mark's soft skin. "I'm sorry for the things I said to you the other day. I have no idea what it must be like to—"

"You don't need to apologize."

"Well then," Jane said, looking up at Paul. "Thank you for the roses. It was very thoughtful."

"Thank *you* for pointing out a couple of very important things."

"Like what?" Jane asked, confused.

"Like the fact that I'm still here with my children, and I don't need to put them up for adoption when I've found someone who is willing to help me care for them." His eyes locked on hers. "Am I right?"

"Yes," she said, relief and happiness flooding through her. "You're absolutely right."

* * *

On Tuesday, Mark had another good day. Off the ventilator and responsive to their voices and touch, he also got to see his sister for the first time since his surgery.

Jane cradled Madison's head as she bent over Mark's isolette. "Say hello to your brother, Madison. He may look a little peaked now, but take it from someone who has two brothers—he'll be chasing you all over in no time."

Paul chuckled.

"And hiding your Barbies, borrowing your bike, reading your diaries and letters," Jane continued. "But you'll be so glad you have him anyway."

"Sounds like you lived a tortured existence," Paul said, his fingers lightly turning Mark's face so he could see his sister.

Jane shook her head. "Nope. Believe me, I learned early on to give out as much as came my way."

"I don't doubt that," Paul said, recalling the earful he'd gotten in the parking garage on Saturday.

"Sorry," Jane said again. "What you see is what you get."

"I'm not complaining," Paul said. "In fact, I have to say that you're refreshingly different from all of the other women I met last week."

"Oh?" Jane asked warily. "Do I want to hear this?"

Paul shrugged. "It's not bad. It's just that right off you didn't seem to care much about impressing me, and later on you didn't get big with the sympathy thing."

"So . . . based on that analysis, why am I here?"

"Well, you didn't care about impressing *me,* but it was obvious right away that you cared about my children. I could tell you had an immediate connection with Madison."

Jane didn't say anything, but she couldn't have agreed more. She straightened and looked down at the beautiful little girl in her arms.

"I feel very privileged," she said quietly, "to be here." She looked at Paul. "I feel terrible that you have cancer—and that is about the most inadequate expression there is. What you've been through with your illness, your wife's death, Mark's heart—it's unfathomable—all of it. I'm amazed you've held together so well, and I do have a great deal of sympathy for you." She gave him a shaky smile. "What I won't do is feel sorry for you because you've got these two beautiful children. I am actually insanely jealous." Her smile deepened. "Maybe that's why I went a little berserk when you brought up the adoption thing. While there's still a chance . . . Well, I just don't see how you could give them up."

Paul rose from his chair and stood across from Jane.

"Maybe with your help I won't have to."

* * *

On Wednesday, Jane rocked and fed Madison while Paul spent time with Mark, who'd had a rough night. Afterward, she and Paul braved the hospital cafeteria once more, and she listened while Paul relayed all that Mark's doctor had discussed with him that day. Jane watched the lines of worry increase on Paul's brow as he spoke. As he swallowed a handful of pills, she wished there were something she could do to take away at least *one* of his problems.

At eleven thirty on Thursday, Jane had the Sweviecs' house inspection. Three and a half hours later, with a notepad full of complaints to bring to the sellers' attention, Jane pulled into the hospital parking garage. When she got to the nursery, Paul had already left, and since a new nurse was on duty, Jane was unable to get in to see Madison. Frustrated and filled again with that terrible longing, Jane spent thirty minutes standing at the window watching a nurse she didn't know feed and bathe Madison.

That night Jane left not one, but two needy messages on Paul's answering machine. She hoped he'd forgive her—hoped he wouldn't go back to the idea that her job always had to come first. Once she made this sale, she could practically forget about her job for a few months. She could prove to him that she was in this for the long haul.

When Paul hadn't returned her calls by 9:30, Jane broke down and made another batch of double-chocolate-chip cookies. She ate seven of them while watching *Sleepless in Seattle*. It always made her feel better to know she wasn't alone in having dreadful, lonely nights. If people as gorgeous as Tom Hanks and Meg Ryan could be lonely too, then maybe there was hope.

Chapter Fifteen

At noon on Friday, Jane shut down her computer and locked up her desk. Paul usually arrived at the hospital around one or two in the afternoon. Today she was going to be there first. As she walked out the office door, her brown-bag lunch in hand, Tara ran up behind her.

"Oh no you don't," she said, stepping in front of Jane. "You've been acting strange for almost two weeks now. I want to know what's up."

"Nothing's *up*," Jane said, looking warily at the cloudy sky as she stepped around Tara.

"You're a lousy liar." Tara walked beside her. "You're not still sore at me about that thing with the Sweviecs, are you?"

Jane shook her head. "I'm not mad. Just in a hurry." She glanced at the traffic, then stepped off the curb and started toward her car, parked across the street.

"Because I'm *really* sorry," Tara said, following her. "I'd never have said anything if I'd known it would cost me your friendship."

When she'd reached the sidewalk again, Jane stopped, turning to face Tara. "I'm still your friend. And when the deal closes, I'll take you out to an expensive dinner to prove it."

"I don't want an expensive dinner—well, maybe I do—but what I really want is for you to talk to me. For us to do lunch a couple of times a week like we used to. It's no fun drowning my sorrows at the bakery by myself."

"I'm sorry." Jane squeezed Tara's hand. "I didn't mean to leave the orange rolls all to you." She began walking again. "So tell me your troubles."

"No," Tara said, her face sullen.

Jane opened her bag, pulled out a cookie and waved it in front of Tara's face. "No? These have the same medicinal qualities as the rolls at the bakery."

Tara sighed and snatched the cookie. "If that's the best you can do." She took a bite. "Mmm," she sighed again.

Jane smiled. "Exactly." Refraining from looking at her watch, she sat down on a bench by her car. *So much for being at the hospital before Paul,* she thought. "Tell me how things are with Zack."

Tara took another bite and closed her eyes in bliss. "Zack? Who's he? These could almost make you forget your problems."

"They work for about an hour," Jane said. "Then you're more depressed than ever—there's a whole pound of butter in that recipe."

Tara's eyes flew open. "A *pound* of butter? That's *awful*. I'll have to stay for the second aerobics class tonight."

Jane laughed. "Well, I'm glad to hear that at least Zack is letting you out of the house again."

"Letting me?" Tara snorted. "He's got me enrolled at two different gyms. I've exercised more in the last two weeks than I did in the past six months."

"Uh-oh." Jane frowned. "Tara, he's doing it again. He's trying to mold you into his idea of the perfect woman." She softened her voice. "If he was the right one for you, then he'd love you just the way you are."

"I know, I know," Tara said, then looked down at her lap as the first tear drop splashed onto her cookie.

Jane hurriedly dug through her purse for a tissue. "Crying is good," she reassured Tara. "Here." She handed her the last tissue from the small package.

Tara took it and blew her nose. "Thanks."

"No problem. Listen, if you'd like to take a break from Zack for a while, you could come stay at my place." She smiled. "I have a full cookie jar right now."

"I can't," Tara said. "Not yet, anyway."

"Okay. But the offer still stands—anytime." Jane rose from the bench.

Tara did the same, staring at the wrapper in Jane's hand. "That was your last tissue," she said, stunned.

"I'll get more," Jane said, walking toward her car.

"No." Tara placed her hand on Jane's shoulder. "I mean that was your *last* tissue. Who else has been using those besides me?"

Jane shrugged. "My niece Megan had a cold last week."

Tara looked at her skeptically. "I thought your family dinners were only the first Sunday of the month. That was two weeks ago, and last week, at the bakery, you had a whole pack of tissues."

"I'm having allergies," Jane lied.

Tara rolled her eyes. "And Zack bought me another cat. What's going on, Jane? You're out of tissues and you're baking in the middle of the month? What gives?"

Jane opened her car door and turned to face Tara. "You know I love chocolate, and *I* used the tissues, okay?"

Tara's eyes widened. "You're seeing Paul."

Jane pursed her lips. "I've got to go."

"But he's making you cry, isn't he?" Tara demanded. She snapped her fingers. "I know. You've been crying because of Madison—because Paul isn't quite over her and—"

"You should be a psychic," Jane said, her voice serious as she sat down in the driver's seat. "You're right. Paul will never get over Madison."

"Oh, Jane. Not you too," Tara wailed. "If you're desperate enough to fall for a guy with those kinds of problems, then I *really* know it's hopeless for me."

Jane closed her car door but rolled down the window a bit. "Don't worry about me," she said as she turned the key in the ignition. "I like Madison too."

Jane smiled with satisfaction as she glanced in her rearview mirror and drove off. It was the first time in her life she'd seen Tara speechless.

* * *

"First Green Taurus beats me every day, and now Paul," Jane muttered as she watched him through the nursery window. After another minute, when he still hadn't looked her way, she crossed the room, grabbed a gown, and began to wash. She still didn't know him well enough to judge his moods, and she could only hope he wasn't too upset that she'd missed yesterday.

Amy opened the door for her, and Jane walked across the room.

"Hi," she said tentatively as she sat in the rocker beside Paul.

"Hi." His voice was quiet and he didn't look up.

Jane launched into her apology. "I'm really sorry about yesterday. I had an appointment that ran way over, and when I got here you were already gone. Did you get my messages?"

"Hmm?" Paul asked, looking at her absently.

"Messages," Jane repeated. "On your answering machine. I was worried when you didn't return my calls."

"Oh, sorry," Paul said. He looked down at Madison again and continued to rock.

Perplexed, Jane sat back in her chair and watched him. Lines of worry creased his brow, and there were dark circles beneath his eyes. In contrast, Madison's eyes were closed, her tiny lips puckering as she slept peacefully.

"Are you mad at me?" she asked after a few moments.

Paul looked at her. "No."

"Then what's wrong?" Jane glanced toward the double doors that led to the other side of the NICU. "Is it Mark?"

Paul shook his head.

"Has your—did you see your doctor? I thought your MRI wasn't until next week. Are you—?"

"Madison is coming home on Monday."

Jane's face broke into a relieved smile. "That's wonderful."

Paul spoke mechanically. "She's doubled her birth weight. Her lungs have matured. She's eating well."

"Well don't sound so solemn about it," Jane chided. "You should be ecstatic."

He shook his head. "No."

"No?" Jane asked, incredulous. "You don't want your daughter to leave the hospital?"

"I can't take care of her."

"Of course you can. If you're worried about diaper changing, making bottles, and all that other stuff, I can help you. Or better yet, we'll get my sister—who has changed about a billion diapers and is the ultimate baby expert—to come teach you everything you need to know." Jane's smile widened. "This is really great. I'm so excited for you."

"That's good," he said, looking up at Jane. "Because I'm terrified.

Chapter Sixteen

Jay glanced at his receipt a final time, then took his bags off the counter and left the bookstore. He scowled, thinking that though the bags were heavy, his wallet was considerably lighter. Who would have thought the average first-year law book went for one hundred forty dollars? It was criminal.

He walked toward his apartment, leaves crunching beneath him. Mentally he added up his expenses for the coming semester. It didn't take a genius to figure out he was going to have to get a second job. For a moment he entertained the idea of making big bucks for little work. He was certain that somewhere in this college town—probably even on campus—there were drug deals going down. It wouldn't take much for him to sniff them out. It would be a piece of cake to get in on the action . . . and the money.

Disgusted with himself for even thinking about it, Jay pushed the thought aside, turning onto the street and away from his apartment. He would stick with the old-fashioned, *honest* way to make a buck. Work—plain and simple. He already had a great job playing weekends at a night-club just south of campus, but that wouldn't pay the rent. There were other jobs around here, but he hadn't gotten any he'd applied for.

He was pretty certain he knew why, so he walked another block, then stopped in front of Clyde's Barber Shop. A quick look at the sign on the door and then at his watch told him Clyde's was open for another half hour. Jay set his bags down on the sidewalk and took out his wallet to see how much cash he had left.

There was just enough.

Too bad, he thought as he put his wallet away and looked at his reflection in the glass. His long hair was a part of him, a symbol that he saw things a little differently than most of the world. It was a symbol of what he'd come from, what he'd survived. But it wasn't, Jay realized suddenly, a symbol of what he *wanted* to become.

A corner of his mouth lifted in a wry smile at this realization. As he thought of Jane, he knew instinctively that she'd see him differently with short hair. She'd noticed the other changes in him already; she'd been unable to hide her surprise—and pleasure, he thought—when they'd met on the ferry. Jay bent down and picked up his bags again, then pushed the barbershop door open with his shoulder.

"Eleven months until I see you again, Jane, and already I'm changing."

Chapter Seventeen

. . . In the weeks since her death, I've been reeling. There are days when the pain seems almost too much to bear . . .

* * *

Jane glanced over her receipt as she walked toward her car in the parking lot.

"How does Caroline do this?" she wondered aloud as she added up the cost of two packs of newborn diapers, a set of bottles and disposable liners, a case of formula, burp cloths, a package of onesies, and some infant sleepers.

It was a good thing the Sweviecs' closing was tomorrow. After this purchase, she could certainly use some money in her checking account.

Jane opened the trunk of her car, then thought better of putting anything in there when she realized she'd forgotten to vacuum out the dirt from the rose topiaries. Instead, she loaded everything into the backseat, then climbed in and headed toward Paul's apartment. Madison had been napping when she'd left, and Jane had promised she wouldn't be gone more than an hour. Even after a week of having Madison home, Paul still didn't like to be left alone with her. But today it couldn't be helped. They'd used up all of the diapers from the hospital, and Paul was feeling too sick to go out. Jane didn't dare take Madison with her. It was cold and rainy today, and the NICU staff had advised them to keep her at home for at least two months.

A twinge of worry nagged at Jane as she glanced at the dashboard clock. She'd been gone for fifty minutes. Stopping at a red light, she drummed her fingers on the steering wheel. Madison was probably up from her nap by now, and Paul would be getting anxious.

It was good for him, she reasoned. He needed to gain confidence in his abilities as a father, and he never would if she kept taking over. Not that she minded spending time with Paul or Madison, but Paul's idea of "help" had certainly entailed more than she'd imagined. The first two nights Madison was home, Jane had been there all night, and in the week since, she'd spent every possible minute at Paul's apartment.

At last the light changed, and four minutes later Jane pulled into one of Paul's two allotted parking spaces at the Olympia Apartment Complex. She unloaded her purchases, entered the building, and climbed the stairs, carefully juggling the diapers in one arm and three bags in the other.

At 42B, she thought she heard a baby crying.

The sound grew louder as she walked briskly past the last two doors. Reaching Paul's apartment, she pounded on the door.

"Paul, I'm back." On the other side of the door, she heard Madison's wails. Her voice sounded hoarse, as if she'd been crying a long time. Panicked thoughts ran through Jane's mind as she pictured Madison as she'd left her, in the car seat on the sofa. *Was she strapped in?* Jane couldn't remember, and her heart lurched as she imagined Madison's tiny body falling to the floor.

"Paul," she yelled again, then dropped her bags and tried the doorknob. It was locked, but Jane twisted and pushed on it as she continued to call out.

Inside the apartment, Madison's cries escalated, but there was no sound from Paul. Jane pounded on the door once more, then pulled her cell phone from her purse and dialed 911. Shaking, she gave the operator the address.

"Send an ambulance. The door's locked. He's sick, and there's a baby," she explained in breathless spurts as she tried the door again and again.

Jane waited just long enough to hear that help was on the way before she ran down the hall. "I'll be right back, Maddie. Hang on, Paul," she cried as she rushed to find the manager's office.

* * *

By the time Jane had located the office and discovered no one was there, she heard the ambulance sirens. She ran to the parking lot, arriving just in time to wave down the two firemen emerging from their truck. The ambulance pulled in right behind them.

"Second floor. This way!" Jane yelled. "There's a locked door."

The two firefighters followed her upstairs, a paramedic right behind them, and another unloading a gurney from the back of the ambulance.

Jane took the stairs two at a time and arrived out of breath at Paul's door a few seconds later. On the other side, she could still hear Madison crying. Jane spoke to the firemen as they worked.

"The baby is only ten weeks old—and a preemie. She just came home from the hospital last week. I left her sleeping in her car seat, and her dad was in the other room. He wasn't feeling well. He's got cancer."

Jane watched as the clawlike tool took hold and had the door open in less than a minute. Practically jumping over one of the firemen, she pushed the door open and ran straight to Madison, who lay exactly where she'd left her over an hour ago—strapped, thankfully—in her car seat on the couch.

"Oh, Maddie. Come here, sweetheart," Jane crooned as her trembling fingers undid the buckles. From the corner of her eye she saw the paramedic's bag as he rushed past.

"The kitchen is to the right. The bedroom on the left," Jane said as she picked up Madison. "I'll be right there."

"Just take care of the baby," the medic called as he disappeared down the short hall. One of the firemen headed for the kitchen.

"No one in here," he shouted a few seconds later.

"Got him." Jane heard the call from the bedroom.

Jane scooped up Madison, who was beyond hysterical, her face red and blotchy, her body tense and shaking. Jane sang softly, to calm both herself and the baby as she walked toward the bedroom. One of the firemen stood at the door, blocking her.

"It's best to let the paramedics work alone," he said.

"But—"

"Doesn't she need to be fed or something?" the fireman asked, looking at Madison.

Jane swallowed, then nodded. She looked past the fireman, toward the bedroom once more. "His name is Paul. You'll get me if you need anything?"

He smiled kindly. "Of course."

Reluctantly, Jane went to the kitchen to make a bottle. Her attention felt divided. She should have been in the bedroom with Paul, but Madison was starving, and her crying *would* probably make things more difficult for the paramedics.

Jane held the baby in the crook of her arm as she filled a bottle with warm water and measured the formula. Instead of being relieved at not finding Paul passed out on the kitchen floor, she found herself even more scared of what might have happened to make him ignore Madison's cries.

She knew he'd had a rough couple of days, but what did that really mean? He still hadn't told her much about his cancer—his treatments, his prognosis, how serious it really was. She assumed he meant to, but there simply hadn't been time. It seemed every moment they were together revolved around taking care of his newborn children—a daunting task for a normal married couple. It was proving an overwhelming one for a widower with cancer and a single, working woman.

Jane screwed the lid on the top of the bottle, shook it several times, then gently nudged the nipple into Madison's open mouth. It took Madison several seconds before she realized she was finally being fed and stopped her screaming enough to latch on.

"Poor, Maddie," Jane whispered. "I'm *so* sorry." What she felt was *so scared*. She leaned forward, peeking over the counter into the living room. It was empty, and she couldn't hear what was going on in the bedroom. *Oh, Paul,* she thought.

Madison hiccuped and began to cry again. Jane hummed a lullaby and rocked her as she worked the nipple into her mouth once more. Madison latched on, sucking greedily.

"I know, I know. You're hungry and you had to wait," Jane said. "But your daddy's sick." She walked out of the small kitchen just as the gurney bearing Paul was rolled through the living room.

Jane gasped. His eyes were closed, and he looked deathly pale. "Is he—?" The words died in her throat as she noticed the IV pole and the tubes running down to Paul's left hand. *He's alive.* Relief flooded her as he was rolled past and out the apartment door.

"Wait," Jane called. "What happened? Is he going to be okay?"

"Brad will speak to you, ma'am," one of the paramedics said as he walked by.

The fireman standing next to her nodded to him. "Go ahead. I'll be right behind you."

The gurney wheels clicked as they hit the concrete and rolled down the hall. She turned to the lone fireman left in the apartment. "What happened?" she repeated.

The man looked her straight in the eye, his expression grim as he held up a plastic bag filled with prescription bottles.

"It looks like a drug overdose."

Chapter Eighteen

The door closed softly behind the fireman, and Jane sank to the couch, her emotions in turmoil as she continued to feed Madison. *A drug overdose? Paul?* True, she'd only known him a few weeks, but he just didn't seem the type—no matter how bad things got—to try and take his own life. He loved his children too much. Jane would bet her *own* life on that. So what had happened?

She'd given Brad, the fireman, what sketchy information she could. Even to her own ears, it had sounded like a soap opera. Man's wife is killed by a drunk driver, his babies are saved, albeit delivered two months early. One of the babies has a critical heart condition, the other is sent home for the man to care for while he deals with his own serious illness. She supposed for some people that would be cause enough to attempt suicide. But not Paul. She was sure of it. During her internship she'd counseled enough seriously depressed people to recognize the warning signs, and Paul had none of them. He was sad. He was worried too, but he was also a fighter. There had to be a mistake. All those pills he took—she'd seen them lined up along the bathroom counter—they were all part of his treatment and nothing more.

The bottle went slack in Madison's mouth, and Jane looked down to find the infant sleeping, her eyelids closed, her breathing slow and steady. Tiny as her features were, Jane thought she could already see signs of her father. The father who just *had* to be okay. Jane kissed the top of Madison's head, then eased her onto her shoulder and began to rub her back while she contemplated what to do next. She ought to be at the hospital with Paul. She wanted to be there when he woke up. Brad had warned her there was a chance Paul would not come out of the drug-induced coma. Jane pushed the thought aside. She would not even consider it.

She continued to rub Madison's back until the infant burped, then Jane lay the baby gently in her car seat, buckled her in—thank goodness she had last time—and went to retrieve her phone. Someone had put her bags and purse just inside the door. As Jane dialed her sister's number, she realized belatedly that she hadn't even thanked the paramedics or the firemen. She made a mental note to do that later, then picked up the grocery bags in her free hand and carried them into the kitchen. It took five rings before Caroline answered.

"Hi, Jane. Long time no talk," Caroline said brightly.

No kidding, Jane thought as she rinsed out a bottle. *You have no idea.* "I'm sorry. I've been kind of busy."

"Mom told me about your big sale. That's great."

"Yeah, well there are a few other things going on right now, too."

"Like what—? Oh just a minute," Caroline said. "Jason! Close that freezer *right now.* Finish the carrots from your lunch if you're hungry."

"Caroline?"

"Sorry. I'm back. Jason thinks he can skip the healthy foods at lunch, then come home and eat ice cream every afternoon."

Jane shoved four diapers and a change of clothes for Madison in the diaper bag. "I need a favor."

"Is your weed eater broken again?" Caroline asked.

"No." Jane thought briefly of her usually immaculate yard—the yard she'd barely had time to walk through, let alone mow during the past two weeks. "Actually—" She half laughed, half sobbed into the phone. "I need a babysitter."

* * *

"I can't believe you didn't tell me about this," Caroline scolded as she looked down at Madison asleep in her car seat.

"Well, it was kind of sudden," Jane said. "You never know what might happen when you answer a personal." She gave Caroline a sad smile and handed her the diaper bag. "Listen, I've got to go. There are diapers in here and a fresh bottle, plus a whole can of formula. I just fed her about—"

"Go," Caroline ordered, shooing Jane toward the door. "I can handle this. I've got a few of my own, remember?"

"Yeah, but keep those *few of your own* away from Madison, okay?" Jane asked, looking back with concern. "The last thing Paul needs is for her to get sick."

"Don't worry." Caroline bent to pick up Madison's car seat. "I'm going to lock her in the bedroom with me while I watch *Oprah* and fold laundry. She'll be fine."

"Thanks," Jane said. "I really appreciate this. I don't know how long I'll—"

"Go," Caroline ordered again, and this time Jane complied. A quick wave of her hand and she was running toward her car, all of her thoughts at once channeled on the man who had come so suddenly into her life.

Chapter Nineteen

. . . During those times I think of you—your loss and how you must have felt . . .

* * *

Hearing the soft knock on his hospital door, Paul opened his eyes and saw that the room was dark. Someone had turned the light off, and the daylight had faded outside. Either it was raining or he'd slept away the afternoon. He looked toward the door just in time to see yet another doctor walk in—the fifth one since yesterday when they'd moved him from the emergency room to a room upstairs. The doctor switched on the light and walked toward the bed. Paul stifled a groan as recognition dawned. It wasn't another doctor—it was the *grief counselor.*

Unexpected anger welled up in Paul. They thought he was crazy—like some psyche patient on an *ER* episode.

"Hi, I'm Collin." The man stepped farther into the room. "May I?" He indicated the chair next to the bed.

"Sure." *You will anyway.* Paul took a sip of water from the paper cup on his bedside tray as Collin launched into his speech.

"I'm a counselor here at the hospital, and I thought it might be helpful if we talked about some of the difficulties you've been having."

Difficulties? Now there's a word, Paul thought. He didn't feel like talking—least of all to this guy. He wished he could say, *Just give me your dumb pamphlet again and let's get this over with.*

Collin settled back into his chair. "Do you mind if I ask you some questions?"

"Shoot," Paul said.

Collin's brow furrowed.

Oops. Poor word choice. Paul found himself holding back a grin. If he didn't feel so lousy, he could probably have some fun with this situation. Tami certainly would have. But she wasn't here.

"Have you been feeling depressed, Mr. Bryant?"

The question was so absurd, so idiotic, so completely ridiculous, that for several seconds Paul stared at the counselor and said nothing.

Collin leaned forward, concern on his face. "Have you been experiencing feelings of overwhelming sorrow, despair, hopeless—?"

"My wife is *dead*," Paul said, interrupting him. "My son has a life-threatening heart condition. I have terminal cancer. Last week's CT scan showed it's spreading." He sat up taller in the bed, wincing as he did so. "I'm in constant pain. I can barely take care of my daughter. I'm unable to work, *and* my lease is up next week. Of course I'm depressed! I'd have to be insane not to be."

"Yes," Collin said in a tone meant to soothe. "You're right. Any one of those things alone would be difficult enough. Together they must—"

"Must be enough to make me think about taking my own life," Paul finished for him.

Collin rose to the defensive. "I wasn't going to say that."

"But it's what you want to know, isn't it?"

"I—"

"Don't bother," Paul said. "I'm well aware that's the rumor going around here. Mr. Bryant tried to kill himself by overdosing on his pain meds. Well I didn't. Depressing as life may be right now, it's still mine to live, and I've got an awful lot of things to take care of before I'm done with it."

Paul lay back on the pillows and closed his eyes, wishing Collin would disappear.

He didn't. "If you could explain what did happen then, Mr. Bryant?"

Paul opened one eye. "You have any kids?"

Collin shook his head.

"Well then, you probably won't understand."

"Try me."

Paul sighed, but after a minute he looked at Collin. "Okay. I've got a ten-week-old daughter to take care of. She needs to drink a bottle or have her diaper changed about every two hours around the clock. I'm not particularly fast at either one of those things, so I'm pretty much up most of the night. Combine that with the pain I'm in, and I've had—oh maybe six hours of sleep over the past three days. Take fatigue, plus stress, plus not wearing my contacts, and I took the wrong medicine. I've only got a dozen or so prescriptions on my counter, and yesterday morning . . ." He shrugged. "Well, believe what you want, but it's the truth."

Collin looked skeptical. "You took the wrong medicine *twice?*"

"Obviously I didn't realize it was the wrong one. I got two new prescriptions last week. Check with my doctor if you'd like."

"I believe you," Collin said, surprising Paul.

"Good. Can I leave then? I'd like to see my son today, and I've got a ton of packing to do."

Collin held up his hand. "Not so fast. Unfortunately, you'll also need to speak with a social worker."

Paul scowled. "*Social worker?*"

"About your daughter," Collin said as he rose from the chair.

"My daughter is well taken care of. I have a friend . . ."

"I know, Mr. Bryant. But it's routine."

"You'll explain to them what I just told you, right?" Paul asked, trying not to sound panicked. Though he'd briefly considered putting Mark and Madison up for adoption, it had never occurred to him they might be taken from him.

Collin, his expression serious, spoke quietly. "I'll tell them that I don't think you're suicidal."

"Thank you," Paul said, though he didn't feel relieved.

"I'll tell them," Collin repeated as he pulled a paper from his pocket. "But I want you to take this pamphlet. There are some numbers on the back. You really should be seeing someone. What you're going through is incredibly difficult, and it wouldn't be out of the realm of normal to have feelings of—"

"I don't have *time* to see anyone," Paul said curtly. "I've either got to be here at the hospital with my son or at home taking care of my daughter. If I've got to see a doctor it's to keep me alive a little longer. And I barely have time to get myself to the doctor for that, let alone to lie on a couch discussing Freud's theories."

"There are people who can help, you know," Collin said.

Paul nodded. "And I've met one of them. Jane's upstairs with Mark right now, and she's been a lifesaver helping me with Madison."

"That's not what I meant," Collin said. "There are agencies that watch out for children when their parents can't. You shouldn't be worrying about your children's care when you're so sick yourself. It might be better for your kids if you got healthy first and *then* took care of them."

Paul swung his legs over the side of the bed. "I'm not going to *get* any healthier than I am right now," he said angrily. "And I'm not letting some agency take my children away."

"I wasn't suggesting that, Mr. Bryant." Collin placed his hands on the back of the chair and leaned forward. "You'd have visitation whenever you wished, and if you're truly not going to recover from your illness, it might be better for the children to become established somewhere else—somewhere permanent," he added softly.

Paul sat on the edge of the bed trying to calm his emotions. Losing his temper with the shrink certainly wouldn't help his case. "Look, I've got a plan for my children's future. I just need some time to work it all out. I'm not going to leave them without care, but until I go, it's *my* care they need—as much as I can give." Paul looked up at Collin, trying to read his face. "Do you believe in life after death?"

Collin nodded. "I do—sort of."

"So do I," Paul said. "And when I see Tami—my wife—again, I'm going to have to tell her about our children. What color eyes they have, how much hair—is it curly or straight, a lot or a little. She's going to want to know how it felt to hold them . . . What I told them about their mother, and who I left to care for them. Anything less than that, and I'm going to be a whole lot more miserable than I am now. You understand?"

Collin's nod was accompanied by a slow grin. "Yeah. I've got a wife too." He crossed the room to the door. "I'll tell the social worker," he paused, "that you need some sleep and you'll be just fine."

* * *

Jane stepped onto the elevator, her heart feeling lighter than it had in the past two days. Paul was coming home today, and after seeing Mark permanently off the ventilator, she felt he'd be joining them soon too. She smiled as she rubbed his beanie between her fingers. Paul would be so relieved to hear her news. Relieved and happy—she hoped.

Her smile faded as she thought of the realities of caring full time for not one, but two infants. It was going to be a demanding, around-the-clock job—one she knew Paul wasn't up to. But she had a plan; she just hoped he'd let her go through with it. Determination in her eyes, Jane got off the elevator and headed for Paul's room.

When she reached his door, she knocked softly, then pushed it open. He was awake, sitting up in bed, with a notebook in his lap and a pen in his hand.

Jane stood in the doorway. "Hi," she said. "Guess what?"

"What?" Paul asked warily as he looked at her, worry on his face.

Jane followed his gaze to Mark's knit hat, still in her hand. "I'm just taking it home to wash," she quickly assured him. "My sister gave me a darling red-and-white striped hat and matching socks. Mark is wearing those now. Look." She pulled her digital camera from her purse. "I took a picture for you. He looks just like an elf." She let go of the door and walked toward the bed, then almost jumped in surprise as she noticed the woman sitting in the chair beside the door.

Jane looked at Paul, her mind racing. *Please tell me you're not thinking of adoption again.* "I didn't realize you have company," she said. "I'm sorry. I'll come back later."

"Please stay," Paul said. "Jane, this is Christina Sands, the social worker assigned to my case."

The woman rose from the chair and held out her hand. Jane shook it and gave her a warm smile, though her heart had gone cold at the words. *You can't take Madison,* she wanted to say.

"Miss Sands and I were just discussing what would be best for Madison."

"And your son as well, Mr. Bryant," Christina reminded him.

"Yes," Paul said, and Jane caught the note of strain in his voice. She hoped that meant he was unhappy with the conversation—that he wasn't thinking about giving up the twins.

"Miss Sands feels that my illness renders me unable to care for Madison right now."

Jane swallowed and decided on a bold move. She hadn't wanted to present her idea to Paul this way—Caroline had advised her it was always best to let the man think any new plan was really *his* idea—but Jane realized she might not get that chance. Looking away from Paul, Jane said, "I agree."

"You do?" Miss Sands and Paul spoke in unison.

"Yes," Jane said, "which is why, this morning, I notified my employer that I would be taking an indefinite leave of absence. I've got the money in my bank account to allow me to do so—you can check if you'd like, and—" Jane took a short breath, then continued on, her voice tremulous. "I've also listed my cottage on Bainbridge with a realtor. I realized, some time ago, that the island was just too far away." She chanced a look in Paul's direction and saw that his mouth was open. "I'm going to find a twin home for Paul and I, so I'll be there all the time to help him care for Madison, and Mark also, when he comes home."

"Well then," Christina said. "That changes the situation a bit." She looked at Paul. "Madison would still need foster care until you're settled though . . ." She turned to Jane. "Is it possible you could take Madison now—before you're moved?"

"Of course," Jane said enthusiastically. "I've been staying with my sister who lives close by and—"

"Jane is wonderful with Maddie," Paul interjected.

Christina glanced at the camera in Jane's hand. "It's obvious you care for the children. And if Madison were to be placed in foster care it would become extremely difficult to remove her. I've got the paperwork—" Christina bent down and picked up her briefcase beside the chair. Opening the case, she removed several papers from a manila folder. She looked up at Jane first and then Paul. "Normally, I would never consider this, but this morning I was not aware, Mr. Bryant, that you had someone helping you with your children. And, as our system is already overloaded . . ." She tore the papers in two. "I think it best that we consider these alternate arrangements. Miss—"

"Warner," Jane supplied. "Jane Warner."

Christina smiled. "Miss Warner, if you will assume care for Madison for the next ten days, I will recommend that she be allowed to stay in your care. At that time, the state will require proof of a primary residence, suitable for both Mark and Madison, and proof that you, Miss Warner, reside at such residence full time with Mr. Bryant." Christina's look grew serious as she turned to Paul. "At *no* time, Mr. Bryant, are you to be left alone with your children. The medications you are on, as well as your current medical condition, dictate that your children have additional supervision. If at anytime you are found alone with either Mark or Madison, I will recommend foster care for both of them. Is that understood?"

"Yes," Paul said. His voice was calm enough, but Jane read the tension in his face.

"We understand," Jane reiterated.

"Good." Miss Sand's face softened. She handed a business card to Jane. "Here is the number to call to set up your first appointment. It needs to be within the next ten days. The state will monitor the children and make periodic home visits. Mr. Bryant, are you certain this arrangement is satisfactory?"

Jane held her breath as she turned to face Paul.

The smile he gave her was full of gratitude. "It's great."

Chapter Twenty

. . . I'm sorry. Though I can't take back the wrong I've done you, I hope you will someday forgive me . . .

* * *

Jane frowned as she looked at the address written on the paper in her lap. "You sure this is the right neighborhood?"

"Yeah. It's older, but hey, the house has the accessory apartment and a yard." Paul grinned at her from the passenger seat of her Corolla. "Weren't those your requirements?"

"I said a yard would be *nice*. Being *safe* would also be nice."

"It's safe. I grew up—" Paul stopped midsentence and looked out the window.

"What did you say?" Jane asked as she turned the corner.

"Nothing," Paul said. "There it is. Third house on the left."

Jane pulled up to the curb of a 1950s ranch-style home and stopped the car. Reluctantly she climbed out and walked toward the house. The exterior siding was gray—a perfect match to the dreary sky. The paint was chipped and peeling, but she could deal with that.

The driveway was another matter. A series of gigantic cracks ran through the concrete, splintering out to various potholes. Pushing a stroller down it would be like four-wheeling, and the sidewalk didn't appear a whole lot better. But she supposed she could live with the driveway if she had to. It was the yard that broke her heart.

She couldn't see a single blade of grass in the entire front. Patches of weeds were interspersed through dirt and pea gravel. Besides the weeds, the only other thing growing in the yard were two enormous junipers, so fat they covered much of the front windows. She hated junipers, especially fat, overgrown ones. *Ugh.*

Jane sighed, thinking of the perfectly sculptured potentillas that framed the curved stone walk she'd painstakingly laid in her yard last spring.

Paul took her elbow. "Let's go inside."

She walked beside him, looking down so she wouldn't fall and twist her ankle. He stuck the key in the front door and, after a good shove, it swung open, hinges complaining loudly. Jane flipped the light switch, but nothing happened.

"No power," they both said at the same time. *Of course,* Jane thought. She'd shown vacant houses many times, and the electricity was almost always disconnected. She walked over to the floor-length drapes and gave the string a tug.

The entire thing—drapes, rod, and shade—crashed to the floor.

"You okay?" Paul asked quickly as she stumbled back.

Jane put her hands over her face as she coughed away the dust. "Fine," she muttered.

"At least we can see now," Paul said brightly. "Come on. Let's look at the rest."

Jane pulled her gaze from the newly formed, three-inch holes on either side of the window and followed him as they completed a quick tour through the 1,200-square-foot house.

The kitchen was tiny, and the psychedelic linoleum and harvest-gold appliances filling the small space made her dizzy. The family room was larger, but it had a rough stone fireplace Jane worried the twins would get hurt on when they started to crawl. The two bedrooms in the main house were decent-sized, though they were all painted baby blue and had gold miniblinds. The blinds, combined with the color of the orange shag carpeting throughout the house, were enough to give Jane the beginnings of a headache.

A glance into the bathroom made it worse. The toilet, tub, and sink looked as though they hadn't been scrubbed for over a decade. Again, she realized these were all things that could be remedied with some heavy-duty cleaners, a lot of hard work, and a paintbrush, so she told herself it would be okay—until she saw the backyard.

It was, if possible, worse than the front.

Foot-high weeds covered the entire yard, except for the space just outside the family room door, where a concrete patio was covered by a sagging, rusted awning. Two sides of the yard had a decrepit wooden fence, but the only thing dividing the yard from the neighbor behind was a three-foot-high chain-link fence—an open gate right in the middle. In *this* neighborhood, that would never do. It was one thing to live in an ugly house, but she'd never feel safe with that fence. *Anyone* could walk right in.

Jane stood at the sliding glass door looking out at the yard when Paul came up behind her.

"There's a door out front and another one in the back to the mother-in-law apartment, and it's got everything I'll need—a full bath, one bedroom, and a small kitchen. And there's plenty of room in the main house for you and the twins. This place is great, isn't it?"

"*Great?*" she croaked.

"Yeah. It even has your yard—"

"Not *my* yard," Jane said.

Paul continued as if he hadn't heard her. "The rent is cheap—"

"It ought to be free."

"And most important, it's close to the hospital," Paul finished. He took Jane by the shoulders and turned her gently toward him. "What do you think?"

She looked him in the eye. "I hate it."

"Really?" He seemed genuinely surprised.

"Yes, really," Jane said.

"But think of the twins," Paul argued. "It's minutes to the hospital for Mark and—"

"Yes, think of your babies," Jane interrupted. "Do you really want your children learning to crawl on *that?*" She turned away from Paul and looked out the sliding glass door again.

He looked down at the carpet. "Well, the shag would need to be cleaned."

"Replaced. And I wasn't just talking about the carpet," Jane said. "Look at the grass—or what's left of it." She pointed at the yard. "And there isn't even a real fence in the back. Just some flimsy chain-link thing that the neighbor behind can see right through."

Paul hung his head and sighed. "We're almost out of time, Jane."

She heard the plea in his voice and closed her eyes against it. He was right, and she didn't want him to be. It was Wednesday. They had until Monday to get settled *somewhere* before the first social services visit. But did that somewhere have to be *here?*

The price of rent everywhere else dictated *yes*. That they would each have their own separate unit was also a plus. But as far as Jane was concerned, that was where the positives ended. And they didn't begin to stack up against the long list of negatives.

But it is close to the hospital. Jane opened her eyes and looked at the yard once more. Living with a sagging fence, cracked patio, and grassless yard were small prices to pay for a healthy baby boy. She imagined them living in a nice house with a pretty yard—a yard without Mark toddling around in it because something had happened to him and they'd been too far away from the hospital. A shudder ran through her.

Jane left the window and walked back into the kitchen. She ran a finger over the dusty counter and looked at the empty breakfast nook. She imagined Paul's table there and the four of them sitting at it on a Sunday morning. She and Paul would each be feeding a baby. Paul would have oatmeal on his chin. She would laugh.

She walked into the family room, imagining a Christmas tree in the corner and four stockings hung at the fireplace. In her mind she heard Bing

Crosby singing "White Christmas," and she saw herself sitting in a rocker with Madison on her lap.

Jane swallowed the lump in her throat as she thought of Caroline's yard with its assortment of children's toys, headless flowers, and ruts from tricycle wheels. She thought of Caroline's house—the toothpaste-smeared sinks, the noncommissioned artwork on the walls, the particleboard furniture her sister said they were "getting by with" until they'd saved enough for what they really wanted. And yet, Caroline had what Jane really wanted. She had the husband and darling children. She had a family of her own to love and who loved her. But things hadn't started out easily for Caroline, and her happy life wasn't without sacrifice. Jane wondered why she hadn't realized that before.

Or maybe she had. She'd known it in her subconscious and even offered it to Paul in the parking garage when she'd told him that her house didn't matter, that she'd give it up in a heartbeat for a chance to be with his daughter. She'd known it and meant it too, and now it was time to make good on her promise.

Folding her arms across her chest, she looked at Paul. He had hope in his eyes, and it gave her the courage she needed. She fished in her purse for a pen, then smiled as she held it up.

"Where's the contract?"

* * *

Jane slipped her cell phone into her purse as she stood on the top deck of the ferry and watched Seattle's receding skyline. The earlier clouds had blown away, and it was a gorgeous, clear night. After sleeping at Caroline's most of the week, she'd left Maddie there for the night, then caught the late ferry. She could hardly wait to get home and climb up on her roof. Nights like this were why she'd bought her house. And tonight, she would enjoy it one last time.

For a fleeting second, Jane felt sad and knew she would feel the same way again tomorrow when she closed the gate on her white picket fence for the last time. But there was no going back. She'd made a decision, and she was going to follow it with all her heart.

Even her parents understood—sort of.

She'd spent the evening at their house, explaining the situation and her choice to move next door to Paul and help him care for his children. Her mother had been shocked at such a sudden turn of events, and her father had expressed his concern over how fast she was jumping into such a difficult situation. To say the least, they had not seemed pleased.

But her parents had called a few minutes ago, not quite giving their blessing on Jane's choice, but instead telling her they loved her and would support her decision. She was relieved and had already phoned Paul with the good news.

At ten tomorrow morning, she would meet him at the hospital. By noon they'd be back at Paul's apartment packing, and by Sunday they would each move in. Madison would be hers to care for—hers to love. Suddenly life seemed full of happy possibilities, and Jane looked up at the sky, counting her blessings as well as the stars.

Chapter Twenty-One

. . . I know I can never make up for my selfishness, but I've left you three presents. One is taller than the others, but all are equally fragile. Take care of them for me . . .

* * *

"Happy birthday!" The chorus around Jane had ended and everyone was clapping. Chants of, "Wish, wish, wish," began from her nieces.

"All right," Jane said, smiling as she looked around at Paul, her mother, sisters, and nieces. Having opted to forgo the traditional girls' birthday lunch date in favor of packing, Jane had been pleasantly surprised this morning when much of the female side of her family showed up at Paul's apartment to help with the move. She could tell her mother was still having a difficult time understanding her choice, but she was trying.

"Blow your candles out, Aunt Jane," her twelve-year-old niece Amber said.

"Let me get a breath." Jane puffed out her cheeks, though looking at the cake loaded with thirty candles she doubted she was exaggerating her need for air. Elbowing Jessica, she pointed to the cake and began to blow. Jessica and Amber leaned over to help until the last candle flickered and went out.

"Phew," Jane said. "I *am* getting old."

"You're not old," Jessica protested. "You're the coolest aunt ever."

"Let me take that to the kitchen to cut," her mother said, whisking the cake away from the pile of boxes it had been resting on. "Amber and Jessica, you girls come help me with the ice cream."

Caroline and Mindy went back to the computer they were boxing up, and Karen and Emily picked up the boxes of CDs and videos and took them out to the truck.

Jane looked at Paul. "Take a five-minute break?" she asked.

He nodded. "Let's make it *fifty.* I'm beat." He sank onto the loveseat, and Jane sat beside him.

"You okay?" she asked, concerned.

"Yeah. Just tired, and we've got a lot more to do." He glanced around the room.

"Not really," Jane said. "The only thing left in the kitchen is the pantry, and that's pretty bare." She looked at him knowingly. "Don't cook much, do you?"

He lay his head back and gave her a wry smile. "No."

"Me neither. I guess we can learn together."

Paul turned to her, then surprised her by taking her hand. "You're really great, you know that?"

"Because I don't cook?" She laughed casually but felt anything but casual as she glanced down at Paul's hand on hers. She was shocked at the boundary he'd just crossed.

"*No.*" He gave her hand a squeeze. "Because of all you're doing for me. Spending your birthday packing up some other guy's mess isn't something a whole lot of people would do."

"I'm not 'a whole lot of people,' and—" She stopped, feeling a slow blush creep up her face.

"And?" Paul prodded.

She met his gaze. "And you're not just *some* guy."

"Birthday girl gets the first piece," Amber called, walking toward them with a plate of cake and ice cream. "I got you a piece with frosting on *two* sides, Aunt Jane."

Jessica was right behind her and held a plate out to Paul. He released Jane's hand and took his cake. Jane took hers as well, feeling strangely both regretful and grateful that the spell was broken and their moment of intimacy had passed.

* * *

Paul hesitated, his hand on the doorknob to the spare room, their last to pack. "You ready for this?"

Jane nodded. "It can't be *that* bad. The room's only what—ten by ten?"

"Yes, but it's a crowded—" Paul pushed the door open a few inches before it caught on something. "—mess in here." He reached into the room, picked a sweatshirt off the floor, then pushed the door the rest of the way open.

"Show me your worst," Jane said with mock seriousness as she peeked through the doorway. Her eyes widened. "Wow." He was right—the room *was* crowded, but not in the sense she'd envisioned. File cabinets lined one wall, and much of the bed was covered with piles of clothes and stacks of papers, but the rest of the room was filled to overflowing with items for what appeared to be the ultimate nursery.

On the far side the pieces for two spindled cribs were stacked beneath the window. Next to the cribs was a double stroller, piled high with dozens of baby outfits. The ones on top even appeared to be newborn size. Jane took a step inside the room to get a closer look. Blocking her way to the stroller was a large box containing a car seat that matched Madison's. An intricately carved, antique high chair stood next to the box. Confused, Jane turned to Paul. "Why didn't you show me all this before? Why has Madison been sleeping in her car seat and wearing the same three pairs of pajamas when she has a beautiful crib and plenty of clothes?"

Paul shoved his hands in his pockets and looked out the window. "Tami spent months shopping for the babies, and the rest is from her shower. She was on her way home when the accident . . ." His voice trailed off. "I didn't want any reminders."

"Oh," Jane said quietly. She ran her finger over the polished wood of the high-chair tray.

"Tami's grandfather made that," Paul said, watching her. "Both she and her mother used it. Tami was glad she had something from her heritage to pass down to our children."

Jane tried, with difficulty, to swallow the sudden lump in her throat. The past few weeks had been a roller coaster of emotions, but overall she'd been happy—happier and more fulfilled than she'd ever been. How could she have forgotten her joy had come at the expense of another woman's life?

Jane sat on a corner of the bed and picked up a pair of baby high-tops. Had Tami picked these out? Had she made the teddy-bear quilts hanging over the sides of the cribs? Had she chosen the names Mark and Madison?

Guilt flooded Jane, and her heart ached. Madison was not *hers*. Paul couldn't love her. He appreciated all she was doing for him, but his heart belonged—and rightly so—to Tami.

"Giving up on this mess already?" Paul asked in a teasing voice as if he were trying to lighten the mood that had descended on them. He sat next to her on the bed.

Jane put the shoes aside. "I don't want to give up. I don't *ever* want to give any of this up."

Paul whistled. "We're going to need more boxes."

"That's not what I'm talking about." Jane chanced a sideways glance at him. "I'm afraid this will all disappear—you, your children, that I'll wake up some morning and find out the past few weeks have been a dream. And yet, how can I want this—even feel happy about it—when it must be your nightmare? It seems so wrong." She picked up an infant dress with crochet around the hem. Her eyes watered as she rubbed the delicate stitching between her fingers. "Why did you choose *me*, Paul? I mean, I *know* you need help with your children, but why me, a complete stranger? What about family?"

"It's like I told you that first day at the hospital. I have no one. Tami's sister was driving the car. She died before the paramedics arrived. The only family left is their grandfather who raised them. He's eighty-five years old and lives in a care center. I visited him after the accident, tried to explain . . ." Paul shrugged. "I don't think he really understood, and I didn't try too hard to make him. As for my family—" Paul reached for a photo on the dresser and handed it to Jane. "This is my mom and my brother Peter."

Jane studied the picture, faded from time. A woman stood on the steps of a house similar to the one Paul had just leased. Her hands rested on the shoulders of the two young boys in front of her. "How old were you when this was taken?"

Paul took the picture from Jane and turned it over, but there was no date on the back. "I'm not sure. Sometime in the seventies though. Look at Peter's shirt." He pointed to the wide collar his brother wore.

Jane smiled. "I remember those. My brother looked like that too." She studied the boys in the photo. Paul wore glasses and was on the skinny side, and his grin revealed a couple of missing teeth. His brother, a few inches taller, wasn't smiling. "Is he older?"

"A bit."

If Jane thought his answer was odd, she didn't say so. "You two were cuties. Peter and Paul and . . ." She raised her eyebrows and hummed a bar of "Puff the Magic Dragon." "No Mary?"

"No." Paul's answer was sharp, and his face grew serious. "My father was killed in Vietnam. It was just my mom, Pete, and I. *No* Mary."

"I'm sorry." Jane watched as Paul set the picture back on the dresser.

"It's all right. It was a long time ago. Mom died of breast cancer in '98. And Peter—" Paul smiled ruefully. "Pete's in Iraq doing what he loves best, flying an Apache helicopter and defending our freedom."

"Does he know about the twins?"

Paul shook his head. "No. The last time I spoke with Pete was just before my wedding. We aren't exactly what you call *close*."

"How sad," Jane said. She couldn't imagine life without her large, involved, caring family. Granted, sometimes they seemed a little *too* involved, but not having them—not having *anyone*—would be awful. "But he's your only family—Mark and Madison's uncle. Shouldn't you . . . ?" Seeing the pained expression on Paul's face, she stopped.

"I know." Paul took her hand in his for the second time in less than an hour. His eyes met hers. "I wish I had a great family like yours, but I don't." He looked down at their hands. "I'm as scared as you are, Jane. Only I'm scared that *you'll* disappear. From that first day at the hospital, there was just something about you—a feeling I had. And now it's hard to believe all you've done already—quit your job, sold your house—"

"It's a leave of absence," Jane corrected him. "And the house hasn't sold yet."

"But that you'd give it all up . . . *Can you?*" He looked at her again. "Can you really? Because this is no dream."

Paul didn't wait for her answer but rose from the bed and made his way toward the corner of the room where a sheet covered a large object. He lifted a corner of the fabric and pulled it back.

Jane's eyebrows rose as she looked at rolled blueprints and a professional drafting table. Her mind raced. *Was Paul an architect? Or did the table and plans belong to Tami?* Jane realized she'd never asked Paul what he did for a living—or had done before getting sick. Their conversations always revolved around the twins—or occasionally Jane's family. Even at dinner with her parents the other night, Paul had steered the conversation clear of anything to do with his past. Somehow, without really saying it, he always made it seem that topic was off limits.

Paul took a thick manila envelope from the top of the table and handed it to her.

Jane's hands shook as she read the words *Last Will and Testament*.

"I need you, Jane." His voice was thick. "I don't have much to offer—not even myself, but your name is in there. If you're willing, I've found the mother my children need."

Before she could change her mind, Jane stepped forward and threw her arms around him. "I'd be honored," she whispered as her tears started in earnest.

Chapter Twenty-Two

"Order what you want. My treat," Jane said, opening her menu.

"Since it's your birthday, *I* should be treating," Tara protested. Her menu remained closed as she scanned the Michelangelo-inspired art adorning the walls of Assagio Ristorante. "This place is great."

Jane smiled. "I'm glad you like it. I chose it because I know how much you love painting."

Tara sighed as she reached for her menu. "I used to, didn't I?"

"Mmm-hmm." Jane took a drink of water and set the glass down. "There is *one* thing you could do for my birthday, Tara."

"I already broke up with Zack."

"*Really?* That's wonderful," Jane said, truly delighted by the news.

Tara looked hurt. "I wouldn't say it's *wonderful,* but—"

"Wise," Jane corrected. "It was a very *wise* decision." She beamed at Tara. "I'm proud of you. Now you'll have time to *remember* that you love painting—and that you're very good at it. You'll be able to have a cat, only take Tae Bo if you want to . . ." Her voice trailed off. "But that's not what I was going to ask." She slid a folder across the table. "I want you to sell my house."

"*What?*" Tara exclaimed, nearly rising out of her chair. "Are you crazy? You love the cottage." She pushed the folder back. "No way. I'm not going to be an accomplice to whatever temporary insanity has gotten into you."

"I am perfectly sane," Jane assured her. "I am also in Paul's will—as guardian of his children."

"Jane, Jane, Jane." Tara put her elbows on the table and buried her head in her hands. "Have you learned nothing from watching my disasters?"

Before Jane could answer, the waiter appeared at their table. Jane ordered while Tara studied her menu.

A few moments later, she looked up. "I'm ready." Tara leaned toward the waiter and pointed a polished nail at her menu. "I'd like the capellini donato—unless you'd recommend something else." She tilted her face up expectantly.

Jane rolled her eyes. Tara couldn't be *that* heartbroken over Zack if she could flirt with a guy who was probably still in college.

"An excellent choice," he said, and reached for Tara's menu.

She stopped him, her hand on his. "Perhaps you will come back later and tell us about the *desserts*." The word rolled off her lips seductively.

"Of course." He gave a polite nod. Tugging at the menu, he backed away from their table.

Jane waited until he was out of sight. "Tara, you're shameless!"

"Am not." Tara put on her best pout. "It's therapeutic, you know. I'll get over Zack much faster if I find I can still attract other men."

"Don't you think that guy's a little young for you?"

"I'm not going to *marry* him. I don't even want to go out with him." Tara picked up her drink. "I just need to know I can get his attention."

"I don't think I'll ever understand you," Jane said, taking a breadstick from the basket the waiter had brought.

Tara tapped her nails on the table. "Then just learn from me. I will *not* sell your house, Jane. You love that place. You love the island."

"You're right. I do," Jane confessed. "But Tara, I can't have everything, and I'd rather have Paul and his children."

"You've only known this guy a month. And here you are, ready to give up your whole lifestyle to suit his? It's crazy. It's—it's something *I'd* do."

"Paul isn't Zack."

"*Hel-lo.*" Tara waved a hand in front of Jane's face. "From my point of view, this is what you're getting. First." She held up one finger. "A sick man—needs pampering." She held up another finger. "Second, he's recently widowed—still loves his wife—not a whole lot of love coming your way. Third and fourth, he's got two needy children—*tons* of work. And fifth, medical bills galore. And you're *quitting* your job?" Tara shook her head. "Wake up, girl. You're always warning me about getting my feet wet in murky water. Well you just dove right in, completely ignoring the sign that says *Strong Undertow.*"

"Sink or swim," Jane said lightheartedly.

Tara didn't return her smile.

"And I'm not quitting. I already talked to Ed, and I can come back when I need to." Jane held the folder out to her again. "*Please,* Tara. I've signed everything, listing you as the realtor. I owe much less than it's worth now, so it should be an easy sale. You can have the whole commission." She flipped open the folder. "I've taped the key right here."

Tara frowned. "You're already out?"

Jane nodded. "We packed the past four days, and my brothers are moving the big stuff tomorrow. I really need you to do this for me. Because I can't."

"You can't because you don't really want to."

"I've made my choice."

Reluctantly, Tara took the folder. "I'm worried about you, Jane. You've always told me I was foolish for jumping into relationships—and you've always been right." She met Jane's gaze. "I wanted to believe in what you said—that you were holding out for someone special and you'd find him. But this can't be it." She shook her head sadly. "Just remember you can always come back to Emerald, and the rolls at the bakery taste even better when you're recovering from a heartbreak."

* * *

Jane sat on one of the stools at Caroline's kitchen counter. "How was Madison tonight?"

Caroline closed the dishwasher. "She was great. Jessica fed her twice and even changed her diaper. I think I've just about got myself a babysitter trained."

"Good timing," Jane said. "Cause I think I'm going to be booked from now on."

"You think?" Caroline teased. She rinsed out the dishcloth and began wiping down the counter. She stopped when she came to Jane's purse and the papers next to it. "What are these?"

"Singles info. Tara made me take them and *promise* to read them in exchange for her listing my house. She thinks I've lost my mind."

Caroline tossed the dishcloth in the sink and picked up the papers. "She's concerned about *your* decision?"

Jane smiled. "Funny, isn't it?"

"Not really," Caroline said.

"Not you too." Jane frowned.

"Nope." Caroline held her hands up. "You won't hear another word from me. Heaven knows I've done enough stupid things in my life that I'd better not judge you."

Jane's frown turned into an outright scowl.

"Anyway, Tara's just trying to be a good friend." Caroline perused the brochures. "Listen to this. My Matchmaker. You get a personal interview where you compose a thoughtful ten- to fifteen-minute video for their library. Says here the success rate is high." She flipped to the next paper. "Or how about this one—Aim-High Adventures. 'Meet the man of your dreams doing everything from horseback riding to hot-air ballooning to cooking Thai food.'"

"Great," Jane mumbled. She kicked off her shoes as she stifled a yawn. "I need to go to bed."

"Wait. One more," Caroline said. "How about Love and Lunch? It's the perfect dating solution for the busy professional."

Jane slid off the stool. "Afraid I don't qualify anymore."

"It's hard to imagine what it would be like being single again." Lost in thought, Caroline set the brochures down and placed both hands on the counter. Her face grew serious as she leaned forward. "If I had ten minutes to describe my perfect man—"

Ryan walked into the kitchen. "About six feet tall, brown hair, great body," he said, sucking in his gut. He flexed his biceps before kissing Caroline on the cheek.

"No." She made a face. "That's not how I'd describe him." She cleared her throat and stood a little taller as if posing in front of a camera. "My idea of a perfect man is one who takes the garbage out every day—without being asked." She threw a glance in Ryan's direction. "He also walks the dog whenever it rains, so his wife doesn't have to, of course."

"Dream on, woman," Ryan said as he opened the freezer and took out a carton of ice cream.

"But the best thing about my perfect man is—" Caroline turned around, facing Ryan. She leaned back against the counter, tossing her hair over her shoulder. "That when he takes his clothes off— "

Jane cleared her throat to let her sister know she was still in the room.

If Caroline heard, she ignored her. She had Ryan's full attention now, and Jane watched as Caroline beckoned him closer with the crook of her finger. Ryan set the carton of ice cream on the table and walked toward his wife.

"When he has *all* his clothes off," she continued in a sultry tone as she ran her fingers down his shirt sleeve. "He . . . puts—them—in—the—hamper."

Jane smothered a laugh as Caroline pinched her fingers together and then opened them as if dropping something.

"Oh yes." Caroline sighed. "That would be one *amazing* man." She turned back to the sink, a dreamy look on her face as she picked up the dishcloth and finished wiping down the counter.

Ryan stood behind his wife, scowling. "Just for that, I'm eating the rest of the Tin Roof Sundae."

"Go for it, dear," Caroline replied. "Just make sure your bowl ends up in the dishwasher when you're through."

"Good night," Jane called, heading down the hall. She'd heard enough of this kind of banter to know where it was heading. A smile touched her lips. Caroline and Ryan reminded her of the movie *Return to Me*. They were the happy—if not somewhat insane—married couple with kids swarming all around. Jane's smile faded. *She,* on the other hand, was the single and lonely sister in the movie.

But, Jane reminded herself, by the end of the movie that had changed. The widowed architect had recovered from losing his wife and fallen in love with the sister—even though she had his wife's transplanted heart. Jane sighed, remembering the poignant moments of the movie and feeling grateful that at least she didn't have the *heart* obstacle to overcome. Still, she couldn't help but hope she'd end up as happy as that. Paul was an architect too. Maybe that was a good sign.

Keeping the light off, Jane tiptoed into the nursery. She leaned over the port-a-crib to check Madison and was surprised to see her bright eyes open, her tiny face looking up expectantly.

"Hello, little princess." Jane reached over and picked up Madison. She held the little girl against her chest and began swaying slowly in the dark, rubbing her cheek against Maddie's soft head and inhaling her sweet fragrance.

"Is there a chance, Maddie? I know it's only a movie, but maybe it *is* possible. Maybe your dad will get well and then . . . Maybe someday he can love me as much as he loved your mom."

Chapter Twenty-Three

"I can't believe the difference a coat of paint makes," Caroline said, standing next to her minivan parked in Jane's driveway.

"Try *three* coats," Jane called, walking out of the house, a baby carrier in each hand.

"And the yard—wow." Caroline looked appreciatively over the front yard of the rental. The junipers were gone, the soil weeded and graded in preparation for sod, and the house had gone from a dull gray to a soft yellow. New white shutters framed the windows.

Jane set the twins, in their car seats, down on the walk and returned to lock the door. "Yeah, now that the monster bushes are gone, it's not too bad."

"Not bad—it's great," Caroline said. "How did you get all this done so fast?"

"I know a few people with backhoes, and Paul helped too. He watched the twins while I painted, and he even arranged a deal with the landlord. We get a hundred dollars off the rent each month, so long as we send the receipts showing our purchases for improvements on the home." Jane smiled with satisfaction as she picked up the twins again.

"If only Ryan and I were so motivated." Caroline shook her head and turned toward the cars. "Can we take my van? I made a last-minute appointment for Andrew. He had a terrible night—I think it's his ears again."

"Sorry he's sick." Jane stopped to give Caroline a quick hug. "You look beat," she observed, moving past Caroline to the van's sliding door.

"Give yourself a couple of months with the two of them." Caroline nodded to the twins as she opened the van door. "You'll look the same."

"I don't know," Jane said. "Mark has been home a week now, and it's not too bad. Paul is pretty helpful." He was *more* than helpful at night, Jane thought as she lifted Mark's seat into the van. It seemed each time she went to take her turn giving a middle-of-the-night bottle or diaper change, Paul was already with the twins. And on those few occasions she'd managed to beat him into the nursery, he was always right behind her, offering to take over—since he was up anyway. Jane knew he didn't sleep at night; what she didn't know was if the pain keeping him awake was physical or emotional.

She unfastened the seatbelt and pushed Madison's car seat next to Mark's. "Doesn't Ryan take his turn at night with Andrew?"

"No." Caroline shook her head. "We made a pact. I take care of Andrew, and Ryan handles all the other kids' nightmares, bed-wetting, and requests for food. Believe me, I have the better deal. "

"Sounds like it," Jane said. "There." She stepped into the van. "We'd better hurry. I don't want to be late for their first appointment with a new doctor."

"It won't matter if you are," Caroline said with a sigh. "We'll have to wait anyway."

* * *

The only seats available were next to the reception desk, so she and Caroline took those after they'd signed in.

"These guys must be good," Jane mused, looking around the room.

"They are," Caroline said, snatching up the latest issue of *Parents* magazine. "Otherwise I wouldn't wait. And they've got good magazines. It's about the only chance I ever have to read." She pointed eagerly to the potty-training article featured on the front cover. "Just wait. You'll have to do two at once. You'll be begging me for advice."

"I'm sure," Jane said, more interested at present in the woman across the room who was openly breast-feeding her infant.

"You could, you know," Caroline said, following Jane's gaze.

"Could what?"

"Nurse the twins if you wanted to. I read about a shot they give adoptive mothers to start their milk. You should ask Dr. Larsen."

Jane looked appalled. "No thanks." She lowered her voice to a whisper. "I think I'd like to be a part of creating my own baby first."

"You *should*."

"Really? Any suggestions?" Jane rolled her eyes. "It's not like I'm the most eligible female and I've got men falling at my feet. I thought I had problems before—just being plain Jane, almost thirty. Now I'm plain Jane who *is* thirty. I'm living next door to a guy who's got cancer, and soon I'll be a mom of two special-needs infants. Quite a catch."

"What about Paul?" Caroline asked.

Jane's eyebrows rose. "What about him?"

"Maybe he could help you out there."

"I can't believe you just said that." Jane stared at Caroline in disbelief. "First of all, we're not married. And he's sick, for heaven's sake. And even if he wasn't— well, he's still mourning his wife. He hasn't even considered a relationship."

"Good," Caroline said, returning to her magazine.

"No, that's *not* good. What's wrong with you? You suggest I get cozy with Paul, and then you're glad we aren't even dating?"

Caroline tried but couldn't hide her guilty look. "I told Mom I'd find out how things are going—you know, how friendly you and Paul are these days."

"I can't believe this," Jane said, incredulous. "And from you of all people."

"Yes, from *me* of all people." Caroline's teasing tone was gone. "I told you before—I almost ruined my life. So who better to watch out for you and make certain you don't ruin yours?"

"But I'm not," Jane protested.

Caroline touched her sleeve. "I know. And I know you love those babies, but I can't lose sight of the vision of you kneeling at the temple altar. And we're all just worried *you'll* lose sight of it. *That* is what you deserve, Jane. Nothing less. Heavenly Father wants to bless you with everything possible."

Jane looked away, angered at the sudden sting of tears behind her eyes. "I'm looking for those blessings," she insisted. "I really am."

* * *

Appointments finally over, they sat in Caroline's van, feeding the babies before heading to the store to get the antibiotic for Andrew's ear infection.

"So what *does* nursing feel like?" Jane asked as she gently nudged the bottle into Madison's mouth.

"Why do you want to know?" Caroline's gaze drifted to Maddie. "I'm sorry I teased you earlier. It's perfectly fine to bottle-feed babies. And just because you didn't give birth to a child doesn't mean you can't be her mother."

"I'm not worried about that." Jane leaned around her seat to check on Mark. "But I may never have the experience of being pregnant or nursing a baby, and I kind of want to hear what it's like."

"All right," Caroline said somewhat reluctantly. "But after this I just discuss bed-wetting, temper tantrums, and nightmares. Got it?"

Jane nodded, smiling.

Caroline looked down at Andrew, a thoughtful expression on her face. "Well . . . The first few weeks—month really—are tough. Ryan always says that I have as much liquid come from my eyes as I do from my breasts because I just sit there crying from the pain."

"Why do you do it then?" Jane asked, perplexed.

"Well, with Jess it was because we were so poor and I knew we could never afford the formula. Ryan had almost three years of college left and there wasn't a dime to spare, so I just did it. But after that, I realized how great nursing was, and I was glad I hadn't stopped."

Jane used a corner of the burp cloth to wipe the milk dribbling down the side of Madison's chin. "What's so great about it?"

"Oh, lots of things—being sore and swollen, milk stains on all your clothes, being the only one who can feed the baby in the middle of the night." Caroline grimaced. "Doesn't get any better than that."

Jane laughed. "You could do a formula commercial."

"I suppose," Caroline said. She looked down at Andrew, linking her finger through his tiny fist. "But I wouldn't. You have this baby—you've really had him nine-plus months already—but now you get to hold him in your arms, sing to him, look at him. Still, you miss him being inside. As absurd as that sounds, it's true. By the end of a pregnancy you're tired of backaches, getting up ten times a night to use the bathroom, wearing tents for shirts—you're sick to death of all of it—yet you miss feeling that child inside you."

"So then you nurse him?" Jane asked, trying to piece together her sister's logic.

"Yes," Caroline said. "You have this adorable infant, a scrunched-up, seven-pound ball who does nothing but cry and mess his diaper. He can't use his hands—doesn't even know he has them. He can barely communicate. He can't even see you very well. But when you pick him up and put him to your breast . . ." Caroline stopped, carefully placing a finger in Andrew's mouth, releasing his piranha-like suction.

Before Andrew could cry, she'd kissed him on the cheek and settled him on the other side, where he promptly latched on, sucking contentedly once more. His tiny hand waved in the air a moment, then settled, palm flat, against Caroline's chest.

Caroline secured her bra, adjusted the blanket covering her, then looked up, her eyes brimming with emotion. "So you put this helpless infant to your breast and immediately he knows what to do. He latches on like it has been done a hundred times before, and your body responds in the most miraculous way, providing what he needs to grow. And then you realize he still needs you. You're still connected."

"It sounds wonderful," Jane said.

Caroline reached out, squeezing her hand. "Hey, you'll have your own children someday."

"What if I don't?" Jane asked.

"You will," Caroline said. "You're going to meet someone. I know it."

"I've met him," Jane said, forlorn.

"Not Paul?" Caroline asked, her brow wrinkled with concern.

Jane said nothing, but nodded, meeting Caroline's eyes.

"Oh, Jane," Caroline said, reaching out. "I was afraid of this. You're not falling for him, are you?"

"I don't know—I don't know what it is." Jane sighed. "But it's great. For the first time in a *long* time, I'm not lonely. Every morning when I wake up, Paul comes over. We sit at the table, share a grapefruit, read the paper—and not the personals either." She gave Caroline a wry smile. "And now that Mark is home, Paul and I are together most of the day. We play with the babies or work on the house. At night we take turns making dinner, and after the twins are in bed we play Scrabble or watch TV." Jane looked at Caroline, trying to make her sister understand what she was saying. "Do you know how *fantastic* it is to have someone to sit next to and share a bowl of popcorn with while you watch the news?" She didn't wait for an answer. "For years I'd see something on television, or I'd read something in the paper, hear a new song on the radio—*anything*—and I'd have a thought I'd long to share with someone. Now I can. I've got Paul, and he's the best thing that's ever happened to me."

Caroline's face was sad as she lifted Andrew to her shoulder. "*Scrabble?* And the *news?* Jane, that isn't love. What you've done is fall *out* of loneliness, but that isn't the same as loving someone. When it's love, you *know* it. You have this feeling, this take-your-breath-away—"

"Chemistry," Jane finished for her. "I felt that with Jay, remember? And it seems I also remember you telling me that love involved more than that. It involved friendship. So what—now that I've found the friendship, that's not good enough either?" She turned away, looking out the passenger-side window as she fought back angry tears. "We can't all find what you and Ryan have."

"What Ryan and I have takes a lot of work, and I think you can have that—when you meet the right person." Caroline took a deep breath. "But you're forgetting one important part of the formula. You need friendship, chemistry, *and* faith. Life is hard, Jane. Don't make it worse by choosing someone who doesn't share your faith, who doesn't know Heavenly Father like you do."

"I think Paul could learn," Jane said. "I even think he kind of wants to. He's asked Mom a few questions while I've been at church and she's over helping with the babies."

"That's good," Caroline said, encouraged.

Jane gave her a sad smile. "I suppose so, except . . ."

Caroline's brow wrinkled. "What?"

Jane looked up at her. "He wants to know where his wife is now. Every question he's asked had to do with Tami. He can't let go of her."

"Should he have to?" Caroline asked softly. "If Ryan had died a few months ago, would you expect me to be over him?"

"That's different," Jane protested. "You're sealed in the temple. You're—"

"And if you truly care for Paul, you'll want him to have those blessings too," Caroline said. "You'll want to ease his sadness by teaching him about eternal marriage."

Jane swallowed the lump in her throat. "That's asking an awful lot of me, don't you think?" She tried to smile but couldn't.

Caroline nodded. "You asked it of yourself the day you moved in next door to him. I'm not saying you've made a completely bad decision, Jane. But what you have done is make life much more complicated. Now you need to be careful to not make things worse. Paul is your friend. That's fine. But if you tangle with the emotions physical intimacy brings, you'll be even more devastated when . . ." Her voice trailed off.

"You can't say it either," Jane accused, setting Madison's empty bottle aside.

"You'll be even more devastated when Paul dies," Caroline said softly. "His cancer *is* terminal."

"We're all going to die," Jane said, angrily wiping a tear away. "Paul may know how, but even he doesn't know when. He's already far outlived his doctors' predictions."

"That's great, but—"

"His cancer could still go into remission," Jane insisted. "He's on this new combination of drugs, and they're administered straight into his liver, so he's not as sick as before. The rest of his body may rally and fight back. And if that happens, then why can't I love him? Why couldn't he be the one?"

Caroline bit her lip and continued to rub Andrew's back. After several seconds she finally spoke. "I hope you're right. Just—be careful, Jane."

Jane gave her a wan smile. "I will. Remember this is *me* you're talking to. The worst I've ever done is share a stolen kiss in the hall at work—and look what that got me."

"Good," Caroline said emphatically.

"You know what I keep thinking of, though?"

Caroline shook her head. "What?"

"Remember in junior high when I was on that *Anne of Green Gables* kick?"

"Yes." Caroline rolled her eyes. "I was ready to shred those videos. You must have watched them twenty times."

"Thirty-two," Jane confirmed. "*Anne of Avonlea* was my first foray into romance." She smiled, remembering. "And now I keep thinking of the scene where Gilbert is dying and Anne brings him her book. She finally tells him she loves him."

"And he gets better," Caroline said.

"He gets better," Jane echoed. She looked down at Madison, asleep in her arms. "Miracles do happen. Paul *could* get better."

Caroline leaned across the seat, putting an arm around Jane. "That was fiction. Real life is usually—different."

"I know," Jane said, a tear trailing down her cheek. She wrapped a blanket around Madison, carefully tucking her tiny hands inside. "But I love his children. And I could love him."

Chapter Twenty-Four

Jane felt like beaming as she sat beside Paul at her parents' table. For the first Thanksgiving in her adult history, she had not come alone. The past several years—especially the last two since her brother Michael had married, leaving her the only one still single—she'd felt out of place at family gatherings. She loved her parents and her siblings, but their well-meaning advice and teasing about her unmarried status had hurt her on more occasions than she cared to count.

And Thanksgiving was always the worst.

Longstanding family tradition dictated that everyone old enough to talk take a minute—or *ten,* as her blubbery sister Karen always did—to tell something they were thankful for. In the past Jane had struggled to come up with something acceptable to say.

The year she'd graduated she expressed gratitude for her education—though her degree wasn't the one she'd really wanted. Jane was also thankful for her job—well, sort of. It paid the bills, but it wasn't what she wanted to do for the rest of her life.

Last year she'd been thankful for her house, and her parents had really frowned at that one. After all, a house was a material thing, and her mother felt she'd be better off living in a tent rather than her run-down cottage.

With painful Thanksgiving memories still fresh on her mind, one of Jane's New Year's resolutions for 2003 had been to disappear on a cruise ship when the holiday rolled around again. But today she was glad she'd postponed booking her passage. Tonight she had something meaningful to say. Tonight there would be no singles jokes directed her way. Tonight her parents would be happy.

Jane glanced at her watch. If only Karen would finish her monologue.

It was a good thing they'd already eaten. Jane remembered when they were growing up and she and her siblings had to express their thanks *before* dinner was served. But the Thanksgiving she was six years old, that had changed.

That year she'd spent all morning at the park, thrilled she was finally old enough to be included in the also-traditional family football game. By the time dinner was served at four o'clock that afternoon, Jane had taken a bath, had her hair braided by Grandma, and had watched most of the *The Wizard of Oz.* Needless to say, she was starving.

Her father said the blessing, and then the grown-ups began the thanking. All of the children from oldest to youngest were expected to follow. Jane sat at the far end of the table, swinging her legs impatiently. The basket of rolls was right in front of her plate, and she thought the fragrance of the fresh-baked bread was going to kill her if she couldn't have a roll *soon*. Unfortunately, it was Karen's turn to talk, and she wouldn't shut up about her favorite teacher, winning the spelling bee, and making first chair in orchestra.

Jane's stomach growled and, ever-so-slowly, her fingers inched toward the rolls. Her parents were at the other end of the table, their attention focused on her chatterbox sister. They probably wouldn't even notice . . . Jane lifted a corner of the cloth. A second later her hand closed over a warm, buttery croissant.

Smack! Her brother's hand came down hard on hers. "No fair," Michael yelled, wresting the croissant away.

"Give it back," Jane shrieked, waving her arms in the air, trying to reclaim her coveted prize.

"*Children*," her mother reprimanded.

Michael stuck his tongue out and tossed the roll toward Trent. Jane leaned forward to intercept it and dragged her new blouse through the cranberry sauce. The croissant missed Trent but hit the gravy bowl, and a drop splashed onto Emily's sleeve.

"Moth-er," Emily wailed. "Look what Michael did." She dipped a napkin in her water glass and accidentally knocked it over. Mom jumped up to get a towel as Emily frantically scrubbed the sleeve it had taken three painstaking weeks of home ec to sew.

"That's enough nonsense," her father said sternly, pointing the carving knife toward their end of the table.

Too late to heed his command, Jane watched as the olive she'd launched with her spoon sped toward Michael and hit him square between the eyes.

"You little twerp." Michael reached for her, but Jane ducked out of the way, and he decked Caroline instead.

Time seemed suspended as Michael, realizing what he'd done, opened his mouth in horror. A chorus of gasps echoed around the table. Jane knew at once that dinner was a lost cause.

Caroline was involved now. She made fights serious. From the corner of her eye, Jane saw her father push his chair back.

Caroline stood and grabbed the bowl of peas from the table. She advanced on Michael.

"I'm going to shove these up your nose."

Michael shrank in his chair. "Help me, Trent," he pled. Trent snatched the serving spoon from the mashed potatoes.

It happened fast—less than a minute, probably. Their father put a swift end to the food fight, spanking most of them and sending them to their rooms—without anything to eat except for whatever potatoes happened to be on their faces. Jane lay on her bed and bawled, distraught that she'd been the cause of such a disaster.

"Don't be a crybaby," Caroline scolded, sitting down on their bedroom floor. "You're not going to starve. I've got enough candy here to keep us for a week." She flipped up her comforter and pulled a box out from under her bed. "What kind do you want?"

Jane shook her head. "I'm n-not hungry. It's all m-my fault. I ruined Thanksgiving." She turned her face into her pillow, sobbing.

Caroline shrugged. "Suit yourself," she said. "I'm going to sneak a soda." She got off her bed and went to the window. Opening it slowly so it wouldn't squeak, she popped out the screen and climbed up on the dresser. "I'll bring you back a lemon-lime."

Jane lay on her bed crying as Caroline jumped to the ground then muttered when her shirt became caught on a Barbary bush. A few moments later two sodas appeared on the windowsill.

"Give me a hand, Jane," Caroline whispered loudly.

Jane got off her bed and went to the window. She moved the sodas, climbed up on the dresser and reached down to Caroline.

"Thanks," Caroline said a moment later when she was safely back in the room. She put the screen in, closed the window, and sat on her bed. "You can quit being upset now, cause guess what I heard?"

"I don't know," Jane said sullenly.

"Mom and Dad and Grandma and Uncle Jerry are all in there *laughing* about what happened."

"Are not," Jane said, scowling.

Caroline popped the top off her soda. "It's true. I heard them through the garage wall. *And* Dad says that from now on we get to eat *before* we thank. Isn't that great? You did a really cool thing, Jane."

"They're laughing about the food fight—really?" Jane asked, hope in her voice.

Caroline nodded. "And they're going to come get us for dinner in fifteen minutes. So either drink that soda or hide it."

Jane stuck the pop in her Barbie box—next to another soda and a pack of Twinkies Caroline had previously snuck for her. But the sudden relief she felt dictated some kind of celebration, so she took out the Tootsie Pop she'd been saving since Halloween. She lay back on her bed, the sucker in her mouth, as she thought again about the scene at dinner. She was glad her parents were laughing now, because the look of disappointment on her mother's face had just about killed her.

Jane hated disappointing anyone. She hated conflict, and it seemed her family had plenty of that with nine different personalities interacting each day. She vowed then and there that never again would she cause a fight like she had that day. She would not let her mother down again.

Remembering that lofty goal she'd made as a six-year-old, a wistful smile touched Jane's lips. Growing up she *had* done a good job of not upsetting her parents. But since then . . . It seemed her whole life was one disappointment after another—until now.

Over the past two months, her parents seemed to have accepted Paul. Today there would be no conflict. With a man at her side and a baby on her lap, she wasn't a disappointment to them. She had something genuine to be thankful for.

"And I'm thankful our 401(k) is doing well again. You know for the past two years we've just watched it decline, and we weren't sure how we'd ever retire or . . ."

Karen was still going strong. Jane turned to Paul and rolled her eyes. "Sorry," she mouthed. Paul leaned closer, his hand draped casually across the back of Jane's chair.

"I guess every family has to have at least one person who drives everyone else crazy," Jane whispered.

Paul smiled mischievously. "Maybe you should launch an olive at her."

"How do you know about that?" Jane demanded.

"I had to do something this morning while you played football."

Jane bit back a smile. "No fair," she whispered. "I don't have any way of learning your family secrets."

Paul's eyes seemed to darken. "Don't worry," he said quietly. "You will soon enough."

She looked at him quizzically, uncertain what he meant. "Do you have an estranged aunt hidden somewhere—or something else I should know about?"

"Just a brother," Paul said. He nodded toward Karen as she finally finished and sat down. "It's almost your turn." He leaned back in his chair, his attention seemingly focused on Jane's brother, who was now speaking.

Jane pushed Paul's confusing comment to the back of her mind and waited for her turn to speak. Michael—as much a man of few words as Karen was a woman who could talk your ear off—finished in about thirty seconds. All eyes focused on Jane.

She looked around the table. "I am thankful for each of you—for such a fun, fabulous, supportive family. And—" Taking a deep breath, she spoke the words it seemed she'd waited forever to say. "This year I'm thankful to have someone special here with me." She turned to Paul and suddenly felt overwhelmed with emotion as her eyes met his. "There aren't enough words to express how glad I am you came into my life. It is my privilege to be your friend, and the gift you've given me in trusting me to raise your children . . ." Jane felt her eyes water as she glanced down at Madison snuggled in her lap and Mark asleep in his car seat beside her chair. She looked at Paul again. "It is priceless—better than anything I could have ever imagined. I love Mark and Madison, and—I love you for sharing them."

For a split second, Paul had a stunned look on his face, but he recovered quickly before an awkward silence could descend on them. He smiled at Jane and took her hand in his as he cleared his throat.

"I'm the one who has the most to be thankful for," he said. "Jane, you've come into our lives like a miracle—an answer to an impossible prayer." He looked at her parents and then around the table. "I am grateful to each of you as well, for welcoming me and my children into your home."

Jane's parents and siblings nodded and smiled in response, but no one said anything—as if they expected Paul might say something more. When he didn't, her mother spoke.

"We're so happy to have you," she said as she rose from the table, signaling the end of the thanking. "Now who's ready for pie?"

Chapter Twenty-Five

"You did *what?*" Tara asked through a mouthful of peanut-butter-and-jelly sandwich.

Jane pulled two bottled waters from the fridge and set them on the table. Looking out at the weed-filled backyard, she sighed. "In front of my entire family, I told Paul I love him."

Tara looked horrified. "Jane, Jane, Jane." She put her elbows on the table and buried her head in her hands.

"I know. I'm a complete idiot." Jane sat down across from her.

After a moment, Tara looked up. "No, you aren't an idiot. You're just ignorant as to affairs of the heart, and *that* we can fix." She smiled brightly. "Fortunately, you've got me to help you. Now tell me what happened after the major faux pas."

"Well, Paul didn't say 'I love you' back, and then the floor didn't swallow me like I wished it would." Jane opened her water bottle and took a drink.

"Never can count on floors," Tara mused. She pointed to a plate of cinnamon rolls in the middle of the table. "May I?"

Jane nodded. "They're all for you. Consider it payment if you can help me get out of this mess."

Tara took a roll and put it on her napkin. "How has Paul been since Thanksgiving? You've had a weekend together. Anything different?"

"I'll say," Jane said, resting her chin on her arms folded in front of her on the table. "Basically, he's avoided me. He went to bed early on Thursday and stayed in his apartment most of Friday—said he had some work to do. I wanted to rent a movie or at least play Scrabble, but he turned me down for both. He was pretty much a recluse Saturday and Sunday. And *then,* after breakfast this morning, he left on his own for his appointment at the hospital. Usually, he asks me to drive him there." Jane sat up straight, then rose from the table. "Just a minute, I think I hear Mark." She left Tara to her cinnamon roll and the quiet kitchen.

A few minutes later Jane returned holding Mark in the crook of her arm. "Would you like to feed him?"

Tara looked scared. "No thanks. I don't want to catch whatever mother-hooditis has infected you."

Jane laughed and handed Mark to Tara anyway. "Then just hold him while I make a bottle." She turned on the faucet and took a can of formula from the cupboard. "What do you think of the rolls?"

"They're fabulous," Tara said as she jiggled Mark awkwardly. "I've eaten two already."

"At least my domestic skills are improving," Jane said. She measured formula into the bottle full of water, then put the cap on.

"But alas," Tara said. "The way to a man's heart is *not* through his stomach."

"Tara," Jane warned. She settled in the chair with Mark.

"All the men I've ever known," Tara said, "need to have some physical connection to start feeling close to you. You have to kiss them." She scrunched her napkin in a ball and threw it in the trash.

"*Fortunately* . . . Paul isn't like any of the men you've ever known." Jane pulled the bottle from Mark's mouth and wiped the milk dribbling down his chin.

"That's what you think." Tara eyed the rolls. "Do you have a Ziploc bag or something I could take those home in?"

"Second drawer to the left of the sink," Jane said. "But not so fast. You haven't given me any hope of fixing things with Paul. I mean, I can't even get him out of his bedroom."

Tara stood, hands on hips, looking at her. "And there's a problem with that?"

"Yes."

Tara pointed her finger at Jane. "You're going to have to be bold, Jane." She took a bag from the drawer and began dropping rolls into it, thinking aloud as she did so. "But how . . . There has to be a natural lead in—something you already have in common." Tara stopped. "Got it," she said, snapping her fingers. "You and Paul play Scrabble together, right?"

Jane answered warily. "Yeah."

Tara's lips curved into a mischievous grin. "Good, cause tonight you're going to play like you never have before. Now listen closely. Here's the plan."

* * *

Paul's fingers gripped the soft leather arms of the wingback chair. He felt sick to his stomach—dizzy—and today it wasn't just the cancer causing him pain. Across the dark mahogany desk, Richard Morgan's brow furrowed as he read the papers from the manila envelope Paul had handed him five minutes earlier.

Richard reached up to loosen his tie, and Paul fought anxiety as he watched the clock tick for another five minutes. To pass the time, he looked around the room, making a halfhearted attempt to notice if anything had changed since he'd last been in the attorney's office. Except for a new family picture on the windowsill, everything seemed the same—exactly as it was the crisp November day nearly two years ago when Richard had called both him and Pete into his office to try to talk some sense into them.

Richard hadn't been successful. And now, today . . . Paul wasn't certain Richard would see his side of things and help.

At last Richard finished reading the first few paper-clipped pages, then scanned through the remaining packet. He looked up, one simple question forming on his lips.

"Why?"

Paul was prepared for this. "Because I haven't got much time left, and it was Tami's last wish." He pulled the bandage wrapper from his pocket and placed it on the desk. "An EMT gave this to me the night she died."

Richard picked up the crinkled paper and read the words scrawled across it. He exhaled sharply as he finished. "I can understand why you think Tami meant Pete, but you don't really think she expected you to go out and find some woman to—?"

"That's exactly what she expected," Paul said, recalling the changed pictures in his apartment and Tami's voice in his head so many times in the past weeks. "And considering Pete isn't here, it makes perfect sense that the twins have a second guardian now."

Richard looked at him intently. "Does Pete know? Have you asked him to come home?"

"From a war?" Paul shook his head. "No. Half the reservists in Iraq probably have circumstances where they should be with their families. And I know my brother. Pete wouldn't ask for any special break."

"Hmm," Richard murmured, neither agreeing nor disagreeing with Paul's statement. He leaned back in his chair, his attention still focused on Paul. "You look terrible."

"Thanks," Paul said sarcastically. "You were never one to mince words."

Richard smiled. "No point. Wastes everyone's time. Pete doesn't know about your cancer, does he?"

"No point," Paul shot back. "I'd rather he forgive me because he wants to—not out of sympathy."

"Maybe he already has," Richard said.

Paul shrugged. "Maybe."

"I'd think—in your shoes—that I'd want to patch things up. Forgive and forget." Richard leaned forward over the desk. "I'd want to see my only brother."

Paul shifted uncomfortably in his chair. He looked out the window, waiting as a wave of pain rolled through his middle. He shouldn't have gone without his painkillers this morning. But who'd have thought stress would hurt this bad. It was all he could do to keep from doubling over.

"I do want to see Pete—or talk to him at least." Paul looked pointedly at the papers on the desk. "It's next on my agenda, *after* I've taken care of the legalities. Now are you going to help me or not?"

Richard leaned back in his chair again and sighed. "Peter is my friend and colleague. It feels like betrayal to set him up in something like this. He'll hate us both for tying him to some woman he's never met."

"He'll get over it," Paul said. "Or maybe he won't. Either way, it's time my brother learned to stop holding a grudge."

Richard met his gaze. "I wonder if Pete is the one with the grudge? He doesn't seem the type. In fact, I'd say he's more the sort to be torn up over the fact that his only living family member hasn't spoken with him in two years."

"Like I said—" There was an edge to Paul's voice. "As soon as everything is in order, calling Pete is next on the list." Trying not to wince, Paul rose from his chair. "So if your answer is no, I'll just find another attorney to help me." He reached for the papers on the desk.

Richard stopped him. "Sit down." It was an order, not a request. Paul hesitated a moment before he eased back into the chair again.

"You don't want some other attorney messing with something as important as this," Richard said. "If handled incorrectly, your nominating joint guardianship could result in a custody battle somewhere down the line."

Paul frowned. "That's not my intention. Trust me on this. Jane is already a terrific mother. You'd really like her. Pete will—"

"Then why isn't she here?" Richard asked. "Why didn't you bring her?"

Paul hedged. "She's with the twins—they don't go out much yet."

A look of disbelief, then genuine anger crossed Richard's face. "She doesn't know—does she?"

Paul didn't answer.

Richard threw his hands up. "What are you trying to pull here, Paul? Do you *want* your children in the middle of a custody battle a few months—or years—down the line?"

"Months," Paul said. "And no, of course not." He looked Richard straight in the eyes. "I've got my reasons for doing things this way, *and* I am going to tell Pete and Jane, but first I want the business end of it complete."

Richard studied Paul, taking in his haggard appearance again. "I'll do it," he said at last. "I just won't like it."

Paul smiled for the first time since he'd entered the office. "Well then, that makes two of us."

* * *

Forty minutes later, Paul left the building and returned to his car. He sat a moment, letting the heater warm up and letting some of the stress ease from his body. He'd done it. If he died this very minute, Mark and Madison would be provided for. They'd have a mother and a father—of sorts.

He'd honored Tami's last wish.

Paul physically felt the tension leave him, felt his shoulders relax, felt some of the pain in his gut and chest subside. He hadn't fully realized what an enormous relief it would be.

"My to do list is getting short, Tami," he said quietly. There were just two things left, and neither would be easy. Paul glanced at the letter on the seat beside him. He put the car in reverse and backed out of his parking space. Next stop—the post office. And then, soon, he would have to talk with Jane.

Chapter Twenty-Six

At eight o'clock Tuesday night, Jane stood outside Paul's apartment, the Scrabble game and baby monitor in one hand and an enormous bowl of popcorn in the other. She hadn't been able to put Tara's plan into action last night, as Paul had come home tired and feeling unwell after his appointment. Turning sideways, Jane rang the doorbell with her elbow.

"Come in," Paul called.

Balancing the popcorn bowl on top of the Scrabble box, Jane used her free hand to open the door. She crossed the small kitchen to Paul's room. Looking inside the open door, she saw him sitting up in bed, a James Patterson thriller in his hand.

"I can't believe you're reading that," she chided, stepping into the room. "Don't you have enough stress in your life already?"

"Makes me feel better," Paul said. "I may have problems, but at least I know I'm not in danger of being murdered." He eyed the bowl in her hand as he sniffed the air. "Unless, of course, you're planning to overdose my arteries with butter."

"Nope." Feeling bold, Jane walked over to the bed and sat down. "Just making sure we have enough to last for a *long* game of Scrabble. I'm planning to beat you soundly."

"I really don't feel like—"

"Uh-uh," Jane protested, holding her hand up. "I know you don't feel like playing. I also know—from things you've told me—that Tami never let you get away with moping in your bedroom. Which is *exactly* what you've done the past several days."

Jane watched Paul's face, trying to gauge his reaction to her playing what Tara called "the wife card." Tara's advice was not to be afraid of talking about Paul's wife. In doing so, Tara assured her, Paul would see that she could move beyond that obstacle and that, intuitively, would help him do the same.

Now Jane was pleased to read mild surprise on his face. *Score one for Tara.*

"You're right," he said, setting his book facedown on the nightstand. "She wouldn't let me stay in bed and mope. Would you rather play in the kitchen?"

Yes. But Tara tip number two was *keep him in the bedroom.* "No," Jane said in what she hoped was a nonchalant tone. "You can stay right where you are with your pillows to keep you comfortable. I've got the monitor with me."

Paul shrugged. "Okay." He leaned back against the headboard, and Jane passed him the popcorn and proceeded to set up the game.

"You sure you're not expecting your sister's kids or something?" he asked, eyeing the large bowl again before taking a handful of popcorn.

"You haven't eaten much lately," Jane said. "I thought the least I could do is ensure that you're getting some fiber—since my cooking hasn't appealed to you this week."

Paul's hand stopped halfway to his mouth. "Your cooking is great. I just thought . . ." He broke off as her eyes met his.

"What?" Jane prodded.

"Nothing." He glanced at the game board. "Let's play."

Jane smoothed the comforter flat and started spreading the letter tiles out on the inside of the box lid.

"Don't bother with that," Paul said. "We can just draw from the bag."

"Oh, right," Jane said, giving him a sheepish smile. She'd planned to spread the tiles out, discreetly taking the six select letters that she'd purposely left at her end of the box. Reluctantly, she began dropping the tiles into the bag.

Paul reached over to help, picking up the rest, including the ones she'd set aside.

Now what? Jane thought. So much for seductive spelling if she didn't get those letters. Reaching her hand into the bag, she counted seven pieces. A, M, S, Q, I, L, and K. She smiled. Four out of six wasn't bad. With a little luck she could spell *kiss me* in no time.

Paul went first. "*Ax.* Nine—times two for double word equals eighteen points." He leaned forward, placing his tiles.

"Ouch," Jane said. She wrote eighteen under Paul's column on the paper. There was still hope—if she could just get another S and an E. She drew on her next three turns, and Paul did the same.

"*Ban,* ten points," Paul said, playing off his A in *ax.*

Jane frowned as she drew another letter.

"Not having much luck tonight, are you?" Paul asked.

"I guess that's what I get for saying I was going to win." Jane looked up at Paul, noting the circles under his eyes were darker than usual. "You haven't been sleeping well, have you?"

He shook his head. "No."

"I'm sorry," Jane said. "I'll get up with the twins tonight."

"I don't mind taking them," Paul said. "Truth is, I'm usually up anyway."

"Please let me know if you need help." Jane reached for a handful of popcorn and then remembered what Tara had said about the way she should eat. Jane suddenly felt guilty. Paul had so much to worry about that he couldn't sleep at night, and here she was, thinking of how to get him to kiss her. *You're not the only one who will benefit,* Tara's voice came, unbidden, to her mind. *Studies have shown that kissing lifts people from depression.*

Jane heeded Tara's voice in her head. Instead of shoving several pieces into her mouth at once, like she normally did, she selected one piece of popcorn from her hand and brought it slowly to her lips. "Mmm," she murmured exaggeratedly.

"You sure you're not the one who needs to eat?" Paul asked, giving her a funny look.

Mortified that she'd so obviously bungled the move, Jane swallowed the popcorn so fast she began to choke. She coughed several times and felt her face turning red. She brought her hands to her chest—as if that would somehow help her breathe—and inadvertently spilled the rest of her popcorn down the front of the sparkly shirt Tara had lent her.

"You want some water?" Paul reached for his cup on the nightstand, but Jane, her face even redder, shook her head, jumped off the bed and ran out of his apartment and back to her own kitchen.

Once there, she bent over the sink, alternately gagging and gulping water from the faucet. When she could finally breathe a minute or so later, she looked up to find Paul standing on the opposite side of the bar, concern on his face.

"You okay?" he asked.

"Fine," Jane croaked. But Paul was giving her a funny look, and she was surprised to see him staring at . . . her *chest*. She looked down and saw that the front of her neckline—aside from holding her spilled popcorn—was now soaked from the spray of the faucet. She felt her face heat with embarrassment again.

"I'll just go change," she said, walking quickly past him and down the hall to her bedroom. She closed the door, then slid down to the carpet, burying her face in her hands as she pulled her knees up to her chest. If Tara could see her now . . . Jane imagined the look of horror on her friend's face when she explained how she'd ruined the evening. Jane stifled a sudden giggle. At least she *had* captured Paul's attention. He'd certainly never noticed her like he had five minutes ago. She rose from the floor, found a T-shirt, a regular crew neck that was anything but romantic— "Tim's Tree Removal" was scrawled across the front—and returned to Paul's room.

"Everything all right?" he asked.

Jane noticed he purposely avoided looking at her shirt. She nodded and took her place at the end of the bed, silently vowing to leave the suggestive eating and Scrabble tactics to people like Tara.

"Your turn," Paul said.

She drew the letter E. *Figures. Oh well. Too late now.* On her next turn she placed her E next to Paul's B in ban.

"*Be.* Five points," she said, marking her own score.

"All those letters and that's the best you can do?" he teased.

"And going the other way it's *ex,* ten," Jane continued.

"Impressive."

Paul's smile was all the incentive she needed to return to Tara's plan. She watched as he studied his letters, then finally drew another tile.

"Ant," she said, her voice still sounding hoarse as she took her next turn.

"Uh-uh," he protested. "Doesn't work going the other way." He glanced down at his tiles. "But I'll give you those measly three points and take seventeen." Paul picked up the x and moved it, adding several more letters. "*Sextant.*"

Jane rolled her eyes. "I think moving letters is a little beyond cheating, but if you want to play rummy instead—" She picked up the S from the board and turned it around, facing Paul. Quickly she added KIS beside it. Before she could change her mind, she grabbed the E from *be* and placed her M in front of it, after the word kiss.

"So that's what this is about," Paul said. He sighed, then leaned back against the headboard and closed his eyes.

"Yes," Jane whispered, looking down at her lap. She pushed the Scrabble game aside and scooted closer, facing him. "Listen, Paul. I'm sorry about Thanksgiving. I know I embarrassed you. What I meant was that I like you a lot. You're fun to be with, and maybe someday—"

"No!"

Jane's head snapped up, and she looked at Paul with trepidation. But instead of the anger she'd expected to see, she read sorrow in his eyes and the lines on his face.

"No," his voice was quieter—tired. "Jane I . . ." He ran his fingers over the top of his head, then quickly brought his hand down and looked at it, as if he were surprised he'd felt no hair. "I forget sometimes," he said. "I forget that I'm bald now. I forget that I'm dying. Once in a while, I even forget about Tami, and I know I start to flirt with you—to tease a little, to have fun."

"There's nothing wrong with that," Jane said.

Paul shook his head. "There's *everything* wrong with it."

"You're not breaking any vows," Jane lowered her voice to a whisper. "Tami is gone."

"So am I, Jane." Paul leaned forward and took her hand. "It's only a matter of time—a *short* matter of time before I'm gone."

"Quit saying that," Jane said. "You can't give up. Mark and Madison need you. They need a father."

Paul gave her a sad smile. "I know they need a father." He squeezed her hand. "But I'm not going to be around to—"

"*Don't.*" Jane blinked rapidly as her eyes filled with tears. "I can't stand it when you talk that way. What happened to the man who beat the doctors' predictions? The guy who didn't give up?"

"He ran out of options," Paul said, his voice solemn. "His doctors ran out of treatments, so he found a kind, beautiful woman to raise his children."

Jane heard only the first part of his explanation. "What do you mean the doctors ran out of treatments?" With her free hand she wiped at a tear trailing down her cheek.

"I'm done," Paul said simply. "There's nothing left. No more radiation. No chemo. There aren't even any experimental treatments they'd recommend."

Stunned, Jane brought a hand to her mouth. "Nothing?" she whispered. He shook his head.

"But your injections . . ." She recalled Paul's hope, just a few weeks earlier, that the weekly Ethanol injections to his liver were doing their job to kill the tumors. "I thought—"

"My whole liver is a tumor," Paul said. "There's just *too much* cancer to wipe out."

Sudden, sickening fear washed over her. Her bottom lip quivered, and her breath came in short spurts. "But you can't just give up—they can't . . ."

"It's over, Jane."

She tugged free from Paul's grasp and buried her face in both hands, shoulders shaking as the tears came in earnest. She stayed that way several moments, sobbing. *This can't be happening. It's not true. It's* not *true.* Her mind fought against the inevitable—what had slowly been becoming obvious over the past month. She cried, each tear washing away more of her hope.

After several minutes when, at last, the initial overwhelming flood subsided, she wanted to ask but couldn't—*How long?*

He must have read her mind. "I don't know how long I have. Weeks maybe—a month or two. Dr. Kline gave me some strong pain meds and the name of a good hospice for when those aren't enough anymore. I won't have you taking care of me at the end." He handed her a tissue.

She took it and wiped some of the smeared mascara from beneath her eyes. "Why not?"

"Because you've already got two babies to care for, and they're more important. You'd never be able to do it all. You know it, and our social worker knows it too."

Jane didn't say anything. He was right.

Paul held out his hand to her, palm up. She placed her fingers in his.

"You said you loved me for sharing my children with you, and I love you, Jane, for taking them—for the amazing sacrifices you've made already. But I can't love you any other way. I won't kiss you." He glanced at the abandoned Scrabble board, the sorrow in his eyes replaced by a spark of mischievousness. "And I *especially* won't have *sextant* with you."

Jane sniffed loudly but couldn't help returning his half-smile. "I should hope not since we aren't married."

Paul grinned. "I play a mean game of Scrabble, but you always give me a run for my money. When you weren't coming up with any words, and you made such a careless mistake, I knew something was up."

Jane felt her face heat with embarrassment again.

"By any chance has your crazy friend been by this week?" Paul asked.

"Yes." Jane grimaced. "I'm afraid I've never been any good at flirting, and the Scrabble thing was Tara's idea."

"Thought so," Paul said, nodding.

"You should have heard her *first* idea," Jane said.

"No thanks. I'll pass." He squeezed Jane's hand. "Listen, I want you to promise me something."

"What?"

"Someday, when you meet the right guy—the one who *will* kiss you—please don't follow any of Tara's advice. Just be yourself."

"I will," Jane said, only too happy to promise never again to try Tara's dating tactics. "But the problem is, when I'm myself, nothing ever happens. Tara's urging 'to get my feet wet' was a large part of the reason I answered your ad."

"Then I'm grateful to Tara, but the promise *still* holds." Paul's eyes met hers.

Jane smiled at him. "Of course." A rush of intense longing and sorrow washed over her, and she felt tears threatening again. She attempted levity to keep them at bay. "You sure you couldn't kiss me—just once?"

He shook his head. "That privilege belongs to someone else. And someday, when you're at that moment, when he kisses you, I don't want you to see my face. I don't want to be a memory that interferes."

Jane reached out and traced her finger down Paul's jaw line. "I'll always remember your face," she whispered. "I'll see it every day for the rest of my life when I look at your children." Her heart ached, thinking of his loss, then filled to overflowing at the thought of Mark and Madison truly being hers. Fresh tears flooded her eyes. "What a gift you've given me, Paul."

And he had. But she'd hoped for so much more. In her dreams Paul recovered from both cancer and the heartbreak of losing Tami. He was healthy again, and he saw Jane as more than a nanny for his children.

It *could* have happened. Their friendship could have grown into love, that magic chemistry suddenly sparking between them. And she would have told Paul about the gospel, would have had the courage to read her scriptures aloud at the breakfast table instead of quietly to herself as she did every morning. Paul might have believed what he heard . . .

He might still believe. And wasn't that even *more* important, now that time was so short?

Jane jumped off the bed suddenly. "I'll be right back."

She raced out of his apartment, back to her house, to her own bedroom. She opened her closet and took out the quadruple combination she'd been hiding there for the past few weeks. She hadn't been able to bring herself to give it to Paul before now, but suddenly she couldn't wait.

Clutching it in her arms, she returned to his room. "I have something for you to read that will make you feel much better than that thriller." She nodded toward the novel on his nightstand as she stepped forward. Holding out the scriptures, she continued, "I marked some pages about what happens after our bodies leave the earth and—and eternal marriage." A smile trembled on her lips. "I'll always wish things could have been different between us, but since they can't . . . Tami loved you first, and these pages will tell you how you can be with her forever."

Chapter Twenty-Seven

Jane stood in the front room, one hand on the doorknob, Madison's car seat in the other. "It's *one* picture, Paul. Just one. You *owe* it to Mark and Madison."

"I've got reasons for my decision, Jane—things you wouldn't understand." Paul made no move to rise from the sofa.

"Try me."

He shook his head, then glanced at the clock on the wall. "You'd better go. You'll be late."

Jane pursed her lips and looked at him a minute longer, then opened the door, picked up Mark's car seat with her other hand, and left the house. She didn't bother returning to close the front door. Paul could do it. She didn't trust herself to face him again without *really* losing her temper or bursting into tears.

After buckling the twins and herself in, she put the car in reverse and looked over her shoulder as she backed out of the driveway. "Your father is *so stubborn*," she said to the infants in the backseat.

Mark was intent on the toy in front of him, but Madison churned her legs in response and looked at Jane.

"Let's hope your brother isn't the same way, Maddie," Jane said, her voice softer as she returned Madison's smile. Jane sniffed loudly and looked in the rearview mirror before putting the car into drive. Her nose was red and her eyes puffy. Everyone would know she'd been crying, and she'd look horrible in the family Christmas photo.

For a brief moment she considered staying home and feigning illness but knew if she did, Mom would come over to check on them. Deciding it would be easier to face her mother when she had a houseful of grandchildren to distract her, Jane drove down the street, her reluctance to arrive with a blotchy, tear-stained face ensuring she stayed well within the speed limit.

Fifteen minutes later she pulled up to the curb in front of her parents' house. Caroline's family was piling out of the van parked in front of her. Seeing that Jane was alone, Caroline came over to help.

"Where's Paul?" she asked as she unbuckled Madison.

Jane lifted Mark's car seat from its base and shut the car door. "At home. He isn't feeling well."

Caroline waited for Jane to walk around to her side. "You okay?"

Jane nodded. "I'm here, aren't I? And that's pretty good considering Paul and I just had our first fight."

"Oh. Is that all?" Caroline let out a relieved sigh. "You had me worried."

Jane walked up the front steps. "What do you mean is that *all?* It was terrible."

Caroline rolled her eyes as she followed. "For Miss I-Don't-Like-to-Upset-Anyone, I'm sure it was. But arguing is part of life. Everyone does it once in a while. Don't be so uptight."

Jane turned to her. "Are you telling me you enjoy it when you and Ryan fight?"

"Of course not," Caroline said, holding the front door for Jane. She grinned. "But I certainly enjoy it when we make up."

Jane scowled at her. "I don't have that option, remember?" She walked past Caroline and into her parent's living room where she set Mark's car seat on the floor by the sofa. The front door shut, and a moment later Caroline came into the room. She set Madison beside Mark and pulled Jane into a hug.

"I'm sorry. That was a really stupid, insensitive thing for me to say."

"It was," Jane agreed. She stepped from Caroline's embrace and sat down on the sofa, motioning for her sister to join her. "Sorry I'm so grumpy," she said. "It's just been a rough couple of weeks."

Caroline sat down and turned toward Jane. "How is Paul—really?"

Jane shrugged. "He seems about the same—though I don't know how I'll even know when it is bad. I never see him. He doesn't talk to me—just holes up in his room, except at night when I hear him get up with the twins. And that's their alone time. I feel like I'm intruding if I join them." She sighed. "We had that one great—and terrible—night a couple of weeks ago, but since then he's just completely closed off to me."

Caroline leaned back against the sofa cushions. "We'd probably do the same in his shoes."

"No we wouldn't," Jane insisted. "We'd spend every moment we could with our family."

"But he doesn't have a family to be with," Caroline gently reminded her. "His wife is dead. His parents are gone. His brother is out of the picture."

"But I'm—"

"A friend he doesn't want to get too close to. A friend he doesn't want to hurt any more than he already has." Caroline continued before Jane could interrupt. "I'm betting Paul's withdrawal isn't just about him. It's protection for you. He's a decent guy, and he doesn't want you to get more attached to him than you already are. He doesn't want you hurting when he's gone."

"And being miserable now is better?"

"Not better," Caroline said. "But maybe easier in the long run." She rose from the sofa. "Wow, I sound like someone else I know." She looked down at Jane. "Someone else who used to charge a quarter for such sage advice." Caroline held out her hand. "Ante up, sis."

Jane smiled. "You guys were always great to pay me. It must have been a pain humoring your little sister like that." She reached for her purse, then stood.

"Humor you, nothing," Caroline said. "You had some darn good advice back then. You have no idea how many scrapes I got out of for a mere quarter."

"In that case, call it even." Jane dropped her purse to the floor.

"Ho, Ho, Ho." Their father's deep voice came from the doorway. They turned around to greet him.

"Why Santa, you're looking rounder this year," Caroline teased as he came toward them.

He glanced quickly to the right, then left, and pulled down his false beard. "Your mother bought new pillows. I feel like a waddling duck—I can hardly move."

"Gotta love Mom," Jane said, exchanging a glance with Caroline, one full of memories of costumes past made by their mother.

"At least you're not dressed as the Tin Man right now," Jane teased.

"Ah. Don't remind me," Santa grumbled. "It took hours to wash all that silver makeup off, but that wasn't half as bad as the years it took the Relief Society sisters to forget I'd worn *tights* under that tinfoil box."

Jane and Caroline laughed. The older Relief Society sisters *still* remembered and talked about Dad's tights the year their mother had decided the whole family would be characters from *The Wizard of Oz* for Halloween.

"Where's the rest of your clan?" he asked Caroline.

"Most likely rearranging your tree and shaking every package beneath it," Caroline said.

"Well, round 'em up for the pictures. I can't stand this suit all day." He turned to Jane. "Where's Paul?"

"At home. He's no worse," she quickly assured her father. "He just doesn't want to be in any pictures."

She turned to Caroline. "That's what we fought about."

"Did you suggest one of just him and the twins?" she asked.

Jane nodded. "I told him that's all I really wanted. I promised he wouldn't have to be in the big family photo or anything. But he wouldn't come. And the worst of it is that I don't have one single picture of him with either Mark or Madison. I've taken dozens of the two of them, but Paul won't even be in one."

Caroline's brow furrowed. "I know it's not the same, but you *could* Photoshop him in."

"That's all well and fine," their father said, grabbing a magazine off the coffee table to fan himself with. "But unless you want to Photoshop old Santa in, I suggest you get those babies and get in the other room."

"Come on," Caroline said, bending down to unstrap Madison. "We don't want a grumpy Santa."

* * *

An hour and fifteen minutes later the family pictures were finally done, and Santa wasn't the only one who was grumpy. Jane excused herself to the quiet of her parents' room to feed Mark and get him to sleep—hopefully—before she drove home. Her nieces were in the other room playing with Madison.

Mark drank half his bottle before his eyelids started to droop.

"Wake up, little buddy," Jane coaxed, lightly stroking the side of his face. He rewarded her with a quick smile and a drool of milk down his chin. Jane wiped up the milk then set the bottle aside and lay Mark, stomach down, across her lap. She rubbed his back, waiting for the burp she knew was there. "You know, your sister is going to be able to beat you up if you don't start eating more," Jane scolded gently. "She's got you by more than two pounds now."

Mark's response was the burp she'd been waiting for. Jane rolled him over and tried the bottle again, but he was sleeping soundly. *Lucky boy,* Jane thought. A nap right now would be great, much better than facing the volley of questions about Paul—and her life in general—that she knew her mother would fire at her.

Jane glanced at the clock on the dresser as she lay back on the bed and positioned Mark on top of her. His head nestled beneath her chin, and she felt his heart beating close to hers. His sweet baby scent washed over her along with warm contentment. She would steal a few precious minutes before returning to the chaos that was her family.

* * *

"Jane. Wake up, Jane." Marsha Warner touched her daughter's arm gently.

Jane's eyes opened. "Mom?" She knew immediately from the look on her mother's face that something was wrong. Holding Mark, she sat up. "What is it? Is Maddie all right?"

"She's fine." Her mother picked up Mark. "Someone just called from Paul's cell phone. He's in an ambulance on his way to the hospital."

Chapter Twenty-Eight

Jane sat at Paul's bedside, half-relieved, half-regretful that he had been given morphine before she arrived. She felt grateful he wasn't in pain, but she longed to talk with him. His organs were failing, the doctors gently explained. And when they asked if she'd ever considered hospice care, she nodded numbly. The paperwork was somewhere in Paul's bedroom. He'd shown it to her the night they'd played Scrabble—*Was that only two weeks ago?* Later, she would go home and find the information needed to get him transferred, but for now she wanted to stay in case he woke up. He'd asked for her.

He'd asked for her, and she'd left the house angry.

Jane rubbed her hands together, chilled by the temperature in the room and the dire circumstances. She told herself this couldn't be happening, but when she closed her eyes and opened them again, everything was very real. *So* real and painful—especially considering she hadn't even known Paul a full four months now. Tara had sure called this one right. Jane felt very much like she was drowning in a strong undertow.

She pulled her sweater tight and watched the steady beep of Paul's monitors. They brought a little comfort. He was still alive. He could still have a little longer.

"No more time," Paul's voice startled her and she jumped in her chair. She brought a hand to her pounding heart as he gave her a weak smile.

"Paul." Her eyes clouded with tears. "I'm so sorry I got mad this morning. I didn't know how sick you felt. I wish you would have told me."

"Should have."

Jane reached for his hand. "I'm the one who should have told you more—about where Tamara is and how our Heavenly Father is anxiously waiting for you to return home. It's true, Paul." She smiled through her tears. "You're almost ready to go home. And until then you just rest. I'll find those papers for the hospice you chose. We can move you there. I'll do exactly what you asked."

"Pete." Paul's voice was barely above a whisper.

Jane stood and moved closer to the bed. "Your brother? Do you want me to call him?"

He nodded.

"Sure. I don't know how, but I'll get my dad to find out."

Paul's brow creased. "Tell Pete—sorry."

"Okay," Jane said. "I'll tell him you're sorry." She glanced at the monitor that registered Paul's heartbeat. Was it her eyes, or did it seem to be slowing? "You rest now. I'm going to go tell the doctor you're awake." She went to the door, opened it, and stepped into the hall just as the alarm on Paul's monitor sounded.

Chapter Twenty-Nine

Atypical of Seattle, it didn't rain the day of Paul's funeral. Jane wore her coat anyway; it was long and black and heavy—appropriate for her melancholy. Her sister Emily came by at nine and took Mark and Madison for the day. Jane had debated taking them to the funeral but thought the better of it. Instead, she decided to write everything down to tell them later.

Her mother, bless her, had made all the arrangements. Jane had only to show up, and even that was made simple. Caroline and Ryan came by for her at eleven, and after the services at the funeral home, a rented limousine drove them to the cemetery.

Jane watched as the dark walnut casket was unloaded and carried over to the newly dug grave. The men of her family, whom Paul had hardly known, were the pallbearers. That was the first thing that started her crying. How was it that such a wonderful man had so few people to remember him?

She'd run the obituary in the paper for three days. A few people had called—two colleagues of Paul's and his attorney. Dr. Kline had come to the funeral home as had some friends of Tami's. But that was it—the sum total of Paul's mourners. Jane was baffled. So what if he'd left his job months ago. So what if he hadn't been able to go out much because of the chemo. Where were the old friends who should have remembered him no matter how long it had been? She knew, from Paul's own admission, that he'd always been somewhat of a recluse. But he'd said that, growing up, his lack of friends never bothered him—having a brother had more than made up for it. And right now, that was what bothered her most . . .

Where was his brother?

The night Paul died, she had placed a call to Iraq. It was early morning there; she'd imagined she might have a chance to actually speak with Peter. But he'd been out on a flight, and the best she could do was a promise that the chaplain would convey her news. She left her phone number but no call had come in return. She had no idea how the military worked, but surely Peter could have at least called if he wouldn't be able to attend his own brother's funeral.

Jane took a seat on the folding chair closest to the casket and pulled a wad of tissue from her purse. Behind her, Caroline gave her shoulder a squeeze. Jane reached back and touched her hand.

"I'm all right," she whispered. But she wasn't.

The next hour was surreal, each scene passing by like a slow-moving motion picture. Paul's associates shook her hand and spoke with her briefly. One of his doctors from the hospital came over to give her a hug. Two couples who'd been friends of Paul and Tami lingered afterward for a few moments but did not speak to her. What was there to say?

Finally everyone left except her family.

Jane looked at Caroline. "Could I . . . ?"

"You bet." Caroline nudged Ryan and took her father's hand. "Come on, let's wait by the cars."

"Are you sure?" her mother asked, her own eyes red with tears.

"Yeah, Mom," Jane said. "I'll just be a minute."

Jane watched as they walked across the lawn, then she moved to the head of the casket. Fingers trembling, she bent and placed the yellow roses she had brought with her on top of the polished wood.

"Well, Paul." She gave a shaky sigh. "Caroline warned me about this, and I didn't listen." She brought a hand to her mouth and bit back a sob. "I brought yellow roses, for friendship. But really . . . I felt red." She wrapped her arms around her middle and lowered her head, letting the tears fall freely to the ground.

"I always believed in fairy tales, Paul. I believed in knights in shining armor and happily-ever-after. I believed in miracles. But now you're there." She gazed upward through the trees to the clear sky above. "And I'm still here. Your children are here. What kind of a happily-ever-after is that?" Jane stepped back from the casket, her head shaking.

"Good-bye, Paul. Be happy with Tami. Thank you. Thank you both for Madison and Mark."

* * *

When Caroline dropped her off after dinner at their parents', Jane felt more exhausted than she ever had in her life. She walked in the door and dropped her purse on the stool and her keys on the counter. Shrugging out of her coat, she let it fall to the floor, then kicked off her shoes on the way to the couch. She sank onto the worn cushions and leaned her head back, closing her eyes.

The house was eerily quiet. She opened one eye and glanced at the clock. There was still over an hour until Emily brought the twins back. Jane lay down on the couch, curling her legs up and wedging her toes under the cushion for warmth. The room felt cold. She looked at the thermostat on the wall above the couch and saw that it was seventy-six degrees—plenty warm for the twins. So what was wrong with her? Was she getting sick on top of everything else? A stab of fear coursed through her. She couldn't get sick—not ever again. She was all Mark and Madison had, their *only* means of support, their only parent.

This solemn thought motivated her to roll from the couch to the floor and crawl on her hands and knees toward her old trunk with the fleece blanket folded on top of it. Jane reached for the blanket and pulled it to her, covering herself. She lay on the floor, curled in a ball, shaking. Whether from sorrow, sickness, or fear, she didn't know and didn't care to analyze at the moment either. Getting the blanket had taken what energy she had left.

Jane closed her eyes once more, thinking she would rest for a few minutes before getting up to prepare bottles and pajamas for the twins. But when she opened her eyes again and looked at her watch, she found that half an hour had passed. She was still alone. She'd been alone her whole life, it seemed, and she hated it.

She was also still cold, and it was too quiet in the house. Jane stared at the television and the remote, just inches away. She should watch something. That would take her mind off things. Jane stretched, her fingers reaching for the remote, when she saw the stack of movies in the entertainment center.

Sitting up, she scooted over to the glass door. She opened it, pulled out the first video and held it in her lap, studying the title. *While You Were Sleeping.*

While I was sleeping, you were dying, she thought.

Jane set the video aside and pulled out a second. *Somewhere in Time.* Again, appropriate.

She reached for a third tape. *Ever After*—how long she'd be missing him. *The Princess Bride* DVD case slid from the shelf. She stared at the cover and her vision began to blur. She was anything but a princess, and *never* a bride. Jane hurled the case across the room, then got to her knees and scooped all the other movies off the shelf. The titles, nearly all romances, mocked her, reminding her of what she'd never have. She began pulling them from the boxes, throwing them at the trash can. When she came to *Sweet Home Alabama,* she snapped the DVD in two, then ripped back the plastic and tore the picture to shreds. *How dare you have two,* she thought, *when I can't even have* one *man to love me.*

Jane grabbed the next movie from the pile. *Serendipity.* She ran her finger over the title. A chance encounter. A moment in time. Fate. She'd experienced such a moment herself—one day a few months ago outside the intensive care nursery at Swedish Medical Center. Only her moment hadn't led to a lifetime of love.

"Liars," Jane shouted, shaking the box until the video fell out. She pried the back open and began pulling until a mound of shredded tape lay in her lap. She pushed it aside and wiped her eyes.

One movie remained on the shelf.

Reverently, Jane pulled *Casablanca* out and clutched it to her chest. She sobbed, rocking back and forth as if she were holding one of the twins.

"You understand, don't you Ingrid?" *You lost him forever, too.* Still holding the video, Jane lay back on the floor, sobbing, amidst her sea of broken dreams.

Chapter Thirty

Richard Morgan glanced up at the woman sitting across from him. Jane Warner's face had gone suddenly pale and her fingernails—painted bright pink with happy face stickers on them—curled into the leather arms of the wingback chair as if she were hanging on for dear life. *And is that a cold sweat breaking out across her forehead?* He was disappointed but not surprised. He'd seen this type of reaction many times before—always when he was reading a will and always when there was a lot of money concerned. Money that shouldn't necessarily be given to the person in front of him.

Richard let out an inaudible sigh and continued reading. "All funds remaining from the sale of property belonging to Paul C. Bryant and Tamara L. Bryant, along with life insurance monies from policy MLB783562, name of insured Paul Christopher Bryant, shall be deposited in a joint account of the legal guardians for Mark Peter Bryant and Madison Tamara Bryant. These monies are to be used for the sole purpose of—"

"Wait," Jane interrupted. "Wait a minute. What do you mean by that—*joint?*"

Richard Morgan laced his fingers together and leaned forward over the desk.

"I assure you there is ample money, Miss Warner, for you to provide for the children's needs for quite some time, so long as you are prudent in your spending. However, Mr. Bryant's will *does* stipulate that the account be in both your name and Peter's, as you will both be providing for the children." Richard frowned at Jane. Her mouth hung partly open, and he could see that her emotions were wavering somewhere between shock and anger. "Perhaps," he suggested, none too gently, "Paul specified the money be shared this way so you would have some accountability as to how the funds were spent."

Jane rose from the chair, her eyes blazing. Richard could see she had moved full tilt to fury.

"I'm not talking about the *money,*" she said. "He can have every last cent, for all I care. I'm talking about Mark and Madison."

"Yes, I am certain you don't care about the money—unemployed as you are. Sit down, Miss Warner," Richard said, trying to contain the irritation in his voice. "We've much more to discuss." To his surprise, she ignored him.

Jane pulled her coat from the back of the chair. "I am not *un*employed. I took a leave of absence to care for the twins so Paul could spend what time he had left with them. Without me, they'd be in foster care. *I* am the one who has been caring for them—day and night. Changing diapers, feeding them, taking them to the doctor, reading stories, washing clothes, taking pictures." Her voice faltered. "I'm the one who loves them. And I know I'm the one Paul specified as their guardian. He told me himself. He never said anything about Peter—their *uncle*." She said the word with disdain. "I appreciate your time, Mr. Morgan. My attorney will be in touch. You may speak with him." She gave a curt nod, then turned toward the door.

"Miss Warner." Richard rose from his chair. "Do you expect me to believe you knew nothing of this arrangement—that Paul led you to believe that you alone were responsible for his children?"

Jane stopped but did not turn around to face him. "Yes," she said, her voice barely audible. Then she opened the door, leaving the office before Richard could ask her anything more.

Nonplussed, Richard returned to his seat. He still didn't like her, but there was something . . . He buzzed his secretary.

"Joan, will you discreetly follow Miss Warner to her car? Then come to my office after she's left." He waited several minutes, his fingers flipping impatiently through the file on his desk. Paul had *promised* he'd tell them both. Surely he had, unless . . . It was only two weeks after their visit that he'd died. Richard looked up to see Joan standing in his doorway.

"Well?" he asked, hoping her information would end his confusion about Jane Warner. It wasn't all that unusual for him to request that Joan follow clients after they left the office. Often a person would give his or her true character away with simple facial expressions or conversations. A person's choice of car and how fast they left the parking lot also told him volumes. Many times he'd wished he could put surveillance cameras in the elevator or outside the building.

Joan pursed her lips. "She's crying."

"*What?*"

"She started before she even left the office. She took the stairs, not the elevator, and she's still sitting in her car right now, bent over the steering wheel. Crying her heart out." Joan looked at him accusingly. "What'd you do to her?"

"I don't think it's what I did." Though, now that he thought about it in a different light, Richard was sure he hadn't helped. "I think it's what Paul Bryant *didn't* do." He looked at Joan, a grim expression on his face. "I'll need a background check on Miss Warner. I want to know everything there is to know—right down to her bank account balance and her shoe size. And I'll also need—" He glanced at his watch. "—well, today if possible, I need you to find a number for Peter's reserve unit in Iraq. It's probably too late, but this call needs to go through as soon as possible. The information you'll need is in here." He handed Joan the folder. She nodded and, mumbling something about insensitive men, left his office.

Richard leaned back in his chair, trying to recall every detail of Paul's funeral. There wasn't much to remember, except . . . an image of a tearful Jane Warner, clutching a bunch of yellow roses. Richard swore under his breath. "If you've done what I think you have Paul . . . it's a good thing you're already dead."

Chapter Thirty-One

Jay propped his feet on the window ledge and leaned back in his chair. He watched the blinking Christmas lights on the house across the street and felt a pang of what he imagined must be homesickness. Funny, he thought, how he should feel something like that, considering the home he'd been raised in. There'd been no stockings hung by the chimney with care. No pies. No mythical jolly old man delivering presents. It had been just Dad and him—celebrating the holidays with Chinese takeout instead of the usual frozen pizza. They'd maybe catch a movie together at the mall theater, and afterward he'd show Dad the computer game or book he wanted for Christmas. It didn't seem like much to miss, and Jay wondered again why it was that his father's death had messed him up so badly. Why had it sent him, during his senior year of high school, straight into his mother's arms and her drug-addicted life?

Jay reached for his guitar and propped it on his lap. His fingers found the chords on their own, and he began strumming "White Christmas." He stared out the window, watching as sporadic snowflakes fell through the twilight. He wondered what the weather in Seattle was like right now.

He wondered what Jane was doing.

* * *

Jane hung the two small stockings her mother had sewn for Madison and Mark on the fireplace mantel. Her own stocking lay on the table—folded and pressed flat from its year of storage in her Christmas box. It seemed silly now that all these years she'd been hanging her stocking each Christmas Eve. It wasn't as if her fairy godmother would put an engagement ring in it and she'd find a prince under the tree Christmas morning. Jane gave an indelicate laugh, then swallowed quickly as a tear spilled from her eye.

"Don't be stupid," she muttered. "Think of the good." She turned away from the fireplace and looked at the twins playing on the new carpet her family had surprised her with for Christmas. Jane still didn't know what she was going to do about the fireplace when the twins started crawling. She knew, for Maddie at least, that wasn't too far away. At five months, she was already trying. A smile lit Jane's face as she watched them.

Mark lay on his back and was doing his best to get a toe in his mouth. Madison had progressed to sitting up and was stretching to get a toy that was just out of reach. She grabbed for it, bending forward until her little body was nearly parallel to the floor. Her fingers brushed the rattle just as she lost her balance and fell over sideways.

"Good try, Maddie," Jane said as she sat down between the babies, handed Madison the toy, and picked up Mark.

"I love you, little guy," she said, placing a kiss on his cheek. "You too, Maddie."

Mark smiled at Jane and grabbed a fistful of her hair. She put her hand over his and felt a surge of joy and protectiveness. She missed Paul so much, but she was going to be okay. She had two beautiful children, and she was going to do everything in her power to keep them. Maybe it wasn't in the cards for her to have a husband, but she could still have a happily-ever-after with her babies.

Still holding Mark, Jane stood up and went over to the stereo. She put in her favorite Christmas CD and danced Mark around the room to "White Christmas."

Part Two

Then Comes Marriage

Chapter Thirty-Two

The plane banked right as they approached the airport, and Peter looked out the window at the beauty of Mount Rainier. After so long in the desert, the mountains and greenery below looked like paradise. *Don't be deceived,* he reminded himself. The last two times he'd been home were far worse than his time spent in Iraq.

Losing Mom had been awful. He still missed her and felt angry and cheated. But his last visit had been even more terrible than Mom's funeral. Peter still wasn't sure how he felt about everything that had happened that November. The hurt from his fiancée's betrayal had faded, but the shame of his own actions and the loss of his brother—both then and now—was still as fresh a wound as if it had happened yesterday.

Peter closed his eyes and laid his head against the seat. *Paul. How is it possible I'll never see you again? I'd give anything to take back what I did—the things I said . . . It should have been me that died. Not you. I'm the one who's been living on the edge.*

Peter opened his eyes, glanced out the window again, then reached into his shirt pocket for the paper folded there. He took it out, pressed it flat on the seat-back tray, and began reading for what was surely the hundredth time since the letter had arrived nearly two months earlier.

> *Dear Pete,*
>
> *It is with much sorrow I share with you the news that Tami was killed in a car accident. In the weeks since her death, I've been reeling. There are days when the pain seems almost too much to bear. During those times I think of you—your loss and how you must have felt. I'm sorry. Though I can't take back the wrong I've done you, I hope you will someday forgive me.*
>
> *I know I can never make up for my selfishness, but I've left you three presents. One is taller than the others, but all are equally fragile. Take care of them for me.*

Peter frowned as he refolded the letter. It made sense now—sort of—or more so, anyway, than it had when he'd received it. The first time he'd read it, he wondered what on earth his brother was talking about. *Presents?* What, did Paul think sending him something expensive and fragile was going to somehow make up for stealing his brother's fiancée, marrying her, and then letting her get killed in a car accident? Peter remembered the anger he'd felt as he stood in the doorway of his tent, shocked at what he'd just read.

Then, two days later, the chaplain had come with the news Paul had died—of cancer. And Peter, his only living relative, his twin, hadn't even known his brother was sick. Pete recalled sitting on his bunk, rereading the letter carefully—aware of how close to death Paul had been when he'd written it. *I've left you three presents* . . . Left you. Of course. What else was there to do but leave everything?

A hollow ache, an awful remorse, had engulfed Peter from that moment on. He had yet to let it go. Too hurt and angry—at himself mostly—to talk to anyone, he had put away the letter and the note with the name and phone number of the woman who'd called to tell him about Paul. He'd spent the next two weeks working like crazy, taking every flight available, volunteering for every job he could—especially the dangerous ones. And why shouldn't he? he'd reasoned. If he died, there would be no family to mourn his loss. No parents. No wife and kids.

No brother.

Pete had noted—on more than one occasion—that he was the only one in his barracks without pictures by his bed. When he flew, there was no good-luck token in his pocket. No endearing words to reread over and over again—except those from his deceased brother that promised him *presents*. Like he had any use for those.

Then Richard Morgan had called—and called again and again until Pete was finally around and had to talk to him. And Peter had discovered what those presents were.

And now he wanted them. Badly.

Well, two of them, anyway. The "taller one"—as Paul had so eloquently referred to the woman—Peter wanted nothing to do with. And therein was the nightmare that lay before him. According to Richard, Jane Warner also wanted Paul and Tamara's children. She'd been caring for them the past five months and had no intention of giving them up. She'd hired an attorney, and Richard said that social services had given her a very favorable report.

Peter groaned inwardly, remembering his insistence during law school and his internship afterward that he would not practice custody law. He would defend sleazy criminals before using his skills to pitch family members against each other in battles over their children. He didn't want a custody battle now, but he certainly didn't want to set up residence with some strange woman, either. Peter wondered what in the world Paul had been thinking when he came up with the idea of joint custody. Had he really believed his brother would go along with the plan for an instant family?

Peter's brow furrowed as he thought of the dilemma he faced. He'd loved his brother. He would love Paul's children too. But if Paul had thought that this Miss Warner could somehow make up for taking Tamara, he'd been sorely mistaken.

The FASTEN SEATBELT sign came on, and Pete felt his ears pop as the plane descended. He folded the seat-back tray into place and handed his cup to the flight attendant. Below him, he felt the landing gear unfolding, and he looked out the window at the approaching runway. He braced himself not for the landing but for the battle that lay ahead—the most important one of his life.

* * *

An hour and a half later, Peter drummed his fingers on the arm of his chair as he sat in his colleague's office and listened to his speech.

"The only thing on your side is the claim of kinship," Richard Morgan said. "And I'm telling you, it isn't going to look good when her attorney mentions to the judge that you weren't on speaking terms with your brother for the past two years—nor did you even attempt to contact Miss Warner after you learned about the babies."

Peter scowled. "What was I supposed to say? Hi, I'm Peter—the other half of this parenting team. Would you like me to pick up some diapers on my way home from Iraq?"

Richard didn't smile. "Joke all you like, Peter, but the fact is, you've shown no interest in those children and, blood relative or not, the court won't give them to you—not when your brother's will stipulates joint custody. What *will* happen—if you're fool enough to drag this into court— is that those babies will end up in a foster home while the system takes its sweet time figuring this mess out." Richard paused, then spoke again, his voice lower. "If you care at all for Mark and Madison, then you won't try to take them from the stable home and loving mother they know."

Pete threw his hands up as he stood. "She's *not* their mother." He walked to the window and stopped, hands in his pockets, looking down on the traffic below. Tamara was their mother. Tamara, whom he'd loved. If Paul had really cared for her, then why had he replaced her so quickly?

After a minute Pete spoke again. "The Service Members Civil Relief Act might work in my favor."

"Why not try to make things work the way they are now?" Richard suggested. "Go see Jane Warner. Meet your niece and nephew. Make it immediately clear that you have no intention of taking the children and—"

"But I do."

"Would you shut up and listen to me?" Richard demanded.

Pete turned to face him. "I'm listening."

"What would you do right now, this very moment, if you had sole custody of the twins? If someone walked through that door and handed them to you?"

Pete shrugged. "Take them home. Take care of them . . ."

"Really?" Richard asked, leaning back in his chair. "Do you have car seats? Do you know what they eat? Do you have any idea of their schedule or the care they require? I told you Mark has already had open-heart surgery. Do you know what medicines he takes, how to administer them? Who his doctor is?"

"No," Pete admitted, running his fingers through his hair. "But I'm certain that, given the right information, I could be an adequate father. I've been operating a fifteen-million dollar machine for the past twelve months. I think I can handle two babies."

"I'm sure you can," Richard said, though he didn't sound all that convinced. "But wouldn't it be easier if you had someone to help you? After all, who's going to watch them when you return to work?"

"I'll hire a nanny." Peter began pacing across the office.

"Why not think of Jane Warner as a nanny?"

"Because . . ." Pete said. He withdrew the letter from his pocket and tossed it on the desk. "I don't think that's what my brother had in mind." He nodded to the letter. "Read it."

Richard picked up the paper, put on his glasses and began reading. "Hmm," he said, looking up when he finished. "You know, Paul was pretty sick the last time I saw him. It's very probable that he wasn't in his right mind when he wrote this."

Pete stopped pacing and returned to his chair. "So you don't think he was trying to fix me up? You don't think this Jane woman is expecting me to marry her or something?"

Richard chuckled. "She's *hardly* expecting that. She didn't even know you were in the picture until I had the misfortune of telling her." He handed the letter back to Paul.

It was Peter's turn to be unconvinced. "You sure it wasn't an act? I mean, she's had a pretty neat package dropped into her lap."

Richard nodded. "That's exactly what I thought, and when she got upset after I told her about the money being put into an account that has both your names on it, I thought for sure I was right. But since then . . ." He shrugged. "Let's just say I feel differently." He glanced at his watch, then rose from his chair. "Sorry, Pete, but we'll have to cut this short. It's my wife's birthday, and I'm taking her out to dinner."

Peter stood. "I'll walk you to your car and you can tell me why you changed your mind."

"I don't want to tell you too much. You can form your own opinions about Miss Warner." Richard took some papers from his drawer and placed them in his briefcase. "Here—I almost forgot." He handed a file to Peter.

"What's this?" Pete asked, opening it.

"Your first assignment. Holland versus Holland." Richard shook his head. "A sixteen-year marriage ending in divorce. You represent Mrs. Holland. She wants to move out of state and wants full custody of their three children. He's protesting it. Weston's his attorney."

"Uh-uh," Pete said, trying to hand the folder back to Richard. "I don't do custody, remember?"

"I remember," Richard said, grinning as he walked away from Peter and the file in his outstretched hand. "I thought this might be a good reminder why. Besides, we're swamped right now. It's good to have you back."

Pete sighed. "I don't know that I *am* back. Word was, before we even left for the States, that reserve units are being recalled after only a few months at home."

The smile left Richard's face. "I've heard that on the news. You ought to think about getting out when your time is up. You're a father now. Those children need you." He opened the office door and stepped through, holding it for Peter.

"First you make me feel like I'm totally inadequate, and now you're telling me I'm *needed?*" Peter shook his head. He walked past Richard to Joan's desk, retrieving the luggage he'd left there earlier. "Any chance I can get a ride?" he asked Richard. "I haven't picked up the Jeep yet."

"Sure," Richard said. "Though maybe I'd better drop you off at a car dealership. Jane has refused to use any of the money left to her. She recently sold her car to pay Mark's doctor bill, and now she drives the Jeep." He turned to his secretary. "Good night, Joan."

"Good night, Mr. Morgan. Good to have you back, Mr. Bryant."

Peter managed to nod and give Joan a wan smile before following Richard to the elevator.

"She has my car, too?" he asked, exasperated.

"Yep," Richard said as he pushed the level-one button. "Remember, you left it with Tamara, and then Paul drove it. Jane has no idea it belongs to you, and I *wouldn't* advise taking it from her."

"Of course not," Pete grumbled. "At least she doesn't live in my house—does she?" he asked, an alarmed look on his face as he glanced at Richard.

"No," Richard said, unable to keep the corner of his mouth from lifting. "She lives behind it."

Chapter Thirty-Three

"Hello, Karen?" Jane called as she walked through her sister's family room and onto the adjoining deck.

"Hi," Karen answered, looking up from the Primary manual she was reading. "How was the appointment?"

"Same as last time. Mark's heart is still holding its own, and he has to grow more before the second surgery." Jane put Mark's car seat down and walked across the deck to the playpen. She reached down and picked Madison up. "Come here, cutie."

"Any word from Iraq?" Karen asked, setting the manual aside. She took a soda from the patio table. "Want a drink?"

Jane shook her head. "No thanks, and I haven't heard anything from Paul's brother."

Karen took a sip of her soda and set it down again. "Maybe you'll never hear from him. Maybe he isn't interested in the children, or maybe something will happen while he's—"

"I've thought of that," Jane said, looking grim. "And then I've thought what a terrible person I am to think such a thing." She frowned. "I don't wish anything bad for him, I just hope he'll continue to leave us alone." She looked across the yard at Karen's husband Scott, who was measuring a length of the lawn with a tape measure. "You guys putting in a garden?"

Karen laughed as she glanced in Scott's direction. "Are you kidding? The yard wouldn't even get mowed if it weren't for the boys." She folded her arms and frowned as she watched her husband. "No. Scott is measuring for a basketball court. Apparently the driveway isn't good enough anymore. We're using our tax return to pay for it."

"Ah—of course," Jane said, nodding. Poor Karen was never going to get that cruise she kept talking about. Every year it was the same story—Scott had some project, all sports related.

"What are you going to do with the play fort?" Jane asked, watching as Scott measured around the attached swings.

Karen shrugged. "I guess we'll put it in the paper—free for anyone who will come and get it. The kids haven't used it for a couple of years, and Caroline's family just got one last summer. I'd offer it to Emily or Michael, but they're both in condos right now."

"I'm not," Jane said, excitement in her voice.

Karen looked at her. "Are you kidding? What would you want with a big swing set? And in that *awful* rental?"

"That *awful* rental isn't so bad anymore," Jane said, choosing to ignore her sister's thoughtless comment. "I can attach a couple of those cute baby swings, and the twins can be outside more when I'm working in the yard." She imagined the fort with a fresh coat of stain and a new awning. And best of all, beneath the fort was a sandbox for the children to dig in. They would grow up, sand squishing between bare toes, running through the sprinkler on the lush lawn and loving the outdoors. Jane looked at Karen hopefully.

"Well . . ." Karen began. "You'd have to take it apart yourself."

"Done," Jane said. She walked past Karen and picked up Mark's car seat and the diaper bag. "Can I just leave the playpen here? I'll go home and feed the twins, change, get my tools, and be back this afternoon."

"Uh, sure," Karen said.

"Thanks," Jane called, feeling like a kid on Christmas morning as she went out the front door.

Chapter Thirty-Four

Peter grabbed a carton of orange juice from the Styrofoam cooler. Replacing the lid, he took a stale muffin from the bag on the kitchen counter and sat carefully on the only piece of uncovered furniture—an old rattan barstool that had been in his mom's kitchen as long as he could remember. Opening the juice carton, he lifted it to his lips and took a couple of swallows. His laptop lay open in front of him as he glanced around the combination kitchen/dining room. *What a mess.* And he wasn't just thinking of the house. Though, after being closed up for more than two years, it needed some serious help too. But he wasn't feeling too motivated to clean, at least not unless the power got turned on sometime in the next forty-eight hours. Right now, he had more pressing matters—like meeting his niece and nephew . . . and Jane Warner.

Peter leaned over to the sliding glass door and adjusted the vertical blinds so he could see into the backyard. He stared out past the recently mowed grass—he'd paid a company to take care of it while he was gone—to the sagging chain-link fence that separated his backyard from the one behind it. The gate in the middle was still there, and Peter remembered the many afternoons he'd walked through it to play with his friend Greg. Peter wondered what Greg was up to these days and if his parents still owned the house. If so, Paul had certainly worked a sweet deal with them for rent. Even in these older neighborhoods, seven hundred dollars a month was unheard of. *And Richard suggested that Paul wasn't in his right mind when he wrote that letter. Ha.* Pete would bet his life that his brother had known exactly what he was doing.

He turned away from the window and reached for the folder next to his laptop. He wasn't ready to go back to work, wasn't even adjusted to the time change yet, but a sticky note on the inside of the folder had shown a scheduled appointment with Mrs. Holland next Wednesday. Knowing he was fortunate to have a job to come home to, Peter focused his attention on the file and sat reading and taking notes for the next twenty minutes until a noise outside caught his attention.

Lifting his eyes from the screen to the sliding glass door, he looked out at the backyard, glanced down at his watch, then looked outside again. It was six fifteen in the morning, and a woman in a Mickey Mouse sweatshirt, jeans, and work gloves was dumping gravel from a wheelbarrow into a corner of the yard. Jane Warner? If so, he was surprised. One of the few things Richard had said about Miss Warner was not to judge her by her nail polish. *This* woman pushing the wheelbarrow in the predawn light didn't strike him as someone who would be concerned with her nails.

Pete watched as she emptied the wheelbarrow, then turned around and headed out the side gate. Curious, he stood and went to the kitchen window where he could see better.

It was a good five minutes before she reappeared, the wheelbarrow full again. Once more, she emptied it, but this time parked the wheelbarrow and went into the garage. A few moments later she returned, dragging a heavy beam. This pattern repeated itself four times before she began carting other supplies into the backyard as well.

More curious than ever about the woman and what she was up to, Peter went into the living room and looked through his duffel bag for his binoculars. He'd been so exhausted after Richard dropped him off last night that he hadn't bothered to unpack anything and had fallen asleep on the couch.

Tossing aside his clothing, shaving kit, and the religious book his friend Shane had given him at the airport, Peter located his binoculars. He returned to the kitchen and watched, realizing that the woman was unloading the makings for a rather elaborate swing set—the great big wood kind with a fort, fireman's pole, and the large yellow slide he saw her struggling with now.

A sudden thought struck him. He left the kitchen, went upstairs to the bedroom, and looked out the window.

"Nooo," he groaned, lowering the binoculars. The woman had transported all that stuff in *his* Jeep. He watched as she unfastened a bungee cord, carelessly letting it spring onto the other side of the car, and pulled more wood from the roof.

She had his car. She had to be Jane Warner. He lifted the binoculars to his eyes again, concern for his vehicle momentarily overtaken by his curiosity about the woman.

He watched as she hefted the wood onto her shoulder and carried it into the backyard. Dumping it by the other supplies, she returned to the side yard, where lay an enormous pile of lumber and parts he hadn't noticed before. Pete had to admit he was impressed by her determination to unload it—albeit one piece at a time. She was not a large woman, but apparently what Jane Warner lacked in muscle, she made up for in determination. Not that she didn't have any muscles, he amended as he watched her shed the sweatshirt in favor of the short-sleeved T-shirt underneath. As she lifted a bag of concrete and carried it to the corner of the yard, he realized her biceps were just fine.

It suddenly occurred to him that he ought to help her, that working together might be the perfect opportunity to break the ice—so to speak. Because another thing Richard had said was to be prepared for ice.

Peter ran downstairs, grabbed his shoes from the living room, and went to the kitchen for another quick drink of juice. *Fortification.*

He swallowed and watched as she brought the last item from the garage—a pink, compact toolkit. *No way she's gonna use that thing to assemble a swing set,* he thought. But it appeared she was planning to do just that. She opened it up and reached for the bag of screws attached to one of the beams.

Choking back laughter, Pete began to cough and splayed orange juice across the sink. A popular credit card commercial came to mind as he used a napkin to wipe up the mess.

New paint job for his Jeep—$1,500

Binoculars—$65

Watching your neighbor attempt to build a fort with a pink toolkit—Priceless.

He tossed the napkin aside and, still smiling, headed to the garage for his tools.

* * *

Jane sat on the ground by the pile of wood and supplies she'd hauled into the backyard. Over half the lumber and the bags of concrete were still out front, but she had what she needed to get started. Opening her toolkit, she removed the pink-handled scissors and began cutting up the instructions she'd downloaded from the company's website. With her little pink stapler, she moved across the lawn, attaching pictures and instructions to the corresponding beams and bags of screws, nuts, and bolts. When that was done she stood up, brushed off her jeans, and returned to the garage for her cordless drill and circular saw. She had a better collection of power tools than any other female she knew, and she took great pride in knowing how to use them. By doing much of the smaller work herself on her landscaping jobs, she'd been able to keep costs down and keep in shape—or justify eating more chocolate, anyway. Jane smiled, happy that today it *was* her yard and project she was working on. But just as she walked through the garage door, she heard cries on the baby monitor.

"Six forty-five. Right on time, Maddie," Jane said as she glanced at her watch. She tugged her gloves off and tossed them on the patio table.

Picking up the monitor as she went into the house, she told herself she'd get to the posts later today—though it would have to be much later.

By the time she had the twins fed, changed, and dressed, it would be time to go to work. A thrill of hope shot through Jane as she thought about her nine o'clock appointment. Last month the Sweviecs had hired her to landscape their yard. Now their neighbors were interested in having their yard done as well. If the couple accepted the plans she presented today, she'd have her expenses covered for another month.

Madison's cries increased in volume, and Jane stifled a yawn as she hurriedly washed her hands. Her day was off and running. It would easily be midnight before her head hit the pillow again, but that was okay.

Being tired and busy meant there was no time in her life to be lonely.

* * *

Marsha Warner hung up the phone and made a neat check by the first item on the list Jane had left for her.

"Next," Marsha said, pleased that she'd so easily found a good price on sod. *Set up mulch delivery from AJ and Sons Ground Covers,* she read on the line below. Adjusting her bifocals, she scanned the address, delivery date, and other details. With a sigh she picked up the phone again. Usually when she babysat for her daughters, they asked her to do things like bathe the baby or fold laundry. Once, when her son-in-law Scott had been unable to tear himself away from bowl games, she'd painted a bedroom with Karen and helped her assemble a crib.

But assembling furniture and painting seemed like normal grand-motherly things compared to the requests Jane made. She needed help locating exotic plants, scheduling backhoes, and finding special sprinkler heads. It seemed an unusual way for a woman to make a living, but, Marsha conceded, as of late it looked like Jane might just make a go of it. *If only she would do well enough to hire a secretary,* Marsha thought. She looked at the babies playing on the floor and, anxious to get down to the real business of being a grandmother, returned to Jane's list.

* * *

Peter glanced out the sliding glass door as he buckled his tool belt and picked up his drill from the table. Outside there was no sign of Jane Warner, only the pieces of the play set that lay strewn across the yard—abandoned. She'd probably given up already.

"Perfect," Pete heard himself say aloud. She may have the diapering and feeding stuff down better than he did, but there were still a few things he could do—things she couldn't—that would benefit his niece and nephew. And it looked like it wasn't going to take as much effort as he'd thought to prove it.

Suddenly feeling better about the forty-five minutes it had taken to locate his tools, and the cold water he'd endured to shower and shave—first impressions were important, and *this* particular one he really didn't want to botch—Peter walked into the backyard. He hummed as the lyrics to a favorite song played in his mind.

He'd saved a lot of money over the years, and after he built the fort he'd stock it with all kinds of great toys. A kind of giddy excitement overtook him as he thought of meeting his niece and nephew. He'd always loved kids.

Opening the gate, Pete walked across the lawn, heading for the side yard. Not wanting to frighten Miss Warner, he'd decided it was better to go around to the front instead of knocking at the patio door.

A few feet away from the house he stopped, confused as he overheard the conversation of a gray-haired woman standing at the kitchen window. Her back was to him, and she had the phone to her ear. He took a step closer, straining to hear.

"The name is Jane Warner. Yes. I'd like delivery Monday morning at nine thirty."

Jane Warner? Peter forced his feet to keep moving. He must have misheard. This woman looked like a grandmother or . . . *Why not think of Jane Warner as a nanny?* Richard's words came back to him. Peter felt his face heat as he recalled their visit yesterday.

You don't think she expects me to marry her or something? he'd asked. And Richard's response had been a chuckle. *She hardly expects that.*

Feeling like a complete idiot, Pete stomped over the uneven driveway. All along he'd thought Paul had been playing matchmaker—trying somehow to make up for taking Tamara, when really he'd found someone to take Mom's place. And of course he'd welcome the help of an experienced caretaker like that.

He reached the front door, pressed the doorbell, and waited. The earlier nervousness he'd felt had left, but with it, he was surprised to discover, came a feeling of disappointment. Pink toolkit aside, the other woman had intrigued him. But if she wasn't Jane Warner, then who? A neighbor or relative maybe?

The front door opened, and he found himself facing the woman he'd seen on the phone. Her hair was short, curly and gray, and she looked at him over the top of her glasses. The floral apron tied around her waist instantly reminded him of his own mother. If this really was Jane Warner, then Paul had done a good job.

"Ms. Warner?" he asked tentatively.

She nodded, her eyes widening as she looked at him. Pete supposed she noticed his resemblance to Paul.

He stuck out his hand. "A pleasure to meet you, ma'am. My name is Peter Bryant, and I imagine you're expecting some explanations. I'll be happy to give them, but first—"

She was shaking her head. "No. You see, I'm—"

"Please," Peter continued. "Know how grateful I am for the care you've given my niece and nephew these past months. I'd like it if—"

A baby's cry stopped him cold.

The woman's face broke into a smile. She gave his hand a squeeze. "Welcome, Mr. Bryant. Come in and meet your niece and nephew." She released his hand and stepped aside. "And please, call me Marsha."

* * *

Peter lay on his side on the floor, a bottle in one hand as he fed Mark. Behind him Madison babbled happily as she tugged at his ear. A second later he felt a drop of drool hit the side of his face.

"You got me," he cried, setting the bottle aside and rolling over to pick up Madison. He lifted her in the air above him and she laughed, rewarding him with more drool. Mark turned his head toward them and waved his arms as if he wanted a turn as well. Peter lowered Madison to his chest and she lay there a moment, her face against his beating heart. He closed his eyes. *This is heaven.* He was holding Tamara's daughter—the closest he'd ever get to holding Tamara herself again.

Mark grabbed at Pete's arm, his tiny fingers pulling out a fistful of hair. "Hey," Pete exclaimed. He set Madison back on the blanket and picked up Mark. "Be a little more patient there, will ya? Just because I held your sister first doesn't mean I don't love you too, little guy." A lump formed in his throat as Peter sat Mark on his chest. He looked at his brother's son. *Paul's son. My son now.* Responsibility, both awesome and terrifying, settled over him. He had so much to learn. There was so much to do—so much to look forward to. It had been a long time since he'd felt any real excitement about his future. Now, with these two babies, it seemed brimming with possibility. The past hour of his life was the best he could recall in years.

"Would you care for a cookie?"

Peter looked up and saw Marsha Warner standing over him, a plate in her hands.

"Sure," he said, remembering that all he'd eaten today was part of a day-old muffin. He set Madison on the blanket and stood. He reached for a cookie, but Marsha handed him the plate. "Take them all. There are plenty more coming."

"Thanks. These are great," Peter mumbled through his first bite.

"Jane's recipe," Marsha said, beaming at him. She looked toward the twins. "You're a natural with them."

Peter swallowed and looked back at the babies. "They're amazing."

"Yes they are," she agreed. "And an awful lot of work as well. My daughter could certainly use some help."

"Then I guess I'd better get busy proving my usefulness," Peter said. Reluctantly he tore his gaze from the twins—from Mark's shock of dark hair and Madison's dimpled mouth, just like her mother's. "Thank you again for the cookies, Mrs. Warner. I'm going to get started on those swings now, and please tell your daughter I look forward to meeting her."

"I will," Marsha said. "You can bet I will," she reiterated under her breath as he closed the sliding glass door behind him and walked across the lawn.

Chapter Thirty-Five

Pete whistled as he mixed cement in the wheelbarrow. He'd already dug six holes and figured he had just enough time to pour the concrete and set the posts for the swing set before the rental car company arrived with his temporary transportation.

He'd chosen what he thought was a perfect location for the play fort—in the middle of the yard, directly in front of the patio. It would be easy to keep an eye on the children from Jane's kitchen as well as his own. A smile crossed his face as he recognized the wisdom of his decision. He hadn't even been on the job for a full day yet, and already he was thinking like a parent. Jane Warner couldn't help but be impressed when she met him.

Pete silently acknowledged that he was impressed by her as well. One hour with the twins had given him a glimpse of what lay in store. And while he was eager to embrace this new life, he was suddenly glad he didn't have to face it alone. Paul must have known that two babies would require two parents, and so he'd found Jane—and her mother.

Mrs. Warner was great, and Pete knew he was warming to the situation largely because of the morning's interaction with her. Playing with the babies had been wonderful, but it had also been nice to sit down at the kitchen table and have someone fuss over him. It'd been a long time since anyone was genuinely interested in and concerned about his life. Paul couldn't have chosen a better grandmother for his children, and if Jane was anything like her mother, then the twins were in good hands. So far it appeared she'd done a great job caring for them. Mark and Madison were happy, healthy babies, and for Mark at least, that seemed no small feat. That Jane was able to manage the child's health care, work part time, *and* think about extras like building a swing set was impressive.

Pete shoveled a couple of inches of concrete into the first hole. Working fast, he set the shovel aside and lifted the post into place. When he had it steady, he began shoveling concrete in the hole around it, stopping often to straighten the post. He quickly realized it would have been much easier had there been someone to hold the post while he shoveled.

He could do it alone, but he could work better—more efficiently—if he had help.

Hopefully, Jane Warner felt the same about being a parent. She'd proven she could do it alone, but if he was lucky, by now she might just be ready for some assistance.

* * *

"How *could* you, Mother?" Jane stood just inside the patio door, hands on hips and a scowl on her face as she looked at what her neighbor had done.

"He was trying to be helpful, dear," Marsha said, putting her arm around Jane. "He saw you struggling with all that wood this morning and he wanted to help."

"Saw me?" Jane asked. "*Spied* on me is more like it. I knew I should have had that fence replaced. And now that I know the owner is home, I'll definitely have it done—and I'll bill him for half." She tugged on the handle of the sliding glass door. "In fact, I'm going over there right now to tell him—"

"I don't think that would be very wise," Marsha said, placing her hand over Jane's. "He's a nice man and he meant no harm. Besides, he isn't even home. Why, this very minute he is out shopping for a car because he gave his away—to . . . to a woman in need." She looked at Jane for any sign of softening. Seeing none, Marsha quickly reversed her earlier decision to tell her daughter all about Peter Bryant and his natural way with children. If Jane was this upset about a neighbor helping with the swing set, she wouldn't handle the news of Peter's arrival well at all. Better to wait a few hours for reinforcements—Jane's father had always been better at getting through to their children. And for Jane's mood to change. "I think, if you'll give him a chance, he'll prove to be an excellent neighbor. Helpful and—"

"I don't need his help," Jane huffed. She walked away from the sliding glass door and into the kitchen. Grabbing a glass from the cupboard, she stood at the sink and turned on the faucet. "I mean, what kind of person comes into their neighbor's yard and *pours cement?* And in the middle of the yard too? Is he some kind of lunatic or something?" She turned off the faucet, lifted the glass to her lips and drank half of it down. She sighed. "If I keep the fort there, then the swings will hit the lilac bush, and I'll have to cut it down. I was really looking forward to enjoying it this spring—a bush that size takes years to grow and keeps the whole yard fragrant."

"I'm sorry, Jane. I didn't think of that. I told him that was exactly where you'd want the swings—where you could easily see the children playing." Marsha gathered her purse and bag of crochet supplies from the table. "Your list is over here. I was able to take care of all but two of the items. You can see the notes I left."

Jane turned to her mother. "I'm sorry, Mom," she said, her tone softening. "And thanks for babysitting and making all those calls. I didn't mean to vent. It was a rough morning, and then—" She glanced out the window again. "This."

Marsha walked over to her daughter and gave her a hug. "Your father and I will come by later tonight. Until then, try to cheer up. Play with the twins. Life is going to get better—you'll see."

* * *

Peter only half listened as the salesman droned on about the features of the 2003 Audi A4. This was the third lot he'd visited, and he was having a difficult time getting enthused about playing *Let's Make a Deal.* Sure the model was a great little car. But the price tag was high, and how could he spend so much when he didn't yet know all the particulars and costs associated with Mark's monthly medications, doctor visits, and forthcoming surgeries?

Then there was the issue of size. At the first lot, he'd found a used Jeep Cherokee that he liked, but after overhearing another couple's concerns about fitting two car seats in a similar-sized vehicle, Peter suddenly wasn't so certain about simply replacing his Jeep. It seemed to be working out for Jane, but maybe it wasn't the safest option, and when he thought about safety, he thought about the accident that had killed Tamara. He would do everything possible to ensure her children never suffered the same fate.

"On top of the great gas mileage, it's really a classy car—great for driving clients around, or business lunches, that sort of thing. What is it you do, Mr. Bryant?" the salesman asked.

Realizing he'd been staring at the factory sticker for several minutes, Peter looked at the man next to him. "I'm an—" He paused. "I'm a parent. What can you show me that has good safety ratings and built-in car seats?"

* * *

Peter used his shoulder to push open the front door. Both arms loaded with grocery bags, his fingers fumbled with the switch for the living room light. A second later it flickered on, and he smiled. *All right.* He'd have a refrigerator and a hot shower tonight.

"Vast improvements already," he said as he walked into the kitchen. He opened the top freezer and placed the bag of ice he'd bought inside. He wouldn't need it in the ice chest to keep food cold now, but it would be nice to have for drinks when Tamara and . . . He caught himself before the thought was complete. Tamara, her sister, Paul, the whole group that used to hang out together—none of them would be coming over. Why couldn't he remember that? Was it this house or just being home again that kept reminding him of the past?

Peter opened the fridge, shoved half the grocery bags inside, and closed the door. He turned the oven to PREHEAT and sat down at the bar. His laptop lay where he'd left it earlier this morning, but he didn't feel like working. He pushed it aside and, with his head in his hands, looked down at the counter. The initials PP stared up at him. He swallowed the lump in his throat and smiled, remembering how angry his mother had been when she'd discovered that he and Paul, using steak knives, had carved double P's into the counter half a dozen times each. They'd probably only been about six years old at the time, and it had seemed hysterical that their initials put together spelled something so naughty.

They'd never replaced the counter, and now Peter silently wondered if his mother had found it amusing too. He thought of Paul as he traced one set of letters with his finger. How was it possible that his brother, his best friend, was gone? His parents, Tamara—everyone—gone. *Not everyone. I have Mark and Madison.*

A need so strong it surprised him surged through Peter. He had to see his niece and nephew again. Tonight. He needed to hold them close, feel their hearts beating against his. He rose from the stool and went to the sliding glass door. Pushing the blinds aside, he flipped the lock and opened the door, then stepped out onto the patio. He stared at the back fence in surprise. For a minute he wondered if he was in the right backyard. White privacy slats were woven through the chain link the entire length of the fence, and though the fence was only three feet high, the slats protruded a good foot or two above.

"What in the world—what does she think she's doing?" Pete walked across the lawn. He reached the gate, grabbed the handle and pulled. It didn't budge. He tugged again and heard the unmistakable sound of chain clinking against metal. Bending a handful of slats down, he peered over the fence. A padlock and three eighths-inch metal chain secured the gate closed.

Stunned and angry, Pete let the slats spring back into place. That gate had been there for years and never, *never*, had there been a lock on it. He looked over the fence and saw that his posts were still standing. He'd spent his morning sweating over a swing set, rescuing her from certain failure, and *this* was how she repaid him?

Pete glanced up at the house. Light shone around the edges of the blinds on her sliding glass door, and he wondered if Mark and Madison were playing in the family room on the other side of that door. He wanted to see them, to know they were okay. He'd already missed seven months of their lives, and he was not going to miss a minute more. Stalking back into his house, he grabbed the car keys and stormed out his front door.

* * *

Jane bounced Mark gently on her hip as she prepared his bottle. He continued to fuss, burying his face in her shoulder, wiping his nose across her white shirt.

"I know, I know," she said as she tried to measure formula with one hand. "I'm sorry. I should have fed you sooner, but we *had* to get that gate taken care of. Right, Maddie?" Jane glanced over at Madison, sitting in her high chair, contentedly spearing Cheerios with her fingers.

Setting Mark on the counter, Jane reached around him to screw the lid on the bottle. His howls increased.

"Almost done, little guy." Jane scooped him up again and shook the bottle as she walked over to the kitchen table. Settling in a chair, she lay Mark back in her arms and began feeding him, unable to stop herself from smiling as he attacked the bottle. "Careful," she warned. "Drink it too fast and you'll throw up."

Paying no heed to her warning, Mark continued to gulp, and Jane used her free hand to open the jar of baby food she'd wedged between her knees. She set the jar on the table.

"Mmm. Sweet potatoes, Maddie. Your favorite." They were *not* Maddie's favorite, but having read that it was good to continue offering your baby foods she had previously rejected, Jane kept trying to get her to eat them. She stuck the rubber-tipped spoon in the jar and then held it up to her own mouth.

"*So good,*" she said exaggeratedly, pretending to take a bite.

Madison reached for the spoon.

Jane held it up, out of reach. "Bzzz." Her voice was hoarse, making her airplane imitation sound sick. *Great.* She'd probably caught a chill working outside in the evening air. *Irritating neighbor,* she thought for the hundredth time.

She whisked the spoon into Maddie's mouth, then watched for her reaction.

Maddie's lips puckered.

"No, Maddie," Jane said, trying to scoot her chair back. She wasn't fast enough, and the bite of sweet potato splayed across her chin and chest.

"*Madison,*" Jane said, more sharply than she should have. She rose from her chair and went to the sink. Maddie began to cry.

Jane set Mark's bottle on the counter, grabbed the dishcloth, and wiped at the stains on her shirt. Deprived of his bottle, Mark started howling.

"How could one little bite go so far?" Jane grumbled as she looked down at the orange splotches. Lifting Mark to her shoulder, she began bouncing in time with her scrubbing.

Maddie's cries escalated, so Jane walked over to the high chair and dropped a handful of Cheerios on the tray. Maddie brushed her arms back and forth over the tray, scattering cereal across the kitchen floor. Her face grew beet red and she started screaming.

"All right, all right," Jane said. She tucked the dishcloth into the front of her sweats. With her free hand, she reached down and lifted Maddie from her chair. "It's okay," Jane spoke soothingly. "You don't have to eat sweet potatoes anymore. Whoever wrote that article probably doesn't even *have* children."

The doorbell rang, immediately followed by a persistent knocking.

Mom and Dad. Thank goodness. With a crying baby on each hip, Jane walked toward the front door. She undid the chain, flipped the dead bolt and grabbed the knob, pulling the door open. She gasped.

Paul stood on her front step.

Chapter Thirty-Six

Jane felt her heart leap, and it was all she could do to restrain herself from running into his arms. She still held the twins, but their crying ceased to bother her. Paul's name formed on her lips, and her eyes welled with tears. She'd pretended she didn't miss him so much anymore, but she had. He looked so good—all tan and healthy. Even his hair was growing back. A Bible verse from a long-ago Sunday School lesson trailed through her mind.

"And not a hair on their heads shall be lost."

A ridiculous thing to think of right now, especially since he was scowling at her.

"What's wrong with them?" he demanded in a voice that wasn't quite Paul's.

Jane's attention was pulled back to the howling twins. Before she could reply, he stepped over the threshold and took Mark from her.

"It's all right little guy. Your uncle's here now. I'll take care of you."

Uncle? The word went screaming through Jane's mind, snapping her out of the trance she'd been under since opening the door a half minute ago. Her heart plummeted as sadness, anger, and fear threatened to overwhelm her all at once. Paul wasn't here. Of course not. It was only his brother shown up at last. His negligent, unfeeling brother—

"Uncle Pete has got you now. Yeah, you're okay."

Jane watched, dumbfounded, as he walked past her, through the living room and into the kitchen. Left with no choice, she followed, but feeling wary about having him in her house, she kept the front door open.

"This Mark's?" He held the bottle up in front of her.

Jane nodded. "Yes, but you can't just come right in here and—" And *what?* She watched as he held Mark in the crook of his arm and began feeding him. Almost immediately, Mark quieted, his attention focused on draining the bottle.

Madison leaned forward, arms outstretched toward the stranger.

Jane handed Madison a cracker and pulled her back, putting an arm protectively around her. She stared hard at Paul's imposter. Piercing blue eyes—nothing like Paul's—stared back at her. How had she possibly mistaken . . . ? How could she have thought . . . ? It didn't matter now. She just needed to get this space-invading uncle away from the twins and out of her house. Best to be polite and usher him out as quickly as possible. She took a deep breath and stuck out her free hand.

"Hi. I'm Jane."

"So I gathered," he said dryly, not bothering to take her hand.

Jane was about to excuse his rudeness and chalk it up to his probably not knowing how to hold a baby and a bottle on the same side, when he ruined it by openly looking her over, frowning, no doubt, at her stained shirt and disheveled hair.

She tried one more time to be nice. "Listen, it's almost the twins' bedtime, and it's really important they stick to their routine. So why don't you just put Mark on the blanket over there, and tomorrow we can work out some sort of visitation schedule."

He sent her a scathing look. "*Visitation?* I don't think so."

Jane suppressed a shudder. No wonder Paul hadn't wanted anything to do with his brother. Why on earth had he involved him in the twins' custody? Were the ties of blood that strong?

She handed Madison another cracker and forced herself to stay calm. She'd read that babies could sense a parent's mood, and she certainly didn't want the twins feeling any of her anxiety.

"Please." She spoke in her soothing therapist voice. "Give Mark to me and leave."

Pete ignored her and walked into the family room, settling in the rocking chair. "You know, I've got as much a right to these children as you do—more in fact. So you can forget any other silly ideas you have about keeping me away."

Jane felt genuine panic begin to set in. What was he talking about? She hadn't done anything to keep him away. He'd kept himself away—off flying his helicopter in some dangerous corner of the world. A sudden thought occurred to her. What if he'd been discharged from the military because of some mental trauma? Maybe *that* was the problem. Maybe that was why he'd shown up out of the blue.

She watched him rocking Mark. He seemed normal enough—though rude—but was it possible he had post-traumatic stress disorder? Jane tried to recall the undergraduate class she'd taken that covered the subject. She couldn't remember much—except that a lot of veterans from the first Gulf War had been affected by it. What were the chances she was dealing with a discharged, deranged military man?

Willing her voice not to tremble, Jane spoke again. "The twins *really* need to get to bed, so it would be much better if we could continue this in the morning." She moved toward the rocker. "Just hand Mark to me and—"

"I'll put him to bed."

"No," Jane said, more loudly than she'd intended. "Please, just—you need to leave."

Pete considered a moment. "All right. I can take Mark with me for the night then."

"No!" Jane exclaimed. "You can't *take* him." She backed up, pulling the phone from its charger on the wall. She blocked the entrance to the living room. "You have exactly ten seconds to put Mark down and get out of my house before I call the police."

Pete shook his head in disbelief. "You are way too stressed out." He took the empty bottle from Mark's mouth and lifted him to his shoulder. Mark began to cry. "Still hungry, little guy?" Pete asked. He looked up at Jane. "Hand me that other bottle, will you?"

She shook her head. "It's Maddie's. Ten, nine, eight—"

"Can't you make her another one?" Pete asked. "Mark is still hungry. Look at him."

"Seven, six . . . I mean it, I'll call the police."

He looked up at her, accusation in his eyes. "Go ahead. Then I can tell them this poor kid is starving. Maybe you ought to try feeding him more often. He might gain some weight."

Jane used her thumb to punch *nine* on the phone. "I do feed him. He has acid reflux and throws up a lot. Now put him down and get out of my house."

Madison leaned forward again, her cries escalating.

Pete smiled at her. "It's all right, darling. You hungry, too?"

"*One*," Jane said punching the button on the phone. "She *was* eating when you interrupted us. Now put my son down and get out."

Pete's smile faded. He rose from the rocker. "He is *not* your son," he said in a voice so chilling it scared her.

"I'm the only mother they've known, and I've cared for them while you've—"

"Served my country. I came home as soon as I could. I've been counting the days until I could be with these kids, and first thing, you try—"

"You never called or wrote," Jane accused. Madison grabbed for the phone, hitting several buttons at once. Jane pried Maddie's fingers from the phone and held it up out of her reach. "I didn't have any idea that you wanted to be a part of their lives. I didn't even know if *you* were alive, and I certainly didn't expect—"

"9-1-1 dispatch. Do you have an emergency?"

Jane stared at the phone in her hand.

"Go ahead," Pete urged, smirking. "Report me. I'm sure my ten seconds are past."

She put the phone to her ear. "Hello." She listened for a moment. "No. There is no emergency. My daughter accidentally pushed the buttons. Sorry to trouble you."

Pete's eyebrows rose and he gave her a look that clearly said he was calling her bluff.

That, along with the dispatcher's insistent questions, was all she needed. Jane spoke again. "Well yes, I'd *thought* about calling the police because a man forced his way into my house," she explained, surprised to find her voice shaking, more from anger now than fear. "Yes. He's still here, and he's holding my son." She paused, listening again.

Pete walked to the counter and picked up Madison's bottle. He gave it to Mark, who began drinking as eagerly as before.

"No. He isn't hurting him," Jane continued. "He's—he's feeding him a bottle." Another pause. "I don't know if he's armed."

She thought she saw amusement flicker in Pete's eyes as he shook his head. She listened to the dispatcher's instructions. "No. I *can't* leave. No, I'm not restrained," she said, exasperated. I just won't leave my baby. Yes. That's the address. But as I said earlier, we're fine. He knows I've called you, and I'm sure he's going to leave *right now.*"

Pete walked closer and leaned toward the phone. "Sorry. I can't talk right now," he said loudly. "I'm feeding a very hungry baby, but you should know I'm this boy's uncle and legal guardian."

Jane frowned at him as she spoke into the phone. "He claims he is, but I've never met him before. He just showed up at my house, walked right in and took my baby. Yes. I'll wait on the li—"

Jane gasped as the phone was pulled out of her hand. She watched as Pete hit the END CALL button.

"Before the police arrive, we need to get a few things straight, Miss Warner. The first being that my name *is* Peter Bryant and I am co-guardian—with *you,* unfortunately—of these two wonderful children. After tonight, I'll be certain to carry documentation with me at all times, lest you should forget."

"I didn't know—"

"Don't lie," Pete warned, narrowing his eyes. "I can't tolerate liars, and I certainly won't allow one to be involved in raising my brother's children. Even if your mother hadn't told you about me, you recognized me. I saw it in your eyes when you opened the door. Paul *was* my twin, and I'm sure our resemblance hasn't changed that much over the last couple of years."

"My *mother?*" Jane asked. "What has she got to do with this?" She didn't wait for his reply. "And, yes. I did see similarities, but you still had no business walking right in and taking Mark. You could have at least had the decency to introduce yourself and then *ask* if you could see Mark and

Madison." Jane stepped around Pete and went into the kitchen. Pointing to the phone she said, "*You* had better call them back and explain, or we're going to have a real mess." She grabbed a bottle of apple juice from the fridge and gave it to Madison. "You're lucky Mark didn't start screaming. Babies this age have stranger anxiety. They need awhile to get to know someone new before they trust that person to pick them up or—"

"They *do* know me. I spent all morning with them."

"You *what?*"

"Didn't your mom tell you?" Pete asked, looking as perplexed as Jane felt. He stood on the opposite side of the counter. "I spent a couple of hours playing with the twins before I went out and worked on your swing set."

"*You!*" Jane exclaimed. "You're the one who came into my yard? Who poured cement too close to the lilac bush? You're my—*neighbor?*" A look of horror crossed her face as realization hit.

"I'm not too thrilled with the deal, either," Pete said, scowling at her. "And while we're on the subject, you're driving my Jeep. And that's my sofa over there too." He nodded to the corner of the family room. "But I'm okay with all of that. In fact, I was trying to be optimistic about the whole situation until this evening when I saw that you'd covered up the fence and chained the gate shut." He spoke the last as they heard the sound of a car out front.

Realizing the police were probably outside, Jane tensed. Hadn't she read somewhere that it was a felony—or at least a misdemeanor—to request emergency services when they weren't really needed?

Peter kissed Mark on the forehead and laid him down on the blanket in the family room. "See you soon, buddy," he said.

Jane followed him.

"Good night, sweetheart." Pete touched Madison's hair as he walked past.

Jane sent him a panicked look. Out front she heard car doors slamming. "The gate key is on the counter," she offered. "You could go out the back, and I'll tell them you got away."

Pete threw her a look of disgust. "You're joking, right?" Footsteps sounded on the walk.

Jane turned and watched as he left the kitchen and went through the living room. She saw him raise his arms just before he reached the front door.

"I'm the man you want, officers. I am unarmed and coming out the front door."

Jane held her breath as he stepped through the door. *You have to stop this,* her conscience demanded. *Don't make him pay for your mistake.* Before she could act on her thoughts, she heard Mark gagging. Whirling around, she saw that he was throwing up—or trying to. Peter had placed him on his back, and now Mark was choking on his own vomit.

All else forgotten, Jane dropped to the blanket, laid Madison down, and scooped up Mark. With one hand she began patting his back while her other hand raised his little arms to open his airway. He continued gagging, and it seemed like forever before a stream of sour milk finally projected from his mouth, splattering across her lap and the blanket. Mark cried, and Jane felt tears running down her own face. She'd never been so scared or so relieved. She pulled him close, rocking back and forth, her head bent close to his. At last he began to calm down.

"Everything all right, miss?"

Jane looked up and saw a policeman standing over her. "Y-yes," she stammered. "He was choking, and I was afraid . . ." Her voice trailed off as she suddenly remembered *why* there was a police officer in her house. She leaned to the side, looking for Peter.

"If he's okay now—" The officer nodded to Mark. "Then I have a few questions."

Still holding Mark, Jane got to her feet. She walked past the officer and into the living room. He followed. The room was empty, so she went to the front door and looked outside.

"That man—the one who came out with his hands up—do you know where he is?" Jane asked.

"Not to worry," the officer said, smiling at her reassuringly. "Right now he's in the back of a patrol car on his way to the station."

Chapter Thirty-Seven

"I can't believe you didn't tell me, Mother," Jane said again. The last officer had just left, without charging her with anything, thankfully. Jane knew it was fortunate her parents had arrived when they did. Her mother's explanation had clarified the situation for Jane and the questioning officer.

Jane ran her fingers through her tangled hair. "I've got to go down there. That's all there is to it. Pete doesn't have a car and—" She looked at her father. "There shouldn't be bail to post, should there?"

"Shouldn't be, since you're not pressing charges." Her father settled on the sofa that Jane now knew belonged to Peter. She looked around the room. What else of his was she using?

"Mom, could you bathe Mark for me and try to get him to take another bottle? Slowly."

"Of course, dear." Marsha rose from the rocker where she'd been holding Mark. Maddie lay asleep on the blanket, juice bottle still in hand. "You really shouldn't give her juice at night, Jane. Her teeth will—"

"I *know*, Mother." Jane pulled her coat from the front closet. "I never do, but I was a bit stressed. First I thought I'd seen Paul's ghost, then I had this pushy guy in my house. I thought he was going to try to take the twins . . . Why doesn't anyone *get* why I was upset?" she asked, feeling angry all over again. She grabbed her purse from the counter. "I'll be back as soon as I can."

"Take your time," Marsha called.

* * *

Jane parked in one of the thirty-minute spaces in front of the police station. She turned off the Jeep and took a deep breath. The whole way over she'd tried to rehearse what to say, but nothing came to mind, except the inevitable "I'm sorry." And she was sorry—for the fence, for calling the police—even if Maddie had dialed that last *one*—and mostly for her behavior tonight. Since learning that Paul had appointed joint custody for the twins, she'd been terrified his brother might try to take them away. Tonight, she'd given him reason to. She could imagine a custody hearing with a psychologist testifying about her absurd behavior.

"Miss Warner is given to extreme mood swings, bouts of hysteria and—" Jane popped a fun-size Three Musketeers bar in her mouth as she entered the police station. "—an unhealthy addiction to chocolate."

Chewing quickly, she walked to the counter and waited until the officer there looked up at her.

"I'm here to pick someone up," she said, careful not to open her mouth too wide in case she had chocolate on her teeth.

"Name?" the officer asked.

"Pau—Peter Bryant." *What is wrong with me?* Placing her arms on the counter, she leaned forward. "He was brought in about half an hour ago. But it was all a big misunderstanding. You see, my mother hadn't told me he was back from Iraq. And I was already worried about this strange neighbor who'd come in my yard while I was at work. So when Peter came over, I wasn't expecting it, and he just walked right in and—"

The officer held up his hand to stop her. "I heard about you. Have a seat and I'll tell Detective Mitchell you're here."

"I thought we'd taken care of everything at the house," Jane said anxiously.

"Just a formality, miss." He picked up the phone.

Jane nodded and took a seat, restraining herself from digging through her purse for another candy bar.

Five minutes passed before Peter walked into the lobby.

"Hi," he said, looking down at her.

"Hi," she said, standing. "Are you um—all done?"

"Free to go," Pete said. "Unless you've come to press charges."

Instead of rising to his bait, Jane clutched her purse and walked past him to the parking lot. Pulling her keys from her coat pocket, she unlocked the passenger-side door. She turned and found herself face-to-face with Pete.

For a split second their eyes met, then he stepped back and opened the car door.

"I should have said thank you for coming to pick me up. I thought I'd have to wait until my boss was back from his date with his wife. "

"You're welcome," Jane said stiffly. "I'm sorry you were here in the first place. I—don't know what came over me tonight."

Pete's eyebrows raised. "Maternal instinct, maybe? You were right. I shouldn't have just walked in your house." He motioned for her to get in the car.

"Oh," Jane said, realizing he meant for her to be the passenger. Reluctantly, she handed him the keys and got in the car. He closed the door behind her.

Pete walked around to the driver's side, got in, and started the engine. "Wow," he said, looking at the odometer as he moved the seat back. "A lot of miles on this thing. I bought it new in 2000."

"It made a lot of trips to hospitals—several times a day even, for a couple of months."

"Mmm." Pete nodded. "Hadn't thought about that. I guess it wasn't just Paul and Tamara out driving off into the sunset." He looked at Jane out of the corner of his eye, trying to gauge her reaction to Tamara's name.

"Probably not," she said. "Listen, I should get home. Mark threw up—right after you walked out the front door. My parents are there now, but I need to make sure he's okay. And I need to get cleaned up." She brushed a hand across her sweats. "Sorry about the smell."

"Mark threw up?" Pete asked, concerned.

Jane nodded. "Yeah. He's got a really sensitive stomach. He has to eat slow and burp often. Otherwise . . ."

"So it was my fault."

"Basically," Jane said with a hint of a smile.

"And you didn't change before coming to get me?" He took in her appearance, from her tousled hair to her stained shirt and sweats.

"No." Jane glanced away. "I thought it was more important I get down here."

He detected irritation in her voice. "I wasn't trying to be critical. I'm grateful—and impressed. Most women I know wouldn't leave the house looking like that."

Jane turned to him, astonishment on her face. "Is that supposed to be a compliment?"

"Yes," Pete said adamantly.

She sighed and leaned her head back against the seat. "Please, just take me home."

Without another word, Pete put the car in reverse, backed up, then left the parking lot. The ride home was silent. He kept his eyes on the road, and Jane looked out her window. He knew he'd hurt her feelings, and he felt bad. It seemed like that was all he was ever capable of when it came to women. *It's why you're still single at thirty-four,* the thought came, bringing to the surface all the guilt he'd carried around the past two and a half years.

For a minute he wished he were back in Iraq where life was, for him anyway, less complicated. But then he thought of the twins. Already, he couldn't bear the thought of leaving them. He was surprised at the pull he felt toward Mark and Madison, and he didn't know if it was because they were Tamara and Paul's, or if it was because he had no one else. Whatever the reason, he had to try harder with Jane Warner if he expected to be a part of their life.

He pulled into Jane's driveway. "Do you have a garage door opener somewhere?" he asked, feeling along the sun visor.

"In the console," Jane said, opening it and handing him the remote. "Aren't you going to take the Jeep with you?"

He shook his head. "And leave you with two babies and no car? You must really think I'm a cad."

"Well," Jane said. "If the shoe fits . . ."

"Okay, I probably deserve that," Pete admitted. He waited for the garage door to open, then pulled the Jeep inside. He turned off the engine and unbuckled his seatbelt, but made no move to get out.

"Let's try this again." He handed the keys to Jane, then kept his hand extended. "Hi. My name is Peter Bryant, and I have the good fortune to be co-guardian of my brother's children with you. I am appreciative of all you've done for Mark and Madison, and I would be grateful if you would teach me all I need to know so I can be involved in their lives. They're the only family I have."

He caught the nearly imperceptible softening in Jane's eyes as she took his hand.

"Jane Warner. Pleased to meet you."

Pete held on. "And I am sorry for offending you tonight. And for future times when I will no doubt do the same. One of my least-endearing qualities is being brutally honest."

Jane chuckled. "Brutal is right. Tonight has probably scarred me for years." She tugged her hand away. "But I forgive you, and as long as we're being completely honest, I have to tell you that I really hoped I'd never meet you. I didn't have any idea Paul would do this to me—to us." She looked down at her lap and began idly twisting her watch. "He told me *I* would be Mark and Madison's guardian. He never said anything about joint custody with you. But right after Paul's funeral his attorney called—"

"Richard Morgan," Pete supplied.

"You know him?" Jane asked, looking up again.

"Met with him yesterday," Pete said, deciding now was not the time to mention Richard Morgan was his boss.

"Oh, right," Jane said. "When he told me about you, I was really upset. And then . . ." She paused. "Then I was scared."

"Of what?" he asked, surprised at the sudden vulnerability he saw in her eyes.

"You. I was afraid you would try to take Mark and Madison away, and by then—" Her breath caught. "I already loved them so much."

Pete looked away, leaning against the headrest. Hadn't he wanted that very thing—been planning it, even—to take the twins away from Jane Warner? "The thought had crossed my mind."

Jane nodded. "You're the blood relative, so I was afraid you would win." She bit her lip. "I've been so afraid of this. *Please,* don't. I know I didn't give birth to them, but I love them as if I had."

The car was quiet as Pete digested this information. He *was* a cad—and a lot of other things for thinking he'd just walk right in and take over the care of the twins. He'd only been thinking of himself and what he wanted. Or didn't want—like a woman complicating his life. Never once, until now, had he considered how that woman might feel or, even more important, what was best for Mark and Madison. He hated to admit it, but from what he'd seen so far, Jane Warner was best for them.

She spoke again. "Did you know I was there the day they were born? It's kind of a quirky twist of fate, but I was at the newborn ICU with my nephew when they brought Mark and Madison in for the first time. I heard the nurses talking about their mother. I felt so bad for them."

"Is that when you met Paul?"

Jane shook her head. "It was about six weeks later. He'd put an ad in the paper."

Pete looked incredulous. "An *ad?*"

"Yes." Jane smiled. "You know, our first meeting was very much like this one."

"You got Paul arrested, too?" Pete ran his finger over the instrument panel, wiping dust away.

"No," Jane said with a laugh. "But it was a disaster. In less than fifteen minutes, he had offended me, and I walked out. Date over."

I don't want to know about Paul's relationship with Jane, Pete reminded himself, but couldn't curb his curiosity. "So how did you end up together?"

"I learned he had a baby in the hospital—I didn't know he had *two* until later—and for some reason I felt compelled to go to the hospital and see his baby."

"For some reason, huh?" Pete said, not buying it.

"Really," Jane insisted. "It was like I was prompt—call it fate if you like. All I know is that I'm so grateful I followed whatever it was and went."

"What happened when you got there?"

"Paul found me standing at the NICU window, staring at Madison." Jane smiled wistfully. "He came up to me, stuck out his hand—just like you did a few minutes ago—and said something like, 'Hi. I'm Paul. I have terminal cancer. My wife died in a car accident, and I'm looking for a woman to raise my children.'" Jane had a faraway look.

"And it was love at first sight." Pete couldn't keep the sarcasm out of his voice. He knew he shouldn't be irritated with Jane. She'd done nothing wrong, but he couldn't help but feel angry with Paul. How could he have forgotten Tamara so quickly?

Jane nodded. "I fell in love with Maddie the first time I held her."

And Paul. What about Paul? Pete wanted to ask. *When did you fall in love with him? And how was it that he loved you, when he'd been married to the most wonderful woman on earth?*

Pete drummed his fingers on the steering wheel. "So what was your first date?"

"We didn't really date," Jane said. "Unless you count visiting the hospital cafeteria. He took me out for macaroni and cheese and Jell-O a couple of times." She grinned at Pete. "Maybe you'll be a bigger spender, huh?"

Pete frowned. "Maybe." Did she think he was just going to step in and take Paul's place?

As if sensing she'd said something wrong, Jane grabbed the door handle. "I didn't mean to imply . . ."

"Forget it," Pete said. A thought occurred to him. "I'm wondering, though, why Paul didn't just put the twins up for adoption? Why would he advertise for a woman and not an adoptive couple?"

"He did think about it," Jane said. "But he changed his mind." She got out of the car.

Pete did the same. He shut his door and walked toward the back entrance to the garage. "What changed his mind?"

Jane looked at him across the hood of the Jeep. "I've thought about that a lot and there's only one reason I can think of." She spoke quietly. "You."

Chapter Thirty-Eight

Saturday morning Pete awoke to noise from outside. He looked out the bedroom window and was pleased to see the gate ajar and Jane pulling privacy slats from the fence. He hurriedly dressed to join her.

Walking into the backyard a few moments later, Pete headed toward the open gate. Stepping into the yard, he watched as Jane wrestled with a particularly stubborn PVC slat. Shania Twain's voice carried across the lawn from the CD player on the porch. Pete smiled to himself as he watched Jane sing along to "Man, I Feel Like a Woman."

Yeah, you look like a woman too, he thought, admiring her curves as she pulled at the top of the fence. She had on jeans today instead of the baggy sweats she'd worn last night, and her hair was pulled back into a ponytail. He wished she'd wear it down. He'd always had a thing for women who wore their hair up. There was something about a woman's bare neck. And right now that was the last thing he wanted—to feel any pull of attraction toward *this* woman. Things were complicated enough already.

Pete walked along the fence toward her.

Jane glanced over at him. "You gonna help me with these?"

Pete shoved his hands in his pockets and shrugged. "It depends on what you're doing. If you're planning to replace the PVC with brick or something . . ."

"I'm *trying* to make amends," Jane said. "You know, good fences make good neighbors, so bad fences must make bad neighbors." She stopped working and looked at him. "And I don't want that. I'm taking the privacy slats out, and I already got rid of the lock on the gate. So will you help?"

Pete tried to suppress his grin. "Am I allowed? Didn't I mess up pretty badly yesterday? Something about concrete and a bush?"

Jane let go of the slat and tugged off her gloves. "Come here. I'll show you." She walked to the center of the yard and stood between the posts Pete had installed. "See this?" She pointed to the large shrub growing a few feet behind. "This lilac was trimmed back in the fall, but already it's starting to get buds. Pretty soon the whole tree will be covered with these." She pinched a cluster between her fingers. "And when they open up, this entire yard will be fragrant. Of course, the lavender color is also beautiful, but it's the fragrance I'll miss."

Pete looked confused. "Why miss it? The posts aren't anywhere near."

"But the swings," Jane protested. "The swings will hit." She moved between the posts, walking front and back in the path a swing would take.

"Well, maybe eventually they'll hit, but it will be awhile before the twins go that high. I see your point though," Pete admitted. "Sorry. I was just thinking about the easiest place to watch the kids."

"And that is more important," Jane agreed. "I know I shouldn't be so upset. It's just that I'm a yard person. You know, some women have the, 'stay out of my kitchen' philosophy. Well, for me it's, 'don't mess with my yard.'"

"I'll be sure to remember that," Pete said.

"But today you *can* help," she added quickly. "I thought these slats were a pain to put in, but they're so much worse to take out."

Pete walked over to the fence, examining the slats and chain link. Putting his palm on one of the metal posts, he leaned forward. The entire fence bent under his weight. "Thought so," he said, turning to Jane. "How about we leave the slats in and just take down the whole fence?"

She looked doubtful. "I don't know if that's a good idea. I'm just renting."

"From the Reimans?" Pete asked.

Jane nodded. "How did you know?"

"They lived here the whole time I was growing up. They put the gate in the fence so their son and I could go back and forth between houses."

"That's your house?" She looked toward the sagging fence and the house behind it. "You *own* it?"

"Pretty much. Mom left it to Paul and me when she died. A couple of years ago Paul planned to purchase some property and build on it, so he mailed me the deed to our house."

"I can't believe this." Jane put her hands on her hips. "What a sneaky, underhanded thing to do."

"What do you mean?" Pete asked warily, sensing she was headed for a mood like she'd been in last night.

"Paul did this," Jane said, as if just fully realizing the implications. "He found this house for us to rent, and *I* didn't want to live here. I didn't like the neighborhood, and the house and yard were in terrible shape—all I've done since we moved in is paint, clean, fix . . ."

"I don't understand," Pete said.

"He tricked me," Jane continued. "He made me feel terrible for not wanting this place. He said it was perfect because it was close to the hospital and we'd always be able to get Mark there quickly if there was an emergency."

"Well, that is true," Pete said.

"Yes, but he said nothing, *nothing* at all about *you* living behind us. He never told me that was the house he'd grown up in or that you would come back there. And I remember—" Jane snapped her fingers. "I remember having a conversation about the sagging fence and gate and wanting to get them replaced, but Paul said no. He told me the owners wanted it kept the way it was." She began pacing back and forth between the swing-set posts. "Which really made no sense, because they let us fix everything else. They even took a big chunk off our rent because we were doing so much to the house." She stopped suddenly. "Oooh. I could just—"

"Kill him if he weren't already dead?" Pete said quietly.

Jane's head snapped up. The look on her face was a mixture of horror and shame. "No. I didn't mean—"

"It's okay." Pete walked over to her. "You think I didn't feel the exact same thing when I found out that Paul had died, that he'd left two *children*—children I didn't even know existed—to me? I didn't even know he had cancer." Pete ran his fingers through his hair.

"I'm sorry," Jane said lamely. She folded her arms across her chest and looked down at the grass. Her head was still swimming with the implications of what Paul had done. He'd set them up perfectly for . . . for joint guardianship? She hoped that was all he'd intended. So far his brother was nothing like she'd imagined. He was a little bit Paul, and a whole lot a stranger still, yet they were thrown into the awkwardness of having these serious conversations and figuring out how to share two children. She looked up at Pete, voicing the questions that had been on her mind for months. "What happened between you two? How come you didn't know Paul had cancer?"

Pete's eyes narrowed. "He didn't tell you?"

Jane shook her head. "He hardly ever mentioned you. It made me sad," she admitted. "I have six brothers and sisters, and I'm fairly close with all of them."

"Then you're very lucky," Pete said.

"I know." Jane looked down at the grass again, digging at a weed with the toe of her sneaker. "You don't have to tell me. I shouldn't have asked." She heard Pete sigh.

"Maybe some other time when—"

Madison's cry on the baby monitor interrupted them, saving him from continuing.

When we know each other better? Jane thought. *Will we know each other better?* "How about breakfast?" she asked, pulling the monitor out of her pocket. "Or have you already eaten?" she added, giving him a way out if he wanted.

"I haven't eaten yet." Pete glanced at his watch. "It's only 6:45. Do you always get up so early?"

"Usually." Jane bent down to pull the weed. "I like to come out in the quiet and work in the yard. It's one of my favorite times of the day. I guess you could say I'm a morning person." She stood again and began to walk toward the house. "What about you?"

"Night owl," Pete said, following her. "Though the military has done its best to change that. But normally I prefer to stay up late. I enjoy being outside then."

"What do you do outside at night? Do you have a garage you like to putter in or—?"

"Stars," Pete said. "I really enjoy watching the stars. I have a great telescope."

"Oh," Jane said, remembering fondly the times she'd sat on the roof of her cottage and counted the stars on clear nights. "I can see how that would be enjoyable too." She reached the sliding glass door and opened it.

"You'll have to wait a bit for breakfast," she warned. "Around here it's babies first, then grown-ups. Come on in and you can earn your food."

Chapter Thirty-Nine

"Hello, handsome," Jane said, scooping Mark from his crib. She gave him a kiss on the cheek and went to the other crib, where Madison stood babbling as she clung to the bars.

"Good morning, beautiful." Jane used her free hand to lift Madison. She turned to Pete. "Okay, pick one."

"Umm—is there a right or wrong choice here?" He looked at the twins. "What are we doing?"

"Changing diapers," Jane said with a smile. "First thing in the morning both babies need to be changed. And, as you can guess by the smell, at least one of them is more than wet."

Pete looked at them warily. "Which one?"

"Don't know," Jane said. "You've got fifty-fifty odds, though—unless they're both stinky." Her smile broadened.

Pete rubbed his hands together. He looked at Mark and Madison. "All right, guys—and girls—sorry, Madison. Actually, you know, I think I'd better start with Mark first. I'm a little more familiar with the anatomy."

Jane laughed. "I understand. You can use the changing table."

Pete took Mark and laid him on the table. He watched as Jane put a blanket on the floor, laid Madison on it, and grabbed a diaper from the shelf. Kneeling beside the blanket, Jane began unsnapping Madison's sleeper. Pete looked back at Mark.

"Maybe, for this first time, I'd better get some coaching over here."

"One second. I'll be right there."

Pete watched carefully as Jane unfastened the diaper, folded it down, wiped Madison, and slid a clean diaper under her. She had Madison's new diaper on, her pajamas snapped up, and the whole process complete in less than a minute.

Pete whistled. "You're fast."

Jane tossed the diaper in a pail next to the changing table and squirted some hand sanitizer on her palms. She gave Madison a toy and stood. "Ready?"

Pete rubbed his hands together. "Ready." *How hard could it be?* He unsnapped Mark's pajamas and pulled them up, out of the way like he'd seen Jane do. *So far so good.* He reached for the Velcro fasteners on the diaper.

"I wouldn't do that if I were you," Jane said.

"How come?" Pete asked, looking over his shoulder at her.

"Little boys are a bit different. The air hits their—their . . . The air hits them and they start to go."

Pete's eyebrows rose. "So what you're saying is—"

"Just have another diaper open and ready to cover him up in case he squirts," Jane said quickly.

"You speak from experience," Pete said, unable to hide his amusement at her word choice. It was nice to know he wasn't the only one feeling a little out of his comfort zone.

Jane pursed her lips and nodded. "Yes, and let me tell you, it *hurts* when you get hit in the eye."

"Good to know." Pete turned his attention back to Mark. "All right. Open and ready." Pete pulled a diaper from the shelf and began unfolding it.

"Uh-uh." Jane took it from him. "This is Maddie's. See the pink edging?"

"Well, yeah, but does it really matter? I mean, we live in a society where women serve right beside men in the military. So what's the big deal with diaper color? Can't Maddie wear a blue diaper and Mark wear pink?" Pete frowned as he continued in mock seriousness. "Is this really what we want to teach these children? Don't you want Maddie to feel she can do anything—even wear blue diapers?"

Jane folded her arms across her chest and suppressed a grin. "Go ahead," she urged, waving Pete on. "Put the pink one on. But you're the one who gets to change Mark's clothes and the crib bedding and do all the laundry when his diaper leaks."

Pete, his hand on the Velcro of Mark's diaper, stopped. "What do you mean?"

"The diapers are different," Jane said. "Boys are different than girls. The diapers are padded differently based on where the absorption is needed."

"Really?" Pete asked. He looked at the diaper, impressed. "I didn't know."

"Now if you'd like to lobby the diaper companies to change their color scheme to include pinks and purples for boys and maybe reds and blues for girls, feel free to do so. In the meantime, the pink and blue trim keeps things pretty simple. Not to mention that Madison is wearing a size larger than Mark right now."

Without a word, Pete put the pink diaper back on the shelf and took a blue one. He unfolded it and laid it aside, ready to grab it should he need to.

"Okay. Here goes." He unfastened the tabs on both sides and peeled back the diaper. "Well, hey. That's quite a mess there." He quickly pulled the diaper back up and turned his face aside. "Now what?"

"Now you wipe *everything* off." Jane walked toward the bedroom door.

"Where are you going?" Pete called, trying not to sound too anxious. "I mean, come on, if I can't even figure out the right diaper to use, I should probably have you demonstrate—"

"You'll be fine," Jane said. "Just make sure to use plenty of wipes and sprinkle some powder on him when you're through."

Pete began pulling wipes from the dispenser. When he had a good-sized wad in his hand, he peeled back the diaper again.

Jane stood in the doorway trying not to laugh. "It's usually more effective if you use one at a time. Otherwise, you'll go through the whole box at one changing."

Pete shook several of the wipes out of his hand. "This *looks* like it's going to take a whole box," he muttered.

"Good luck," Jane called. "I'm going to get the twins' breakfast ready. Bring them to the kitchen when you're done." She paused in the hall and turned back. "Oh, and Peter—"

"Yes?"

"Mark always has a messy diaper first thing in the morning."

* * *

"Where do you want them?" Pete asked somewhat grumpily as he walked into the kitchen a few minutes later, a twin in each arm.

"In the high chairs. Mark needs to sit in the one with all the rolled-up towels." Jane stood at the counter, mashing something in a bowl. "Everything go okay?"

"Fine. It only took me five tries to line up the snaps right on Mark's pajamas. How come they design baby clothes to be so confusing? Whoever heard of pants that snap all the way down to your foot?"

Jane laughed. "I never thought of it that way."

"What's on the menu?" Pete asked. He walked to the breakfast nook and tried putting Madison in her seat. The tray was pushed in too far though, and he couldn't figure out how to get it off without putting one of the twins down. Reluctantly, he asked for help again. "Jane, could you come here a minute?"

She wiped her hands on a towel, walked across the kitchen, and took Madison from Pete. "Observe," she said, putting her free hand behind her back. "With practice, many things can be done while holding babies." Balancing Madison on her hip and putting her arm around her, Jane bent over and used the same hand to spring the tray loose. "Now you try," she said, nodding to Mark's high chair.

Pete put one hand behind his back, secured Mark with his other arm and tried to unlock the tray. It wouldn't budge. Mark began sliding down Pete's leg.

"It's okay," Jane said as she buckled Madison into her chair. "It takes practice, and women do have better hips for the job." She walked over and unlatched Mark's tray.

"It would seem I can't do anything right," Pete grumbled.

"Oh don't say that," Jane said brightly. "You haven't tried feeding them yet." She went into the kitchen and returned with two bowls. "Mashed bananas with rice cereal for Mark." She handed the bowl to Pete. "And Maddie can feed herself banana slices and Cheerios for a few minutes." Jane put the other bowl on Maddie's tray. "If you'll supervise here, then I'll go make french toast for us."

Pete looked at the bowl of mashed banana and cereal. It didn't look very appetizing, and he imagined Mark would feel the same way. "Any tips?" Pete asked hopefully.

"Airplane noises and small bites," Jane called as she returned to the kitchen.

Pete picked up the spoon. "Airplane, huh?" he asked. "How about a helicopter, Mark? Those are more fun." Pete dug the spoon in and began twirling it around in his fingers, making a whirring noise. Mark's eyes followed the motion, and after a few seconds Pete flew the bite into Mark's open mouth. Surprisingly, he ate it. Encouraged, Pete tried another "helicopter" bite and got the same results. Remembering to keep the spoonfuls small, he continued feeding Mark, and in a few minutes' time the entire mashed concoction was gone. Pete looked over at Madison and winked. "I think we've got this one down," he whispered.

He turned around in his chair to watch Jane. She stood at the stove with her back to him, flipping french toast. She'd brought the CD player in from the patio, and Shania was still singing. This song he was less familiar with—something about a woman not being impressed by money, nice cars, or Brad Pitt. Curious, he listened as he watched Jane gather the syrup, butter, plates, and silverware and bring everything to the table.

"So if movie stars, rocket scientists, and nice cars don't impress, what does?" he asked.

"Hmm . . ." Jane considered as she set the table. "I'm not sure."

"There must be something," Pete coaxed.

Jane returned to the stove and took the last of the french toast from the skillet.

"I really don't know." On the way back to the table, she grabbed a carton of orange juice and a half-eaten jar of baby food from the fridge. "Maybe nothing does. Maybe that's why I'm single."

"Ever been married?" Pete asked.

"No. You?" Jane set the plate of steaming bread in front of him.

Pete shook his head. "Never." *Engaged once,* he could have added but chose not to. He used his fork to take a piece of bread from the plate.

"This looks great. My mom used to make french toast on really thick bread like this."

"Texas toast," Jane said. "I grew up with it too. Good stuff." She reached for the butter, then stopped, seeing Mark's empty bowl. "He ate it *all?*" she asked, astonished.

Pete grinned. "Every bite."

Jane got up and walked over to the high chair. She made a point of looking in Mark's hair, under his chin, beneath his bib, and at his lap. Finding nothing, she folded her arms and smiled at Pete.

"Now *that* impresses me."

Chapter Forty

Monday morning Pete walked into the office and went straight to Joan's desk.

She smiled up at him. "Good morning, Mr. Bryant."

"Morning," he said, returning her smile. Leaning closer, he spoke in a quiet voice. "I was wondering if there might be a file on Jane Warner. I thought maybe Richard—"

"Right here." Joan held a folder out to him. "Richard said you'd ask for it."

"He did, did he?" Feeling chagrined, Pete took the folder.

Joan nodded. "Yes. And I'm also supposed to break the news that your office has been temporarily taken over by the interns. Richard suggested you use the library until they finish up next month."

"No problem," Pete said. "Thanks." He waved the folder and headed in the opposite direction, reminding himself he was simply grateful to have a job after spending so many months away.

Once in the library, he resisted the urge to look through Jane's file and instead got busy preparing for his Wednesday meeting. He still couldn't quite believe Richard had given him a custody case. Pete grimaced as he opened his laptop. He didn't particularly enjoy court, and this time it was likely to be downright unpleasant.

He'd been working for about half an hour when Richard strolled into the room.

"So, aside from getting arrested, how was your weekend?" He put a stack of folders on the table and sat in the opposite chair.

Pete leaned back and put his hands behind his head. "It was incredible. Absolutely incredible."

"Really?" Richard seemed surprised. "Tell me about it. And sorry I missed your call on the cell Friday night. I'd promised Candice I'd turn my phone off during dinner."

"Don't worry about it," Pete said. "Everything worked out fine. Jane gave me a ride home."

"Wasn't she the one who put you there in the first place?"

Pete nodded. "Yeah, but it was just a misunderstanding."

"Some misunderstanding," Richard said sarcastically. "What else *incredible* happened this weekend?"

Pete leaned over the table. "I have two adorable children. They're a hoot—so fun to watch—so much work to care for," he added. "Seeing them for the first time, the whole experience, everything was amazing—and very overwhelming."

"Most people have a bit more time to adjust to the idea of parenthood."

"I've had a couple of months," Pete said. "But nothing could prepare me for this. I had no idea . . ."

"I told you," Richard reminded him.

"Yes, you did," Pete agreed. "But I'm not just talking about all they require. I didn't realize how fast I'd become attached to them. I spent Friday morning with Mark and Madison and then a short while that night—until the police said I had to go." He grinned, knowing Richard was curious to hear the whole story. "Then I was with them most of the weekend. I changed diapers and fed them. We rolled around on the floor. It was the most fun I've ever had. I can't wait to see them again tonight." Pete tapped his pencil on the desk and looked at Richard expectantly. "Is it always this way with babies? Or do you think it's because I see a bit of Paul and Tamara in them?"

Richard shrugged. "Don't try too hard to figure it out," he advised. "Just enjoy it. They become teenagers fast enough." He frowned as if thinking of the teens in his house. "Meanwhile, remind yourself how much those cute little babies cost. You're going to use your paycheck like never before. So earn it. Here are a few more files for you to look at."

"Not custody, I hope," Pete said, reaching for the folders.

"No," Richard said. "Just some probate that needs to be taken care of. It's enough to keep you busy for a while. Sorry about your office, by the way."

"This is all right." Pete glanced around the library. "I'm just grateful to be employed."

"You wouldn't be if you weren't such a good attorney." Richard eyed Jane's folder as he rose from the table. "Read about Miss Warner yet?"

"No. Thought I'd do that at lunch. Anything in there that'll make me lose my appetite?" Pete asked, joking.

Richard gave him a curious look. "No. But more than likely, you may find something that will whet it."

Chapter Fourty-One

Jane parked the Jeep in front of her parents' house. Getting out, she took Madison from the seat behind her, then walked around the car and got Mark from the other side. After the gagging incident last week, she'd switched their car seats, wanting to see Mark all the time in case he ever threw up like that again.

With a baby on each arm, Jane walked to her parents' door. She felt a little guilty she hadn't invited Peter to come to the monthly family dinner, but he'd only been home a short while—she'd only known him a *week*—and she was afraid her family might swarm him like a bunch of hungry vultures.

It was better, she reasoned, for her to come alone today so she could explain to everyone about the change in her circumstances. She'd simply tell them that she was trying to be a willing participant in this whole co-guardianship thing. If anyone in her family interfered or tried to make it something that it wasn't, everything would be ruined.

Jane extended her thumb to hit the doorbell. She knew the door was probably unlocked and she could just walk right in, but now that she wasn't always carrying the twins in their car seats, she couldn't set them down for a moment to open the screen and the door. A high-chair tray was one thing, but she couldn't do everything by herself while holding both babies. Sometimes a little help was nice.

She smiled, thinking about the previous day. Pete had stayed over for most of it, helping with mundane things like folding the twins' laundry and changing their sheets. He'd played with Mark and Madison, worked on the swing set, and gotten Mark to eat solid food for all three meals. Jane was thrilled and felt he'd more than made up for their rough start the Friday before. She'd told Pete so and thanked him before he finally left at nine o'clock, after they'd put the twins to bed and shared a pizza.

Life was good, Jane realized. Really good. Instead of the nightmare she'd envisioned, she found herself genuinely happy to have some help. The past week had given her hope. Joint custody might just work after all.

Jane's mother opened the door. "Hello, dear." She gave Jane a kiss on the cheek. "Where's Mr. Bryant?" She peered around Jane.

"I didn't invite him, Mom. I didn't want to overwhelm him with the mob." Jane walked past her mother and into the living room.

"Shame on you," her mother scolded. "We're not a mob." She closed the door and followed Jane.

Jane handed Madison to her. "You know what I mean. Everyone will think it's a romantic thing—that he's my boyfriend or something—when that's not it at all. I'm on a bit of precarious ground here. Peter's already admitted he's thought about trying to win sole custody of the twins. If he felt pushed—"

"Nonsense, Jane. He's not going to take these babies away from you. But never mind." Marsha walked toward the family room. "I knew you wouldn't invite him, so *I* did."

"*What?*"

Her mother stepped aside just as they entered the family room. Pete sat on the couch between Caroline and Jessica.

Jane tried to hide her shock and horror at seeing him there.

"Hi." Pete rose from the couch and took Madison from Jane's mom.

"Hi." Jane's voice sounded hoarse. Behind Pete, Caroline flashed her a thumbs-up. Jane felt her face grow hot.

Jessica mouthed, *"Lucky."*

Jane turned away from the couch. "Uh . . . could we go in the living room to talk for a minute?" she asked Pete.

"Sure."

"One sec." Jane took Mark over to the couch and handed him to Caroline. "I'll kill you if you've said *anything*," she whispered fiercely.

"Me?" Caroline asked, feigning hurt. "How could you think—?"

"Later," Jane said, cutting her off. She walked away, leading Pete into the relative privacy of the living room. Once there, she turned around to face him. "Please don't think I'm rude for not inviting you," she began. "But my family—"

Pete held his hand up. "I know. You're the youngest of seven—the only one unmarried—and they all give you a terrible time about it."

"Yes," Jane exclaimed. "But how—?"

"Your sister—Caroline?"

Jane nodded.

"She warned me. Said not to take anything too personal and to know you had nothing to do with anything that was said. She told me that any male who accompanies you is fresh meat for digesting."

Jane smiled. "Unfortunately, that's a pretty apt description. Once I arrived at the same time as the carpet cleaner, and everyone got all excited."

Pete chuckled. "Well, don't worry about it today. A little teasing is no big deal, huh, Maddie?" He tickled her chin. "Besides, your mom invited me before I'd even met you. I was pretty taken with her—she reminds me a lot of my mom—and I promised her I would come. When you didn't mention dinner, I couldn't think of a way to tactfully bring it up. So I figured we'd just deal with it here, which we have."

"Thanks," Jane said, still feeling terrible about the whole thing.

"No problem," Pete said. "Now if you'll excuse me, I was invited by your brother-in-law to watch a tape of Thursday night's game."

"That'd be Scott," Jane said dismally.

"I'm going to teach Maddie the finer points of basketball," Pete said.

Jane frowned. When had he started calling her Maddie? "Have fun," she said without much enthusiasm.

"Nice picture," he said, as he walked by a faded watercolor print of Jesus surrounded by children.

Is he joking? Like the rest of the mauve and blue living room, it seemed to Jane that the picture was very old and out of date. Both she and her sisters had suggested to their mother several times that the room could do with redecorating, but their mother always insisted she liked the colors— and that picture. Shrugging it off, Jane decided to go to the kitchen to see if her mother needed any help—and to talk to her about what she'd done.

She found Caroline at the island mashing potatoes.

"Mother, you really should get a mixer," Caroline complained. "These hand mashers are a pain to use and leave too many lumps."

"The potatoes are better with a few lumps in them," her mother insisted. "Hello again, dear," she said, noticing Jane. "Would you like to make the gravy for me?"

"Sure." Jane grabbed an apron from the hook by the refrigerator.

Caroline started right in. "So, tell us about *the man*."

"There's nothing to tell," Jane said. "He came home. We're working on being nice to each other and sharing the care of the twins." She took a pot from the cupboard. "Mother, I *really* wish you hadn't invited him today. Do you know how awkward this makes things?"

"I invited him as a friend of the family," her mother said. "And besides, you never know what may happen."

"But he's *Jane's* friend, Mom," Caroline said, surprising Jane by defending her. "And you know she's sworn off men. They either end up getting their tongues stitched or getting her fired."

Or they die. Like Paul. A swift, familiar pain tugged at Jane's heart. She set the pot on the stove.

"Stitches? I don't think I've heard about that one." Her mother arched an eyebrow. "But never mind. Mr. Bryant only got arrested," she said brightly.

"Arrested?" Caroline's head snapped up. "Ooh, I've missed something good."

"Not a word, Mom," Jane warned.

"My lips are sealed," Marsha said, then pressed them together. She opened the oven to check the rolls. "Perfect," she murmured, reaching for a hot pad. "Hurry with the gravy and potatoes, girls. I want everything on the table to be hot."

"Oh it will be," Caroline teased. "Jane's *friend* will keep us all melting, I'm sure."

* * *

"Do you have the stroller with you?" Pete asked as they cleared the table after dinner. "I was thinking we could take the twins on a walk."

"I've got the stroller," Jane answered. "But it's my turn to wash the dishes. This probably sounds silly, but we still follow the old rotation from when we were all kids. I'm up this month, then I'll be free for another six."

"I'll help," Pete said. "It shouldn't take long." He took the last plate from the table and headed toward the kitchen, pleased with the look of surprise on Jane's face.

She'd probably expected him to say he'd take the twins on a walk by himself. Part of him wanted to do just that—he'd yet to have any time alone with them. But he knew if he went without Jane, it would make her really nervous. He'd heard her speaking to her mom earlier, and he knew she was worried he might try to take the twins from her. The fact that she'd learned he was an attorney—and Richard Morgan's colleague—probably hadn't alleviated any of her fears.

Pete set the dishes on the counter and opened the dishwasher. "I'll load," he offered. "Time me. I've never done this many dishes before, but Paul and I used to have races when we were growing up. It's been awhile, but I bet I'm still pretty fast."

"Well . . . since I wouldn't want to deprive you of practice time . . . Okay," Jane said. She looked at her watch. "On your mark . . ."

Pete held his hand over the faucet.

"Get set," Jane said. "Go!"

Pete turned the water on and began rinsing plates and loading them into the dishwasher. Jane returned to the dining room to wipe off the table.

Caroline was on the ground, peeling food from the floor beneath Andrew's high chair. Seeing Jane, she looked up. "Pete's trying to impress you."

"He's trying to impress Mom," Jane countered. "He's smitten with her. She reminds him of his own mother." Jane leaned over the table, gathering crumbs into the dishcloth.

"That may be so," Caroline said, standing up. "But *you* should be impressed by any man who does dishes."

"I am," Jane said nonchalantly. "I feel sort of like Meg Ryan in *You've Got Mail*—you know, when her character realizes that Joe Fox is actually not her worst enemy." Jane scooped the crumbs into her hand and straightened, meeting Caroline's gaze. She lowered her voice to a whisper. "Truth is, I've been impressed by Pete all week. He's great with the twins. He's helpful and kind and funny . . ."

"That's good," Caroline whispered back, keeping an eye on the kitchen doorway.

Jane smiled sadly. "Yes, but—"

"But *what?*" Caroline demanded.

"I'm no Meg Ryan, and like you said earlier, I've sworn off men, because it *always* ends in disaster."

Chapter Forty-Two

"I'll push if you'd like," Pete offered, lifting the stroller from the Jeep.

"Um, sure," Jane said reluctantly.

"What's wrong?" he asked, balancing the stroller against his leg while he closed the hatch.

Jane shifted the twins on her hips. "Nothing," she assured him. "It's silly."

"Try me," Pete said as he attempted to open the stroller. "It can't be as ridiculous as my not knowing how to put a diaper on—or open this thing." He looked at Jane for help.

"There's a lever on the right side. You've got to unlatch it first."

Pete located and released the lever, and the stroller unfolded. He stood behind it, holding the handle while Jane situated Mark and Madison in their seats. When she was finished, he stepped aside, motioning for her to take over.

"I thought you wanted to push."

"I do, but so do you. Go ahead."

"Thanks," Jane said as she took the handle and checked the brake. "Where to?"

"You tell me," Pete said. "This is your old turf." Jane thought for a moment, then turned the stroller around. "There's a little park a few blocks away—not that Madison and Mark are going to get out and run around."

"Soon enough," Pete said. "Did you see Maddie pull herself up on your parents' couch?"

"I did," Jane said. "Watching the basketball game must have inspired her. She's ready to take on the court."

Pete grinned. "Nah. I bet she'll be a dancer like her mother was."

"I didn't know Tamara was a dancer." Jane gave him a sideways glance. "What else do you know about her?"

"Quite a bit," Pete said, wishing he hadn't mentioned it.

"You should write it down," Jane said. "And everything you can remember about Paul too. It's important for the twins to know as much as they can about their—parents."

Pete heard her hesitation and felt a rush of guilt. "Hey, about what I said the other night," he began, "about you not being Mark and Madison's mother—that was way out of line. I apologize. I was just angry about the fence and . . ." *What else had he been so uptight about?* Pete struggled to remember why it was—just a little over a week ago—he'd been so against Jane Warner's having anything to do with Mark and Madison. Now all he could think of was that she was a godsend, a miracle who allowed him to be involved in the twins' lives. "Anyway, I'm sorry. You're a great mother to them, and if it weren't for you, I *would* be looking at visitation rights with some adoptive couple."

"Thank you," Jane said sincerely. "You're great with them too. I certainly can't get Mark to eat like you do."

They walked in silence for a moment, and Pete's thoughts drifted back to Tamara. He knew she was Mark and Madison's biological parent, but seeing them with Jane, it was easy to see *her* as their mother. Still, Jane was right. He should write down Paul and Tamara's story.

"I suppose I could do something like that," Pete said. "Write about Paul and Tamara, I mean. Maybe in a few months . . . I doubt I'll forget too much between now and then."

"Whenever you're ready." Jane gave him a mischievous look. "You could write about the dishwashing races the two of you used to have. By the way, your loading time was seven and a half minutes, but your hand-washing time was *seventeen.*"

"That's because I had a slow dryer," Pete complained, rolling his eyes at her. "Remind me to get better help next time."

Jane laughed. "Then I'll wash and we'll see how fast *you* can figure out where everything goes. It's not my fault Mom rearranges all her cabinets once a month." She stopped walking. "Here," she said, stepping aside. "You can push now."

"You sure?" Pete asked. "You're not afraid I might run off with the twins?"

"No. Did you think that was why I . . . ? You did!" she exclaimed, looking dismayed. "Okay, the thought may have crossed my mind the first day—or two—but since then I haven't been worried. I—trust you."

Pete took the handle and began walking. "You're not very convincing."

"I mean it," Jane insisted. "I wanted to push because I *like* to. My sisters all married young and had children right away, but I've had to wait until I'm thirty to have the privilege of taking babies on a walk."

She hung back, and Pete glanced at her out of the corner of his eye. She looked embarrassed, and he wasn't sure if it was because she'd told him her age or the fact that she had wanted a baby for a long time. Neither surprised him. He'd already known that much and more from reading the file Richard had prepared. The file that *had* piqued his curiosity more than he cared to admit.

"I'm enjoying Mark and Madison too," Pete said. "But I also have to have a job, so I know I couldn't do it alone. I'm glad they have you."

"Thank you," Jane said again.

"You're welcome."

She laughed. "Aren't we the polite patrol today. We aptly fit the description I gave my sister just an hour ago—'trying to be nice to each other and learn how to share the twins.'"

Pete nodded in agreement. "That's us."

They walked in silence until they reached the park. Mark began fussing, so Jane took him out of the stroller. Pete picked up Madison, and they moved over to a bench.

Pete pulled Maddie's hat down over her ears. "Her nose is a little pink. Do you think it's too cold for them? I could run back and get the car."

"They've got all those layers. They're probably fine," Jane assured him. "But use this if you're worried." She handed him a pink, fuzzy blanket and leaned against the bench, enjoying the scenery.

Pete wrapped Maddie in the blanket, then watched Jane out of the corner of his eye. "Can I ask you something?"

She nodded warily.

"How come you didn't tell me you're Mormon?"

"I—I don't know," Jane stammered, looking embarrassed again. "I guess I was afraid it might be one more thing to make you want to take the twins. That and I wasn't a very good example of a member of the Church the night we first met."

"Oh." Pete looked down at Madison.

"Does my religion bother you?" Jane asked.

"Not at all." Pete spoke honestly. "The unit I serve with is based in Utah—I joined the Reserve to help with expenses when I was attending law school there. Anyway, I know quite a few members of your church. Good people. Great families—like yours."

"Thank you," Jane said, unmistakable relief in her voice.

"It's true." Peter leaned back against the bench, thinking of his buddies going off to what they called a sacrament meeting each week. He'd guessed that was where Jane was headed this morning when he'd watched from his upstairs window as she, all dressed up, loaded the twins in the Jeep. By then, he'd known she was a lifelong member of the LDS Church. Richard's research revealed that and much more.

Pete's thoughts shifted to the book Shane had given him when their unit came home this last time. Pete hadn't opened it until this morning, and then only because he was feeling restless since Jane and the twins weren't around. On the inside cover he'd found a brief note:

*In these marked passages lies the peace you're seeking. Good
luck with your new life.*

Shane

As much bored as he was curious, Peter had found himself flipping
through the book, reading a marked section here and there. Then he'd
come to a part about Jesus Christ's visit. Probably because he was so
focused on Mark and Madison, the verses about Christ blessing the children had caught his attention. That afternoon, the picture in the living
room at Jane's parents' had reminded him of those verses. It all seemed very
appropriate and good, Pete decided, that Jane belonged to a church so
focused on children. Maybe that was what made her so great with Mark
and Madison. Had Paul sensed that in her?

An image of his brother smiling at them came suddenly to Pete's mind.
Goose bumps sprang up on his arms, and for a moment he had the extra-
ordinary feeling that someone was watching over them.

Chapter Fourty-Three

"Ready to go?" Peter asked, walking through Jane's front door.

"Almost." Jane handed him Mark. "Maddie had to be changed last minute." Reaching down, Jane picked up the diaper bag, giving that to Peter too. "Go ahead and get in the car. I'll be right there." Racing to the bedroom, she grabbed her shoes and collected Madison from her crib. They needed to hurry to get a good spot for the St. Patrick's festivities on Fourth Avenue. Jane couldn't remember ever being this excited to go to a parade before, but today she was eager to watch Mark and Madison experience one for the first time.

She hurried to the Jeep, buckled Madison, and got in.

Pete grinned. "My, you're looking . . . *green* today." He took in her appearance, from her green socks and hoodie to her dangling green earrings and the green scrunchie in her ponytail.

"No pinching. I grew up with brothers and learned early to be prepared."

"Ah—you take all the fun out of things," Pete complained as he put the car in drive and headed downtown.

After several minutes searching for a parking space, Jane finally spotted one. Pete maneuvered the Jeep along the curb, and Jane climbed out of the car and opened the door to get the twins.

"Did you see your surprise?" Pete asked, looking across the seat at her as he unbuckled Madison. He nodded his head toward the back of the Jeep.

Jane glanced behind the seat and saw that instead of the large double stroller, there were two smaller, compact strollers. She looked at Pete questioningly.

"Now we can each push," he said. "Let's hurry. I think I see the start of the parade."

Jane held Mark and Madison while Pete popped open the strollers. "See? One hand," he bragged. "I tried out every single model at the store, and these were the best."

"Does the fact that they have *Jeep* written on the side have anything to do with it?" Jane teased.

"Maybe," Pete admitted. "It's good to feel manly when taking your children on a walk. But that's not the only reason. Look how great they are." He pointed out the different features. "Lightweight, yet they recline. And they have this cool storage pouch. You know, for all the Cheerios and stuff? And check out the tread on these tires."

Jane couldn't help but smile at his enthusiasm. "You chose well. And it was very sweet of you." *Sweet.* Where had *that* come from? Sweet was something you said to a boyfriend when he brought you flowers. She mentally cringed at her choice of words.

Thankfully, Pete didn't seem to notice. He'd already strapped Mark in and waited for her to tuck Maddie's blanket around her. Jane nodded that she was ready, and they took off at a brisk walk, heading for the parade route. They'd gone about a block when Jane heard someone call her name.

She looked over to the curb and was surprised to see Tara walking toward her. She was wearing a very tight lime-green miniskirt and matching sweater with some sort of boa thing attached—and she was holding hands with Zack.

"Jane, I haven't seen you in forever," Tara exclaimed, giving her a hug. "What have you been doing the past few weeks? You look—different."

Pete stopped and turned around, heading back to her. *Oh no,* Jane thought. He'd survived her family thus far, but Tara was another matter entirely. "We've been running to make it to the parade on time," she said, praying Tara would shut up.

"No," Tara shook her head. "That's not it. You have a look like—Who is this?" she asked as Pete stopped beside Jane.

"Tara, Zack, this is Peter Bryant. He recently returned from Iraq." Jane looked at Pete, apology in her eyes. "Pete, this is my friend Tara, and her friend Zack." She could have introduced them as 'my friends, Tara and Zack,' but she'd never counted Zack as one of her friends. Any guy that would hit on his girlfriend's co-worker was a creep in her book, and Zack had earned that distinction early on. For the life of her, Jane could not imagine what had possessed Tara to see him again. Had she forgotten about the loss of her cat, her art classes, her freedom?

Tara's eyes were huge. "*This* is Peter?" She smiled at him, exposing every one of her recently whitened teeth.

"That's me." Pete shook hands with Zack and then Tara, who, Jane noticed, held on a second longer than necessary.

"So," Jane said. "What are you two up to today?"

"We decided to go out to brunch—you know for the holiday," Tara said. "And then I'm going to show Zack some property. He's thinking of buying a house."

"Oh," Jane said, nodding her head, silently sending Tara the *Are you out of your mind?* look. Jane turned to Pete. "Tara is a realtor. In fact, she is *my* realtor. How's that going, by the way? Any offers on my cottage?"

"Not yet," Tara said brightly. "You know what I say. If it's meant to sell, then it will."

"It's *meant* to sell," Jane said. "And soon. Because if it doesn't, I'm going to be living on macaroni and cheese."

"You're so funny, Jane," Tara said. "You'll just have to come back to work, that's all. Did you know Jane is also a real estate agent?" Tara asked, looking at Pete. "She's given up a very promising career to stay home with those babies." Tara glanced at the twins. "Though they are getting cuter."

Jane rolled her eyes, and she noticed Zack shifting uncomfortably at the mention of babies. She watched his gaze drift to Madison and Mark and noticed his look of boredom change to one of outright repulsion.

Run, Tara, Run, Jane thought.

"It was nice to meet you, but we'd better get going," Pete said. "The parade is supposed to start in a few minutes, and we don't have a spot yet."

"Good to see you," Zack said, looking at Jane.

"Nice to meet you too," Tara murmured, taking a last, lingering look at Pete. She turned to Jane. "Call me."

"Sell my house," Jane replied, then hurried to catch up with Pete.

"Interesting friend," he commented as soon as she'd caught up with him.

"Yes," Jane agreed.

"Why are you having her sell your house?"

"Because she'll give me a break on the commission, and because she took care of everything with the listing so I didn't have to."

"No. I mean, *why* are you selling your house?"

"Because I couldn't live there with Mark and Madison." Jane started to jog, trying to match Pete's pace. "It's on Bainbridge—not very close to the hospital."

"But if you're a realtor, why not list it yourself?" He looked over, slowing his stride as he noticed her running. "Wouldn't it be worth the paperwork not to have to pay *any* commission?" He stopped suddenly. "Let's cross here. I think I see a place on the other side."

Jane followed across the street. They walked another half block before finding some free space along the curb. She spread out the thick blanket she'd brought while Pete lifted the twins from their strollers. They settled on the blanket just in time to see the last of the pre-parade activities.

"All right, Mark. This is it." Jane bounced him on her knee in time to the music of the approaching band. As the drummers walked by, she pulled the earflaps of his hat down to muffle the sound.

"You never answered my question," Pete reminded her. "Don't take this wrong, but it seems kind of strange for a realtor not to list her own house."

"I suppose it does," Jane said. "But you have to understand that before Mark and Madison came along, that cottage was the love of my life. It was a miracle I was ever able to afford it, and then I put all my spare time and money into the yard. It was very hard to leave—I don't think I could show it to people. So you see, Tara *will* earn her commission."

"Why not just rent it?" Pete asked.

"I am, sort of, for now," Jane said. "Tara's been staying there since she broke up with Zack. But she can't afford the whole mortgage payment, and after what I saw today, I wonder if she'll move out altogether." Jane sighed. "In any case, the cottage isn't practical anymore. With Mark's health problems, it will be a long time before I would feel like I could stay there—even on weekends. I'd never forgive myself if something happened and I wasn't close enough to the hospital."

Pete nodded and returned his attention to Madison and the parade. Her eyes were wide as she followed the activity down the street. Beside him, Jane beamed as she snuggled Mark close and pointed out all the exciting things to see. Pete watched her from the corner of his eye, irritated with himself that he *was* intrigued by her. Richard had been right on the money. The more Pete learned about Jane, the more he wanted to know. She was the most unusual woman he'd ever met, and he still couldn't fathom all she'd given up—the life she'd left behind to care for Paul's children.

Pete forced himself to look away, silently acknowledging that his curiosity, admiration, and respect for Jane were growing day by day.

* * *

"Today was a lot of fun," Jane said as she turned on the night-light and left the twins' room. Pete followed right behind her.

"It was," he agreed. "I think I got some great pictures. I really love this new digital camera. I can take hundreds of shots of Mark and Madison and store them on my computer."

"Strollers, a new camera . . . Aren't you just the proud dad?"

Pete laughed. "I guess I'd better be careful I don't become the *broke* dad."

"I know what that's all about," Jane said. She went into the kitchen and got two glasses of water. "And believe me, it's no fun."

"Then why don't you use some of the insurance money?" Pete asked. He sat at the counter across from her.

Jane frowned as she handed him a glass. "How do you know about that?"

"About what?" he asked, taking a drink. "About the money we can draw on, or the fact that you haven't used a cent of it?"

"I assumed you knew about the account," Jane said. She took a long drink of water, then looked directly at Peter. "Richard Morgan thought I was in this for the money. He thought that I'd preyed on Paul or something and was just waiting to pounce." She sounded indignant. "I'd much rather struggle than have him thinking—"

Pete held a hand up, cutting her off. "Richard *thought* you were after Paul's money, but that was months ago. Believe me, he's changed his opinion since then. Besides, taking some money out to pay Mark's doctor bills—instead of selling your car, for example—would in no way implicate you're after any money."

Jane's brow furrowed. She set her glass aside, folding her arms across her chest. "How did you know about my car?"

"Richard told me—only because I wondered what became of my Jeep," he added quickly.

"Hmm." Jane turned away, her ponytail flipping behind her, driving him crazy again. He watched as she carried dishes from the counter to the sink. "Speaking of the Jeep . . ." Pete said.

"Yes?" She opened the dishwasher.

"What would you think if I waited awhile on purchasing a car?"

"What would I drive?" She turned on the faucet and began rinsing out bottles.

"The Jeep, of course," Pete said. "Richard has an old Mercedes parked in his garage he said I could use. He was going to let his son start driving it, but his grades dropped and the insurance is too much."

Jane shrugged. "Sounds like you don't need to buy a car right away." She turned to him. "Unless you'd rather drive the Jeep, that is. It seems to me you're pretty attached to it, and pushing around a Jeep stroller isn't quite the same."

"No," Pete agreed. "It isn't, but those *were* some pretty good off-road tires through the grass." He grinned.

"How did Paul come to have your car, anyway?" Jane asked.

She returned to loading the dishwasher, and Pete was glad she couldn't see his face. He cleared his throat, wishing the unbidden memory of Tamara would clear away as easily.

"It was a wedding present."

Chapter Fourty-Four

Jay stuck the paper in his folder, shoved the folder in his backpack, and left the room. Instead of feeling self-conscious—as he usually did—about his inexpensive backpack next to the leather attachés he saw his classmates with, he felt great. The professor's remarks on the top of his paper burned into his mind.

Brilliant. At the end of the semester, see me about an internship.

What a wonderful thing that would be, Jay thought. Most internships paid considerably more than he made now, and with a little luck he'd have a great start to his résumé *and* a leather attaché by the time school started again next fall.

Jay left the building and zipped up his jacket as he walked across campus. For late March, the air felt bitter cold; he was still accustomed to the more temperate climate of Seattle. He thought—as he did every day—of the ocean, the city, and Jane. The promise of spring was in the air. Soon he'd have finals. Summer would be here before he knew it. Over half the time had passed until he would see her again.

He wondered what the past seven months had been like for her. Had she met someone? Did she ever think of him?

He'd dreamed of her again last week. She was downtown, walking around, looking at different vendors, milling through a crowd. She'd had a smile on her face—the prettiest he'd ever seen. And though they hadn't spoken in his dream, he could sense her happiness.

Jay waited for the light to change, then crossed the street. Dreams usually came to him for a reason. It had been that way in his family for as long as their history had been recorded. He found himself grateful for this dream now and hoped it was a sign of things to come.

Chapter Fourty-Five

Jane walked into the family room and handed Mark to Peter. "I've just changed both their diapers, so they're good for a couple of hours. Their pajamas are on the top shelf of the changing table, and you could probably skip their baths tonight." She took a can from the counter. "The formula is right here—you remember it's one scoop for every two ounces, right?"

Pete nodded.

"There's half a jar of peaches in the fridge and another of applesauce," Jane continued. "Try to feed them those before their bottles, okay?"

"Mmm-hmm," Pete answered, his attention on Mark and his toes. "This little piggy went to Pizza Hut," he began, wiggling Mark's big toe.

"Remember, after you've fed Mark, please watch him carefully if he's on his back. And just in case, I've written down the pediatrician's number and poison control. Of course, you know 9-1-1."

"I'm vaguely familiar with that one," Pete said dryly. He pulled his attention from Mark's toes to Jane's anxious face. "I'm not twelve."

Jane set the paper on the counter. "I'm sorry." She sighed. "I'm a little nervous is all."

"A *little?*" Pete asked. "All morning you've been acting like you've never left them before."

"Well, I haven't," Jane said. "At least not for this long, or . . ."

"With me?" he guessed.

Jane looked out at the backyard. "Well yes, that too," she admitted.

Pete got up from the couch and put Mark in his exersaucer—the latest in the string of toys Pete had purchased in the past month. He walked over to Jane. "Listen," he said, gently turning her face to him. He was surprised to see her eyes glistening with unshed tears. He'd known she was worried, but . . . "I'm not *that* bad, am I?" he teased.

She shook her head. "You're not bad at all. You're great—the perfect dad." She took a deep, shaky breath and looked into his eyes. "I . . . I need to know that Mark and Madison will be here when I get back."

"Of course they'll be—" His eyes widened as understanding dawned. "You're still worried I'll try to take them." It was his turn to feel hurt.

"Well you see it all the time on those flyers in the mail," Jane's voice wavered. "And you admitted you'd thought about it."

"Whoa. Wait just a minute." Pete held his hands up and took a step back. "That was over a month ago. I'd hope by now you'd know I could never do that. I *love* Mark and Madison, and I want what's best for them. I know that's you. How you could even think . . . ?" Shaking his head, Pete returned to the couch and sat down.

Jane stood silent a moment, her arms folded across her chest, head down. Finally she walked over and sat on the opposite end of the couch. "I'm sorry," she said. "This whole situation is just so strange—and difficult. My *life* has been so strange and difficult since I met your brother."

Pete looked at her but did not say anything.

She tried to explain. "Paul never talked about you, and because you weren't around to help him during those last weeks of his life, I really made you out to be the bad guy. When you didn't come to his funeral, or even call, I was downright incensed. I felt justified in raising the twins by myself, which is why I wouldn't use any of the money or do anything else that might be used against me in court. I hired an attorney, and I was ready to do whatever it took to keep *my* children." She looked down at her lap, fingers anxiously twisting her purse strap. "Then you came, and you were nothing like I'd imagined."

"Thank goodness," Pete said, his voice dripping with sarcasm.

"From that first day, you were great," Jane continued. "A natural with the twins—truly the perfect father. And now I know I'd never win in court against you. Even if you weren't an attorney yourself—" Jane bit her lip. "I'd never *want* to win, because Mark and Madison deserve to be with you. You're family. You're how I believe Paul would have been."

Pete leaned back against the sofa cushions but did not look at her.

"I'm sorry," Jane said again. "But I can't imagine my life without Mark and Madison. They're everything to me."

Pete sat up and reached for her hand. "They'll be here," he said quietly, looking into her eyes. A slow grin lit his face. "I hate court, and besides, *you'd* win."

* * *

Exhausted, Pete sank onto the couch. He looked over at the clock in the kitchen and saw it was two in the afternoon. *So much destruction in so little time,* he mused, looking at the family room strewn with toys. Maddie's newest game was to take everything out of the toy basket and throw things as far as she could. She actually had a pretty good arm. *There might be a softball player in her.*

Glancing in the breakfast nook, he remembered that he'd left the high chairs and table messy from lunch. Globs of banana stained the kitchen floor, and mashed cracker pieces reached all the way to the refrigerator. *Yep, that's some arm, Maddie.* Empty bottles lined the counter, and a small stack of messy diapers balanced by the back door, waiting to be taken to the big garbage can outside. Pete looked at the clock again.

Jane had only been gone *four* hours.

She'd be away the rest of the day, all night, and most of the day tomorrow, trying to finish up a landscaping job at Sequim Bay. She'd been excited about her work, he could tell, but she'd also been a wreck about leaving the twins. Whereas he'd been fine with the whole arrangement— eager, in fact, to have some time alone with Mark and Madison and prove to Jane that he could handle the weekend thing just fine.

Fool. He frowned at his own naivety. Coming over to play for a couple of hours each night wasn't the same as caring for two babies all day—alone. Still, he planned to have the twins fed and bathed and the house clean when Jane walked in the door tomorrow night.

With that goal in mind, Pete knew he should get up and clean before things got any worse, but the twins were napping right now, and . . . He kicked his legs onto the couch and adjusted the pillow behind his head. He'd take care of the mess soon—right after a short nap of his own.

Chapter Fourty-Six

Pete backed quietly out of the twins' bedroom. He paused in the hall, waiting to see which one of them would cry this time. Two minutes passed without a sound and he smiled with relief. Victory—*finally.* It was 10:30, though. An hour and a half later than Jane managed to get them to bed each night. What had he done wrong?

He stretched, his muscles complaining about the hours he'd spent on the floor today. Of course, falling asleep on the lumpy old couch hadn't helped any either. He ought to buy Jane a new couch. *You ought to buy her a lot of things,* he thought. *No, you shouldn't,* he argued with his conscience. Jane wasn't his girlfriend, she was . . . a wonderful mother to his niece and nephew—something just *slightly* more important. *You should be providing for her, or at the least helping her more.* Plagued by such guilty thoughts, Pete turned in the hall and headed toward the laundry room. He pulled the baby monitor off the shelf and checked that it was working, then went out the back door and walked over to the door of the attached mother-in-law apartment.

Paul's apartment. He'd never once seen the door opened, and Jane had confided that she hadn't been in there since Paul died, hadn't so much as changed the sheets. She'd simply closed the door, leaving it to be dealt with later. It seemed that later was tonight. He would do it for her.

Pete remembered Jane's hesitation this morning when she'd told him he was welcome to sleep in her room while she was gone.

"If you're bored tonight, you might visit Paul's apartment—and go through his things."

He'd caught the hint of suggestion in her voice and knew she hoped he would take over the task of going through Paul's belongings. Still, it was a job he was loathe to do. Only the thought of doing something to please her made his hand turn the key and twist the knob of the door. He opened it, reached inside, and flicked the light on.

The galley kitchen appeared bare, and the door to the bedroom was slightly ajar. Reluctantly he crossed the small room and went inside. Seeing the bed stripped bare, he let out a sigh of relief. A neat stack of blankets and sheets lay folded at the foot. A note was on top.

Peter,

If you're reading this, then you've decided to go through Paul's things. Thank you so much. It was something I simply could not do. I am learning there are many things I can't do without your help. Thank you for giving it so freely.

Jane

Pete picked up the note, folded it carefully, and put it in his pocket. He was touched that she'd thanked him, that she'd braved coming in here to get the bed ready. *Thoughtful,* he added to the mental list of characteristics he'd been keeping about her for the past six weeks. Jane was thoughtful and brave, and he would be too. Looking around the sparsely furnished room, he imagined Paul's last days. The books piled up beside numerous pill bottles on the dresser painted a clear picture. With a sigh of resignation, Pete crossed the room and opened the closet door.

* * *

The last number on the digital clock on the nightstand turned over, making a subtle click. If the room and apartment were not so eerily quiet, Pete would have missed the sound. But he didn't, and looking up he saw it was 1:45 A.M. After more than three hours, he was almost done.

Paul's belongings, clothing mostly, lay sorted into piles to be donated to Goodwill. Tomorrow, Pete decided, he would load up the Mercedes and take as much of it over as he could. Then he'd vacuum the room, open the window, and air everything out. Even if the rest of the house was a mess when she got home, Jane would be grateful he'd taken care of Paul's things.

Returning to the closet, Pete reached for the last item hanging on the rack—Paul's letterman jacket. He swallowed the sudden lump in his throat. Thus far he'd held it together. He'd been brisk and businesslike about the whole experience—quickly gathering up the more personal items, like Paul's toothbrush, razor, and prescriptions, and taking them out to the trash. But for some reason, the jacket—identical to the one hanging in the back of his own closet at home—stopped him cold.

It seemed like both a lifetime ago and yesterday that he and Paul had received their jackets. It was their junior year, and they'd both been star players on the varsity baseball team. He'd pitched. Paul was first baseman. Together they'd played an amazing season, leading their team to the state championship.

Clutching the burgundy wool, Pete felt his eyes begin to sting as the reality of Paul's death sank in.

His best friend—his brother—was gone.

Memories were the only thing left of all their years together—and Pete knew he'd shortchanged them both on those. Holding the jacket a minute more, he brought it to his face and inhaled, letting the musty fragrance take him back in time to the glory days of high school when he was the big man on campus, and his brother was always right there at his side.

At last he set the jacket by the door, in the small pile of things he wanted for himself. Blinking rapidly, Pete returned to the closet for the remaining items on the shelf. Reaching up, he pulled down an electric blanket and a plain, brown grocery bag. He tossed the blanket in the pile of things to be donated and carried the sack over to the bed. Laying the bag on its side, he noticed Paul's writing on the brown paper.

Tamara's things. Keep for Mark and Madison.

Pete stared at the words on the bag and realized, for the first time, that Paul would have been the one to go through Tamara's things after *she* died. What had that been like?

Sympathy was an emotion Pete had not felt toward his brother in a very long time, but he allowed it to surface now as he thought about the anguish Paul must have felt at losing his wife, fighting cancer, and knowing he wasn't going to be around to raise his children.

Pete's fingers trembled as he reached for the first item in the bag. He knew he didn't need to go through these things—if Paul had wanted them saved, then they would be saved—but something compelled him to reach for the tissue-wrapped package that lay on top of everything else.

Carefully unwrapping it, Pete was surprised to find nothing but a large bandage inside with a piece of paper stapled to it. Folding back the paper, he began to read.

December 1, 2003

Dear Mark and Madison,

You were the love of our lives, even before you were born. How your mother and I looked forward to meeting you, how we wanted to be with you. Please know we tried. Your mother held on long enough for you to be born safely. And I stayed as long as I could. We will always be watching over you. Be happy. Love your parents. There isn't a better father or mother on earth than those we have chosen for you.

Love,
Dad

The burning in his eyes returned as Pete reread the last line of his brother's letter. *There isn't a better father . . .* Had Paul really *felt* that? How could he when the last time they'd met—

Pete pushed the memory aside. He didn't want to remember that time of ugliness between them. Wasn't it better to dwell on the good times they'd had?

His eyes watered as he lifted the paper to read the blurred writing on the bandage beneath.

> *God must have known I couldn't live without you, Paul. Find our babies a mother. You know who their father should be. I'll be waiting.*
>
> *I love you.*
> *Tami*

Pete's fingers shook as he held the bandage and read it again. When had this been written—and by who? The writing wasn't Tamara's, and why a bandage for paper? He glanced at Paul's letter again.

Your mother held on long enough for you to be born safely . . .

Pete hadn't considered before that Tamara might not have died instantly in the accident. But the note implied she hadn't. She must have held on—long enough to tell someone her wishes. And one of her last thoughts had been of him. Astounded by that knowledge, Pete's trembling fingers released the bandage, and it fell to the floor.

It had been *Tamara's* idea first. *She* had chosen him to care for their children. And Paul had agreed.

I stayed as long as I could.

Stayed and found Jane, Pete could have added. His brother had done the best he could with what little time he had. *You took the gamble of your life, and your children's, that I'd come through for you,* Pete thought. He remembered the strange email he'd received from Paul—the missed opportunity for reconciliation.

All the foolish words Pete had said, the anger he'd harbored. The guilt that still weighed on him rushed to the surface, bringing a pain so great he could hardly bear it. If only he'd had one more minute with each of them. If only he'd forgiven them sooner . . . If only.

Burying his face in his hands, Pete bent over on the bed and wept.

* * *

Sunlight streamed through the window, and Pete cracked open an eyelid to look at the clock. It was 6:40 A.M. The twins would be awake any minute now. Kicking off the covers, he rose from the bed. He had a lot to do today and a new determination about him. Last night, after going through Paul's room and the bag of Tamara's belongings, he'd made peace with at least some of his demons.

Paul had loved Tamara, *really* loved her, to the bitter end. And Tamara had been one hundred percent devoted to her husband. The pages from Tamara's journal that Pete had read in the wee hours of the morning told the story from her perspective and made him realize things he never would have. Contrary to the original angst Tamara's love for Paul had caused him, Pete now felt oddly comforted by it. He found himself grateful she'd been with Paul through most of his ordeal with cancer. Pete had read of her sorrow and fear for his brother, and the long hours and days she'd stayed by his side through one gruesome treatment after another.

He'd seen the note and the box with the pacifier in it and felt a portion of the joy Paul and Tamara must have had, knowing a miracle had happened and they were going to be parents after all. He saw the plans for their dream house that Paul had so carefully drafted.

Pete knew he'd loved Tamara—still did in some measure—but he finally realized it wasn't with the same depth Paul had. Instead of feeling it was his ex-fiancée who had died in that car accident, Pete now thought of his brother's wife who had died—his sister-in-law. His old sorrow was gone. In its place were regrets that he hadn't forgiven earlier and spent what time he had with the two of them.

Pulling up the comforter, Pete tossed the pillows onto the bed. He cast a last, cursory glance in the direction of the brown bag on the floor—the bag that had revealed so much about Paul and Tamara's life—and his own.

Wedged in amongst the myriad emotions was a feeling of relief; the scene he'd made at their wedding, his bitterness, hadn't ruined anyone's life. Paul and Tamara—in all the roller coaster of their brief marriage—had been happy.

He felt awed and inspired that they had *both* chosen him as Mark and Madison's father. It was no accident or last-minute decision made out of desperation. Paul could have found a loving, adoptive couple. He could have given full custody to Jane. But he hadn't. He'd wanted them both.

The question was, what else had Paul wanted? Pete mulled over the last letter—long since memorized—he'd received from Paul.

I've left you three presents. One is taller than the others, but all are equally fragile.

A corner of Pete's mouth lifted. Fragile wasn't exactly the word that came to mind when he thought of Jane—following through with her threat to dial 911, showing off her arsenal of power tools, telling him in vivid detail the intricacies of Mark's heart condition. Yet fragile she was where the twins were concerned. He'd seen that yesterday when she'd tear-fully asked him if they would be here when she returned. Pete wondered if she was also fragile with matters concerning her own heart. Given what he knew about her, he guessed she might be. She might even be lonely and scared . . . like he was.

Take care of them for me.

Paul had known he wasn't going to be around very long. Pete wondered suddenly if his suspicions about Paul and Jane's relationship had been all wrong. Maybe the only thing between them had been a mutual love for the twins. And what if Paul *had* intended Jane and him to end up as more than co-guardians? Pete struggled to decide if Paul's intentions really mattered to him anymore. What good was there in avoiding such a thing at all costs, just to spite his brother? There wasn't. But what might be lost if he didn't at least explore the option? Much. A relationship like Paul and Tamara had shared. A mother and father—together—for Mark and Madison. A family.

Pete finished making the bed and left the room. As he closed the door behind him, he remembered his mother's words of wisdom after he'd had a fight with Paul when they were teenagers.

"When you hold a grudge like that—against your own brother—all it's doing is cutting off your nose to spite your face. Now you march up to your room and think about that."

He'd had a lot of years to think and knew she was right. Pete also knew, with sudden clarity, that he was interested in Jane Warner, and it didn't matter to him at all what Paul had or hadn't thought about that. The real question was what would Jane think about it, and what had she felt toward his brother?

A large dose of apprehension mixed with a thrill of anticipation surged through Pete as he thought of Jane. It had been a very long time—over three years—since he'd tried to get a woman to be interested in him. He wondered what his chances were now. Was it possible Jane felt the same tug of attraction he did?

Pete had no idea, but he intended to find out tonight.

Chapter Fourty-Seven

Jane pulled the Jeep into the garage, unloaded her tools, and entered the house through the back door.

"Hi," she called, walking into the kitchen. She bent to unlace her shoes, but not before her eyes caught a glimpse of the sparkling kitchen and her nose got a whiff of—*clean.*

"We're in here." Pete's hand waved to her from behind the bar. "How'd it go?"

"Really good," Jane said, tugging off her sneaker. "We finished the Malones, and I got the other contract."

"That's great," Pete called.

Jane left her shoes on the mat and walked toward the family room. She found Pete on the floor using Maddie's teddy bear as his pillow.

"The house looks great," she said, smiling as she looked around. The kitchen floor had been mopped, the family room vacuumed, and other than the small pile of toys that Mark and Madison were playing with, the whole house looked picked up.

"Do I pass?" Pete asked mischievously.

"Definitely." Jane shrugged off her jacket and knelt on the floor beside Mark and Madison. "Hey guys." She leaned forward, scooping them in a hug. "I missed you."

Mark immediately grabbed for the hair that had come loose from her ponytail, but Madison clapped excitedly and made her happy, spitting noise—the latest in her speech accomplishments.

"Hey," Jane said, turning her face away from Maddie's mouth at the same time she tilted her head away from Mark. "Just pull my hair and spit on me. Nice greeting." She hugged them both a second time, then leaned forward and set them back on the blanket.

Pete couldn't help smiling as he watched Jane. *Buy her new socks,* he thought, noticing the holes in her heels as she bent over. She had her back to him, and as she bent to put the twins down again, his grin widened in appreciation of her curves. He thought she looked adorable with her holey socks, denim overalls, and messy ponytail. Jane turned to lean against the couch and caught Pete watching her. "What?" she asked warily. Her hand went to her hair and she tucked a few straying pieces behind her ear.

"What are you thinking? I know I'm a mess."

Pete shook his head. "Not at all. I was thinking you look very good in overalls."

Jane laughed as she stood. "Thanks. *That's* a compliment I've never received." She picked up her jacket and went to the closet to hang it up. "Are you hungry? I can fix us something to eat."

Pete sat up. "You haven't had dinner?"

"No. We finished late, and I just wanted to get home."

"You go shower. I'll fix something." Pete stood and went to the kitchen.

"You don't have to," Jane said. "I mean, you're probably exhausted—either that or you hired a cleaning lady."

"No to both of those," Pete said. "And I *want* to fix you something."

Jane looked at him questioningly, but he'd already turned around and was rummaging through the refrigerator. "All right," she said at last, then headed toward her bedroom.

* * *

Jane pulled the towel from her head and shook her hair loose. She worked quickly, brushing out the tangles. She would have liked to blow her hair dry, but felt she'd already taken too long showering and cleaning all the dirt out from under her fingernails.

Normally she wouldn't have thought too much about wet hair or her nails, but tonight—something made her care. The way Pete had looked at her . . . the things he'd said . . . Even more than that, it was the way she'd felt. An undercurrent of tension seemed to be running through the whole house, zipping back and forth between the two of them.

Yesterday morning things had just been comfortable. Jane was Jane. Pete was Pete. And they were both doing their jobs taking care of the twins. Jane wasn't sure what had happened to make that change. She wasn't sure she *wanted* it to change. A comfortable friendship was how she would have described the evolution of their relationship over the past month and a half. If they left that behind . . . then what?

Bending over the sink, she looked at her reflection critically in the mirror. *Average* stared back at her. Brown hair. Brown eyes. Roundish face. Nothing exciting about that. Hoping to improve what she could, Jane reached for her toothbrush and mascara. If nothing else, she could smile with confidence and bat her eyelashes if called upon. The idea was absurd, as was her mood, Jane decided as she brushed her teeth. She'd probably imagined the whole thing.

She carried her dirty clothes to the laundry room and tossed them in the hamper, noticing the key in the lock to the outside door. *Did Peter leave it there?* She hadn't really expected him to have time to clean out Paul's apartment. Curious, she opened the door and stepped outside. The door to the apartment was slightly ajar and, like her house, it smelled of pine-scented cleaner. Turning the light on, she went inside and was delighted to find the cupboards cleaned out and the closet completely empty. The dresser and nightstand were cleared off and had been dusted. The floor was vacuumed. Seeing a piece of paper on one of the pillows, she walked over for a closer look.

Jane,

Thank you for being such a great friend to my brother—and to me. Hope you like the apartment.

Pete

"Do you like your surprise?"

Startled by his voice, Jane jumped. The paper fluttered to the floor. She turned to find Pete—wearing one of her aprons—leaning against the doorframe.

He looked at the bed. "Now that it's clean, I guess I can sleep over whenever I want."

"Uh—"

He grinned. "Just kidding."

Is he? Jane experienced a moment of panic as she bent to retrieve the fallen paper. Paul had lived here, but somehow the thought of Peter spending even one night in such close proximity seemed entirely different.

"The place looks really great." She straightened, biting back a laugh as she took in Pete's appearance. "You look good too. Maybe you should wear pink more often."

"You're just trying to get me to cook more," Pete accused. "First you abandon me to diapers and feedings, then, next thing you know, I'm slaving away at the stove."

"*You* offered." Jane's hands went to her hips.

"I know." His grin widened. "Come and get it while it's hot."

Jane turned the light off and followed him outside. "What are we having?"

"My one and only specialty," he called.

Feeling off-kilter, as she had since coming home forty-five minutes ago, she followed him back to the house and into the kitchen. "Do I smell—breakfast?"

"You do." Pete carried a steaming plate to the table. "I was planning to come over and make you breakfast tomorrow morning—since you're always feeding me—but I decided we could just as well have it tonight."

"It smells heavenly." Jane took a seat at the table and offered the prayer.

"I didn't know I had any bacon. Did you go shopping?"

Pete nodded. "Yes I did, brave man that I am."

"I'll say." Jane looked at him in admiration. "And tell me, how was it, shopping by yourself with two babies?" She poured herself a glass of orange juice.

"An adventure." Pete set a plate of toast and the butter on the table. "I found one of those two-seater carts and stuffed blankets all around the sides. Everything was great until Mark grabbed Maddie's hair."

"Uh-oh," Jane said over the rim of her glass.

"Uh-oh is right. I thought I might get arrested again, Maddie was screaming so loud."

Jane laughed. "How did you calm her down?"

"Um . . ." Pete mumbled, then took a bite of his eggs.

Jane folded her arms and sat back in her chair. "*What* did you do?"

"Bacon?" Pete held the plate out to her.

She took a piece. "Let me guess. Some beautiful woman took pity and came to your rescue."

He shook his head. "Actually, it was—"

"*More* than one woman? My goodness," Jane said. "I'll bet you had a whole gaggle of them following you around the store."

"Nobody helped me," Pete said. "Why would you think that?"

"Because it's a well-known fact"—Jane waved her hand in the air— "that women find men with babies very attractive. I can only imagine with you having two . . ."

Pete took a bite of bacon and leaned forward over the table. "You never told me that men with babies are chick magnets."

Jane grimaced. "I hate that term."

"Chick magnets?" He grinned. "Sorry. Funny though, how you failed to mention such an important piece of information. Why, I could have gone to the park, or the mall, or . . ."

"I didn't want to feed your ego." Jane rolled her eyes.

"You think I *have* an ego after a month and a half with you?" Pete stabbed a bite of scrambled eggs with his fork. "I've been humbled to the depths by you, woman. It's very hard for a guy who flies a multimillion dollar piece of machinery to admit he can't change a diaper or snap a onesie correctly, or do any other number of things I've messed up."

Jane laughed. "Yeah. You look real humble. I feel just terrible." She reached for the plate of toast and the butter. "Now, fess up. If it wasn't a woman, then how did you get Maddie to stop screaming? I know what it's like when she gets going."

Pete took another bite before answering. When his eyes finally met Jane's, he looked chagrined. "I gave her a candy bar."

"A *candy bar?*" Jane asked in disbelief. "Peter, she's only nine months old!" Her eyes narrowed and she pointed the butter knife at him. "What kind? Were there nuts in it?"

"Three Musketeers. I've seen them around here, so I thought maybe she had a preference . . ." Seeing Jane's exasperated look, he broke off. "I suppose those were for you."

"Of course they were for me. I've *never* given anything like that to the twins."

"Well then, that would explain it," Pete said.

"What?" Jane asked again, almost afraid to hear the answer.

"Now I know why they both preferred my Milky Way."

* * *

"He's finally asleep." Pete let out an exhausted sigh as he sank onto the couch.

"Thank you. Thank you. Thank you," Jane said as she struggled to balance a set of plans and two open books on her lap. "You are officially relieved from weekend duty." One of the books slid forward and she grabbed for it.

"Let me help." Pete scooted next to her, taking one of the books and half the blueprints.

"Thanks," Jane said again. "I'll be done in a few minutes. I just need to get a quick overview of the yard so I can start thinking about the possibilities."

"Does this mean you'll be gone next weekend too?" Pete asked.

Jane looked up at him. "Oh no. I'm at least two months out on this one—probably three—before I get started. The Saunders will have to approve the final plans first—and if they're anything like the Sweviecs or the Malones, that will take a month in itself. And after the plans are approved, I'll need to line up the larger work I sub out."

"What?" Pete teased. "You don't have a backhoe hidden somewhere in that tool jungle you call a garage?"

"I wish. But alas." She sighed. "That will have to wait much longer. Though I do have a marvelous drafting table now—thanks to Paul."

"I'm glad it was put to good use. By the way, everything of his that I saved is packed in plastic boxes in my garage. Your garage seemed pretty crowded, but if you would rather have them here . . ."

Jane shook her head.

"Well, if you ever want to go through any of it, just ask."

"Okay. Thanks again for doing all that." She began rolling up the plans. "Plastic was a good idea. It should keep out the moisture."

"That's what the beautiful woman who helped me at the store suggested," Pete said.

Jane looked at him again, her mouth partly open. "*You* are—"

"Don't say it. My ego, remember?"

Jane finished rolling the plans and made a point of hitting Pete on the legs before setting them on the floor. "I'll take that book now." She held out her hand and he returned it.

"Mind if I turn the TV on mute?"

"Go ahead," Jane said. "I need to mark a few pages of some of the plants they liked."

Pete turned the television on, and Jane continued to scan her landscape books, her mind already planning the layout of the Saunders' yard. Beside her, Pete clicked the remote until he settled on the news.

She finished with one book and started on the second, noticing Pete made no move to return to the other end of the couch. They were sitting side by side, his shoulder next to hers, legs brushing up against each other.

Jane stared at her book, trying to refocus her attention to deciduous tree selection, but her mind was elsewhere. How long had it been since she'd sat close to a man like this? *Since Paul.*

Memories of their movie nights, shared popcorn, and Scrabble games came flooding back. Her fingers stilled on the papers in her lap as she closed her eyes against the unexpected tide of sadness.

"Thinking about Paul?" Pete asked quietly.

Not trusting herself to speak, Jane looked up at him and nodded.

"I can always tell. You get that sad look in your eyes. It catches you off guard, doesn't it?"

"Yes," Jane said, astonished at his perceptiveness.

"That's the way it always is when you lose someone you love. Trust me, I've had plenty of experience."

"Tell me," she coaxed.

Pete turned the television off and set the remote aside. "Well, I can't remember my father—he died in Vietnam—so I can't say I've had those moments of intense memory and sorrow about him. But I still do with my mother—it happened a couple of times recently around *your* mom. Something just reminds me, you know?"

Jane nodded. She *did* know.

"And, of course, there's Paul. Last night when I was going through his things, I was doing great until I found his letterman jacket. Then for some reason . . ." Pete shrugged.

Jane resisted the sudden impulse to reach for his hand.

"Of course, maybe it's worse when you lose someone you loved romantically." Pete's eyes sought hers. "So when you lost Paul . . ."

"I was devastated," Jane finished. She wasn't certain, but she thought she glimpsed disappointment in Pete's eyes before he looked away.

She hastened to explain. "In my other life—before I decided to dig in the dirt for a living—" She gave him a shaky smile. "I was going to be a therapist. I've always had this need to help people. And no one needed help more than your brother. He filled that need for me very nicely. But the thing is, when you're doing so much for someone—like I was for your brother—you can't help but love them." Jane looked down at her lap, slowly closing *Treasury of Trees*. The book of Paul was over and done with—had never really begun, she realized suddenly. Was it possible her story with Peter could be different?

"I loved Paul," she repeated. "But it wasn't a romantic kind of love. His feelings were all for his wife, and I loved their children, and that was it."

Pete looked at her, unconvinced.

"You lived beside each other for how long?"

"A couple of months," Jane said. "But it was only so I could help with the twins—so they wouldn't end up in foster care. Anyway, it wouldn't have mattered if we spent a couple of *years* together. In Paul's mind, he was still married. He told me so once."

"I see." Pete wished very much he knew the circumstances that had led up to that conversation. He was certain she was telling the truth—about Paul's feelings, anyway. What he'd read last night had extinguished any doubts he'd harbored about Paul's loyalty to Tamara. But had Jane really only cared for him as a friend? Pete remembered her reaction that first night they met. He'd seen the same thing again from time to time and was certain, when she got that faraway, teary look, that she was holding onto some fond memory of Paul.

From the corner of his eye, Pete watched as Jane folded and refolded a sticky note. *I'm not the only one who's nervous. Good.*

"Nothing happened between you two?" he asked. "Not even one little kiss?"

"Not a one," Jane confirmed.

In a bold move, Pete reached for her hand. Holding it on his lap, his thumb began caressing her palm. "Do you know what I think?" he asked.

She shook her head but didn't look at him.

He reached for her chin and turned her face to his. "I think my brother was a fool."

Jane's eyes widened and she pulled her hand away from Peter's. Grabbing her books, she stood. "What a—a terrible thing to say. Paul was kind and good and—I've wondered, this whole time, why on earth you two were at odds because you both seemed so nice, but now I see—"

"Whoa," Pete said, standing to face her. "I didn't mean anything like that. I just meant that I couldn't have lived so close to you and not kissed you."

"Well then, I guess it's a good thing you don't live in the apartment."

"Jane—" Pete raked his fingers through his hair. *How did I mess this up?*

"I'm going to bed now. Please lock up when you leave." She tried to step around him, but he caught her arm.

"Look at me, Jane." She did, and he saw through her mutinous expression. *She's scared.* "I only said that about Paul because I was trying to find a way—I was trying to tell you I wanted—to kiss you."

"Please don't," she said, her voice trembling.

"Why not?" Pete asked. "Didn't you just tell me earlier that women find men with babies irresistible?" He risked a smile.

"And women find men with big egos particularly *un*attractive."

"Ouch." Pete brought a hand to his chest, and Jane tried to move around him again.

He blocked her. "Let me kiss you, Jane."

She shook her head and crossed her arms in front of her, books and papers clutched to her chest.

Pete took a step closer. "Why not?"

"Because bad things happen when people kiss me. It's disastrous—"

"Nothing bad is going to happen." He reached for her hands. Gently he pried her fingers open and placed her things on the side table. "Have you ever had a kiss that was *good?*"

She didn't answer.

Pete put his hands on her shoulders and his eyes locked on hers. "A kiss that made your breath catch and made your heart feel like it stopped for a minute? One you wished would never, ever end?"

Jane nodded slowly.

"Me too," Pete said. "A long time ago."

"What happened?" Jane whispered.

"She died," Pete said, knowing now was not the time to tell her about his past with Tamara. "What about you? Why aren't you with the man whose kiss swept you off your feet?"

"I got fired," Jane said with an embarrassed smile.

Pete smiled back, sensing her resistance melting. He knew she'd gotten fired—it had been one of the most curious things he'd found in her file. He longed to hear the whole story but didn't want to take them from the moment they were in now. "If you kiss *me,* I can guarantee you won't lose your job. In fact," he paused as if just then considering the possibilities. "You might just get a promotion."

"How so?" Jane asked, licking her lips nervously.

"Well," Pete drawled. "I have this theory that Paul wanted us to be together—to be more than Mark and Madison's co-guardians. To be . . . a couple. And I just want to see if that's possible. One kiss is all it will take—

just one."

"Just one?" Jane repeated, looking down at the floor, shifting from one foot to the other.

Pete nodded and worked hard to keep a straight face. "How well two people kiss is high up there on the compatibility measure."

He could see her struggling to contain a smile.

"So are you willing to give it a try—for Paul's sake?"

Jane was silent for a minute, her brown eyes glistening as she looked up at him. Finally she whispered, "For Paul's sake." Her eyelids closed expectantly.

More nervous than he would have liked to admit after all the hype, Pete took her face in his hands and bent to kiss her, praying he could remember how, hoping he could be half as good as the guy whose passionate kiss had cost her so much. After all, he didn't want to take away from that experience. He only wanted to give.

Her lips were soft, warm and . . . *still*, giving him the impression at once that it had either been a long time or she didn't know how to kiss. He endeavored to teach her, holding her face tenderly, gently increasing the pressure on her mouth. And suddenly, she responded.

He felt her arms move hesitantly around his shoulders, the light touch of her fingertips driving him crazy. Pete moved one of his hands to the back of her neck. Threading his fingers through her damp hair, he pulled her closer.

After that, he couldn't have said who was the one being kissed. But suddenly *he* was the one who couldn't breathe and was certain his heart had ceased to beat.

At last, Pete lifted his head, but kept his arms around Jane. She lay her face against his chest, and he bent to kiss the top of her hair. After a moment, she tilted her face up to his. Her eyes were sparkling with mischief and something else.

"Do you have your answer?" she whispered.

He nodded slowly, then pulled her tightly to him. "Yes."

A resounding yes.

Chapter Fourty-Eight

"Look at them," Karen said, standing at her parents' family room window. She watched as all the grandchildren and *Jane* hunted for eggs in the backyard.

Caroline came up beside her. "Mom said Peter came over early this morning and hid a bunch of eggs just for Jane. Can you imagine that?"

"And she gave him an Easter basket." Karen made a face. "Disgusting."

"Completely revolting," Caroline agreed. She sighed. "I'm so jealous. When's the last time you got something for *Easter?*"

"Last year. Play-off tickets," Karen said dismally. "Though I ended up giving mine to one of Scott's friends, so I suppose that doesn't count."

Caroline snorted. "Has that husband of yours *ever* given you anything that wasn't sports related?"

"Once." Karen held out her hand. "A wedding ring. He tricked me."

Caroline laughed as she put an arm around her sister. "Poor Karen. Ryan's no saint, but at least he doesn't have an addiction like Scott's. You really need to do something about that."

"I'm working on it," Karen said. They both looked out the window again.

"You don't suppose Pete put a ring in one of those eggs, do you?" she asked.

Caroline shook her head. "It's too soon, but I think it's coming." She watched as Jane opened a large plastic egg, and Hershey kisses spilled out on the lawn. She bent to pick them up, and Pete walked over to help. He knelt beside her, and Jane handed him a candy. In return, Pete grabbed her arms, pulled her close, and kissed her soundly.

Looking over at her mom, Caroline fully expected her to scold Jane and Pete for kissing in front of the grandchildren. Caroline remembered that was all *she'd* heard whenever Ryan was at the house and they'd been too friendly. Instead of scolding, she found her mother eagerly watching the couple, her hands clasped together, a look of joy on her face.

"I can't believe Mom is encouraging this," Caroline said. "It's not like Peter's a member of the Church."

"Not yet, anyway," Karen mused, turning away from the window.

"What do you mean?" Caroline asked.

"He's reading the Book of Mormon, and . . . Mom invited him to church tomorrow."

"Really?" Caroline's eyebrows shot up. "Does Jane know?"

Karen shook her head as she left the room.

Caroline looked outside again. "Maybe Jane *has* finally met her prince charming."

* * *

"Hi, Mom." Jane sat down on the second to last pew and leaned over, handing Maddie to her father. Since moving from her cottage, she'd attended church with her parents—she needed the help with the twins, and it wasn't like she could go to a singles' ward with two babies in tow.

"You're alone?" her mother asked, looking past Jane toward the chapel doors.

Jane turned around, following her gaze. "I'm always alone, Mom. Nothing has happened to change that."

"But it's Easter," her mother chided. "It would have been nice of you to invite Mr. Bryant."

"He knows I go to church on Sunday. If he wanted to come—"

"Morning, everyone." Peter's voice interrupted.

Jane turned to him, her mouth open. He smiled as if it were the most natural thing in the world for him to be there.

"Mind if I sit between you and your mom? I need to ask her something."

Jane nodded numbly. Peter squeezed past her and sat on the bench. Jane realized her mouth was still open and shut it.

"I'm so glad you could make it, Peter," her mother said warmly.

"Me too," he said. "Though my ride left a little earlier than I'd anticipated." He grinned at Jane before returning his attention to her mom. "If there's a minute before the service starts, I want to ask you something." He held up a Book of Mormon.

Jane's eyes nearly popped. *Where did he get that? What else don't I know?*

Beside her, Peter's head was bent toward her mother's as their conversation continued.

"There's a part in Mosiah . . ."

Jane's head whirled as she tried to listen and couldn't. Mark wiggled on her lap. She pulled out a board book and handed it to him. Conversations and greetings carried on around her. The prelude music ended, and a member of the bishopric came to the podium. Pete stopped talking to her mother and reached over, taking Jane's hand.

"You look great. Happy Easter," he whispered.

She tried to return his greeting but only managed a weak smile. She looked at the book in his lap, then met his gaze, questions plainly written on her face.

"It's from one of my buddies in Iraq. I've only read a bit. On days your mom babysits, she and I talk about it when I come home for lunch. That's all."

That's all. The words spoke volumes. *Don't make it more than it is. Don't get your hopes up.* She hadn't—hadn't even considered the possibility.

Until now.

But with Pete beside her, a baby on each of their laps, she could suddenly think of nothing else. Jane closed her eyes and bowed her head for the prayer, savoring a perfect moment, knowing it probably wouldn't last but wishing that it could.

Chapter Fourty-Nine

"Have fun tonight," Pete said, giving Jane a light kiss on the lips.

"You too." She climbed into the Jeep and sat down. "Remember—no turning Mark into a sports maniac."

"It's not Mark I'm worried about," Pete joked. "I fear what Maddie may learn in that houseful of women."

Jane laughed. "Don't worry. I'm sure a twelve-year-old's party won't be *that* bad."

Pete placed one hand on the car door and one hand on the roof. He leaned in toward Jane. "It's not the twelve-year-olds I'm worried about—but those aunts of hers." He gave Jane another quick kiss and shut the door.

She backed out of the driveway and waved as she drove off.

Whistling, Pete returned to the house to collect Mark and the bags of chips he was bringing to the "guys night" at Scott and Karen's house. The men of the Warner family were looking forward to enjoying the Sonics/Jazz game at a female-free house, while Jane and her sisters and nieces were spending the evening at Caroline's, celebrating Jessica's twelfth birthday.

A contented happiness surrounded Pete as he packed the diaper bag. He reflected on how quickly he'd become accustomed to life with babies, how fast he'd learned the names—and quirks—of Jane's family members. He was even starting to get a handle on the whole Mormon thing. He was surprised at how much he was enjoying the Book of Mormon, though he wasn't entirely sure he bought into the Joseph Smith story. He'd told Jane as much last Sunday after he'd gone to church with her. She'd said she understood and hadn't brought the subject up since. He appreciated that—appreciated her, and realized each day how much he'd come to care for her. The couple thing was working out better than he could have ever imagined. If this was what Paul had envisioned, then Pete knew he might very well end up owing his brother a lifetime of gratitude.

* * *

"Oh, Mom—I love it!" Jessica finished tearing the wrapping paper from a large box containing a karaoke machine. "Can we use it tonight?"

"I think you scored with that gift." Jane sat on the couch beside Caroline, watching as Jessica opened the rest of her presents.

"She's wanted one forever," Caroline whispered. "I had to get it—that and a half dozen CDs. Wait until she sees those. She'll be ecstatic." Caroline scooted to the edge of the couch and leaned forward over the girls on the floor. "Open that next, Jess." She pointed to a Winnie the Pooh gift bag.

"Who are those CDs for?" Jane whispered knowingly. "Seems like you were the one always singing into a curling iron while you listened to the radio."

Caroline looked at her. "You know, we probably *should* try it out—to help the girls get up their nerve. After all, if a bunch of thirty-somethings can get up and sing, then anyone can."

"No way," Jane said with a shake of her head. "I'm too old for that sort of thing—and if I am, you definitely are."

"Age is a state of mind, and my mind says we're both plenty young." Caroline rose from the couch, tugging Jane behind her. "Come see the costumes I chose for us."

* * *

"I don't understand," Scott grumbled. Kneeling behind the television, he fiddled with the cables. "It worked fine an hour ago. The kids know better than to come in here . . . What could have happened?"

Ryan looked at his watch again as he turned the radio up. "Shh. I think—yep, we just missed the tip-off."

"Who has the ball?" Scott demanded.

Ryan shrugged and put a finger to his lips.

"Chili dog, anyone?" Jane's brother Mike came in from the deck. "They're hot off the grill."

"Quiet," Scott barked. "We don't know who has the ball."

"TV won't work," Pete said, filling Mike in.

"What about the one in your bedroom?" he suggested.

Scott shook his head. "It only gets local channels. Karen uses it to watch those dumb craft shows on PBS while she sews."

"Maybe it's not your television. Maybe it's the satellite," Mike suggested, drawing the same conclusion everyone else already had.

"Trent's on the phone with the satellite company right now," Pete informed him.

Trent covered the phone. "There's an approximate wait of eighteen minutes. Maybe it *is* the satellite company."

"Great." Scott smacked the television as he stood. "We can't wait eighteen minutes. We'll miss most of the first quarter. Who has cable?"

Pete shook his head. "Neither Jane or I do."

"I've got the same dish as you," Mike said.

Scott looked hopefully at Trent.

Trent shook his head. "Uh-uh. Amy says when I quit buying stocks that end up worthless, then I can spend more money on cable or other things I want."

"We're doomed," Scott concluded.

"We've actually got cable right now," Ryan said, surprising everyone. "Just for the next three months on special—then we'll cancel again."

"But that's where the girls are," Pete protested. "We can't crash their—"

"Too bad." Scott strode to the coffee table, scooped up the bags of chips, and headed toward the door. "They'll have to understand. This is an emergency. Mike, bring those chili dogs and let's go."

* * *

"Aunt Jane! Aunt Jane! Aunt Jane!" Jessica and her cousins and friends chanted, slapping their hands against their thighs as they sat cross-legged on the lawn before the makeshift stage that was the back patio.

"In a minute," Jane called to the girls. Turning to Karen, she said, "I can't *believe* we're doing this." Standing just to the side of the cement, she watched as Caroline—dressed as outlandishly as she was in bell-bottoms, a psychedelic large-collared shirt, and heels—set up the karaoke machine.

Caroline held one of the microphones to her mouth. "Listen carefully, ladies, to the wisdom of the next song as Jane and I perform . . . *Cher!*" Taking the CD off pause, she held one of the microphones out to Jane, who reluctantly walked across the patio, her lime-green polyester fringe swishing.

Jane took the microphone. "*Where* did you get these awful clothes?" she whispered.

"They're Mindy's," Caroline said. "She's got a bunch of stuff like this in her old closet at Mom's. Now sing."

Deciding she'd look just as ridiculous whether she got into her performance or not, Jane turned to face the girls and began swaying her hips, her only consolation that at least the men weren't around to see them.

* * *

"I smell estrogen," Trent said, walking up the steps to Caroline and Ryan's house.

"I just smell chili dog," Mike said, letting go another belch.

Pete shook his head as he carried Mark, bringing up the rear of the party. Imagining Jane's sister Caroline, he smelled *disaster.*

Ryan unlocked the front door, and they went inside. The living room was deserted, but sleeping bags and pillows lay spread across the floor, and a pile of discarded wrapping paper and bows was stacked by the television. *The Princess Diaries* DVD lay beside the remote.

"Uh, guys," Pete tried again. "I've never had any sisters, but I'm telling you, I don't think this is such a great idea."

"You know, I think Pete is right," Ryan admitted as he looked around the room. There was a basket of nail polish on the coffee table along with a tray of small paper cups filled with mints and an enormous bowl full of assorted bite-size chocolate bars. Beside the chocolate was a book, *The American Girl Guide to Boys.*

"It doesn't look good," Pete said.

Scott grabbed the remote, knocking *The Princess Diaries* DVD to the floor. "I know," he said. "Pete, you and Ryan go find the girls and tell them our predicament. If anyone can smooth things over, I'm sure you can." He flipped the television on, then quickly found the right channel.

"Man, we're still down," he grumbled, his attention at once focused on the game.

Pete glanced at Ryan.

"Sure, why not." Ryan had a look that said he knew he'd pay for this later.

Pete followed him into the kitchen, which was also deserted, but music and laughter came through the open back door. He walked over to investigate.

Peering through the window, he saw the yard was ablaze with tiki torches and little flower lights hanging from the patio awning. A dozen or so pajama-clad girls were scattered across the lawn, sitting on blankets, kneeling and standing—all of them squealing with delight at the duo on the patio.

Curiosity winning out over caution, Pete pushed the door from the garage open and stepped into the yard so he could see exactly what held their attention. Ryan walked out behind him and they stood together, mesmerized by the sight before them.

Caroline and Jane, in full '70s regalia, from wigs to bell-bottoms and silver heels, were dancing around the patio. A small TV screen displayed the words to Cher's "It's in His Kiss," though it looked to Pete like neither of them really needed the prompt. Amused, he watched Jane wiggle her hips and pull the microphone close for her next line. He'd never seen her like this—never would have imagined she had such a wild, uninhibited side.

"Man, my wife is hot," Ryan muttered under his breath.

Pete was thinking the same thing about Jane, but said, "Her temper is gonna be hot if she finds us here."

"Yeah—*yeah*," Ryan agreed, snapping out of his trance. He began slowly backing into the shadow of the house. "We've got to get the guys out of here quick," he said, just as Caroline spotted them. "Uh-oh."

Pete saw the instant change on her face—the smile replaced by a ferocious scowl. Her eyes narrowed as she walked toward the edge of the patio. Knowing what he did about Caroline, Pete realized he had to do something quick or else be party to a major fight.

"Take Mark." Pete thrust him into Ryan's arms. Striding toward the patio, he put a finger to his lips to silence Caroline. He took the microphone from her and snuck up behind Jane, who continued to sing.

"How about my kiss?" Pete croaked into his microphone.

Jane stopped suddenly, turning to him, a horrified look on her face.

Pete stepped forward and pulled her into a crushing embrace, kissing her before she could protest.

After a few seconds, Jane's arms twined around his neck and she kissed him back. The girls erupted into cheers and applause. He ignored them, ignored everything else except the woman in his arms and the stir of emotion she was causing. At last he felt her pull away.

Jane looked up, giving him a sheepish grin as she pushed the wig back on her head.

"Well?" he asked, quiet enough that only she would hear. "What does my kiss tell you?"

Still reeling, Jane looked into his eyes.

"Heaven help me," she whispered, echoing the words so many heroines in her romance novels said when realizing they were completely, hopelessly in love.

Chapter Fifty

"No peeking." Pete led Jane out the sliding glass door to the back-yard. He stepped behind her, putting his hands over her eyes to ensure she didn't see. "Now the way this game works is you have to *smell* your way to your present. Go."

Jane put her hands on her hips and breathed in deeply. "This is impossible. Everything smells of lilac."

"Yee-es," Pete said.

Confused, Jane stayed where she was, her toe tapping on the cracked cement. "How am I supposed to find another scent over that?"

"Use your nose to follow the lilac," he suggested. "Find where it's strongest."

"What good will that do if I'm supposed to—?" she broke off, twisting out of his grip to face him. Her eyes opened. "Did you—?"

He spun her back around, pointing to the three new bushes in the yard. "One for each baby, and a third for me—I realize I'm at least as much work as Mark and Madison."

"They're beautiful," Jane exclaimed. She ran from the patio and went to examine the nearest plant. She leaned over, her face close as she inhaled the heady fragrance. "Where did you find such mature ones?"

Pete smiled. "In your little black book of landscaping. The people at Gearson Nursery were especially helpful when I told them who the lilacs were for."

"Aren't you sneaky!" She went to the other two plants, bending over to inhale their fragrance. "I love them. Absolutely love them," she said, returning to Pete.

"I'm glad. I know tradition is cut roses, but I thought you'd like these better. He took her in his arms. "Happy Mother's Day, Jane."

* * *

Jay rose from the stool and put his guitar in its case. He was surprised to have been called into work today—it being Mother's Day and all. Normally Sundays were slow, but maybe today sentiment had driven more men to the bar, hoping they could drown their sorrows in a beer or two. It wasn't a half-bad idea.

As if she'd read his mind, Diedre, the bar attendant, sidled up to him, a drink in her hand. "Share a beer before we close up?"

She looked up through long lashes, and Jay studied her face with as much longing as he did the beer. She was pretty, and was he ever thirsty.

"No thanks," he said, snapping the clips on his case. "I've got to study."

"You always say that," she whined, sliding her arm around his waist. Jay stiffened at her touch.

She took a sip from the glass in her hand. "What's one little drink going to hurt?"

Plenty. An ache—no, an urgent *need*—coursed through him. He looked down at her again. Her face tilted up to his—expectant, pleading, offering.

"I can't," he said, his voice not sounding as sure as he would have liked. Gently, he pried her fingers away and stepped from her embrace. "See you Tuesday." He lifted his hand in a casual wave but did not look back.

"Jay?"

Against his better judgment, he paused in the doorway. "What?"

"She must really be something."

"Huh?" He turned back and was troubled to see her eyes were glossy.

"That girl you love, she must really be something," Diedre repeated.

Jay looked at her, unfairly making comparisons with Jane. "She is," he said finally. He turned and headed out the door again. "She really, really is."

Chapter Fifty-One

Jane returned the last of their dinner to the picnic basket and brushed the sand from her jeans. Scooting closer to Peter, she lay on the blanket and looked up at the stars. "This was supposed to be your Father's Day surprise, but I didn't want to wait that long."

Pete leaned up on his elbow beside her. "I must say this is way better than the standard tie my boss gets every June. We'll come out here again for Father's Day. I'll give you a quiz to see what you can remember."

"I'll do my best," Jane said, sounding doubtful. "I never realized there were so many constellations." She lifted her hand, pointing to the black sky and the thousands of tiny lights sprinkled across it. "Big Dipper. Little Dipper."

"Everyone knows those," Pete teased.

"Let me finish," Jane ordered. "I was about to say 'or more scientifically known as Ursa Major and Minor.'" She pointed her finger to the east. "And over there is Hercules. Big brawny guy that he is."

"Not to be confused with Orion, farther west," Pete said. "Go on."

"Cassiopeia," Jane continued. "Perseus."

"Good," Pete commended. He took her hand. "You skipped a few though." Handing her the binoculars, he pointed to a smaller cluster of stars. "Name that one."

"Long name or short?" Jane asked.

"Short. Just remember it's small—so is the name."

She frowned in concentration. "Lyra?"

"Excellent," Pete said. "That deserves a kiss." He leaned over her, placing a chaste kiss on her forehead.

"That's all?" Jane complained. "Not much of a reward."

"Name that one." Pete took her hand, moving it across their line of vision. "Just southwest of Cassiopeia."

Jane studied the six points for a full minute. "I give up," she said at last.

"Camelopardalis," Pete said. "You owe *me* a kiss now."

Jane rolled to her side, facing him. "Of course. And for such a *long* name, I should think a long kiss is in order." She leaned close, and Pete pulled her to him. After a few minutes, her hair came loose from its ponytail, and the blanket wrinkled, the sand encroaching on them. The stars were all but forgotten.

Beneath her touch she felt Pete's heart beating as rapidly as hers. He deepened their kiss as his leg looped over hers, pulling their bodies together.

Breathless, Jane suddenly pulled away. *What am I doing? I haven't waited thirty years to ruin my future in one passionate night on the beach.* She lay back, knees bent, eyes half closed as she listened to the gentle lapping of the waves. Her toes edged off the blanket, curling into the sand.

Pete looked at her from the corner of his eye. "You okay?"

She shook her head. "No." Above them thousands of stars twinkled brightly, reminding her of the vastness of eternity—an eternity she didn't want to spend alone.

He reached down and took her hand, entwining their fingers. "Scared?" he guessed.

Terrified. Of myself. Of the path that led me to this moment. "Yes," she said simply.

"Me too," Pete said.

Surprised, she turned to him. She doubted that at thirty-four he was inexperienced in these matters. He'd certainly taught her enough about kissing, and she imagined there was much more he would willingly share. "Why are *you* scared?"

He didn't answer right away, but his fingers tightened around hers, warm and reassuring.

She knew he would always be the gentleman. If she wanted to stop, he would. Trouble was, more and more, she didn't want to. When Pete held her, kissed her, put his hands on her face or shoulders or waist, the world outside ceased to exist. It was even difficult to think of Mark and Madison during those times. But Jane knew she had to—had to choose a course that would allow them both to continue caring for the twins. Was there such a course?

Would Peter eventually ask her to marry him? And if he asked, could she say yes? *Could I be happy?* He made her deliriously happy right now, but would it always be this way? Would their religious differences eventually cause problems? She imagined sitting alone in church with the twins as they grew older. Who would baptize them? Would they even want to be baptized, or would they choose to believe as their father did? Jane imagined herself at forty, fifty, sixty . . . alone at church. Alone for eternity.

Tears gathered behind her eyes and she turned away from Peter, not wanting him to see.

He said nothing more about being scared, but instead asked her a question. "Did you know my father died in 'Nam?"

"Yes." Jane hoped her voice didn't betray that she was on the verge of crying.

"He flew a helicopter there—he was a medic. Got the Purple Heart for his heroic efforts risking his life to rescue the injured, those left behind."

"I didn't know that," Jane said, immensely grateful for the change of subject.

"Paul and I were just babies when he was shot down. It was April 1969. Witnesses saw his helicopter go down, but they never found his body."

"Did anyone else survive?" Jane asked. "Did they find his helicopter?"

"No and yes," Pete said. "He'd had one injured man on board, and the men who found him figured he'd died when they crashed—though his throat had been slit too—probably the Vietcong did it for extra measure."

"But your dad . . ."

"Wasn't with his chopper or anywhere else they searched. There was no sign of him. He just vanished. There are still about eighteen hundred MIAs from the Vietnam War, and my father is one of them."

"That's awful." Jane sat up, hugging her knees to her chest. "I can't imagine not knowing what happened to my father."

"My mother couldn't either, so for the first twelve years of my life, she simply pretended he was still coming back." Pete leaned up on his elbows, looking out at the ocean. "Every Christmas she'd buy him a present—some of them are probably still up on a closet shelf somewhere at the house. And on his birthday, we always had pork chops, mashed potatoes with gravy, and German chocolate cake for dessert." Pete paused, and Jane glanced over at him.

"There was a movie a few years back," she said. "With Cybil Shepherd. She'd lost her husband on their first anniversary, and for the next twenty years she still pretended he was around."

Pete nodded. "That was my mom."

"*Chances Are,*" Jane said with a sigh. She owned that movie—or had, anyway, until she'd destroyed half of her video collection during her breakdown after Paul's funeral. "It's a very sad, funny, romantic movie."

"There wasn't anything funny or romantic about my mom," Pete said quietly.

"No. Of course not." Jane sat silent for several minutes, watching as the waves lapped the shore. She looked at Peter again. "You said for the first *twelve* years of your life your mom was like that. What happened then?"

"We met Mary." Pete picked up a handful of sand and let it drift through his fingers. "She showed up at our door one day the summer Paul and I were twelve."

"Mary?" Jane asked, certain she'd missed something. "I'm confused."

Pete's fist closed around the pebble that was left in his hand. He looked at Jane. "Mary was a Vietnamese refugee. She was eleven years old . . . and she had a note from my father."

Jane's eyes grew wide. "What did the note say?"

Pete shrugged. "It's been a long time, and I don't remember all of it—but the gist was that if my mother was reading the note, then it meant my father hadn't lived. He said he was sorry—that he'd gotten lonely and made some mistakes. He hoped she would forgive him and take care of Mary, that she was just a little girl and innocent of his sins."

Jane's hand covered her mouth. "Your poor mother. What did she do?"

"Fell apart." Pete hurled the pebble toward the water, and it was lost in the foam. "She took one look at Mary, saw my father's eyes, and closed the door. I remember she went to her room and stayed there the rest of the day. I was worried about her, so I slept on the floor outside her door all night. She cried for hours." Pete's brow creased. "I'll never forget that sound."

Jane watched him with concern. She was touched he was sharing so much of his past with her, but she wasn't quite certain why he'd chosen *this* particular time to tell her about his parents. She sensed there was something he wanted her to understand—but what?

Peter continued. "When I came home from baseball the next afternoon, all the pictures of my father were gone—every last one." He paused, as if recalling something else. "She never mentioned him again, and if we did . . . well, it was bad. Once, I asked for a German chocolate cake for my birthday, and it sent her to bed, crying, for two straight days."

"Oh, Peter." Jane reached out and touched his arm. He didn't respond to her touch, and after a minute had passed, she asked, "What happened to Mary?"

"After my mother had gone to her room, I went out front. Mary was still sitting there on the step. She couldn't speak any English, but the escort from the refugee organization did. I had to explain that we couldn't keep Mary as they had hoped."

Jane looked at Pete with new admiration. "And you were only twelve when all of this happened?"

He nodded.

She rested her chin on her knees and stared at the water again. Something clicked as she suddenly remembered a conversation she'd had with Paul shortly after they met.

"Peter, Paul, and *Mary?*"

"Yep," Pete said without emotion. "My parents got engaged after one of their concerts. They thought that would be the perfect family. Two boys first, then a little girl—"

"Named Mary," Jane finished.

"Yeah." Pete picked up another rock and hurled it toward the water. "We should go now. Your mom will be tired." He rose from the blanket and extended a hand to Jane, pulling her up. They stood facing each other.

"That was quite a story," she said. "Why did you share it with me?"

Pete shoved his hands in his pockets and looked up at the stars. "Before I was twelve, I always wanted to be like my father. I dreamed of flying a helicopter into Vietnam and finding him—alive. Then, when Mary came, when I saw how my father had broken my mother's heart—I didn't want to be like him at all."

Jane touched his sleeve. "But you *do* fly a helicopter—in strange and dangerous places all over the planet."

The corner of Pete's mouth lifted. "That sounds like something Paul would have said."

Jane looked down at her toes buried in the sand. "Guilty," she confessed.

Pete lifted her chin and planted a swift kiss on her lips. "You're both right, that's what I do, though it has more to do with other things than with my father."

"What do you mean?"

"The Reserve paid for school, and later, when I had an opportunity to get out of the military, well it just didn't seem right. Anyway, that's a story for another day. What I told you tonight, about my dad, was about something else entirely—about you being scared—of me."

Jane took his hands. "I'm not scared of you."

"No?" Pete's eyebrows rose. "What was that all about, then?" He nodded his head toward the crumpled blanket.

"Okay, maybe a little," she admitted. "But I'm also scared of myself. You make me feel . . . You make me forget anything else exists but the two of us."

A genuine smile lit his face at her confession, but sadness quickly swept it away.

"You don't need to be scared of either of us," Pete assured her. "I decided long ago that I would never be like my dad. I'd never hurt any woman the way he hurt my mom. And there's only one way I can be sure of that." He pulled Jane close, turning her to face away from him. They stood silent, his chin resting on her hair, his arms wrapped around her as they watched the surf.

It wasn't that he was embarrassed or ashamed by his choice—his virtue—but he was afraid to see Jane's reaction.

"I decided long ago that I would wait until I married . . ." His voice trailed off, leaving her to draw the obvious conclusion. "There have been times when I've wished I *hadn't* made that decision, but then I've thought of my mother—the pain my father caused—and I always remember that I would never want to hurt a woman like that. Especially one that I love."

He waited, felt Jane catch her breath, and was grateful he couldn't see her face. He knew, in this day and age, that the announcement he'd just made was something akin to declaring insanity—or sexual dysfunction at the least.

"You're thirty-four years old, Peter," she said at last. "And you're telling me you've never—*ever* slept with a woman before?"

"At fifth-grade camp I snuck into the girls' cabin and stayed there all night. Does that count?"

She shook her head. "Afraid not."

He heard the tremor in her voice and turned her to him. "Jane, it's nothing to cry about. I promise you, I'm normal. Everything works—and I'm attracted to women—you ought to have figured that out by now."

"I wasn't worried—" The first tear rolled down her face.

He pulled her close, pressing her to his chest. He couldn't understand why she was so upset, unless . . .

"Oh, hey, you don't have to feel guilty." He rushed on. "You had no reason to feel as I did—to make the same choice. It doesn't matter what you've done." *Liar*, his conscience roared. "I only wanted you to know that I'll never cross that line, that I—ouch!" He stepped back, shocked that she'd pushed him away so violently.

"What is it that you think *I've* done?" she demanded.

Pete shrugged. "Well you're thirty years old, you're gorgeous—"

Jane laughed, then her eyes narrowed. "Go ahead and dig yourself deeper."

Pete scowled and moved forward, capturing her arms. "You *are* beautiful," he said. "And I'd be a fool if I thought I could be the first guy to have touched you."

Jane stomped her foot on top of his. "Well you are!" Her eyes brimmed with more unshed tears. "The most I've ever done was linger too long on that blanket with you tonight."

Astonished, Pete stared at her, reading the truth of what she said in her eyes. He caught her up in a hug, swinging her around in a circle. "So I don't have to be afraid of you, either?" he joked, setting her down again.

She tried to punch him, but he held her hands fast at her side. She sniffed again, refusing to look up, staring instead at his chest.

"I wanted to believe you were—that you'd waited," Pete explained. "You seem so different from the other women I've dated. I don't know what it is exactly . . ."

"I do." She spoke so quietly he could barely hear her. "It's my faith, Peter." She lifted her head to look up at him. "My knowledge of God's plan. I've always wanted to wait until I'm married—to save what is most sacred for the one other person I'll share my life with."

"Then I'm awfully grateful to your religion." Bending down, he pressed his lips to hers in a tender kiss, trying to convey the depth of his feelings.

Jane looked up at him, and he saw the flicker of hope in her eyes. It was one of her most endearing qualities—that trusting, open honesty. She couldn't hide anything from him even if she tried. Not wanting to dampen her spirit, he smiled, then kissed her once more, knowing all the while that he could not marry, *would* not marry while the chance still lingered that he might someday be gone and never come home.

Chapter Fifty-Two

Pete loosened his tie as he stepped from the Mercedes. Whistling, he walked toward the mailbox. It felt great to be home from work at one o'clock on a Friday—even though he'd taken the afternoon off because Mark had an appointment with his pediatric cardiologist. The twins' first birthday was a month from today, and he and Jane were hopeful Mark's recent progress would bring good news.

Opening the mailbox, Pete reached in and grabbed a slim stack of envelopes. Aside from the normal utility bills and bank statements, he didn't get much mail, so it took him just a second, as he walked back up the driveway, to scan through the letters. Stopping midstep, he swore under his breath as he saw the return address on the third envelope.

Ripping open the top, Pete pulled the paper out and unfolded it. He didn't need to read the letter to know what it said, but his eyes roamed over the page until he found what he was looking for—the date—July 26, 2004.

One month.

They'd let him have almost six at home, and now they'd given him one month to prepare to go back. Feeling numb, Pete unlocked the front door and walked into the house. He tossed his briefcase on the couch and crumpled the paper in his hands and let it fall to the floor. Walking past the table to the sliding glass door, he pushed the blinds aside and stood, staring into the backyard—his and Jane's. The fence had been gone for months.

She was outside as he'd expected. Maddie, wearing a yellow sundress with a floppy hat to match, toddled around the yard, pushing a Sesame Street car he'd bought. Mark was in the airplane swing, and Jane was pushing him, pretending to catch his toes every time he came forward. Mark's head leaned back, and Pete heard his laughter through the open window.

Jane looked over at him just then, her face lighting in a smile. Instead of her usual yard overalls, she wore a skirt and blouse, and they ruffled in the afternoon breeze. She reached up to push a strand of hair from her eyes and beckoned for him to join them.

More than anything in the world, Pete wanted to—wanted them—but he couldn't move. Instead he stood motionless, watching, as he swallowed the sudden lump in his throat.

* * *

Peter looked up from the stack of business cards on the desk and tried again to focus on what Mark's cardiologist was saying. He didn't think he'd missed anything too important yet. He and Jane had been commended on Mark's remarkable growth the past few months.

"It was all Peter," Jane said, looking at him affectionately.

Pete knew that wasn't true but he couldn't seem to find the words to refute her compliment—just as he hadn't been able to find the words to tell her he would be leaving.

The doctor continued, and Pete came to attention when he heard *Bidirectional Glenn Procedure*—the name of the second of three surgeries Mark needed.

"Really, Mark should have had this done several months ago," Dr. Ray continued. "And now that he's doing so much better, we don't want to delay." He pulled out a date book. "How about Thursday, August twelfth?"

"Do you have anything sooner?" Pete asked. "Anything in July, maybe?"

"Hmm," Dr. Ray flipped the calendar back a page. "I don't, and it is best to have this lead time. We'll need to change some of Mark's medication routine, and he'll need to go on antibiotics before the operation—there's always the risk of infection." He turned to Jane. "Of course you know that, Miss Warner."

Jane nodded. "I've told Peter how close it was after Mark's first surgery."

Dr. Ray continued. "And Mark will need some additional appointments beforehand—lab work and such."

Jane shuddered.

Pete squeezed her hand. *How could he leave her to face this alone?*

"August twelfth is fine," she said, giving Pete a brave smile. "I need some time to prepare for it too."

"Good." Dr. Ray penciled it in his book. "It will be a morning appointment, though I'm not sure what time exactly. Elaine handles the details with the hospital. She'll also talk to you about finances. But before you leave, let's go over what needs to happen in the next six weeks."

Pete half listened to the conversation. Jane had her PDA out, taking copious notes, so he knew they'd have all the needed information. His mind raced with possibilities. *Could* he postpone his return by a few weeks? What circumstances justified such a thing? He knew acceptable reasons were out there—but they were scarce. Being with a unit based in religion-and-family-oriented Utah, almost all the men he served with had families. Several of their wives had given birth while their husbands were in Iraq, and he knew others whose families had suffered through all sorts of hard times—serious illnesses and surgeries included—while their husbands and fathers were gone.

Pete knew his chances of a delayed return were slim to none.

Jane rose from her chair, and he followed. Shaking Dr. Ray's hand, they left the office and went to talk finances with the office manager. The news was not encouraging. The twins were now on his insurance, thankfully, but when he returned to Iraq, Pete wasn't sure how that would work. Richard had been more than generous, and Pete didn't want to abuse that generosity by asking for benefits when he wasn't around to earn them. He hated feeling so obligated to the firm.

He sighed aloud as they finally left the office.

"Are you feeling okay?" Jane asked. Mark slept in her arms.

"No. In fact, I think I'd better skip tonight."

"Oh." Jane looked away, but not before he saw the disappointment in her eyes. They walked in silence to the parking garage, where he opened the door for her after she'd put Mark in his car seat.

"Thank you," she murmured as she sat down.

Pete closed the door and walked around to the driver's side. The ride home was quiet. When they reached Jane's house, he opened her door again and carried Mark up the walk.

"If you change your mind, just come over . . . I made a big lasagna."

"I know, and I'm sorry." He'd raved about her lasagna and had seconds and thirds the last time she'd fixed it. He leaned forward, handed Mark to her, and gave her a kiss on the cheek. "I'll call you tomorrow."

Jane nodded and turned to go into the house. Pete waited until she'd closed the door, then returned to his car. He knew he'd hurt her, but his head *was* pounding, and he couldn't think about being around Jane or Mark or Madison until he'd come to terms with the thought of leaving them.

Chapter Fifty-Three

Pete rang the doorbell, then shoved his hands in his pockets as he waited outside Richard's house. Inside, he heard screaming and a shuffle. A moment later the door flew open. Richard's teenage daughter, Chloe, stood there.

"Beat you," she called to her younger brother who stood panting behind her.

"Whatever . . . cheater." He stuck his tongue out before retreating into the house.

Chloe turned back to Peter. Recognition dawned and she gave him a flirty smile. "Hi. You wanna see my dad?"

Pete nodded.

"Come on in. He and Charlie are having an argument about grades right now. Dad will be glad for the break."

Smiling at this information, Pete followed her into the house. Chloe led him through the formal living room into Richard's study.

"I'll get my dad."

"Thanks," Pete sat on the leather couch as she left the room. The study was immaculate, as the living room had been. Richard's volumes of books were alphabetized on the surrounding shelves, his desk clear, and the rug looked like it had never been walked on. But Pete knew that just outside the double French doors, the rest of the house was a different story. He couldn't hold back a grin as he saw Richard's youngest, thirteen-year-old Chris, zoom by on roller blades.

"Now ya won't beat me, Chloe," Chris yelled.

Pete caught a flash of the hockey stick trailing behind Chris, and the kids' Labrador followed in hot pursuit. Pete tried to imagine Mark as a rambunctious teenager and couldn't. Would he and Maddie fight like that? Peter remembered that he and Paul certainly had. He guessed sibling rivalry was probably pretty normal—even traceable back to the beginning of time. Cain and Abel hadn't exactly been best friends.

Peter's lips twisted in a wry smile. Funny how his thoughts had turned to scripture so easily. Attributable, no doubt, to the discussions he had with Jane's mother several times a week during his lunch hour. He thought about the video she'd shown him on Thursday, and he wondered if Joseph Smith had ever fought with his brother Hyrum.

What does it matter, and why are you thinking about it?

Pete watched as Chris flew past the door again. He looked like a pretty normal, sweaty, self-absorbed, thirteen-year-old boy. It was difficult to imagine that the most important revelation in modern history would have been entrusted to a teenager like him.

A minute later, Richard's wife Candice walked by with a laundry basket balanced on her hip. Seeing Peter, she stopped in surprise.

"Hello, Peter." Her hand went self-consciously to the bandanna tied in her hair. "Does Richard know you're here?"

"Chloe went to tell him," Pete said, glad for the interruption. He had enough to deal with right now without the added stress of throwing religious indecision into the pot.

Candice frowned. "Chloe's still here? She was supposed to go babysitting twenty minutes ago. I'll see what's keeping Richard." She waved a hand at Pete as she left the room.

Pete leaned back on the sofa and put one leg up on his knee. He looked around the room at the pictures on the wall, keeping his mind focused on the happiness that was Richard's chaotic family.

"Peter." Richard walked into the room. He had sweats and a baseball cap on—entirely different from his office attire—but Pete rose to greet his boss just the same.

"Sorry to interrupt your Saturday."

"No problem." Richard reached behind him to close the French doors. He walked across the room. "What's up?'

Pete withdrew the wrinkled paper from his shirt pocket. "My unit's been called up again."

"When?" Richard looked somber as he sat behind the desk.

"End of July. I've got a month to put everything in order."

Richard looked at him steadily. "What isn't in order?"

"My job," Pete said. "I've left you twice before."

"And proven your worth each time you've returned. Don't worry about your employment," Richard assured him.

"Thank you." Pete hesitated. "I was also wondering what it would take to continue my health insurance while I'm gone. I'm willing to pay a COBRA if I can maintain the same benefits."

Richard's eyebrows rose. "Has the military stopped covering its own?"

"It's not me I'm worried about," Pete explained. "Mark is having open-heart surgery in August. It's going to wipe out almost all of Jane's account if Mark's coverage goes down."

"She doesn't have health insurance?" Richard guessed.

Pete shook his head. "She's not going back to her old job. Her landscape business is doing really well lately, but not so much that she could afford to insure herself or the children. And Paul left too much money for the twins to qualify for Medicaid. We're caught right in the middle."

"I see." Richard leaned back in his chair, a contemplative look on his face. "I think we can work something out with the insurance. But have you ever thought about what might happen if *Jane* became sick or injured?"

Pete refolded the paper and stuck it in his pocket. He looked at Richard. "I have."

"She really ought to be covered, too."

"Are you offering?" Pete asked, suddenly uncomfortable with the conversation.

"I'd like to," Richard said. "But you know my hands are tied. Unlike Mark and Madison, Jane isn't related to you. Now, were you to marry her before you go . . ." He let the possibility hang in the air.

"I can't."

"Why not?" Richard leaned forward over the desk. "You're crazy about her, and she's in love with you. That much was obvious at the dinner last week. You couldn't keep your eyes off each other, and every time she spoke to Dave or Cameron, you looked like you were going to rip their heads off."

Pete frowned. He had wanted to rip their heads off, or at the very least whisk Jane away each time he saw one of the firm's career bachelors talking to her—or stalking her as he'd seen it. He wanted to protect her from guys like that, from everything. Yet . . . "I *can't* marry her," Pete reiterated.

"Why?" Richard demanded. "Because you're leaving? People do it all the time, Peter. Men have been going to war for centuries, leaving their families behind. It's tough, but it's done."

"I've seen the other side of that," Pete reminded him. "I've seen what happens when those men don't come home. Their families suffer—for years. I won't do that to Jane. I won't tie her heart up until I know for sure I'm going to be around to keep hold of it."

"That's a fine sentiment," Richard said. "But I think it's a little late. Married or not, that girl has already given her heart to you. It seems the responsible thing now would be to protect it as best you can while you're gone."

"Dad?" Chloe stood on the other side of the French doors, knocking.

Richard beckoned for her to come in.

Chloe opened one of the doors and poked her head inside the room. "Can you give me a ride? I'm late for a babysitting job."

"Sure, honey. We're just finishing. Grab my keys and get in the car. I'll be right there."

"Thanks, Dad. Bye, Pete." She backed out of the room.

Richard stood. "I'll talk to Joan on Monday. She'll let you know what we need to do to continue the twins' coverage while you're gone."

"Thanks." Pete rose from the couch.

"When is your time with the Reserves up?" Richard asked as he walked around the desk.

"Supposed to be next October," Pete said. "But right now there's a moratorium of sorts—no one can get out as long as we're still this involved in Iraq. I don't know how long it'll be before that changes."

"But you will get out when the opportunity comes?" Richard asked.

"Yes," Pete said. "No doubts. I've had enough. I wish I were done now."

They went through the living room to the front door. Richard walked him to the Mercedes.

"Interesting, isn't it," Richard said, "how you were so adamant to reenlist and had no reservations about leaving Tamara."

"And played the perfect martyr when my brother stepped in," Pete finished.

Richard nodded. "Yet now you don't want to go. Are you sure it's all about those babies?" he asked. "Think about it, Peter. You've got one month. Use it wisely."

Chapter Fifty-Four

Jane sat in bed next to a half-full box of Kleenex and a wad of moist, used tissues—bags of fun-size candy bars on either side of her. She'd cried enough tonight to make Tara look like a dry well.

Savagely, she unwrapped another Three Musketeers bar and shoved it in her mouth at the same time she bit into a Milky Way. She'd started buying bags of those too, for when Pete was around. Which had been every day—until recently. Since their night on the beach nearly two weeks ago, an unspoken pact had been made between them. The passionate kissing had ceased, replaced by chaste kisses and infrequent hand-holding. There were no more dates without the twins, and Pete left immediately after Mark and Madison were in bed each night. Jane knew it was good they were keeping to such boundaries, and yet . . . She hadn't wanted it to be the beginning of the end.

After Pete's silence at Mark's appointment yesterday, and missing him last night, she'd held onto the hope that their Saturday would be good. But his blinds had remained closed all morning, and when Jane took the twins for a walk around the block, his car was gone. He'd finally called at five to tell her he wouldn't be over that night or the next day.

Jane tore the wrapper from another candy bar, musing that if she couldn't have the man, at least she could have his chocolate. She sniffed loudly, then sneezed. Reaching for the remote, she turned up the volume and tried to concentrate on the movie she'd chosen to torture herself with—her Clean Cinema version of *An Officer and a Gentleman*. She was just about to the part where Richard Gere, dressed in full uniform, came into the factory and swept Debra Winger off her feet—literally. It was a scene that always made her heart soar. Today it just made her heart *sore*.

Jane blew her nose again. She wanted to be swept off her feet. Actually, she had been. The only problem was, she'd been dropped on the floor at the end—and she was pretty certain she knew why. At the beach, Peter had told her he was grateful for her religion, but even as he'd spoken the words, she'd sensed his hesitation. He began pulling away from her that night, and instead of feeling devastated, Jane knew she should be grateful. She'd been praying for the strength to do the right thing, and it seemed Heavenly Father was helping her out by having Peter end their relationship. It looked like she wouldn't be faced with the agonizing decision of marrying outside the Church after all.

Fresh tears squeezed from her eyes, and Jane fell over on the bed, landing on the crumpled tissue and wrappers. Would it have been so terrible if she'd married him? She loved him. He'd almost said he loved her. Together, as a real family, they would be better parents for Mark and Madison. *Is that so wrong, Heavenly Father? I love him so much. And he* is *a good man.*

"He is," she said. "I will," she whispered, knowing that's what she'd say if Peter asked her to marry him at this very moment. But something inside told her he wasn't going to ask.

She reached for her pillow and curled herself around it. She felt hopeless. Not all the chocolate in the world could fix her broken heart.

Chapter Fifty-Five

Jane glanced again at the paper on the seat beside her. The pink parchment was still there, date, time, and location emblazoned across the middle. She hadn't imagined the whole thing—which was very good, considering she'd spent the last three days exfoliating her face, doing hours of Tae Bo, and eating nothing but grapefruit. It took a lot of effort to make up for Saturday night's consumption of nearly two entire bags of fun-size chocolate bars.

It had been a weird week since then. Peter came over Monday, but he hadn't stayed long, hardly speaking to her, not even offering an apology or explanation for being out of the picture all weekend. She'd fed him dinner, but their meal was awkward, so she decided she wasn't going to bother cooking anymore. If he was so disenchanted with her, then he could fix his own meals.

Tuesday morning a bouquet of mixed roses was delivered to her door. The accompanying note from Peter apologized for his strange and distant behavior. He said he needed a couple of days to take care of some things and asked her to meet him Wednesday night at the Emerald Bay address on the card.

So here she was.

But where was Peter? It was five minutes after six, and she saw no sign of him. Deciding she might as well get out and look around, Jane stepped from the Jeep, careful to make sure her black skirt cleared the door. Peter had invited her on a bay cruise—that much she was sure of after looking up the address on the Internet. She'd worn her best skirt and borrowed a blouse and a strand of pearls from Karen for the occasion. But what the occasion was, she still didn't know. Why hadn't Peter just picked her up at the house? And what about the roses? She knew yellow stood for friendship and red for love, but what were yellow, red, white, and pink all mixed together supposed to mean?

She felt utterly confused.

Jane wandered across the nearly empty parking lot to the ramp, toward an elderly gentleman standing at the base.

"Miss Warner?" He smiled at her, giving a slight bow.

"Y-yes," Jane said. "Is there a message for me? It seems my date isn't here and—"

"No message," the man said. "Allow me." He held his elbow out, inviting her to take his arm.

Feeling foolish and more than a little leery, Jane placed her hand lightly on his sleeve. "Is Peter here, then?"

The man winked at her. "Not yet, but soon." He began walking up the ramp. Jane held back. For a second she wondered if it was all some wild plot—maybe Peter was planning for her to *accidentally* fall into the bay—leaving him with full custody of the twins. She supposed, given his recent weird behavior, that anything was possible.

The man turned back to her. "I assure you, Mr. Bryant is on his way."

Jane hesitated another second, then finally pushed her misgivings aside. She'd told Peter she trusted him, and she meant it. Other than acting strange the past few days, he'd never been anything but a perfect gentleman with her. Forcing a smile to her lips, Jane took the man's arm and proceeded to board the boat.

He led her through the main cabin—empty now, though Jane could see that it could easily accommodate at least fifty people. Linen-covered tables for two lined the windows on either side. The room smelled of new paint and carpet. She followed the man across a plastic walkway and up a set of winding stairs, then found herself in a smaller room, this one set with only one table at the far end of the cabin.

He led her there, held out one of the two chairs, and beckoned for her to sit. Jane slid into her seat, then looked up.

"We'll be under way shortly," he said. "May I offer you some wine to begin with tonight?"

"No, thank you." She imagined the headline. *Intoxicated mother falls to her death.* "A bottled water would be great."

The man nodded and left the cabin, leaving Jane alone in the quiet. She looked around the room. Plush velvet couches, covered in plastic, lined the walls. A crystal chandelier hung from the ceiling, and laying on a table in the middle of the room was a telescope. She let out a breath of relief. A *telescope*—of course. The stars would be much brighter out on the water, away from the lights of the city. Remembering the times they'd counted stars, she felt herself begin to relax.

Pushing back her chair, Jane rose and walked around the room, checking out the view from each bank of windows. She took her phone from her purse and called Caroline.

"Has he asked you yet?" Caroline sounded breathless, like she'd just run up the stairs.

"No," Jane whispered, though she was still alone. "I really don't think that's what this is about."

"But you *are* on a boat?" Caroline asked. "Is it nice?"

"Very," Jane assured her, looking around. "I'm all alone right now, though. This old guy escorted me on board, and no one else is here. It's a little creepy. Call me in, say, twenty minutes, okay?"

"I will. I've got to run to the store. The guys are here again tonight, and they need snacks." Caroline sighed into the phone. "Apparently, there's some really important baseball game on ESPN. I wish Karen would just give in and get their stupid satellite fixed. I'm sick to death of sports."

Jane laughed. "You're getting soft. Used to be, you wouldn't put up with stuff like this."

"The things we do for the men we love," Caroline said.

Thinking of all she'd been through the past week, Jane silently agreed. "Talk to you later, then." She disconnected the call and put the phone back into her purse just as footsteps sounded on the stairs. She turned to find Peter dressed in a suit and tie, standing across the room. He came toward her, an unreadable expression on his face. A few feet away, he stopped. Reaching into his coat pocket, he pulled out a bottled water.

"Tim said you asked for this." Pete handed the bottle to her. "Hopefully it's not to clobber me with, though I'm sure I deserve it after the last few days."

"I wasn't thinking of anything that violent." Jane unscrewed the cap. "Though I imagine it would be immensely satisfying to pour the entire thing over your head." She took a drink.

Pete leaned forward. "Be my guest, if it will make you feel better."

"No thanks. Your suit looks new. I wouldn't want to ruin it."

He straightened. "In that case, let me start by saying I'm sorry." His eyes caught Jane's.

She quickly broke their gaze. "Apology accepted—maybe." Her tone was intentionally flippant. Turning away she said, "It depends on the menu."

Peter put his hand on the small of her back and guided her to the table. He held her chair as she sat down. "Chicken cordon bleu, a fresh vegetable medley, sourdough rolls, and spinach salad with feta cheese and raspberry vinaigrette dressing. And for dessert, New York cheesecake topped with a rich caramel sauce."

"Mmm," Jane said, giving him a hint of a smile. "That could weigh in your favor."

Pete slid into the chair across from her. "Would you care to start with some wine?" He reached for a bottle chilling in a stand to the side of their table.

"No, thank you." Remembering her resolve to share more of her beliefs with him, Jane added, "Mormons don't drink any alcoholic beverages. We believe they aren't good for our bodies."

Pete put the bottle back. "Wisdom words, right? Your mom told me about that. I can't believe I forgot. Sorry."

"The Word of Wisdom. It's all right," Jane quickly assured him. "My water is great, but go ahead if you want some wine."

He shook his head. "Actually, I don't drink anymore."

Her eyebrows rose. "How come?"

Pete decided he might as well tell her. She should know what she was getting—good, bad, *and* ugly.

"The last time—a few years ago—I got drunk and tried to stop a wedding."

"Whose?" Her eyes were wide.

"Paul's."

Jane's mouth opened in an O.

"I decided my penance should include not drinking for a very long time." He shrugged. "I really haven't missed it."

"But you've missed your brother," she surmised.

"Yes." Pete followed her gaze out to the bay.

"You didn't approve of the bride?" she asked.

Pete cleared his throat. "Something like that." He knew he should tell her all of it, but not tonight. He wanted this evening to be all about Jane. The ghosts of the past would keep until another time.

They sat quietly, the silence neither uncomfortable nor familiar. They'd backtracked, Pete realized, and he had a lot of work to do tonight to regain Jane's trust and favor. Somehow, he had to succeed. After taking the weekend to think things through—as Richard had suggested—Pete knew what he needed to do—what he *wanted* to do, he admitted to himself. He hoped it was what Jane wanted too. At one time, he would have bet on it, but right now, he wasn't so certain.

"Why are we the only ones here?" she asked suddenly, breaking the silence. "Is this a new boat?"

"Not new. Remodeled." Pete glanced around the cabin, seeing the covered furniture and carpet for the first time. In his anxiety over tonight, he hadn't noticed the boat's details. "One of my clients owns this boat and several others in the fleet that run dinner cruises on the bay. This one starts up a regular schedule again this weekend."

"It's very nice," Jane murmured. "You went to a lot of work." She looked at him for a second before glancing away.

"I would have liked to do more. You're worth this and so much more, Jane." Pete reached into his coat pocket, withdrew an envelope, and set it in front of her. "I wish there was time to show you."

Jane picked up the envelope and opened it. Pete watched as she withdrew the letter and began reading. He saw the moment her fingers stilled on the paper and her breath caught. She looked up at him, eyes glistening with unshed tears.

"I should have known it was something bad."

He reached across the table and used his thumb to wipe the first drop from her cheek. "You couldn't have known or done anything."

She shook her head and gave him a sad smile. "You are so much like your brother. When things got really bad for Paul—when the doctors said there was nothing more that could be done—he didn't tell me. He just withdrew, stayed cooped up in his apartment, and wouldn't talk to me. You've done the same thing these past few days."

Pete got up and pulled his chair around to Jane's. He wiped another tear from her face and tried to lighten the mood. "You know us Bryant men—we're like turtles, always retreating into our shells when the news is bad."

"Terrible, stubborn turtles," Jane muttered.

"We are, aren't we?" He put his arm around her and pulled her close. "But the good thing is, we've got these really hard shells, and we're tough. I'm going to be fine while I'm gone, Jane. And so will you."

She sniffed and nodded, leaning her head against his shoulder.

Pete continued. "But I'll feel better leaving if I know you and the twins are taken care of."

"We'll be okay," Jane assured him.

He took her hand. "I want you to be better than that. I want to know you'll have everything you need—that you're provided for."

Jane tilted her face up to his. "What do you mea—?"

"Marry me, Jane," Pete whispered. "I know I shouldn't ask until I'm done with the military, but I don't want to wait. This is the right thing to do . . ." *Was that the right way to ask?* Judging by the look on her face, he didn't think so.

Inwardly he grimaced as she continued to stare at him without saying anything. He shouldn't have asked her so quickly—that hadn't been his intention. They were supposed to have dinner first, to be out under the stars, to have everything as nice as it could be for her, but he'd started, and he couldn't stop now.

"If we marry, then you'll be entitled, as a spouse, to my military benefits. And Richard has promised to keep my health coverage going while I'm gone. The three of you will be covered—Mark's surgery bills won't amount to anything more than co-pays. And if you get sick you can go to the doctor."

"*Insurance?*" Jane asked incredulously as she pulled away from him. "You want to get married so we'll have health benefits?"

"Of course there's more to it than that. We like each other, we—"

"We *like* each other?" Jane pushed her chair back. Fresh tears coursed down her face.

"I thought we did." Pete rose from his chair as she stepped around him. He caught her arm. "If you don't feel the same as you did—if that's changed, then we could continue as we are. You could live in your house, and I'll stay in mine. We don't have to be like a normal married couple. I'll be gone soon—"

"No," Jane cried. She wrenched her arm free. "No." She ran across the room and down the stairs.

"Jane," Pete called, following her. "Wait."

She shook her head and kept running through the main cabin and down the boat ramp. She made it to her car and quickly dug through her purse to find the keys. Pete came up behind her. Jane whirled on him, pointing the key at his chest.

She was sobbing. "Marriage isn't about insurance. It's about sharing friendship and faith and—and life-altering love. I can't marry without those things, Peter."

He took a step toward her, then stopped. He wanted to pull her to him, to hold her tight and kiss away her tears. He'd done it again, he realized. He'd upset her just like he had when they first met, and the night they first kissed.

"If you want to see the twins, call my mom. But it's my turn now. *I* need some time to—to deal with . . ." She threw her hands up. "This." Wrapping her arms around herself she looked down at the asphalt.

"I warned you," he reminded her. "That first night, after the police station, I apologized for future times when my mouth would likely function separate from my brain."

"Brutal honesty," Jane recalled. She pursed her lips together, took a deep breath and looked up at him. "I remember." Turning away, she climbed in the Jeep, slammed the door shut, and hit the lock button. Jamming the key in the ignition, she started the engine and drove forward through the empty space in front of her and out of the parking lot.

She allowed herself a last glimpse of Peter through the rearview mirror and saw that he'd already turned his back and was walking in the opposite direction.

Chapter Fifty-Six

Jane stopped at the red light and rummaged through her purse for a tissue. Unable to find one, she carelessly wiped the back of her hand across her eyes, paying no attention to the mascara trailing down her cheeks. It didn't matter what she looked like now. It didn't matter if she went home and consumed two more bags of chocolate—every night for the next month.

Fresh tears sprouted, and she sniffed loudly. The blurred traffic light turned green, and she stepped on the gas, taking off faster than she should have into the intersection. A horn blared, and Jane gasped. Jerking the wheel to the right, she narrowly avoided colliding with a car turning left. This sent her careening toward a minivan going right. Another horn blared as she braked and cranked the wheel in the opposite direction.

Miraculously, the Jeep jetted between the two cars. Glancing up, Jane realized it was only the left-hand turn arrow that was green. She'd almost caused an accident.

"Sorry," she whispered sheepishly as her heart pounded. The driver of the minivan glared at her as he drove by. She wished the street would swallow her whole and keep her awhile. A second later, she really wished it, when she heard sirens and saw the flashing lights of a police car behind her.

"Oh, no." Another torrent of tears unleashed themselves. Jane pulled to the side of the road and parked the car. She leaned over to the glove box and opened it. The spare diaper she kept in there tumbled out. Jane grabbed it, along with the envelope of papers she hoped held the car's registration.

Glancing in the rearview mirror, she groaned as she saw her face—a blotchy, puffy, red-and-black mess. *At least you didn't drink anything,* she tried to console herself. Though with her luck, and looking as she did, the officer would probably think she was intoxicated anyway. If he asked her to get out and walk a straight line, she might be in trouble. Jane doubted she was capable of doing much right now. Her head pounded, her stomach was in knots, she hadn't eaten dinner, and it felt like she'd cried out a third of the water in her body. She'd likely collapse on the pavement, and they'd cart her away for psychoanalysis.

Jane looked around for a tissue or a napkin. Finding nothing, she grabbed the diaper and opened it. Wiping it across her face, she tried to mop up her tears.

A knock sounded at the window and she jumped, giving a little shriek and dropping the diaper. The police officer knocked again, and she turned the key so she could roll down the window.

"License and registration," he said, holding out his hand.

Jane nodded and grabbed her purse from the seat. With shaking fingers, she pulled her license from her wallet and handed it to the officer.

"Just a moment and I'll find the registration." She took the envelope from the seat and opened it. *Please be in here,* she prayed. The tags didn't expire until next month, so she hadn't bothered to renew them or change the car over to her name. She unfolded the first paper and found a warranty for the car battery. The second paper was a record of tire rotation.

Jane glanced up at the officer and gave him a shaky smile. "I'm sure it's here."

"This your car?" he asked.

She shook her head. "No. It belongs to my—friend." Despite her effort to hold them back, new tears tumbled down her cheeks. Her chest heaved twice until finally, embarrassed but unable to stop herself, Jane leaned her head forward on the steering wheel and began to cry in earnest.

The officer cleared his throat. "Ma'am, why don't you get out of the car and—?"

Jane lifted her head. "I'm okay. Really, I am." She used her sleeve to wipe her face again. "It's just my friend—the one who owns this—he broke up with me, or I thought he did, but he was just upset because he's going back to Iraq. He's flies an Apache." Thinking of Pete in his helicopter made her upset all over again. She took several short, jerky breaths. "It's so—dangerous, and he was upset about leaving the children, so he didn't talk to me." She looked up at the officer, a plea in her eyes. "But now he wants to *marry* me." Her voice rose to a high, trembling pitch "But only so our children will have *insurance.*" Jane hiccuped loudly, taking several more short, gasping breaths as she tried to get her emotions under control.

It was a futile effort. All she could think about was Peter leaving and the fact that he didn't love her. She didn't know which had her more upset at the moment. Looking out the front window at the blurred street lamps, she spoke quietly to herself.

"It's so dangerous there. What if he crashes and never comes home? His father never came home."

The officer bent down close to her window. "Why don't you—?"

"He said we *liked* each other," Jane turned her face to the officer. "But I *love* him. I love him so much it hurts, and yet I shouldn't, and he has no idea . . ." She began to cry again.

The officer let out a long, frustrated sigh. "Just a minute," he mumbled. Straightening, he studied her driver's license then walked back to his patrol car.

Jane picked up the diaper and blew her nose into it. She fought to regain some of her control and began looking for the registration again. She finally found it, folded with a pink paper, cut in the shape of a heart. Opening it, she began to read.

December 22, 2000

Tamara,

I still can't believe you agreed to be my wife. I'm counting the days until you walk down the aisle to me. We'll speak our vows and drive off into the sunset together. I thought this Jeep would do nicely—getting us to some pretty remote places. Until then, think of me every time you get behind the wheel.

All my love,
Peter

Jane dropped the paper as if it had scorched her. Peter and *Tamara?* She read the names again just to be sure. This whole time his heart had belonged to someone else? She remembered his strange confession at the start of the evening.

"I tried to stop a wedding."

Jane knew she should have made him tell her why. But at the time, she'd only been thinking that she finally understood the mystery of why the two brothers had ceased their relationship. She realized the wedding must have been only the tip of the iceberg. She'd had no idea how deep or serious their animosities must have run—each in love with the same woman. Earlier conversations floated through her mind, seeming now like obvious clues she should have recognized.

"She'll be a dancer like her mother."

"I didn't know Tamara was a dancer. What else do you know about her?"

"Quite a bit."

Jane's face was dry now. She sat stiffly in her seat—Pete's—no—*Tamara's* seat.

"A lot of miles on this thing. I bought it new in 2000 . . .

"It made a lot of trips to hospitals . . ."

"I guess it wasn't just Paul and Tamara driving off into the sunset."

Jane pounded her fist on the wheel. "I am *so* stupid."

"How did Paul come to have your car, anyway?"

"It was a wedding present."

"You failed to mention *whose* wedding, " Jane muttered. "Why did I have to fall in love with a *twin?*" Paul and Peter were *so* alike that they'd each fallen for the same woman. Jane stared out the windshield, sobered by the realization that they'd also each settled for her, recognizing what she was—a good mother to the twins.

A good mother. That was it. Not a *wife.*

Jane leaned her head back against the seat, too tired and too angry to cry anymore. The ache in her heart went beyond tears or chocolate or anything else that had helped her cope before.

The officer returned. "Miss Warner?"

"Yes." Jane handed him the registration.

"Please step out and—"

"No problem." Jane unlocked the door and got out of the car.

The officer nodded to the yellow line painted along the side of the road. Jane walked over to it and placed one foot in front of the other on the line.

"I promise I'm not intoxicated or under the influence of drugs." She walked a few feet, turned and came back. *Just a simple broken heart that has me out of whack.*

"That'll do." He beckoned her over. "By chance does this car belong to—and does your earlier crying and subsequent running of a light—happen to have anything to do with a—" the officer glanced down at his clipboard. "Peter Bryant?"

"Yes," she said slowly. "How did you know?"

"Checked the computer. Seems there was an incident back in February."

Jane's mouth hung open. "I have a *police record?*"

"Not exactly." Unfolding the registration, the officer finished writing out the ticket, then tore off her copy and handed it to her. "I know you've had a rough night, but you did run a red light and could have caused a serious accident."

Jane clutched the ticket and nodded. "I know, and I'm terribly sorry."

He looked at her. "I'd advise you to stay away from this fellow. He seems to be trouble." Jane opened the door and got back into the Jeep.

"That's very sage counsel, officer, and I assure you, I plan to follow it."

Chapter Fifty-Seven

Caroline slammed down the phone and stormed into the living room where Ryan and Scott were watching the game. Hands on hips, she stood right in front of the television.

"Ah c'mon Caroline. Bases are loaded, and it's the ninth." Scott leaned to the side, trying to see the TV.

Caroline didn't move. She looked at her husband. "I'm going out for a while. Listen for Andrew. He'll need to be changed and have a bottle when he wakes up."

"You don't want to take him with you?" Ryan asked, hopeful as he loaded a tortilla chip with salsa.

"No, I don't." Caroline walked toward the door, grabbing her purse from the table and her keys from the hook.

"What's wrong, Mom?" Jessica looked up from the coffee table where she'd been doing a puzzle.

"Where you going?" Ryan asked, his attention more focused on the television in front of him than his wife's errand.

"Jane is upset, and I am going to have a little chat with Peter," Caroline said, answering both their questions.

"What'd *he* do?" Scott asked, looking sideways at Ryan.

"Asked Jane to marry him," Caroline said, her hand on the doorknob.

Ryan looked confused. "Isn't that what we expected him to do?"

"Yes," Caroline said matter-of-factly. "He just didn't do it the *way* we expected him to." She opened the door, stepped outside, and slammed the door behind her. Ryan stared at it a moment, then returned his attention to the game.

"Whoo-ee," Scott whispered under his breath. "Wouldn't want to be Pete just now."

"Me either," Ryan mumbled appreciatively through another bite of dip.

Jessica walked over to the window, pulled back the curtains, and watched her mother drive off. After a minute, she looked over her shoulder at her dad. "Don't you think we should call Uncle Pete and warn him that a madwoman in a minivan is headed his way?"

Ryan and Scott looked at each other a moment, then said, "Naw," at the same time.

"It'll be okay, Jess," Ryan assured her.

"Yeah," Scott echoed. "It will be a good test of whether Pete really wants to be *Uncle* Pete."

* * *

At the stop sign at the end of their road, Caroline dug through the CDs in her console. Finding the one she wanted, she ejected *Disney Favorites Vol. 3* and put in *Blondie.* Scanning to the right song, she waited until it came on before she hit the gas again. Her hands gripping the wheel, her eyes focused on the road, she thought of Peter as the lyrics blared. "One way or another," he *was* going to get it.

Her mind whirred with the exact words she planned to share with him. But first, she had to make a couple of quick stops.

* * *

The doorbell rang a second time—a long, grinding noise that prompted Peter to hurry down the stairs. He hadn't been asleep—couldn't begin to get his thoughts to settle after the disastrous evening with Jane. He hoped that was her at the door now and that they could straighten this whole mess out. It was barely nine o'clock, and he'd expected to still be on the boat, looking at the stars, his fiancée in his arms. Instead, he was alone again, and knew full well that *somehow* he was responsible. Unsure what he would say if it was Jane, Pete flipped on the front porch light and opened the door.

She came at him before he even had the door all the way open, her right fist connecting with his jaw.

"Ow," he cried, stepping back as his hand automatically went to his cheek. "*Caroline!* What'd you do *that* for?"

In answer, she swung a bulging bag toward him, catching him in the gut. "How dare you treat my sister like that."

Pete caught the bag of what felt like encyclopedias before it hit the floor. He took a step back, his foot pushing the door closed on his would-be sister-in-law.

"Oh, no you don't." Caroline's own foot stopped the door, and she threw her whole weight into fighting to keep it open.

Pete let her think she was winning—just enough so that he could hear what she had to say. No way he was letting her in the house.

"Do you have *any* idea what you've done?" Caroline demanded.

"Apparently not," Pete said. He tossed the bag aside and it landed with a thud on the carpet. "Is that a bomb or something?" he asked, only half joking.

"No, but good idea," Caroline said. "You certainly deserve it after what you pulled tonight."

"Enlighten me," Pete said, growing more annoyed by the minute. "Because in my mind I don't see that I've committed any crime—going to great lengths to arrange a moonlit cruise along the bay so Jane and I could have a nice, romantic night."

"Romantic?" Caroline scoffed, shoving the door into his shoulder. "You told her you wanted to marry her so she and the twins would have insurance benefits."

"What's wrong with that?" Pete asked. "I care about them, and Mark has major surgery coming up. I don't want Jane to have to cover that on her own."

"How noble of you," Caroline said sarcastically. "Those are the words every woman longs to hear when she's proposed to. Much better than, 'I'm counting the days until you walk down the aisle to me. We'll speak our vows and drive off into the sunset together.'"

Pete stood in stunned silence for nearly a minute. At last he opened the door and looked at Caroline. "How did you know about that?"

"About Tamara, you mean? Jane was crying so hard she ran a red light on the way home tonight."

Pete took an anxious step forward. "Is she okay?"

Caroline nodded. "She got a ticket and found your little note with the car registration."

Pete let out a long sigh. He ran his fingers through his hair and looked steadily at Caroline. "All right. Let's have it."

"*How* could you do this to Jane? Do you have *any* feelings for her—or has this whole thing just been a joke?" Caroline stepped across the threshold, jabbing her finger into his chest. "Because she is in love with you, and Jane has *never* been in love with *anyone* before. She wants to marry you—more than anything. She's even decided you're worth marrying outside the Church. But now she thinks you don't love her—that you're willing to settle for her for the sake of the twins."

Pete shook his head. "That's not true. I do—I do love her," he admitted quietly.

"Then you better figure out a way to prove it." Caroline looked up at the living room ceiling, blinking rapidly.

Pete was surprised to see tears in her eyes. *Oh no, not again—not another one.*

Caroline continued. "You know, when Jane was a little girl and we'd play Barbies together, she always wanted to play getting married. We'd plan these big elaborate weddings. Ken would get shoe polish on his head so his plastic hair would shine. We'd make Barbie this great tissue-paper gown.

All the other dolls sat in rows on our lunch boxes listening to the ceremony . . . It was her favorite thing to play." Caroline smiled sadly. "Jane loved all the Disney fairy tales—couldn't watch them enough, even when she was older. She asked for the *Beauty and the Beast* video for her sixteenth birthday. She's always been a hopeless romantic." Caroline sighed, then looked steadily at Peter.

"Jane has been a bridesmaid *seven* times—once for each of us and once for one of her friends. She has dreamed of her own fairy-tale love story— and despaired of ever having one—for years . . . And now you've broken her heart."

Chapter Fifty-Eight

Peter sat at the kitchen table, surrounded by the texts for his crash course in wedding education 101. Stacked to his right lay *Modern Bride*, *Martha Stewart Weddings*, *Cosmopolitan Bride*, and *Weddings in Style*, demanding to be read. He'd already spent over two hours going through *Town and Country Weddings*, *Elegant Bride*, and *Relationships for Dummies*. The latter had been insulting, though not as insulting as the note he'd just read inside the book that lay open in front of him. Caroline's handwriting was sprawled across the title page of *The Idiot's Guide to Romance*.

> *Yes, Peter. You are an idiot! Read this and learn what you*
> *need to do to fix things with my sister—soon.*
>
> *Caroline*

"Ouch," Pete said as he flipped to the table of contents. *She didn't chastise me enough when she was here?* He scanned the chapter titles, not really focusing, instead thinking more about Jane, a stone's throw away literally but miles away in the progression of their relationship. Caroline had left a couple hours ago, but not before making it clear what she thought of him.

Reliving the evening from Jane's point of view, he *was* an idiot.

But he wasn't certain what reading all of these books and magazines would accomplish. In less than a month, he'd be thousands of miles away—so what were the chances he could mend his relationship with Jane between now and then? What would it take to bring them back to the point where they were on the beach a few weeks ago?

Pete rose from the table and walked to the sliding glass door. Opening it, he walked outside, wandering in the yard, careful to stay on his side of the swing set. He looked up at Jane's window. Like the rest of the house, it was dark. He thought about tossing pebbles at it. She'd come to the window and he'd kneel and profess his love for her. Better yet, he could sing. His favorite band had a great song titled "Jane." Half serious, Pete mulled the thought over in his mind. It didn't take long to conclude that it was going to take much more than a song at a window to change her mind about him. He had to convince her that he wanted to marry her because he loved her. Because he couldn't live without her.

And there, he realized, was the crux of the matter. He hadn't really wanted Jane to know all of that before he left. He'd used the word *like* on purpose tonight. You could like someone and still recover from it if something happened. But when you loved someone—like his mother had loved his father—that could be fatal.

Pete shoved his hands in his pockets and turned away from Jane's window. Somehow he'd wanted to marry Jane yet spare her the depth of emotion that was supposed to come with the wedding vow. Or had he really been hoping to spare himself? Insurance for her and the twins had been a paltry offer, and the moonlit boat that he'd billed as so romantic now seemed cruel. And for Jane, finding his old letter to Tamara must have been like the final nail in the coffin of their relationship.

He returned to the house and sat at the table again, willing to flay himself with bridal magazines all night and forever if the answer to this mess lay hidden in the pages. He glanced at the covers then reached for the last item in the bag Caroline had thrown at him. Taking it out, he saw that it wasn't another magazine or book, but a flat box with a thin, white ribbon tied around it. Someone had scripted in fancy letters, "My temple time capsule" across the top of the box. Peter swallowed uncomfortably, suddenly knowing that someone was Jane.

For a long moment he stared at it, feeling he was invading her privacy by just holding the box in his hands, but then he remembered Caroline was the one who'd given it to him, and curiosity won out. He untied the delicate ribbon and lifted the lid. A pair of white lace slippers lay on top, and beneath them was a postcard of a rather fancy-looking church—a temple, he assumed. Beneath the picture was a lined paper with writing on it. Peter set the other items aside and picked up the paper, looking at the date—June 29, 1986. Eighteen years ago—to the day, almost. Jane would have been twelve.

His eyes moved farther down the paper. It was a list. Only five items were numbered below the underlined title. Peter read them twice, fascinated by the thought of twelve-year-old Jane writing them and thinking about marriage at such a young age.

The kind of man I want to marry.

1. Worthy to take me to the temple and bless our family and home.
2. He loves me with his whole heart.
3. Funny. He makes me laugh.
4. Kind. He doesn't yell or do bad stuff.
5. He's handsome (or at least I think so). It's nice when we kiss.

Peter read the list a third time, realizing that there was no number six—makes lots of money and has a good insurance plan. He lowered his head to his hands, thinking again of how badly he'd messed things up. He turned away, unable to bear looking at the evidence of his failure any longer. But the bridal magazines were on his other side, mocking him.

Through bleary eyes he stared at their covers and saw women in beautiful gowns, scads of flowers, a horse-drawn carriage, an ivy-covered church, hands interlaced, gold bands sparkling.

How . . . obvious. The clock in the living room chimed midnight—it had taken him three hours to figure this out. He *was* an idiot. For the first time all night, the corner of his mouth lifted in a smile.

Mentally, he began assembling his list. Diamond ring, beautiful gown, church, horse-drawn carriage, castle. The last two would be a bit trickier than the others, but he had a few ideas already. He could still fix this. He could give Jane all that she wanted—well, almost all. He'd learned enough about the Mormon Church to realize he couldn't take Jane to the temple . . . Her number-one requirement.

For a long moment, Peter leaned back in his chair, thinking. He *liked* her religion—a lot, actually. But liking something and really believing it were two entirely different things. And he still couldn't get past the Joseph Smith thing. Which was really too bad, Peter thought, because he was enjoying the Book of Mormon. He liked what he read there, and he had no trouble accepting that God would provide scripture for all people on the earth. It was *how* he provided the record that Peter was hung up on. Why would a fourteen-year-old farm boy be the one chosen to restore something so important?

It didn't make any sense.

Peter pushed his conflicted feelings aside and returned to the dilemma of winning Jane back. The temple wedding definitely wasn't an option, but Caroline said that Jane loved him enough she was willing to give that up. Guilt nagged at the back of his mind. He pushed it forcefully away. He'd make it up to her. He'd be numbers two through five on her list and so much more. And he'd start it all with the wedding of her dreams.

Pete went to the counter and took his phone book from the shelf beneath. Not caring about the time, he flipped to the number for Caroline's cell. He dialed, mind racing with plans as he waited for someone to answer. If he was going to pull this off, he would need some help.

Chapter Fifty-Nine

Jay held his guitar case in front of him and made his way down the Jetway into Seattle Tacoma International Airport. After six hours in the air, he was grateful to stretch his legs.

Walking past the gates and into the terminal toward baggage claim, he saw people greeting each other everywhere. *How would it be?* he thought, watching as a young couple shared a lingering kiss. Would he ever have the luxury of someone to greet him, someone who'd miss him while he was gone?

Arriving at the carousel, Jay tried to focus his attention on the bags going around instead of the people hugging, kissing, and chatting beside him. Loneliness had been his companion for as long as he could remember, so he didn't understand why it bothered him so much right now.

Maybe it was being back home. More likely it was because Jane was close. Two months and three days and he could see her again—his crummy luck it had been a leap year and he'd had to wait an extra day. Until then, Jay promised himself, he wouldn't so much as call her on the phone. Every morning he'd go to his internship at the courthouse, and he'd come straight home each night. Though, Jay mused, if he happened to see Jane and she *didn't* see him, would that be breaking his promise?

Grabbing his suitcase from the carousel, Jay strode over to the rental-car booth. He'd planned to call a friend when he arrived but decided suddenly that, seeing how it had been ten months since he'd been home, the least he could do was take the ferry out to Bainbridge and drive around the island.

* * *

Tara brought a hand to her forehead, shielding her eyes from the afternoon sun as she looked up at the most likely buyer she'd had for Jane's cottage. He descended the ladder.

"Well, what do you think?" she asked.

"It'll do." He dusted his hands off and strode past her toward the front of the house. Tara lagged behind, admiring his backside, wishing it were her he was attracted to instead of the cottage. He reached the front gate and his car. With a long, lustful sigh, Tara hurried after him.

He unrolled his sleeves and buttoned the cuffs. "What's the balance on the mortgage?"

"The asking price is $249,900." Tara pulled a flyer from the box attached to the sign.

"No way." He shook his head. "It's only what—eleven hundred square feet? Not to mention that the entire house needs to be completely rewired. You've let what was probably a gorgeous yard become completely overgrown, and the walls—what walls there are in that mess—are painted *fuchsia* and *turquoise.*" He opened the passenger door of the car and retrieved his suit coat.

"Yes, but look at the view," Tara protested. "On a clear night you can climb up and see the entire Seattle skyline."

"If you don't fall through the roof doing it." He looked pointedly at her. "I'm on a very limited time frame here. And this is going to take much more work than I'd planned, so either tell me the balance of the mortgage, or I'll look elsewhere."

In a last feeble attempt, Tara reached over the gate, lifting a section of the white picket fence. "The owner installed these herself just last year. They were much more costly than your regular old fence. Each eight-foot section is easily removed for planting and mowing."

He rolled his eyes. "Apparently the *renter* forgot that part—about the mowing. I imagine the owner would be particularly sad if she knew what her yard looked like now—or the inside of her house for that matter."

Tara pursed her lips. He knew he had her. "Oh, all right," she said at last. "Jane still owes about a hundred and fifty-four thousand."

"You marked it up almost a hundred thousand?" he asked, incredulous.

"What?" Tara whined. "First I'm too high, and now you don't believe me? Jane had an inheritance from her grandmother so she made a large down payment, plus she's put oodles into this yard."

He looked at the cottage again and ran his fingers through his hair. "It's still too much for this dump, but I guess that's more like it. I'll have a check for you in forty-eight hours. Get the paperwork ready."

"A check?" Tara's mouth hung open. "You're going to buy it outright?"

"Yes. And remember, I don't want Jane to know." He walked around to the front of his car.

"But—but she might want to be there at signing, and—"

"Let her sign first. Tell her the buyer is from out of town and you have to fax him the papers." He flashed her a smile. "I'm sure a smart, attractive woman like yourself will think of something."

"Well, okay." Blushing, Tara looked down at the flyer still in her hand. "Hey, wait a second," she called, stopping him just before he shut the car door. Heels clicking, she ran around to the driver's side. "If I sell it to you for the balance owed, then what's in it for me?"

He pulled the door shut, turned the ignition, and hit the power button for the window to go down. "Aside from the near-free rent you've enjoyed the past nine months . . ." The corner of his mouth lifted. "You'll have a warm, fuzzy feeling that you've done the right thing."

Chapter Sixty

Peter lifted his hand to knock on the door again just as Jane opened it. He studied her face for any trace of sadness or anger. They hadn't spoken in four days—since he'd majorly botched the marriage proposal. Every time he'd come over to see the twins, she had left. And only today, at Caroline's coaxing, had Jane reluctantly agreed to go with him to her family's monthly dinner and Fourth of July celebration. Hopefully it wasn't to torch him with a firework, though after last week he couldn't blame her.

"You ready?"

She nodded. "Will you help me with the twins?"

"Of course." Peter followed her into the family room.

"If you'll take Mark and the diaper bag, I'll get Maddie and be right there."

Pete reached down and plucked Mark from the floor. Swinging him high in the air, he turned around, then brought him close, kissing his chin. "Hey, buddy."

Mark giggled and leaned his head back.

"Like that, do you?" Pete asked, then kissed him twice more.

"Oh, and if you wouldn't mind—" Jane stood in the doorway, holding a wiggling Maddie on her hip. "Could you please get their bottles out of the fridge?"

"Sure thing," Pete said, wishing Jane would quit being so formal and—nice. He much preferred the way she used to treat him—ordering him around, scolding and teasing when he did things wrong. Taking the bottles from the fridge, he followed her out to the car, knowing that he'd travel to the ends of the earth to melt her defenses and prove his feelings were for her and her alone.

* * *

Pete set a stack of glasses on the counter beside the sink. "I thought we were off the hook for dishes for a full six months."

"The rotation got mixed up. You don't have to help." Jane's voice was muffled as she searched under the sink for her mother's gloves.

"I want to," Pete said. "We're a team, remember. Joint custody of the twins *and* the chores."

Jane shrugged as she turned on the faucet.

Pete reached from behind her and shut it off. Placing one hand on either side of her on the counter, he leaned forward and whispered in her hair. "We need to talk." He felt her stiffen.

"I don't think that's a good idea."

He put his hands on her shoulders, trying to get her to face him.

"Don't," she said, shrugging out of his grasp.

He sighed. "I know you found out about Tamara—and don't be mad at Caroline for telling me. In fact, if it makes you feel any better, she decked me good on the side of my face. You can still see the bruise a little."

"I'll have to thank her." Jane reached for the faucet handle again. Pete's hand over hers stopped her.

"There never seemed to be a good time to tell you. And Wednesday night, when I wanted to talk about *us* getting married, was certainly no exception."

Jane drummed the fingers of her free hand on the edge of the sink. "I can easily think of half a dozen times that would have been appropriate— *including* Wednesday night." She wrenched her hand away, turned on the water, and began scrubbing plates.

Pete held his hand out to catch the first one she'd finished. "You're absolutely right," he said. "So will you let me tell you now?"

"No thanks." Jane slapped another dish into his hands.

"I insist," Pete said.

"I've lost interest."

"Prove it." He took her shoulders and turned her to him before she could protest. Water dripped on the floor between them. Pulling her close, he bent to kiss her.

"I bit a guy's tongue nearly in half once," Jane threatened, her lips mere millimeters from his. "I bet *that* wasn't in my file."

Pete's eyebrows rose. "It wasn't, but I'll take my chances." He pressed his lips to hers, praying she'd respond, praying the rest of her crazy family would stay outside awhile longer, leaving him and Jane alone to work things out.

Her eyes welled with tears. "Stop it, Peter," she mumbled against his mouth as she pushed him away, the soapy gloves leaving prints on his shirt.

He released her. "Don't cry. I didn't want to make you cry again."

"As if—I have a choice." Jane choked out the words. "If Tamara really didn't matter anymore—if you were over her—then you would have told me."

"You're wrong. Listen to me, Jane." He grabbed her gloved hands and pulled her over to the kitchen table. Sliding a chair out, he waited until she'd sat down before he sat in the chair across from her and began to speak.

"I'll tell you all about it—about Tamara and me—right now."

"It doesn't matter. It's too late."

"Really?" He searched Jane's face.

She shrugged and, glancing at the clock, began removing her gloves. "Go ahead, then."

It was his turn for the deep breath. "Tamara and I got engaged at Christmastime. We planned to get married on Valentine's Day, but we both decided it was too soon. The following September, when 9/11 happened, we still hadn't set a date for our wedding. *Both* of us kept coming up with one excuse or another. My last—and best one—was the surge of indignant patriotism I felt after watching the Twin Towers fall. I told Tamara I'd decided to reenlist and go to Afghanistan to root out terrorists."

Jane looked down at the table as she picked at the chipped Formica with her nail. "Go on."

"Tamara asked me to stay, and I didn't. Honestly, I didn't think twice about leaving." Pete looked at Jane, remembering their conversation at the beach. "Maybe it was part of me—something from my dad or in my blood—but whatever it was, I didn't feel all that bad about leaving Tamara. She was the first girl I ever really loved, but by that time, the love—or infatuation—we'd felt was fading, and we both knew it." Pete paused, wishing Jane would say something or at least look at him. When she didn't, he continued.

"Only I wasn't man enough to admit things were over, and when, less than two months later, she called to tell me that she and Paul were getting married, I lost my temper. I felt betrayed by both of them, and I went to some pretty ridiculous lengths to win her back—including my drunken scene at their wedding."

Jane looked up at him. "I appreciate you telling me." Her tone was matter-of-fact. She rose from the table. "I'd better get the dishes finished so we have enough spoons and bowls for the ice cream."

Pete reached out, his hand on her arm. "I *want* to marry you, Jane." He stood and faced her, taking both of her hands in his. "And it has nothing to do with the twins or insurance. Richard promised he'd keep them on my plan before I even asked you."

He watched helplessly as her eyes filled with tears again. "But this is exactly what I *didn't* want—you crying, your heart broken if something goes wrong in Iraq—so I thought that if we married as more of friends I might spare you some heartache if the unthinkable happened."

Jane pulled her hands from his. Walking away, she tore a paper towel from the roll on the counter. She wiped her face. "So you make me kiss you to prove I don't care?"

"No—yes. I don't know, Jane." He ran his fingers through his hair again. "All I know is that we should get married. There's no one else for me, alive or dead. It's you I want to spend my life with."

Jane blinked to clear her eyes. Her fingers gripped the edge of the counter. "Yes, then. Let's get married." She didn't sound too excited.

"Great," Pete said, his voice also lacking enthusiasm. "Could you look at me?"

She shook her head. "I need a few minutes alone. I'll finish up. Why don't you go out back and feed the twins some watermelon. Make sure they wear bibs."

"Sure," Pete said, nonplussed. Jane had just agreed to marry him—but he didn't feel their conversation had been entirely successful. But at least, he consoled himself, she was ordering him around again. He left the kitchen, nearly running into Caroline, who'd been eavesdropping on the other side of the wall.

"How'd I do?" he whispered.

"I feel like punching you again." Caroline grabbed his arm, dragging him toward the living room. "If that was better, then I shudder thinking of your first proposal. Come on. We have a *lot* of work to do."

Chapter Sixty-One

"Kind of hard to see the stars from the city," Robert Warner remarked as he joined Peter on the deck.

"It is," Pete agreed, "but I think the grandchildren had fun trying." He turned the knob on the telescope's frame and began the process of disassembling it. "Fireworks are cool, but nothing beats a real shooting star." As he worked, he was conscious of Jane's father beside him, watching. An hour earlier, Jane had told her parents of their wedding plans, and Pete had suspected her father would want to talk with him.

Minutes had passed without further conversation when Pete ventured, "I imagine there are a few things you'd like to say to me."

"And some things I'd like to ask," Robert said.

"Sounds fair." Pete bent over, securing the straps on the telescope case, then stood and faced his future father-in-law. "Go ahead."

Robert placed his hand on the railing and looked him in the eye. "How much do you know about temples?"

The question caught Pete off guard. He'd expected to be asked if he loved Jane and how he planned on treating her—maybe even if he'd support her in the Church—but temples . . . He answered as best he could. "I know Jane wanted to be married in one."

Her father nodded. "What else?"

Here goes, Pete thought. "And if she marries me, that won't be the case."

"Hmm." Robert folded his arms.

"I love your daughter, Mr. Warner, and I'll do everything I can to make her happy. But I won't pretend to be something I'm not. I respect your religion, but it's not for me."

"I see." Robert revealed a hint of a smile. "I appreciate you sharing that, but what I was really wondering was if you've ever seen the Salt Lake Temple."

"I have," Pete said, feeling more confused by the minute. What was Jane's dad getting at?

"Did you know it took forty years to build?"

"Seems like I heard that somewhere." During the time he'd lived in Utah it was hard *not* to hear about Mormons or the temple.

"The foundation took just over fourteen years. First time around they used sandstone, but some of the small rocks and mortar between the blocks cracked. President Young preferred the sandstone but realized granite would prove more stable, so the entire eight-foot foundation was removed and rebuilt."

"Sounds like a lot of work." Sensing he was in for a lesson or something, Pete set the telescope on the table and turned to lean against the railing and look out over the yard.

"It was an incredible amount of work. I'm certain some grumbled about starting over, some who thought the *prophet*, of all people, should have gotten it right from the get-go." Jane's father paused, letting his words sink in. "I imagine it was pretty difficult for President Young to tell the Saints they had to start over. Fortunately, he didn't let his pride get in the way. He understood that a building is only as good as its foundation."

Peter looked up to find Jane's father staring at him.

"A marriage is much the same way—as good as its foundation. And," Robert continued before Peter could speak. "That's all I'll say about that. One thing more and I'll let you pack up and get home. I know the twins are sleepy."

Pete glanced toward the house and caught a glimpse of Jane and her mother, each holding a baby as they sat in the matching recliners in the family room.

"It may interest you," Robert said. "To know that Orson Pratt, one of the prominent early Church members, was also an astronomer. He took great care to make certain the symbols chiseled on the outside stones of the temple were correct—even going so far as to set up an observatory."

"What kind of symbols?" Peter couldn't help asking, though he knew he was taking the bait Jane's father held out.

"The sun, moon, and stars—each with a particular meaning relating to the gospel." Robert leaned back, looking up at the sky. "My favorite has always been the Big Dipper, with the pointers ranging to the North Star, symbolizing that the lost may find their way by aid of the priesthood."

"Interesting," Pete said. "Next time I'm in Salt Lake I'll have to take a look."

"You do that." Robert stepped away from the railing, signaling the end of their conversation. "Just remember, if you run into any rough patches while taking good care of my daughter, there's always the North Star to guide you home."

Chapter Sixty-Two

Sniffing the air exaggeratedly, Pete walked through Jane's family room into the kitchen. Jane's mom stood on the other side of the counter, a frilly apron tied around her waist as she stirred something on the stove. Three loaves of bread sat cooling on the nearby cutting board.

"Homemade bread? You're the best, Mrs. Warner."

Jane's mom smiled at him warmly as she picked up one of the loaves and began slicing it. "I know it's summertime, but with it being overcast, I thought bread and soup would be a nice lunch."

"You shouldn't spoil me so much," Pete chided as he took a seat at the counter. "I'm going to have terrible withdrawal when I return to Iraq."

"*Hopefully* from more than just the food," she said, giving him a knowing look.

Pete grinned. "Definitely." He took the thick slab of warm bread she handed him. "I'm going to miss Jane and Mark and Madison more than I can imagine." After slathering butter on the slice, he brought it to his mouth.

"Ah-ah," Jane's mom scolded. "Aren't you forgetting—"

"The prayer." Pete set the bread down beside his bowl, folded his arms, and bowed his head, waiting expectantly. After several seconds of silence, he lifted his head, opening one eye just a little. Marsha Warner, her arms also folded, stared at him.

"Go ahead," she urged.

Pete swallowed, suddenly uncomfortable. In the past six months of their shared lunches, she'd never once asked him to bless the food. "I'm not sure—"

"Nonsense," she cut him off. "You've heard dozens of prayers, *and* you've now heard all of the discussions. It's time—"

"Discussions?' It was Peter's turn to interrupt. "What are you talking about?"

She looked away guiltily, wiping crumbs from the cutting board. "The discussions cover the basic gospel principles. I memorized them with the boys before each of their missions." She turned to Peter again, her warm smile back in place. "I always felt I would have a chance to use them someday."

A part of Peter wanted to feel angry that she'd tricked him into hearing these so-called "discussions," but he had to admit he'd enjoyed their conversations. Aside from that, Jane's mom seemed so similar to his own mother it made his heart ache sometimes. Getting angry would only hurt them both. He'd learned that lesson the hard way with Paul.

He decided to make light of the situation and finagle his way out of the prayer with a distraction. "And here I thought you just enjoyed my company and liked to cook."

"I do," she said, nodding. "I enjoy your company so much that I wanted to share the two things most precious to me—the gospel and my daughter."

Unsure how to respond, Pete looked down at his bread and soup, growing cold.

Jane's mom surprised him by reaching across the counter, placing her soft, aged hand over his. "You've heard all of it, Peter. The plan of salvation, the restoration of the gospel, the fulness and truth in the scriptures. There's only one thing more to be done now, and *you* must do it."

With a will of their own it seemed, his eyes sought hers.

"You have to ask," Marsha said. "Get down on your knees and ask God if it's true."

"I can't," Pete said.

"I know." She squeezed his hand, then pulled away. "I can only imagine how difficult it must be if you haven't prayed before, and that's why you have to start small—today—blessing this meal." She glanced toward the hall, listening for sounds of the twins waking up from their naps. "I'm going to go check the babies. I'll leave you alone." She paused, looking at him intently. "Promise me you'll pray."

He found he was powerless to deny such a simple request. "I will."

* * *

Pete crawled into bed, sighing as his head hit the pillow. He was exhausted. Today he'd wrapped up the Holland custody case—no happy resolution there—and after work he'd headed straight over to the house to see how it was coming along. It was coming—just not fast enough—and before he'd realized it, he'd spent two hours on the roof laying shingles. Now his head ached from the mental strain of the day, and his back ached from the physical labor.

Reaching his arm out, he pulled the chain on the lamp. Darkness flooded the room, and he was certain he'd be asleep in minutes.

Promise me you'll pray.

Pete groaned and rolled onto his side. *Not now.* He tried thinking of the things he needed to take care of at the office tomorrow. He needed to go over his probate cases with the new intern. Then he'd need to tell Richard about the stipulations for—

There's only one thing more to be done now, and you must do it.

Pete pulled the pillow over his head and made a mental list of things he still needed to buy for the house. Paint for the front door. A mirror for the new vanity in the bathroom. A rug for the entry. Another box of cobble-stones to finish the path out back.

Promise me you'll pray.

"I did," Pete said aloud. Sitting up in bed, he scowled into the dark. Jane's mom was making him crazy—except that it wasn't really her mom. It was a figment of his imagination, a memory of their conversation two days earlier. He *had* prayed, a hasty, whispered prayer thanking God for the food. Peter felt he deserved a clear conscience about his promise. Except . . . The promise she extracted from him had referred to much more than a blessing on his lunch.

And they both knew it.

He'd avoided lunch at Jane's the past two days, certain Mrs. Warner would ask the inevitable and he wouldn't know what to say. He hadn't prayed about the things she'd shared with him, didn't know if he could.

Pete ran his fingers through his hair, then got out of bed and walked to the window, looking over the backyard toward Jane's house. She loved him as he was, and he was grateful for that. Her family accepted him too. He and Jane, Mark and Madison, were going to make a great little family. If it wasn't for Iraq looming before them, life would be perfect. Everything was good the way it was.

He knelt down and looked up through the window at the few visible stars. "I'm a good person," he whispered. "I'll love her. I'll love the twins. But—" He swallowed, aware of the sudden lump in his throat. "But if I'm supposed to be something else, *know* something else, you're gonna have to let me know somehow. Not a sign," he added hastily, recalling what happened to sign seekers in the Book of Mormon. "No sign," he repeated. "Just a little help."

Pete waited quietly for another few minutes. He tried closing his eyes and listening. He opened his eyes and looked up at the ceiling, then out at the stars, waiting for something to happen. When nothing did, he returned to bed.

It was a long time before he fell asleep.

Chapter Sixty-Three

Caroline rapped on the dressing room door. "Come on out, Jane. Let's see it."

"This is silly," Jane protested from the other side. "There's really no point—"

"You're Mom's last bride, Janey." Mindy held a finger to her lips as she and Karen showed Caroline the veils they'd found.

Caroline pointed to the one in Karen's left hand. "Do it for Mom."

Jane frowned at her toes, barely peeking out beneath the hem of the heavy satin gown. If she came out they'd only ooh and aah over her and try to convince her—for the hundredth time in the past five days—to have a traditional wedding. And she couldn't do it. She'd agreed, for Mark and Madison's sake, to marry Peter, but it would be simple. The white suit she'd already chosen would do fine for the vows they'd exchange at the courthouse.

Her fingers brushed the delicate scallop of the neckline. To wear a gown like this would only raise false hope—and make her look a fool in front of Peter. He'd made it so very clear that they were marrying as friends. This marriage was all about what was best for the children. She was still plain Jane—no princess.

And this was no fairy tale.

Another knock sounded on the dressing room door. "Jane, dear."

Mom. Oh, no. Jane's left hand went to her waist over the fitted bodice as the fingers of her right hand began massaging her temples. She leaned forward, racking her brain for an excuse to deny her mother what she felt was her due.

"Please, just let me see. I know you don't want to wear it to your wedding, and that's fine. But I've waited a long time to see my baby in a real wedding gown."

"It's not a *real* wedding," Jane muttered under her breath, but she grabbed the handle of the dressing room door and pulled.

"Oh," her mother gasped. "It's beautiful. Perfect."

"Come see." Caroline reached in and grabbed Jane's hand, pulling her toward the pedestal and surrounding mirrors.

"This is silly," Jane protested again, but Karen was right behind her, pushing her along. "For Mom," she whispered in Jane's ear.

Reluctantly, Jane gathered the full skirt and stepped onto the dais. Karen climbed up beside her and began buttoning the row of pearls down the back of the gown. When she'd finished, she placed the veil in Jane's hair.

"Let's attach the train too," her sister-in-law said. Kneeling beside Jane, Amy fastened the train to the back of the dress. Caroline and Emily fanned the fabric out across the pedestal.

Jane lifted her eyes to the mirror and felt her breath catch. The dress *was* magnificent—everything she'd ever imagined her wedding dress would be. She stood silent for a full minute, allowing herself the luxury of feeling truly beautiful, imagining how heavenly it would be to own this dress, to kneel across the altar from Peter, love and adoration in his eyes.

The saleswoman returned. "I've spoken with our seamstress and the alterations to your suit will be finished by noon Monday . . ." She broke off, seeing Jane in the gown surrounded by her mother and sisters. "Oh my, you look positively ravishing. Have we changed our minds, then?"

Jane turned to her, the spell broken. "No, I still want the suit. We were only—pretending. I was just going to change." She reached up, removing the veil from her hair. Caroline took it from her, and Mindy unfastened the train while Amy helped with the buttons. When they were finished, Jane retreated to the dressing room.

Caroline waited until the door had closed before glancing at the price tag on the veil. She looked up at her sisters, whispering. "Who's got a credit card with them? With the veil, I'm going to be over my limit."

"Give it to me," her mother said, reaching through the circle of her daughters. "I've had a long time to save for this." She smiled as her fingers examined the flowers on the circlet. "Keep your sister busy while I pay and arrange for everything to be delivered."

* * *

"Are you happy, Caroline?" Jane asked, frowning as she sat across from her sister at the small table in Waterfall Garden.

Caroline chewed her bite of sandwich as she contemplated how to best answer that question. Since leaving their mother and sisters a half hour ago—they'd all had excuses lined up as to why they couldn't go to lunch, and only Caroline knew they were really heading to the bakery and florists for more wedding preparations—Jane had seemed particularly melancholy. Caroline was pretty sure the wedding gown she'd tried on had something to do with it.

"Sure, I'm happy. Why do you ask?"

Jane shrugged. "I don't know. It's just that you and Ryan had a rather unconventional start to your marriage."

Caroline snorted. "You mean how we almost didn't *get* married? Ryan was an hour late and Dad was ready to murder him." She made a face. "What a disaster."

"I thought your wedding was nice," Jane said.

"As nice as it could be, considering the circumstances." Caroline took a drink of her smoothie. "It was after the reception things really got ugly." She picked up a french fry and bit it, her face bunched up as she remembered.

"What happened?" Jane asked.

"We had a colossal fight, that's what," Caroline said. She reached for another fry. "Ryan felt trapped. I just felt nauseated. For some reason when I was pregnant with Jessica, I got night sickness instead of morning sickness. The super-control-top nylons I'd been wearing all day only made things worse." She waved her fry in the air. "Anyway, I told Ryan what an insensitive jerk he was—a little more explicitly than that, but we're in public—and then I threw up all over his rented tuxedo. After that I spent most of the night in the bathroom. I remember putting towels all over the floor so I wouldn't have to lie on the tile."

"That's *awful*." Jane looked horrified.

"It was pretty bad, but about two in the morning—when I finally felt better and I'd fallen asleep—Ryan came in and got me. He carried me to bed and apologized profusely. We stayed up the rest of the night talking . . . and we prayed together for the first time. Afterward, I felt that we actually might be okay." A faraway look came to Caroline's eyes. "Love, combined with the gospel, is amazing. You'd be surprised what it pulls you through."

"Peter and I are getting married as friends—his words—remember?"

"I know," Caroline said. "But I've seen the way he kisses you. You don't walk around kissing *friends* like that." She took another drink. "Peter's problem is that he's worried about leaving you—and a small part of him is worried you'll dump him like Tamara did—so he protects himself by saying you'll just marry as friends."

Jane frowned. "Since when did you become a therapist?"

"Since I married Ryan, but don't ask me to figure myself out."

"Well, whatever you're doing, it must be working." Jane leaned back in her chair. "Everything turned out good with your marriage. Ryan is active in the Church, you were sealed in the temple, and all these years later, you still seem madly and passionately in love."

"I have Mom and Dad to thank for Ryan's activity. They were really great that first year. When we told them I was pregnant, they were both so hurt and angry, but from the day we married, they accepted Ryan and made him feel an important part of the family. I don't know if we'd have made it without them."

A half-smile curved Caroline's lips as she remembered the good and bad of their early marriage. She looked at Jane. "You're right though. *Mad* and *passionate* certainly describe our relationship. I'm either furious with Ryan—especially lately with those stupid baseball games—or I can't keep my hands off him." A warm contentment flooded over her as she thought of her husband. She *was* happy with her marriage, especially those precious times she and Ryan had alone.

Across from her, Jane was staring absently into space, sorrow in her eyes. Caroline focused her attention back to her sister.

Normally, Waterfall Garden was one of Jane's favorite places in the city. The tiny alcove was surrounded by a rock wall, and a cascade of water tumbled over the stone. Caroline knew it was one of the places Jane used to come for her First Friday romance indulgences. She'd once confided that sitting in such a peaceful place she could imagine good things happening to her, romantic things, like the heroines in her romance novels experienced.

Today, Caroline saw no trace of the hopeless-romantic sister she loved so much. Instead, Jane seemed depressed. She'd hardly touched her lunch, and by the expression on her face, Caroline guessed she was a million miles away. Peter was doing his best to make things right, but Caroline knew that wasn't going to matter if she didn't figure out what was wrong with the bride.

"What are you thinking?" Caroline asked.

Jane faced her. "I keep thinking about Tamara. I don't know how I'll ever compete with a ghost, so why should I even bother? I've convinced myself to marry Peter for the twins. Unfortunately he's right—with Mark's surgery coming up, that whole insurance thing *is* a big deal. But I don't think I can go through with it. When I tried on that dress . . ."

"Go on," Caroline urged, pushing her sandwich aside so she could lean closer to Jane.

"I love him," Jane said miserably. "I can wear a plain suit and marry him at the courthouse, but that won't change a thing. I'll be dying inside because I'll have him, but not really. I'll have him as a friend for mortality, but nothing more."

Caroline reached out and squeezed Jane's hand. "This much I know. Tamara isn't a ghost, and Pete doesn't love her anymore. As for having him only while on earth . . . that *is* how it stands now, but don't give up. He's a really good person, Jane. And he loves you."

Jane looked doubtful.

Caroline rose from her chair. "You've got to have a little faith—and keep dreaming. Some happy endings just take a little longer and are harder to come by."

Chapter Sixty-Four

Jane couldn't restrain her smile as she watched Mark and Madison splash in the International Fountain. Maddie, clad in her pink polka-dot bathing suit, bounced in time to the music, the ruffles along her bottom flapping up and down. Mark sat a few feet away. Nestled safely between Peter's outstretched legs, he leaned forward, trying to catch the water when it spurted out of the hole in front of him.

Jane snapped one more picture of the three of them, then returned the camera to the diaper bag in the stroller parked nearby. Walking back to the fountain, she didn't notice Peter watching her or redirecting the flow of water from a spout near him. A second later she shrieked when it hit her square in the chest.

"Peter!" Half mad, half laughing, she marched toward him.

He'd already turned around and was whistling nonchalantly as he played with Mark. Jane stood over them, hands on hips.

"Uh-oh, Mark. Mommy's mad at us," Pete said, grinning as he tilted his head up. "Maybe we'd better give her a kiss to make up for getting her *all wet.*"

"Your daddy's been a *bad* boy, Mark." Jane squatted, pulling Mark close, no longer caring what his soaked shorts would do to her shirt. "*You* can kiss me." She brushed her lips against his cheek.

Pete looked confused. "I thought women were supposed to *like* bad boys."

"Whatever gave you that idea?" Jane set Mark down again.

Pete gave her a mischievous smile. "I've been doing some reading."

* * *

Jane rubbed her hands up and down her arms, trying to rid herself of the goose bumps. Though her shirt was mostly dry now, the cool air of the monorail was giving her chills.

Pete looked over, then scooted closer and put an arm around her, pulling her close.

She was about to protest but decided his warm hand felt too good on her skin. "Thank you," she said instead, closing her eyes and leaning her head back. The whole day had felt good—felt like things were back to where they used to be when Peter had announced he wanted to explore the whole couple idea. They were a good couple, Jane realized. She'd had a great time today with Mark and Madison and Peter. If only it could last.

A week from today was the wedding. A week and a day after that, he would be gone.

Deciding she didn't want to waste another minute of the time they had together, Jane pushed the thought of friendship to the back of her mind and snuggled closer to Peter. She felt his arm tighten around her. Madison slept in her lap, and Peter held Mark, also asleep. If only they could stay here forever—together . . .

"Westlake Center." It seemed just a few minutes later that the announcement came over the speaker. Jane sat up straight, and Pete lifted his arm from around her. The monorail slowed, then came to a stop. Jane held the twins while he got the strollers ready. They left the car and walked out onto the fourth floor of the mall.

"Hungry?" Pete asked.

"Not really." Jane looked around the food court. "Can you wait another half hour or so for the twins to wake up? We could get them some fries or something."

"Great idea. Let's go shopping." He set out, pushing Mark's stroller, glancing behind to make sure Jane followed.

"What are you looking for?" she asked, somewhat surprised at his enthusiasm. It had been her experience that most men—her brothers and brothers-in-law, anyway—didn't particularly enjoy the mall.

"Something," Pete answered vaguely and continued walking. Rounding a corner, he slowed their pace, then finally stopped—in front of a jewelry store. He turned to her. "I don't want to blow this like I did everything else, so I'm not going to say much, other than I want you to pick out whatever ring you like."

Jane looked from Pete to the store window beside her. Diamonds nestled on velvet, winking at her. In the chaos and upheaval of her life and emotions over the past week and a half, she hadn't thought about a ring. A diamond was usually romantic—and given during the proposal. So what was appropriate for a marriage based on friendship and joint custody? A simple gold band, she quickly decided.

Trying not to care too much that her hair was wild and curly from their water adventure, Jane walked past Peter into the jewelers. Slowly, she pushed the stroller along the glass cases, studying the contents. At the very end of the row, she came to one that contained plain, gold bands. *Plain Jane. Plain band,* she thought with a twinge of sadness as she forced her eyes away from the sparkling solitaire in the next case over. Lifting her hand, she pointed her unpolished nail at a pair of simple gold bands. "Something like that would be nice."

Peter leaned in for a closer look. "Are you sure?" He sounded disappointed. She nodded.

Pete glanced at the price tags. "They're not very much. Do you want to get some earrings or something to go with your dress, then?"

The thought of her white suit and the gorgeous dress she'd left behind made the lump in her throat swell. She shook her head and looked away.

Pete studied her a minute, then finally conceded. "All right. I'll get someone to help us."

As if on cue, the two jewelers who'd been watching them since they entered the store swooped in for the sale. One was tall, blonde, and curvaceous, the other a Danny DeVito look-alike.

"Can I help you?" they chorused.

Pete looked at them both, then settled his gaze—wisely, Jane thought—on the short, bald salesman.

"We'd like to look at these his and hers bands."

The man nodded, took his key out, and opened the case. Jane noticed that tall-blonde-and-curvy was still lingering, staring rather openly at Peter.

"Renewing your vows?" she guessed, sidling closer.

"Saying them for the first time," Peter said, giving Jane a mischievous wink.

"O—oh," the saleswoman said, glancing at the twins.

"It's not what you think," Pete assured her. "These are my brother's kids—his and my fiancée's." He turned to Jane, giving her a poignant look. "My *ex*-fiancée's."

At this, Danny DeVito looked up. "What size?" he asked, contemplating Jane.

"I'm not really sure," she said. How should she know? She didn't own any rings. Jewelry generally got in the way when she was doing yard work. Though, she thought sadly with another glance at the solitaire, she wouldn't have minded if a ring like that slowed her down a bit.

"So, you're helping out your sister-in-law to be," nosy blonde said, obviously unable to contain her curiosity.

Business must be slow, Jane thought.

"Oh no." Pete reached for Jane and pulled her to his hip. "Not my sister-in-law. She's going to be my wife."

"I see," the saleswoman murmured, though she clearly didn't see as she kept looking from Jane to Peter to the twins, then back to Peter.

Jane used her elbow to jab him in the side. Holding out her hand, she let the salesman slip a band on her ring finger. It was too big.

"Are they twins?" the saleswoman asked, looking at Mark and Madison now.

"Yes," Pete said enthusiastically. "Isn't it great? I'm a twin too. My brother and I, we shared everything." He looked pointedly at Jane.

"That's right," she said, not missing a beat. She smiled sweetly at the saleswoman whose mouth hung open, revealing several fillings in her back teeth.

"Yep. Shared just about everything," Peter repeated. Jane turned into his side to keep from laughing out loud.

"Thanks a lot," she muttered. She doubted they'd get any kind of a deal now—seeing how she was a woman living in sin and all.

He gave her a quick squeeze that tickled, and Jane looked up. His eyes caught hers, and for a split second she thought she saw something more than laughter.

On the other side of the counter, Danny DeVito cleared his throat. Pete took the gold band from him, took Jane's hand, and slipped it on her finger. It fit perfectly.

Jane held her hand out, admiring the band. Plain though it was, it was thrilling to be wearing a wedding ring.

"Do you like it?" Pete asked quietly.

She looked up at him, and a genuine smile lit her face. Warmth and contentment washed over her. In that moment, marrying a friend felt nearly perfect.

"I do."

Chapter Sixty-Five

Peter slipped into the pew beside Jane. She gave him a grateful smile before handing Mark over to her mother. The bishop rose to give the announcements, and Pete leaned back, draping his arm across the bench behind Jane. He'd agreed to attend church with her the next three Sundays until he left. He wasn't certain what he'd do when he returned, but he could deal with that later. For now, he was making Jane happy and appeasing her parents.

The opening song was announced. Jane reached for a book and opened it to hymn eighty-five, "How Firm a Foundation." After glancing quickly over the words, Pete looked over at Jane's father, but he was staring straight ahead, his eyes on the chorister at the front of the chapel.

Sneaky, Pete thought, certain her father had requested this particular song. Raising his voice, Pete sang out loud and strong, not willing to let on that he suspected anything. The second verse began, and he found himself caught off guard again. *"In sickness, in health"* certainly brought to mind his impending marriage.

The third stanza stopped him cold.

"At home or abroad, on the land or the sea—As thy days may demand."

A strange feeling came over him. He recognized it as the same he'd felt the first time he and Jane had taken the twins to the park. Someone was watching him. *Watching out for you,* an inner voice whispered. Unable to stop himself, Pete turned and looked behind him but only saw a family with several small children, each busy coloring and consuming Cheerios.

He faced forward again, willing himself to pull it together for the last verse.

"Fear not, I am with thee; oh, be not dismayed, For I am thy God and will still give thee aid."

"Thy God." He thought of the unorthodox prayer he'd uttered a few nights earlier and told himself this couldn't be the help he'd requested. It wasn't an answer or a sign.

As the hymn ended, Pete took the hymn book from Jane and snapped it shut, telling himself once more that the song, those words, were merely coincidence.

Nothing more.

* * *

Loosening his tie, Pete walked across his room and sat down on the bed. When the knot was undone, he pulled the tie completely off, tossing it at the foot of the bed. He lay back, looking at the ceiling and thinking about the past three hours.

Was church always so exhausting? Sacrament meeting alone had about done him in today, what with the songs—the closing hymn had been "Families Can Be Together Forever"—and speakers—a married couple who'd recently gone through the temple. Pete thought he'd done pretty good keeping his cool when the topic had been so obviously arranged for his benefit.

He was all right, that is, until he'd looked over partway through the husband's talk and seen a tear sliding down Jane's cheek. From that point on things went downhill fast. Jane left hurriedly under the guise of changing a diaper, and then Madison, whom she'd left behind, really *did* have a messy diaper. Pete changed her in the too-small bathroom and then spent the next two hours chasing both twins up and down the hall—back and forth past the Seattle temple picture hanging on the wall. By the time church was over, he'd had a splitting headache, and he guessed Jane did too, if her red eyes were any indication.

Remembering her wounded look, Pete raised his hands to his face, covering his own eyes. It didn't help. He imagined he could still see the words from the hymns parading across the front of the temple while Jane stood beside it crying.

It was no good, he realized. He was going to have to pray again to make certain what had happened in church was really just a coincidence. Reluctantly, Pete rolled to the floor, his forehead resting on the side of the bed. He folded his arms and waited, gathering courage to speak when he was so obviously alone.

"Heavenly Father." He'd say a real prayer this time—with the right words and everything, just like the Warners did. "I kneel before You, asking—*begging*—to know if You're there. If Joseph Smith was a prophet. If the Book of Mormon is true. Can I really see Paul and my mom again? Jane believes I can—that You're real, and it's hurting her that I don't feel the same. But I don't." He paused, listening. Waiting.

Nothing.

"I just don't," Pete said, hearing the anguish in his voice. "I don't understand, but I really wish that I did."

Chapter Sixty-Six

The ringing phone woke him from a fitful sleep. Pete glanced at the clock, and seeing it was only 6 A.M., had a moment of panic as he reached across the nightstand. *Is something wrong with Mark?* The caller ID showed an out-of-area number, and he gave a silent sigh of relief when he heard Shane's voice.

"How are you, man?" Shane asked, his loud voice carrying through the line as if he stood right beside Peter.

"Great," Peter said. "Except for the part where I have to report in two weeks."

"Yeah, I know," Shane agreed grumpily. "So, how are those kids of yours? Do I dare ask how the custody thing is going?"

Pete smiled, remembering how he'd spouted his frustrations to Shane, telling him he'd stop at nothing to get full custody of Paul's children. "It's going pretty good, actually. I'm marrying the co-guardian."

"You're *what?*" Shane seemed to recover from his shock quickly. "That's just great. Congratulations. I take it she's a nice girl."

"She's wonderful." Pete paused, debating whether to tell Shane any more. After a few seconds' hesitation, he decided it couldn't possibly hurt. "She's a member of your church."

"She's LDS?" The incredulous tone was back in Shane's voice.

"Yeah," Pete said. "Funny, isn't it? I've even had the missionary lessons the past few months."

The other end of the line remained silent.

"Shane, you still there?"

"I am," Shane said. His voice had gone from loud to quiet and thoughtful. "There's really nothing funny about it, Peter. See, I've had this feeling—this prompting—for weeks now, that . . . that I should call you. I'm sorry I didn't listen earlier."

"No worries," Pete assured him. "We'll see each other soon enough and can catch up then."

"That's not what I mean," Shane said. "I kept having this feeling I should call—and ask if you'd read the Book of Mormon I gave you."

Peter glanced at the book on his nightstand. "I have," he said. "Thanks."

"What—what did you think about it?" Shane asked.

"Well," Peter sat up in bed and turned on the lamp. The strange sensation he'd felt at church was back again. This time he welcomed it.

He took a deep breath. "Actually, I have a couple of questions."

Chapter Sixty-Seven

"We're kidnapping you, Aunt Jane," Jessica announced as Jane opened her front door.

"What?" Jane asked, glancing from Jessica to Caroline.

"For your bridal shower," Jessica continued. She held up a purple bandanna. "Now turn around so I can blindfold you."

"What's this all about?" Jane asked, looking directly at Caroline this time.

Caroline shrugged. "Jess is the boss. She put this whole thing together. You'll have to ask her."

Jane looked down at her niece's expectant face. "Let me call Peter," she said. "Maybe he can stay with the twins."

"He's having a bachelor party tonight, so the twins are coming with us." Jessica pushed past Jane into the house. "Come on, Mom, and help me get them. We've got to get this party going."

Five minutes later, Jane, the purple bandanna tied over her eyes, sat in the back of Caroline's minivan. Jessica chatted merrily on the drive to the *unknown* destination—what Jane quickly recognized, by the route they drove, as her parents' house.

Caroline parked the van, and clutching Jessica's arm, Jane climbed out. Not wanting to spoil the fun for Jessica, she didn't let on that she knew where they were.

The front screen opened, followed by the door, and Jane let Jessica lead her through the house to the backyard. There, Jess pulled out a chair for her and helped her sit down.

"Now stay put, but don't take your blindfold off yet. We'll be ready to start in a few minutes."

Jane sat quietly as Jessica walked off.

"Is this the part where everyone jumps out and yells surprise?"

Jane *was* surprised and nearly did jump at the sound of Pete's voice, mere inches from her.

"What are you doing here?" She reached up to lift a corner of the bandanna.

"Ah-ah." Pete said, putting a hand on hers to stop her. "No peeking."

"Then how come you get to look? And I thought you were supposed to be at some sort of bachelor party."

"I think it's an all-in-one deal," Pete said.

"Or, knowing my parents, more likely it's a plot to make sure neither of us skips town before tomorrow."

"No second thoughts on my part," Pete said. "How about you?"

Jane shook her head. "No." She'd hardly seen Pete all week as he was busy wrapping things up his last few days of work. Every night she poured out her heart in prayer, asking for confirmation she was doing the right thing. And, strangely, every night that confirmation came. She was going through with this marriage. She loved Peter for who he was, and she'd have faith that someday he would be hers forever.

"Here comes Jessica—she says you can take off the blindfold now." He reached behind Jane to untie it. She opened her eyes, blinking several times to adjust to the lights blaring from the patio.

"Ladies and gentlemen," Jessica began, speaking into her karaoke microphone. "We are pleased to gather this evening to celebrate the impending marriage of Aunt Jane and Uncle Peter!" She began to clap and others joined in. Jane looked around the yard and saw her whole family in attendance. Everyone sat at small, round, red-and-white covered tables. A single taper candle flickered in the center of each table. Jane recognized the mints—probably leftover from Jessica's party—sprinkled around the candles, and each table held a disposable camera and a small, dollar-store container of bubbles.

Overwhelmed, Jane looked again at her twelve-year-old niece, who was explaining the program for the evening. Dinner would be buffet-style, served by the other cousins, at the long table by the side gate. After dinner, there would be the opening of presents. Shocked, Jane glanced at the patio table covered in pink- and red-wrapped gifts.

"And finally, after the gifts have been presented, we have some very special entertainment planned." Jessica giggled and looked over at the television set up beside the karaoke machine.

"Oh no," Jane whispered. "Please tell me Caroline isn't planning another Cher concert."

Pete grinned as he rose from the table. "I don't think so." He placed a hand on the back of Jane's chair. "The bride is supposed to be served first, so let's go eat."

* * *

Dinner consisted of barbeque chicken, salads, and fruit-and-marshmallow kabobs with chocolate fondue. Caroline said that, with the exception of barbequing the chicken, Jessica and Amber had planned and carried out the whole party themselves.

When Jane sought the girls out to thank them, they each gave her a hug.

"Everyone deserves a bridal shower, Aunt Jane," Jessica said.

"Especially you," Amber added. "You had to wait *so long*." She rolled her eyes.

Instead of feeling hurt or offended, Jane laughed. "You're right, I did."

"It's time to open presents now," Jessica said, pulling Jane to one of two chairs set up on the patio.

Feeling embarrassed, Jane sat next to Peter and began opening packages from the pink pile. In addition to the traditional dish towels and cookbooks most brides received, she opened a large package of stationery for writing to Peter, and several bags of chocolate.

"The chocolate is for the first week Pete's gone," Caroline explained. "You're on your own for purchasing the repentance grapefruit."

"Thanks, Caroline," Jane said, a catch in her voice. "This is so nice. I can't believe you guys went to so much work."

Pete opened all the red-wrapped presents next, and the gifts he got were even more unusual. Caroline had given him a copy of *Ladies Home Journal* and *Women's Day*. An attached note said that she was arranging for a subscription to each to be delivered to his unit in Iraq.

"I expect you to read up," Caroline said. "Learn all you can while you're away, so that by the time you come home you have a better understanding of women and their feelings."

"Good luck," Ryan called.

"Should have gotten him *Sports Illustrated*," Scott shouted.

Jane's mother gave him a large bag of her homemade brownie mix. "I'm sure if you give it to the cook over there, he'll be able to bake those up for you."

Rising from his chair, Pete walked over and gave Marsha a hug. Jane guessed that if she'd been closer, she would have seen tears in both their eyes.

Karen's gift was an eight-by-ten of the whole family that she'd taken at Easter. Peter and Jane were in the middle of the picture, each with a baby in their arms. Looking at the photo, Jane was struck by how normal they looked—a regular little family, just like everyone else.

Pete thanked everyone again, then turned to her. "And now I've got something for you."

"Me first," Jane said. "Just a minute." She returned to the table where they'd been sitting earlier and pulled an envelope from her purse. She walked back to the patio and handed it to Peter. He glanced up at her, then opened it, removing two tickets.

He grinned. "All right. Barenaked Ladies."

"*Jane!*" Her mother rose from her chair and started marching toward them. "This is not that kind—Why would you—?"

"They're just concert tickets, Mom."

Grinning, Pete held them out for Marsha to examine.

Jane giggled as she tried to explain. "They're a Canadian band—Pete's favorite—and I read last month they were coming to town, so I decided to surprise him with tickets."

"They're all men and completely clothed," Pete added. He reached for Jane's hand and pulled her onto his lap. "Thank you," he whispered, then kissed her. A familiar thrill shot through Jane. They hadn't kissed for weeks, but the chemistry between them was still there—as strong as ever.

"Well, all right, then." Marsha returned the tickets, and Pete slid them into his shirt pocket. "What a name." Shaking her head, Marsha went back to her table.

Ignoring her mother, Jane bent to kiss Peter again.

"Ah-ah. Enough of that," Jessica said, walking onto the patio. "It's karaoke time."

"I am *not* singing tonight," Jane said.

"Of course not." Jessica rolled her eyes. "It's *your* party. *Uncle Peter* is going to sing."

Jane's eyebrows rose. "Really?" She looked at Peter. He shrugged and gently moved her from his lap.

"Did Jess put you up to this?" she asked.

"Nope. It was all his idea." Amber handed Pete the microphone. "The CD is ready to go."

"You sit here, Aunt Jane." Jess pulled her back into the other patio chair as the music started.

"Oh no," Jane murmured, quickly recognizing the tune. "How appropriate," she said, attempting a joke as she looked up at Peter. He wasn't smiling anymore, but looking at her as he had that night on the beach. She read desire in his eyes and tenderness and something else she couldn't quite place.

The lyrics started. The song was "Jane," from his *Best of BNL*—as she liked to think of the band—CD. He'd played it for her the first time when they'd driven out to the beach to look at the stars.

Folding her arms, Jane squirmed uncomfortably in her chair. Why on earth would Pete choose to sing a love ballad in front of her entire family? But glancing out at the yard, she was astonished to see they were nearly alone. Caroline was herding the last of the cousins out through the side gate, just as Jessica and Amber snuck in the house through the back door. Slowly, Jane looked up at Peter again. He sang as he walked toward her, his tenor voice on perfect pitch with the song, the words seeming to be his own.

The music trailed off, and he got down on one knee in front of her. She felt her heart pounding as he took her hand.

"Jane," he said. "Would you do me the honor—of attending my baptism next Wednesday?"

"Wha-at?" She brought her free hand to her cheek. "Did you just say ba—?"

"Baptism," Pete confirmed, a smile breaking out over his face. "I finally understand Joseph Smith. I know he restored the gospel. I *know* it."

Jane read the excitement in his eyes. "You're serious?"

He nodded. "The answer was right in front of me the whole time. I can't believe it took me so long to see the truth."

"What happened?" Jane asked.

"I remembered," Pete said. "I've never told you about the year I was fourteen, but it was really rough. Mom was having her first bout with cancer, and Paul was having his time of rebellion. I had to hold everyone and everything together . . . and I did."

He squeezed her hand as his grin widened. "I've tried to forget that year, almost had, until I was talking to my friend Shane last week and he reminded me. The thing I remembered most was the time I spent asking some divine being for help and guidance—as I paid the bills, gave Mom her medicine, had words with Paul. And I got the help, the answers." Pete paused, looking at Jane intently. She leaned forward, trying to understand what he was telling her.

"I realized that if I could ask and get an answer at such a young age, of course Joseph Smith could too."

Jane sat frozen for another several seconds, then she threw herself forward, into Peter's arms. "I love you, Peter. You've just made me the happiest woman in the world."

"And I'm not even done yet." He laughed as he removed her arms from around his neck and set her back in the chair. Reaching into his shirt pocket, he withdrew a small, white box. He opened it, revealing the solitaire she'd admired at the jewelry store.

"Marry me, Jane," he whispered. "I mean, *really* marry me. I'm in love with you, and I want nothing less than to spend forever proving it."

Jane brought a hand to her lips as words failed her. Tears spilled over her eyes and she nodded. She couldn't even think of a movie scene this moment compared to. It was everything she'd ever dreamed of.

Peter took the ring from the box and slipped it on her finger. It fit perfectly.

"How did you—?"

"I'm a bit slow at first." A corner of his mouth lifted. "But after that I catch on very quickly."

"I love it. I love you," Jane exclaimed, then leaned forward and kissed him.

From around the corner of the house, and just inside the back door, applause broke out. Jane laughed as she looked up and saw all the faces pressed to the glass at the door and window. A moment later they were surrounded by Jane's family, her sisters and nieces clamoring to see the ring, while the guys slapped Pete on the back and congratulated him.

Jane longed to be alone with Peter but found she couldn't even reach him across the sea of her family. But for a moment their eyes met, and she saw in them the promise of tomorrow.

Chapter Sixty-Eight

Jane's fingers fumbled with the alarm as she tried, half asleep, to shut it off. After several annoying seconds, she found the right button, and the shrill beeping ceased. With a moan, she rolled over and stretched, her arms reaching out beneath the canopy of her old bed. For a minute she wondered why she was home, but a glint of sunlight peeked through the frilly curtains and caught the sparkle of the diamond on her finger. Jane froze.

She stared at the ring, not quite believing it was there. Slowly, she lowered her hand and touched the very real diamond. Her face broke into a smile, and a squeal of delight escaped her lips. She sat up, hugging her knees to her chest. Today, she was marrying Peter. In only a few more days, he was getting baptized.

Resting her chin on her knees, she closed her eyes and allowed herself the luxury of reliving the previous evening—especially the last part when Peter had proposed to her. *I'm in love with you*, he'd said. Words she'd begun to believe she'd never hear from any man. *I love you. I love you. I love you.* Her heart sang, remembering Peter's love and sincere testimony. *Joseph Smith restored the gospel. I know it's true.*

Kneeling on her bed, Jane closed her eyes, folded her arms, and offered a prayer filled with gratitude. That she was so blessed seemed a true miracle. She could hardly wait until next Wednesday, and she could hardly wait until ten o'clock when they were supposed to meet at the courthouse.

Jane stretched again, then swung her legs over the side of the bed. It was only six thirty, but she decided she'd shower now before the twins woke up. She wanted plenty of time to make sure she looked her best today.

She stopped midstep, mouth hanging open at the sight before her. Instead of the white suit she'd purchased, a gown—long, white, and flowing—hung from the back of the door. On unsteady legs, Jane padded across the floor to see if the dress, too, were real. Reaching up, she lifted the hanger from the door. Gently, she pulled the plastic off and laid it on the bed. She ran her fingers down the back of the gown, tracing the pearl buttons. Looking at the door, she saw the train billowing out from a second hanger.

It was the dress from the store.

Holding it up to her shoulders, Jane walked across the room to look in the mirror. She stared at her reflection and saw past her tousled hair and plain brown eyes. It was the dress of miracles—even at six thirty in the morning, it made her feel beautiful.

"Jane? Are you awake, dear?" The door opened and her mother stepped into the room. She held the matching veil in her hands.

Jane turned to her. "Oh, Mom . . ." Her voice caught as she saw the tears already flowing from her mother's eyes.

* * *

Jessica bounced up and down on her toes as she waited. "Hurry, Aunt Jane. You're not going to believe this."

"Oh, I might," Jane said, laughing. At this time yesterday, she certainly wouldn't have believed anything about a diamond ring, a real wedding dress, a gorgeous bouquet that included her favorite flowers ordered from Hawaii, or the customized CD Pete had made for her to listen to as she got ready this morning.

She leaned over the counter for a last glance at her lipstick as "I'm a Believer" played in the background. Yes. A believer she definitely was. She turned to Jessica. "Let me guess, there's a limo parked outside?"

"Not even close," Jessica said.

"A horse-drawn carriage?"

"Still cold." Jessica grabbed her hand and pulled her from the bedroom down the hall.

"Slow down," Jane begged as she gathered the layers of her gown. Jessica continued towing her to the open front door.

Jane stepped over the threshold to the porch. Her eyes widened in disbelief. "A *backhoe*? No way." She wouldn't have been more surprised to see a pumpkin-turned-coach parked in front of the house.

Beside her, Jessica jumped up and down. "Isn't it great?"

Jane could only nod her agreement as she looked at the shiny backhoe, covered in flowers and ribbon. A similarly decorated open carriage was attached by heavy chain to the back. Lifting the hem of her gown again, Jane hurried down the walk. "Max?" she asked, surprised, as she recognized the tuxedo-clad man standing beside the front tire. She was used to seeing him in denim and behind the counter at the equipment rental company she often used.

"At your service." He gave her a little bow.

Jane ran forward and hugged him. "What are you doing?"

He grinned. "Heard you needed an escort to your wedding, and horses are in short supply in these parts—more messy too," he added with a chuckle.

"It's perfect," Jane exclaimed, running her finger over the new paint. "Much better than a horse."

"She's a beaut, ain't she?" he agreed. His face fell. "Shame I won't be seeing much of you anymore though."

Jane tore her gaze from the decorated machine to Max. Her brow furrowed. "What do you mean you won't be seeing me? I'm your best customer. And Peter is very supportive of my business. So don't you worry."

"Oh I ain't worried—'cept maybe 'bout you getting hurt driving this thing. But you won't be needing me anymore, seeing as how you own this baby now."

Jane's mouth opened in astonishment. "I *own* it?"

"Yes-siree." Max nodded. His grin was back. "Though the groom told me specific that you're not to drive it today. He wants you safe to the church."

"Does he now," Jane mused. She glanced at the driveway where her mother was unlocking the car. "Someone want to tell me what happened to the courthouse?"

"Oh, you couldn't get married *there*," Jessica exclaimed. "Everything is all ready for you at the church. Grandma and Grandpa took care of it."

"I see," Jane said, her lips pursed in amusement.

Max walked over to the carriage and held the door open for her. "Ladies." He gave a little bow.

"Can I ride with you, Aunt Jane?" Jessica begged. "Please. It's only a few blocks, and Grandma says the twins can't come because they have to be in their car seats, so can I—please?"

"Of course," Jane said. "You can be my lady in waiting." She stepped aside, allowing her exuberant niece to board first. When they'd both settled on the velvet-covered seats, Max shut the half door.

"Mind your hair bobs. We won't go too fast, but I'd hate for you to lose them." With a quick nod, he returned to the backhoe and climbed up.

"He bought me a backhoe," Jane said once more.

Jessica giggled. "I know. Isn't it silly?"

"Not silly," Jane corrected her. "*Romantic.* I bet I'm the only girl who ever had a backhoe drive her to the church for her wedding."

"Probably," Jessica agreed. She looked at Jane. "You're *so lucky.*"

Jane squeezed her niece's hand. "I know."

All too soon, the stake center came into view, but not before Jane had waved to the few cars that drove by, honking their horns as they passed. She wondered vaguely if Pete was planning the same mode of transportation when they left the church. Was there a Just Married sign on the back of the carriage?

Max parked the backhoe, turned it off, and came around to let them out. "How was the ride?" he bellowed.

"Wonderful," Jane said, lifting her gown as she descended the steps to the sidewalk. "Maybe you should think about doing this as a side job."

Max pretended to consider it for a moment. "Nah," he said at last. "I don't think many women would appreciate it like you did. It takes a mighty special female . . ." His voice trailed off and he gave her a wink. "I'm going to go park this around back. See you inside."

Jane gave him another quick hug. "Thank you." Gathering her gown in both hands, she began the walk that led to the open doors of the building. Behind her, Jessica followed, holding up her train.

Reaching the entrance, Jane hesitated. Was she supposed to go right in? Her parents' car was already here—their Volvo traveled a bit faster than a backhoe. Glancing at the parking lot, Jane recognized several cars belonging to other family members.

"Why are we waiting?" Jessica asked, impatient. "You're not scared, are you?"

"No. Of course not." Jane climbed the last step and entered the foyer. She paused, waiting for her eyes to adjust to the change in light.

Jessica fanned the train out behind her, then gave a little wave and hurried away. Jane stood still, unsure what to do next, when suddenly her father was beside her.

He held out his arm, and Jane placed trembling fingers on his sleeve. Her father patted her hand reassuringly. Leaning close, he whispered, "Nice of you to spare us all that bridesmaid and line business we had with the other kids."

"No problem, Dad." Jane gave him a peck on the cheek.

"I love you, sweetheart." He looked into her eyes a moment, then turned his head to the doors of the chapel. "And so does that man in there."

Jane walked with her father to the chapel doors, following his gaze down the aisle to Peter, standing stiffly—tall, dark, and handsome—in his tuxedo. He had known about this, had planned it all.

Matching her father's footsteps, Jane started the walk toward *her* groom. For the first time in her life, she understood what it meant to have a heart swell with happiness. Hers felt near to bursting beneath the magnificent gown that floated around her. Behind, she felt the weight of her train as it glided across the floor. Her hand clutched the exquisite bouquet that had been delivered that morning.

Glancing to the side, Jane saw the pews filled with family and friends. Tara, wearing a bright orange pantsuit, waved a tissue. Jane noticed a whole box on the empty seat beside her.

Wait, Jane thought. *Wait for the right one, Tara. It's so worth it.*

Jane looked to the front of the chapel again. Her father escorted her the last few feet, gave her a kiss on the cheek, and stepped aside, sitting next to her mother and the twins, who were dressed in new, matching outfits.

Jane lifted her face to Peter's, love and adoration in his eyes. It seemed they both caught their breath at the same moment. She wouldn't have believed he could look more handsome than he normally did—but standing there in his tuxedo, he literally stole her breath away. She felt beautiful as he studied her, unabashed longing in his gaze.

"I love you," he whispered.

He held his hand out. Without hesitation, Jane placed hers in it. His fingers closed over hers. They lingered, looking at each other, savoring the joy of this moment—theirs alone.

A loud hiccup-sob, followed by a mournful wail, came from somewhere in the congregation. Recognizing the cry as Tara's, Jane felt the corner of her mouth lift in a smile. Pete grinned back and gently squeezed her fingers. Together they turned to the bishop, ready to speak the vows that would begin their happily-ever-after.

Chapter Sixty-Nine

Peter escorted Jane past interested passengers to the top deck of the ferry. Her heels long since abandoned for sandals, Jane picked up her train so it wouldn't trail behind her. Driving in their wedding clothes in the Jeep—decorated with signs, streamers, and cans—had been embarrassing enough. But Jane was truly shocked when they'd boarded the ferry and Peter insisted they walk around.

"How long do you get to wear this dress?" he'd asked when she balked at getting out of the car.

Jane felt her face heat with embarrassment. "I think that sort of depends on you."

Pete chuckled. "That's not what I meant. You only have one time—one day to be a bride. Why not enjoy it as long as you can? Besides, I want every man on board this ferry to see what I've got and be jealous."

Now, walking across the deck, Jane wasn't sure if *jealous* was the right word. More likely, the other passengers thought she and Peter were insane.

"I still don't see why we couldn't change," she whispered, feeling herself blush as row after row of people stared at them.

Pete grinned. "Because this is every woman's dream—the stuff of romance novels." He pulled Jane over to the rail. "Or so your sister told me. Look." He inclined his head toward the receding shoreline.

Jane followed his gaze. Silhouetted in the setting sun, the Seattle skyline *was* amazing.

"It's been so long since I've been on the ferry. I'd forgotten . . . The view is beautiful."

"I was thinking the same thing," Pete said, looking intently at her. "About you."

Jane rolled her eyes. "Now there's a pickup line if I ever heard one."

He looked offended. "No line. Just the absolute truth." He bent to kiss her.

A couple of teenagers snickered as they walked past.

"Jealous. I told you." Pete said, his lips still hovering over hers.

"I know." Jane kissed him quickly, then turned to look out at the bay. They stood in companionable silence for a few moments, her thoughts a mixture of anticipation and anxiety for the night ahead.

As if he'd read her mind, Pete took her hand and began rubbing his thumb across her palm. The seductive motion unnerved her even more.

"You know," he began. "I'm as nervous as you are."

Jane looked up at him." Really?"

He nodded. "What if you don't like the place we're staying at? What if dinner is not to your satisfaction? What if—?"

"Stop," she giggled, then felt herself blushing. "People are already staring at us." She took a step to the side—away from him.

"Then it really doesn't matter what we do, does it? And anyway, I'm reminded of a movie, just now," Pete said.

"You're mocking me." She tried to frown at him.

"Not at all," Pete said. "I'm completely serious. Name this film. I'm on a boat, and . . . I'm king of the world!" His voice carried across the deck.

Jane turned away, laughing. Another couple smiled at her sympathetically as they walked past.

"He's ill," Jane said, nodding in Pete's direction.

"Liar," he whispered as he came up beside her. "And I can't believe you didn't guess *Titanic*. Pete put his arms around her. "Well, no worries about this boat sinking. I see the shore already. Come on, we'd better get back to the Jeep."

* * *

"Watch your dress," Pete said, holding the car door open for Jane. Draping the train over her arm, she slid into the passenger seat. Pete tucked in the last of the fabric and closed the door. A minute later he was seated beside her, waiting for the ferry to dock.

"So," Jane asked casually. "Where are we staying?"

Pete grinned. "Nice try, but you have to wait. I was actually hoping you'd show me your cottage first. I'd like to see it before it's sold—it is on Bainbridge, right?"

She nodded. "I don't know if Tara could handle seeing us again though. She was pretty torn up today—I think I was her last single friend."

"We wouldn't have to go in. Besides—" He glanced at his watch. "We have some time to kill before our dinner reservations."

"Please tell me we're going to change first," Jane said.

He shrugged. "I guess that depends on your behavior. Show me the cottage?"

Jane leaned her head back against the seat. "It sounds like I'd better unless I want to risk getting dinner all over my gown."

Pete drove the Jeep off the ferry, and Jane pointed him in the right direction. She smiled as she watched him from the corner of her eye. They came to a stop sign and the people behind them beeped and waved. Turning around in her seat, Jane waved back. "Was it Caroline who suggested decorating the car?"

"I think that was all Jessica and Amber." Pete looked at her. "And for your information, beyond Caroline suggesting I learn how to propose properly, she had nothing to do with any of this."

"Any of what?" Jane asked. "Turn left here. It's the second house on . . ." She blinked to make sure she was seeing things properly, then leaned forward in her seat.

Peter parked in front of the cottage, and Jane opened the door and got out before he could come around to get her. Holding her dress up, she ran to the gate and opened it. Walking across the grass, she stopped at several different plants and trees, examining them. Finally she turned to the house and saw Peter, standing on newly poured steps—leaning against a post on an also-new porch.

"I don't understand," she began. "The yard is exactly like I'd planned—right down to the very last bush and tree I had listed in my black book. But there's no way Tara could have . . ." Her voice trailed off. Realizing there was something to the mischievous smile on his face, she moved closer to Peter.

His eyebrows rose. "Yes?"

"Did you—did *you* do this?"

"Depends on how you look at it. If you're asking if I'm the one who mowed and planted and dug and poured—then no. At least not most of it." He came down the steps to Jane. "However, I will say that you aren't very particular about where you keep your little black book, and I may have stolen an idea or two from there."

"But Peter—" Her eyes filled with tears. She turned around in a circle, arms out as she looked at the yard again. "This must have cost thousands of dollars. And it's only mine for a couple more weeks."

He came to her, tipping her chin up. "It's yours forever, Jane. The loan is paid off. You own it one hundred percent."

Her eyes were wide with astonishment. "*You* bought the cottage?"

Pete nodded. "I haven't got the title yet, but all the paperwork is inside. I'm the mysterious out-of-town buyer."

"You *bought* the house," she said again, then threw her arms around him. Peter swept her up and whirled her around in a circle. When he set her down again, she took his face in her hands and pulled him close for a long, lingering kiss.

When their lips parted, he was surprised to find Jane frowning at him.

"We can't live here, Peter. It's too far away from the hospital, and if Mark were to need medical attention . . ."

"I know," Peter said. "For now it'll just be our vacation home."

"Can you afford it?" Jane asked.

He chuckled. "I'm thirty-four years old," he reminded her. "I've been an attorney since I was twenty-seven, and I've never had a mortgage or any other large expenses. I've been saving—for you."

She blushed, and Pete knew she'd caught the double meaning. He bent and picked her up, cradling her in his arms. "Now, it's time to see the inside."

"The *inside?*" Jane asked. Her feet kicked excitedly like a little girl's.

"I didn't have time to finish the whole thing," Pete admitted as he carried her up the steps. "But you're going to love the bedroom."

Chapter Seventy

"You sure you're not hungry?"

Jane shook her head. She knew going out to dinner would prolong their evening, but she felt way too nervous to eat anything. "How about you?"

"Starving." Pete looked at her with undisguised longing.

Jane bit her lip. "In that case, let's go out." She started toward the door.

He caught her arm and their eyes met. "You *know* what I mean."

Jane swallowed the lump in her throat. She looked around the bedroom again, still not quite able to believe the transformation. The four-poster bed, fireplace, and lavish draperies reminded her more of an elegant bed and breakfast. It was the brand-new, oversized Jacuzzi tub in the bathroom that was making her feel faint though.

"The house is perfect," she whispered. "I can't tell you enough how—I love it."

Peter looked at her tenderly. His fingers slid down her arm, and he took both her hands in his. "I wanted you to know how much you mean to me. I want to give you everything in my power. You deserve a fairy tale, Jane."

Freeing one of her hands, she placed her palm on the side of his cheek. "I love you too. I wish I had something spectacular to give you like the house—"

"You do." The mischief returned to his eyes. "Since you're not hungry, we can get right to the business of your tutoring me in the art of love-making."

Jane rolled her eyes. "*Please.*"

"Please what? Please kiss me right here?" He leaned forward and kissed her earlobe. "Please do that again? I'm afraid you're going to have to be more specific tonight."

Jane giggled. "You're terrible—positively wicked."

"I told you women like the bad guys."

"Oh no." She shook her head adamantly. "You've got it all wrong there. It's really the *good* ones we're after, and I waited a *very* long time to find mine."

He turned her around and began unbuttoning her gown. Jane closed her eyes, enjoying the bliss of his fingers brushing against her skin.

Pete whispered as he bent to kiss her neck.

"Take as long as you need to get ready, but leave your hair up. It drives me crazy."

* * *

A few minutes later, Jane stood on tiptoe, looking in the bathroom mirror at her white silk nightgown. Tara's note lay on top of the box the gown—and mask, snorkel, and fins—had come in.

> *Jane,*
>
> *When you decide to take the relationship plunge, boy you take it! I'm so happy for you, so glad the strong undertow turned out to be a swift current to the Mediterranean.*
>
> *Tonight I want none of that Gertrude's Mystery Flannel you usually wear to bed. However, I tried to think of your tastes when I picked this out.*
>
> *Love,*
> *Tara*
>
> *P.S. Remember, while you're swimming in that sea of love, come up for air occasionally.*

Jane hugged her arms to herself, feeling feminine and beautiful—and awkward and jittery.

"Jane?"

Startled by Peter's voice on the other side of the door, she jumped, stubbing her toe on the tile. He knocked again. "You okay?"

"Just a minute," she called in a squeaky, uncertain voice. Taking a last look in the mirror, she opened the bathroom door and glanced toward the bed where Peter sat, looking less at ease than she'd ever seen him. "You can't possibly be as nervous as I am."

"More so," he said half serious. "As the guy, I'm supposed to know everything."

"Well, do you?" Jane asked, her nerves soothed by his endearing confession. She stepped into the room, but lingered by the door.

Peter rose from the bed and walked over to her, pulling her into a gentle embrace. "I know that I love you, and I'm pretty certain that'll be enough."

Chapter Seventy-One

Pete wrapped the blanket around Jane and pulled her close beside him on the roof. The night air was chill around them, but with her by his side he was warm. He looked up at the stars as Jane snuggled against him.

"Careful," Pete warned. "You wouldn't want to pitch your husband off the roof the very first night you're married. The insurance company might find that suspicious."

"Don't worry," Jane assured him. "It was way too much work to find you in the first place. I'm not about to push you to your death."

Pete chuckled. "I'll remind you of that the first time you're angry with me."

She leaned her head on his shoulder. "We shouldn't joke about dying."

"You're right," he agreed. His smile fled. "But it would be a good idea to talk about it—before I leave."

"Don't do it," Jane said. "End of discussion."

"Yes dear," Pete said. "How was that? I've been practicing."

Jane looked up at him, eyes filled with love. "You don't have to practice anything. You're already perfect."

"I'm not," he insisted. "And don't you go thinking that." He tilted her chin to him. "If something happens, don't you dare remember me as a perfect guy. Think of all the times I made you mad instead, okay?"

"I forgot them already."

"Try to remember," he coaxed gently. "And count the stars." He released her and looked up at the night sky. "I've always thought that when someone dies, there's a new star—not forever, and not for everyone—but just for a short while, kind of a sign for those left behind."

"Have you ever seen one?"

He nodded. "I know every constellation, and after my mom died, and then again with Paul—I swear I saw a new star for three nights in a row. If angels can appear, then why not extra stars?"

He glanced down at Jane, but her expression was unreadable in the dark. "If something happens—you give me ten days. *Just* ten days," he reiterated. "And I'll do everything I can so you'll know I'm either alive or . . ."

"Count the stars," Jane said quietly. "Like *The Lion King*."

"You're right." Pete smiled. "I guess life really is like the movies."

"Just not my life," Jane whispered. *Please, not my life.*

Chapter Seventy-Two

Reluctantly, Pete set Mark on the blanket and reached for his duffel bag.

"I'll walk you to the door," Jane said, stoically holding back a dam of tears.

"Come on, then." He took her hand and towed her to the front door just as the shuttle pulled up out front.

"You should have let us take you to the airport," Jane said again.

"I want to remember you here, at the house, just like you were the first night I came home."

She gave him a sad smile. "I hope you can think of better nights than that one to remember."

"I don't know . . ." Pete grinned. "How many couples do you know who can say they spent their first date getting arrested?" He set his bag down and pulled her close for a last hug and kiss.

Madison toddled from the family room to the door, trying to squeeze in between them as she clung to their legs. Pete looked down at her.

"Da-da," she babbled, holding her arms up.

Pete knelt and kissed the top of her head. "Not much of a birthday present, your dad leaving like this." When he stood again, there were tears in his eyes. He looked at Jane.

"I came home six months ago to nothing—no one. Today, I'm leaving a new man with a family and the gospel." He touched her face one last time. "Thank you."

"Come home to your family," Jane whispered, her heart breaking as she watched him walk across the lawn toward the shuttle. "Please, come home."

* * *

Date: Tue, 27 July 2004 8:14 AM
From: "Jane Warner" <janegardengirl@hotmail.com>
To: "Peter Bryant" <petesdragon2@hotmail.com>
Subject: I miss you

Peter, you've ruined me. Thirty years of sleeping alone is all down the drain after one week of sharing a bed with you. I couldn't sleep ALL night. The bed seemed so empty. Everything is empty. The house is too quiet. I cooked too much dinner. It's hard to imagine you're so far away when just last week was the happiest day of my life at your baptism. Please tell me this is going to get easier . . .

Date: Sat, 31 July 2004 4:10 PM
From: "Peter Bryant" <petesdragon2@hotmail.com>
To: "Jane Warner" <janegardengirl@hotmail.com>
Subject: You too

Jane, I'm sorry you're having trouble sleeping. Honestly, I've been so exhausted that hasn't been a problem for me—yet. I put our wedding picture up, and all the guys told me what a hot wife I have. I also won the award for "most accomplished while off duty." Another guy got married, and a couple of other guys' wives had babies, but no one could compete with getting married, getting baptized, and having twins—not to mention getting arrested . . .

Date: Tue, 3 Aug 2004 7:35 PM
From: "Jane Warner" <janegardengirl@hotmail.com>
To: "Peter Bryant" <petesdragon2@hotmail.com>
Subject: Elephants and ice cream

Caroline and I took the kids to Woodland Park Zoo today. Maddie was wild for the elephants and threw a major fit when we finally (after twenty minutes) left them to go see the other animals. Mark's favorite thing was the ice cream. He got it everywhere—his hair was stiff and sticky for half the day . . .

Date: Sun, 8 Aug 2004 4:34 PM
From: "Peter Bryant" <petesdragon2@hotmail.com>
To: "Jane Warner" <janegardengirl@hotmail.com>
Subject: Miss you—a lot

It's hot, dusty, and lonely here. Every time I see a little kid, I think of Mark and Maddie. I miss playing with them and going in to check on them at night when they're asleep. I'd even take changing a diaper right now, just for a couple of minutes to see their smiles and feel their hands pat my face. Which brings me to the person I miss the most—you. It's like you said, thirty-plus years of living single, all down the drain. I think of you every hour of the day. I can't wait to come home . . .

Date: Wed, 11 Aug 2004 10:12 AM
From: "Jane Warner" <janegardengirl@hotmail.com>
To: "Peter Bryant" <petesdragon2@hotmail.com>
Subject: Mark

Peter—I'm so worried about Mark's surgery tomorrow. I wish you were here to tell me everything is going to be all right. I keep telling myself that his doctors are wonderful, that he's been through this before, but none of that brings any comfort. I just want to call and cancel the whole thing . . .

Date: Wed,11 Aug 2004 4:07 PM
From: "Peter Bryant" <petesdragon2@hotmail.com>
To: "Jane Warner" <janegardengirl@hotmail.com>
Subject: You can do this!

Jane, don't cancel. Mark will do fine. He's made it through worse, and he's strong. I've arranged to call you—don't know if it will actually be tomorrow or the next day, but I'll call sometime after the surgery. I can't wait to hear your voice. Give Mark and Maddie hugs for me. I love you.

Pete

Chapter Seventy-Three

Jane reached across the hospital bed, capturing Mark's toes. "This little piggy went to McDonald's, this little piggy went to Burger King . . ." She wiggled each one as she tried to remember the silly jingle Peter used to play with him. She had it wrong, or she simply wasn't as funny—either way Mark wasn't laughing as he usually did. Instead, his face was sullen, and he leaned forward, arms outstretched, a pitiful cry begging her to take him away from this strange, scary place.

More than anything, Jane wished she could. Watching the nurses draw Mark's blood, and seeing him poked and prodded for the early morning lab work, had been enough to bring them both to tears. He was so little, and they'd already hurt him so much. And the awful part hadn't even begun. She tried not to think about that, about the scar that ran down the center of his tiny chest, or about the scalpel that would open it once again.

Fighting the terrible, gripping fear that had been building all week, Jane leaned forward, wrapping her arms around Mark in a tight embrace. She whispered soothing words in his ear, patted his head, and pulled his hospital gown closed at the back so he wouldn't get cold.

But she didn't take him and run away. *Help us, Heavenly Father,* she prayed silently. *Please comfort Mark, and give me the strength I need to see this through.*

Mark's arms wrapped around her neck, clinging as he almost never did. A sad smile touched Jane's lips as she remembered how diligently she'd worked with him, teaching him how to give hugs. At home he wasn't much for snuggling, but the cold, sterile environment at the hospital had made him as clingy as a koala.

Holding Mark securely with one arm, she leaned down to the chair beside the bed and picked up the large shopping bag she'd brought with her this morning. Opening it, she removed the teddy bear—nearly as big as its new owner—and held it up for Mark to see. She'd planned to give it to him after the surgery but decided there was no point in waiting. She could buy another stuffed animal to celebrate then. In fact, she'd buy a dozen. That's exactly what Peter would do if he were here.

"Look at the bear, Mark," Jane cooed. She pried one of his hands from her neck and ran his fingers down the bear's arm. "Feel how soft."

Mark didn't seem impressed with the fur but eagerly poked a finger at one of the large, plastic eyes. Grateful he was distracted for the moment, Jane eased him back onto the bed and glanced up at the clock.

8:50 A.M. Any minute now they would come get him. Could she really let him go? It had taken her over fifteen minutes just to sign the papers this morning. Words like *liability, release,* and *death* had jumped out from the pages, making her wonder yet again if this was the right thing to do and the right time to do it.

Mark looked up at her again, his lips puckering in another cry. Jane smiled and rubbed his arm reassuringly.

Sitting in the big bed with the oversized bear beside him, he looked even smaller and more vulnerable than he had before. The sleeves of the hospital gown came nearly to his wrists—the whole thing was drowning him. It wasn't made for such a miniature patient. For some reason this panicked Jane even more. *If they can't get the hospital gown right, how are they going to perform surgery on a fifteen-pound one-year-old?*

Tears burned behind her eyes, and she blinked them back. *He shouldn't be here. He's too little. How did you do this the first time, Paul?* She looked up at the ceiling, sending a silent prayer heavenward. *Please watch out for Mark today. Be with him when I can't.* Jane wrapped her arms around her middle and bit down on her lip, trying to hold the tears at bay. It was all she could do not to scoop Mark into her arms and whisk him away from here. *What I wouldn't give to have this all over and Mark safely at home where he belongs.*

But she forced her feet to stay rooted to the spot, her eyes glued to her baby, savoring every minute she had. *Most parents think taking their babies in to be vaccinated is difficult—and it is,* she thought. *But it's nothing compared to this, to knowing such trauma must be inflicted on your child in order to sustain his life.*

Mark wrapped one arm around the bear's head and held his other out to Jane. She bent over the bed, holding him again. *What will you think when they take you away and I stay behind? Oh, Peter, I wish you were here.*

The door swung open and Jane let out a breath of relief when she saw it was her parents. Mark recognized them too, and his face seemed to light up at more familiar faces. Her mom took one look at her and came over and held Jane tightly, much as Jane had held Mark a few minutes earlier.

"Everything will be all right." Her mother whispered the soothing words in Jane's ear as she stroked her hair.

In that moment Jane had a glimpse of understanding she'd never felt before. "I love you Mom.

"Eh-hm," Robert Warner cleared his throat loudly.

"And you too, Dad." She stepped from her mother's embrace and wiped a tear away. "I never understood how hard being a parent is."

"You still don't." Her dad's voice was teasing, and he smiled at her. "And you won't until you've raised a teenager like Caroline."

Jane laughed, grateful for the distraction, and leaned forward to give her dad a quick hug.

The door opened again, and two nurses entered, their hair covered, blue gowns on, and looking ready for surgery. Jane had met one of them previously and knew she would be attending Mark today.

"All ready?" the familiar one asked casually—as if Jane were sending Mark off to a birthday party or his first day of kindergarten—or some other completely normal activity. But there was nothing normal about this. She'd never be ready.

"Not quite," her father said, stepping close to Mark. "If you'll let us have another minute, I'll give this boy a blessing, and we'll have a word of prayer."

The nurses exchanged awkward glances. "We'll be right back then," the second one said, and the two left the room.

"I know we just gave Mark a blessing yesterday," Robert said. "But on the way over, I kept thinking that maybe he should have one more—for comfort."

"That would be nice." Jane felt another swell of gratitude for her parents and the priesthood.

Her father stepped forward and tousled Mark's hair. "How ya doing today, little guy?"

Mark looked up at the three of them, his eyes large in his pale face. He smiled, revealing his two new teeth on top. Jane felt her throat constrict as her father placed his hands on Mark's head. She closed her eyes, listening to the words of comfort, and felt a quiet peace wrap itself around her heart. The strength she'd prayed for so fervently was suddenly hers.

The prayer ended. The nurses returned. A last-minute check of Mark's blood pressure and temperature was all it took to start him crying again. Jane carried him to the bed waiting in the hall, and she walked beside it as they wheeled him toward the doors at the far end. At the last minute, the nurse took his teddy bear and handed it to Jane. Mark cried louder, his arms reaching toward her. Jane blew him a kiss as tears streamed down her face.

A second later he disappeared through the doors. Jane clutched the bear to her chest and closed her eyes, listening as Mark's cries continued on the other side.

* * *

Caroline bent down, picked up Madison, and moved her away from the open dishwasher—for the third time.

"You're a determined little girl, aren't you?" Caroline said, moving the kitchen chairs to form an arc around her. "I dare you to get through that," she said as she returned to the sink full of last night's dishes. It had been Jessica's turn to wash them, and she'd conveniently forgotten.

Madison toddled over to the first chair, climbed up, and held onto the back, shrieking as her little fingers gripped the spindles. Right behind her, Andrew dropped his bottle on the floor and followed, though he wasn't quite as adept at climbing. After a couple of tries, he too was successful, and both babies jumped up and down on the chairs, screeching like a couple of caged monkeys.

Caroline fit the last dish into the washer and closed the door. She turned around, shaking a finger at Madison and Andrew. "You two—" The words caught in her throat. She wasn't used to seeing just the two of them together. At family gatherings there were always *three* babies to keep an eye on—Andrew, Madison, and *Mark*. Caroline's gaze slid to the clock on the wall. It was almost noon. His surgery should be well under way by now. She looked at the phone and wondered if she dared call to see how Jane was holding up. Caroline knew how she'd feel if it were Andrew having open-heart surgery. She reached for the phone.

She needs you. Jane needs you—right now. The thought hit Caroline so forcefully that without a second's debate she turned away from the phone and grabbed the diaper bag from the counter. Mom and Dad were at the hospital, but they weren't parents of a baby right now. They hadn't lived through having an infant in the NICU like she had last year. Jane needed her.

Caroline scooped Madison and Andrew off the chairs and ran to find her shoes.

* * *

Breathless, Caroline walked quickly through the hospital. It had taken her forty-five minutes to get the babies over to Karen's and then to get here, but it looked like everything was going well. Jane appeared calm as she sat between Mom and Dad on a couch at the end of the waiting room.

Caroline hurried over. "Hi." She held out a white paper bag. "I brought orange rolls. I know they're your favorite."

"Thanks," Jane said. She took the bag but made no move to open it. "Aren't you missing a couple of kids?"

"No worries. Maddie ran out of things to destroy at my house, so I took her over to Karen's. She said she'd keep her as long as you need. I wanted to be with you."

Their dad reached for the bag. "Well I, for one, *am* hungry." He scooted over on the couch, and Caroline squeezed in beside Jane.

"How you holding up?"

"Okay," Jane said, sounding anything but okay. "I'll just be so glad when it's over. Then we'll only have one more surgery to go, and that won't be for at least another year and a half."

"And Peter will be home by then," Caroline said, assuredly.

"He'd better be." Jane gave her a wry smile.

"Isn't that Mark's surgeon?" their mother asked, looking up from her needlework.

Jane nodded. "Yes." She rose from the couch, and Caroline and her parents followed. Together they walked toward the doctor. Jane rubbed her palms together nervously.

"Mrs. Bryant," Dr. Ray spoke as soon as they were close enough to talk. "We've got a room over here for you and your family. If you'll just follow me." He held his hand out to indicate the direction.

Jane didn't move. "How is Mark?"

Dr. Ray again pointed to the room on the far side of the waiting area. "We'll have more privacy in there."

"Why? Has something happened?" Jane's voice trembled.

Caroline placed a gentle hand on her shoulder. "Come on. It's okay."

The four followed Dr. Ray into one of two smaller rooms. A nurse joined them, shutting the door after they were all inside.

"Please, have a seat," Dr. Ray said.

"How is Mark?" Jane asked again. "Is the surgery over? Were you able to connect the artery—?"

"Mrs. Bryant," Dr. Ray said. "We have many things to tell you. Please, sit down."

Caroline took Jane's hand and tugged her into the closest chair. She sat down beside Jane, and her parents took their places on either side.

Dr. Ray pulled up a chair of his own and sat directly across from them.

"As you know, most babies with Mark's condition have the Bidirectional Glenn Procedure at around six months of age. With him, we had to wait because of his other problems, and simply because he hadn't gained enough weight and his heart wasn't big enough."

Jane nodded. Caroline kept hold of her hand and squeezed gently.

"The problem with waiting as we did—and I believe we discussed this at several of his appointments—is that—"

"The single ventricle is overworked longer," Jane finished. "I know all of that. How is he now? Did something go wrong with the surgery?" her voice escalated, and Caroline could tell her sister's worry was edging into panic.

"The ventricle was worn out. He had a heart valve infection on top of that." Dr. Ray's words were quiet—sad.

"But he took the antibiotics," Jane said. "I made sure of it. He never missed a dose."

"The endocarditis has probably been present for some time," Dr. Ray said. "The antibiotics were simply too little, too late." He leaned forward, elbows on knees, a pained expression on his face. "Mrs. Bryant, Mark's heart failed during the operation. He—"

"Failed!" Jane rose from her chair, tugging her hand free from Caroline's. "How long was it stopped? Is he all right? Is he going to have brain damage?"

"He didn't make it through the surgery, Mrs. Bryant." Dr. Ray also stood. "We tried for over twenty minutes to revive him, but the combination of the overworked ventricle and the infection was too much for your son's heart."

Jane's hand covered her mouth but it didn't muffle her anguished sob.

The doctor's words shocked Caroline, but she forced herself out of the chair and wrapped a comforting arm around Jane, who was shaking.

"Who's with Mark now?" Jane demanded. "Are they still trying? There must be something? Do *something!*"

"I'm sorry, Mrs. Bryant. But there is nothing more we can do. If there was, believe me, I would be in there now."

"No!" Jane wailed. "No, you're wrong! I was just playing with him this morning. He was healthy. He was fine."

"Mrs. Bryant," the nurse said calmly, "Mark wasn't healthy. His heart has been struggling since before he was born, and the evidence of infection we saw today indicates that it could have failed anywhere. That it happened here—with Dr. Ray and his medical team able to do all they could—instead of at your home or the park, is something to be grateful for."

"Grateful!" Jane screamed. "There's *nothing* to be grateful for when your son's heart fails." She swung her gaze over to Dr. Ray. "I want to see another doctor. I want to see Mark. I want my baby."

Dr. Ray nodded.

"It might be better if you took a minute to yourself first," the nurse suggested, holding out a box of tissues.

Jane shook her head angrily. "No. I have to see him right now." Behind her, Caroline heard their mother crying softly.

"Jane," their dad said quietly. "I think the nurse is right. Let's give ourselves a minute—"

"No, Dad." Jane stepped free from Caroline's embrace. "You can stay here, but I have to go. Mark needs me." She moved toward the door.

"I'll go with her," Caroline said.

"All right." Dad said, looking toward their mom with concern. "I'll be along as soon as I can."

Caroline followed Jane toward the door.

"I'm very sorry, Mrs. Bryant," Dr. Ray said quietly as they left the room.

They followed the nurse, but soon the hallways and doors blurred as they walked past. Caroline felt her tears rolling down her cheeks. She glanced at Jane and was surprised to find her face unnaturally pale but completely devoid of tears.

Finally the nurse stopped outside one of the doors. "Take as long as you like," she said. She looked at Caroline. "Perhaps you can assist with the necessary arrangements afterward."

Caroline pressed her lips together and nodded. The nurse held the door open for them, and Jane practically ran inside, then stopped beside the bed. Caroline prayed for strength as she followed her.

Looking tinier and more fragile than ever, Mark lay still and lifeless on the long table. His eyes were closed, his hair matted from the surgical cap. A single sheet was tucked up to his chin, and Caroline was grateful that all evidence of the surgery had been removed.

Jane reached out and touched his cheek. "He's cold," she whispered. "He needs another blanket." She turned back to the nurse. "Could you get him another blanket, please?"

The nurse sent a pleading glance toward Caroline, then backed out of the room.

"Jane," Caroline began. *What can I possibly say?* She swallowed the lump in her throat. "I'll get him one." She turned away, hand over her mouth, holding back a sob.

"And bring his teddy bear," Jane said. "I just gave it to him this morning."

Caroline nodded mutely. She stepped out into the hall to try to compose herself. When she looked up a minute later, her dad was coming toward her.

Gratitude coursed through her, sending more tears cascading down her face. She wasn't strong enough to help Jane by herself. "I don't know what to do," she admitted to her father as he stopped outside the door. "I think she's in shock."

"We all are," her father said, kissing Caroline's forehead quickly before walking into the room.

Caroline watched through the glass window as her dad went to Jane. He put his arm around her, and the two stood that way, looking down at Mark's body as the minutes ticked past on the clock. Tears tumbled down Caroline's face, and she brought her hand to her chest, feeling her own heart ache for her sister. For Mark, Peter . . . all of them. Blindly, she turned away and somehow made her way back to the waiting area. Her mother was nowhere to be seen, but Caroline found the teddy bear, and she brought that, along with another blanket, back to the room.

Taking a deep breath, she pushed open the doors and went inside. Her father and Jane stood just as they had ten minutes earlier.

"I brought the things you asked for," Caroline said quietly.

Jane reached for the blanket. Caroline walked to the other side of the bed and helped her lay it carefully over Mark. When they were finished, she handed Jane the teddy bear. Jane hugged it to herself for a brief second, then placed it on the bed, her face close to Mark's.

"I don't think he's going to wake up," she said at last, her voice choked.

"He's not, honey," their dad said. "But he's in a better place—no pain. Surrounded by those who love him."

"*I* love him," Jane said. She bent and kissed Mark's forehead, then turned into her father's embrace and wept.

Chapter Seventy-Four

Peter looked out the right side of the Apache. He didn't need his night-vision helmet to see the spectacular display lighting the distant city.

"Looks like Fallujah is having a late Fourth of July celebration," Raymond, his copilot and gunner, remarked dryly.

Peter grimaced. "Somehow, I don't think they're feeling all that celebratory about America just yet."

"You're probably right," Raymond said.

Peter checked their coordinates on the computer once again. Cruising along at 140 miles per hour, the thirty-mile trip from Baghdad International Airport took only minutes. But it was the third such trip they'd made tonight, and he was tired. He spoke into his headset. "A little farther and we ought to see the unit we're supposed to cover."

"Near Al-Askari," Ray confirmed. They both already knew the coordinates, but after flying upward of five hours, talking kept them focused.

The Apache banked left and continued toward Fallujah. Peter stifled a yawn. He was anxious to complete this assignment and return to base for some sleep. That was the best part of his day now—sleep and dreaming of Jane. He still got the adrenaline rush from flying—especially when it was on the dangerous side—but with Jane he'd experienced something infinitely better, a high he hadn't come down from. He held onto that every night in his dreams, often falling asleep with their wedding picture in his hand.

As they drew closer to the city, the antiaircraft fire grew heavier. Pete wasn't worried. As he'd reassured Jane many times, the Apache Longbow was a flying tank. He was sitting on a bulletproof Kevlar seat, mounted on a thickly armored floor. The Longbow's smart-shooter radar located, assessed, and retaliated at almost all enemy fire before it could reach them. He felt safer in the air than he did sleeping at the base.

"First target lock on," Ray spoke into his headset.

"Go get 'em," Pete said.

"Bye-bye warehouse." A rocket fired from the pod on the right side of the Apache. At the same moment, the helicopter swung wildly to the left. "What was that?" Ray yelled. Behind him, Pete tried to get the Apache back in control.

"Tail rotor," he said, grappling with the controls as the helicopter spun wildly. "She's slowing—acting like she's jammed."

"Someone's sending out the welcome mat in the form of a couple of rocket-propelled grenades," Ray said. "Get us up."

"I'm trying. Just take care of those rockets." Pete lowered the nose, and the Apache's spin slowed as it banked away from the city.

"Done," Ray said a few seconds later as he affectionately patted the equipment in front of him.

Pete felt some of the stress leave his body. "You fired from the right, didn't you?"

"Yep, and it wasn't a Hellfire," Ray said. "What're you thinking?"

"I don't know." Pete attempted to get the tail rotor going again. Their most recent training had included an update on the problems some of the Apaches had when firing Hellfire missiles from the left pylon. Following the launch of a missile, fragments had flown into the tail rotors of at least two of the AH-64Ds, causing the rotors to jam. Consequently, they were now only launching from the right. Up to now, there had been no problems with the rockets. Was it possible they'd been hit?

Their altitude had steadied, and Pete put the Apache into hover mode.

"We gotta go back," he said, his voice somber.

"Back to base or back there?" Ray asked, jerking his head toward the distant lights of Fallujah.

"Back there," Pete said. "I can't maneuver as well, but we're only a couple of minutes out, and that unit is counting on us. You know what the sarge says."

Ray sighed. "'When we're flying, our men on the ground aren't dying.' Let's do it."

With much more care this time, Pete turned the Apache around and headed back toward the city. They'd take out the targets they had to and then get back to base. Tired as he was, he was eager to find out what had happened to his tail.

"You gonna radio base and tell them?" Ray asked.

"Yeah—when we're done," Pete said as he mentally reviewed the most recent Apache losses. The stats were heavily on their side. Still, this flying with one rotor was a whole new ball game. He thought of his dad—he'd probably had a temperamental bird to deal with all the time.

"Second lock-on," Ray said quietly. Around them, bullets pierced the air. The few that hit were not a concern—they would do little more than nick the surface. It was the bigger stuff they had to worry about. Pete kept his eyes glued to the panel in front of him.

"Third target," Ray said. "Oh, baby, here they come. Can we go any high—?"

Before he could finish his sentence, a powerful force hit the side of the Apache. She keeled and began to spin again.

"Base, this is AH-17. We've had a direct hit," Ray's voice shook. "Unable to complete mission. Returning to—"

Pete swore as the Apache lurched forward, losing altitude quickly. "Now the main's going out. What're the odds?"

His hands gripped the controls as the helicopter rushed toward the desert floor. "We're gonna hit."

In the seconds before impact, he calculated the distance they were from Fallujah and the hours left before dawn. If they survived the crash, it would only be a matter of time before they were found—by the enemy.

Chapter Seventy-Five

Jane woke with a start. Disoriented, she sat up on the couch and rubbed her eyes. They felt puffy, and her head hurt—the terrible aching kind of hurt she always got after a good cry. Her hands stilled on the blanket covering her lap, then clenched around the crocheted edge as memory returned with vicious force.

Mark.

She closed her eyes as the room spun dizzily. Images from the day before replayed through her mind. *Mark, looking small and fragile in the hospital gown as he played with his new teddy bear. Mark crying as they'd wheeled him away. Mark, still and lifeless on the operating-room table.*

Jane struggled to breathe as a crushing weight seemed to squeeze the air from her lungs. She couldn't shake it off, nor could she shake the last, imagined scene from her mind—*Mark, her little baby boy, alone and cold in the hospital morgue.*

Burying her head in her hands, Jane leaned forward, letting the tears fall silently.

Across the room in her parents' den, Madison stood up in the port-a-crib. "Da-da," she babbled, happily unaware of the crisis surrounding her.

Peter. As desperate as Jane was to hear his voice, she dreaded his phone call and the burden she would have to share. Wiping her eyes, she pushed the blanket aside and slid from the couch. Uncertain whether she had the strength to stand, she crawled across the floor to Maddie, who clapped her hands and held her arms out expectantly.

"Da-da," she said again.

"Oh, Maddie, how am I ever going to tell your daddy?" Tears coursed down Jane's cheeks. She lifted Madison from the crib, knelt on the floor, and held her on her lap.

Head bowed, Jane offered a quiet, desperate prayer. She thanked Heavenly Father for her beautiful little girl and the time they'd both had with Mark. Then she pled with Him for comfort and understanding. *Help me know how to tell Peter,* she said. *And when I do, please send Thy comfort to him. He's all alone over there, and he has a job to do and needs to stay safe.*

She finished her prayer just as her father came into the room.

Her dad put an arm around her and pulled her up into a hug. She saw his own eyes glistening and watched his Adam's apple bob as he swallowed. Jane knew her parents—her whole family—were devastated by Mark's death.

Her father's voice was gruff as he spoke. "You need to come with me in the other room, sweetheart. There's someone—this isn't going to be easy— it isn't—" His voice broke off as he tried to compose himself. Jane was touched by his obvious love for his grandson.

She took a deep breath as she leaned into him. She sniffed loudly, thankful that, for the moment, anyway, her tears had subsided. "It's okay, Dad. I was expecting our social worker today. She's always been very kind."

He shook his head and tightened his arm around her. "It isn't social services, Jane. It's someone from the military."

Chapter Seventy-Six

The last rays of twilight slanted across the patio, catching the sparkle of Jane's diamond. Her heart ached as she looked down at her wedding ring, checking once again to make certain it was real. The proof was there, but it did not alleviate the fear that her entire, brief marriage would fade away into bittersweet memory.

Unless Peter came home.

Hands shaking and feeling dizzy again, Jane took a couple of steps backward and sank into the nearest chair on her parent's patio. She closed her eyes, waiting for the spell to pass, and when she opened them again, the first thing that caught her attention was a scrap of red wrapping paper stuck to the wrought iron table. Jane reached for it, then clutched it in her hand, another piece of evidence, indisputable proof that Peter existed. His fingers had touched this paper. If, despite weather, active grandchildren, and her mother's cleaning, the paper remained all these weeks later, then surely he too had survived . . .

Jane let her gaze drift around the yard, remembering when it was filled with tables and family. Food and presents. Laughter and love. Peter and Mark. If she could go back to that night, she'd hold onto them both and never let go. But she'd already had to let go of Mark. This morning she had kissed his forehead one last time. This afternoon she had watched as his tiny casket was lowered into the ground beside Paul's. Tonight, along with the crushing sorrow, she felt the smallest measure of comfort, knowing he was with his parents.

The last blessing her father had given Mark at the hospital had promised that his parents would be with him to comfort him throughout the procedure. With all her heart, Jane believed that Tami and Paul had been there to take their son from this world back to his heavenly home. Clinging to that knowledge was all that had gotten her through the past five days. His body was resting, but his spirit—that sweet little spirit that had so blessed her life—was home.

What haunted her now—what she needed to know and understand— was if Peter was there with him. Had her father's blessing about Mark's parents meant Peter as well? With the time difference in Iraq, Jane realized his helicopter had gone down sometime toward the end of Mark's surgery.

Was *that* part of Heavenly Father's plan—that both father and son be taken home at the same time?

Jane brought her hands to her mouth, lips pressed together as she attempted to halt another flow of tears. She didn't know if she could endure losing Peter as well. And hadn't Heavenly Father promised He would never test her beyond what she could endure?

"I can't," she whispered. "I can't lose them both." Wrapping her arms around her middle, she rocked back and forth on the chair. "Please," she begged. "I can't."

The back door creaked, then swung open and Robert Warner stepped outside. His wife followed, concern in her eyes as they looked at their youngest daughter.

"Jane."

"No, Robert." Marsha placed a hand on her husband's sleeve. "It won't help anything. Look at her—she's overwhelmed already."

"It's closure," Robert said quietly as they crossed the patio toward Jane. "We don't have a choice but to tell her."

Jane lifted her tear-streaked face. "What are you two whispering about?"

"There are some leftovers when you feel like eating," Marsha said. She gave a last, pleading tug on her husband's sleeve.

"Caroline just called." Robert pulled up a chair beside Jane. "There was a report on CNN about an Apache that went down a few days ago. A militant group has pictures . . ."

Jane gripped the arms of her chair. "Was it Peter? What did—?"

"It isn't good," her father said.

"It's on! It's on again." Karen poked her head out the back door. "Dad, they're replaying it—" She stopped short. "Jane. I didn't realize you were out here."

Rising from her chair, Jane ran toward the house. "Do they have Peter? Is he alive?" She pushed past Karen and ran into the family room. Blurred images paraded across the television, and Jane knew it was more than just her watery eyes causing the pictures to appear so grainy.

She felt her father's hands on her shoulders as the British reporter explained what they were seeing.

"—the group claiming responsibility for Thursday's crash outside of Fallujah is also claiming that both pilots are dead. It is believed this footage was shot early Friday morning."

One of the men in the video held his fist out toward the camera, two sets of dog tags jingling in the air. The camera swung back toward the grounded helicopter, which was keeled over on its side. Jane gasped at the blurred images of the two bloodied soldiers within.

"—the U.S. military has not confirmed that these are the two pilots who were listed as missing in action late Thursday night, but there have been no other reports of Apache losses since then."

The three men in the video continued to shout, fists pumped in the air, celebrating their victory.

Jane felt nauseated and faint all at the same time. She stumbled backward, and her father caught her as the final image of the helicopter faded to complete black.

Chapter Seventy-Seven

Jane wrapped a blanket around her shoulders and stepped out into the cool night air. Gathering her courage, she began climbing the ladder that was propped against the back of the cottage. When she reached the roof, she scooted away from the edge and lay back on the new shingles—shingles Peter had laid himself in the weeks before their wedding.

"Where are you?" Jane whispered to herself, the night, and God. The ten days he'd told her to wait had already come and gone. Peter's copilot had been found dead near the wreck of their downed Apache. But they had yet to recover Peter's body. It had simply vanished. Was that the sign he'd left for her? Was she supposed to believe he was dead?

Sitting up, Jane hugged her knees to her chest. She thought of Peter's mother and how she must have felt, wondering all those years what had happened to her husband. Jane couldn't blame her for her inability to move on with life. Some things there was no getting over.

Like Peter . . . and Mark.

Jane let her sorrow shift from her missing husband to the loss of their son. Two weeks after Mark's funeral she still felt numb, though the ache in her heart grew each day as she faced the reality of life without Mark. She yearned to hold him again, to feel his baby-soft face nestled against hers, to hear his laugh.

Even Maddie had seemed lost the past two weeks as she toddled around the house and then the cottage where Jane had fled in an effort to escape the constant reminders of Mark. Maddie's playmate was gone, and she knew it. Without her companion, she had taken to mischief of all sorts—getting into everything her little fingers could reach. Instead of being angry, Jane was grateful for the distraction. It was difficult to unlearn the pattern of caring for *two* babies. Maddie's antics, at least, helped fill a small part of that void.

A drop of rain touched Jane's cheek, and she looked up at the overcast sky, thinking again of Peter. Hope stirred in her heart, and she could not tamp it down. She bowed her head and prayed for strength, then thanked God for the rain, for the clouds, for the past week of misty Seattle nights permitting her no chance for counting stars.

Part Three

Last Comes Love

Chapter Seventy-Eight

Holding the phone in the crook of her neck, Jane glanced at the flight times on her September calendar. She needed to hurry.

"I haven't changed my mind, Mom." Jane rushed around, shoving things in the diaper bag, grabbing a couple of bottles from the fridge. "I'll be fine, and I'll be that way because Maddie is with me."

"But you've never traveled with a baby," her mother protested. "And a six-hour flight—"

"She's all I've got left, and I can't bear the thought of being away from her for three days. Besides—" Jane stopped. Leaning on the counter, she took a deep, steadying breath.

I will not cry. I will not *cry,* she thought fiercely. She spoke into the phone again. "Mom, you and Dad have been wonderful. Everyone has. I couldn't have made it through the last few weeks without such a great family. But I *have* to do this, and taking Madison with me is the right thing. I want to be able to tell her about her father someday, to have her know she was there to honor his name." Jane paused, expecting to hear her mother agree with her. Instead Marsha protested again.

"She'll never remember, Jane. And Washington D.C. is no place for a baby."

"It's more than bringing her to honor Peter," Jane admitted quietly. "Taking care of Madison helps keep me focused on what I have—not what I've lost. I'm afraid if I stop—even for a day or two—I'll fall apart." Jane listened as her mom finally accepted her decision and dished out some last-minute travel advice.

"Love you too, Mom. I've got to go or I'll miss the ferry. Don't worry about us. I'll call you when we land. We'll both be okay." Going to the bedroom to retrieve her suitcase, Jane prayed she was right.

* * *

Jay felt his heart pounding as he walked down the aisle to the last row of seats. Since seeing the for-sale sign in Jane's yard two months earlier, he hadn't been certain she'd be on the ferry this morning. But, early and predictable as she always was, Jane sat in the far seat by the window, her back to him. Her brown hair was longer than it had been a year ago, and it lay smooth and shiny, pulled back in a simple ponytail at the nape of her neck. He allowed himself a brief fantasy of untying the yellow ribbon that held it in place and running his fingers through the silky tresses as they sprang free.

Instead, he sat down opposite her, on the far end of the row, near the aisle. He would wait for her to notice him. Unfortunately, after several minutes, it became apparent Jane's mind was elsewhere. She wasn't looking anywhere but out the window or occasionally at the toddler in her lap.

Jay chuckled to himself. Apparently, Jane had remembered he'd told her to bring her sister and/or her sister's kids for protection. He glanced around the ferry but didn't see any sign of Jane's sister—and he was pretty sure he'd recognize her. It was difficult to forget the face he'd seen staring him down from the other side of a minivan steering wheel. Her voice was etched on his memory as well—it had scared him when, gunning the engine, she'd rolled down the window and threatened to run him over if he ever went near Jane again. He was pretty certain she'd meant it. As she drove off, the driver's side mirror had nicked him, and one of her kids had thrown a rock out the window that hit him in the legs.

Jay scowled at the memory. The little girl on Jane's lap looked harmless enough though, so he decided to take his chances before the ferry ride was over. Standing, he glanced down at his suit coat to make sure it was buttoned right and his tie was straight. Quickly he crossed to the other side of seats and walked toward the window.

He eased into the seat beside her. "Hello, Jane."

She turned to him, confusion in her eyes for an instant before recognition dawned.

"*Jay?*"

He'd succeeded in surprising her. He reveled in the moment as she took in his appearance—from his short hair and his suit down to his polished wingtips.

"I'm glad you remembered," he said. "A year is a long time, and I was afraid you might have forgotten—or met someone—any number of things," he rambled on. "But you're here, and you look fantastic." He caught her gaze. "Gorgeous, actually. Ravishing."

"I—" She looked like she was about to cry. "You look—different. Nice. Great."

She seemed to be having trouble putting words together, and he took that as a good sign. "I see you don't have the personals with you like last year. I'm glad. You deserve better than that, Jane." He saw her stiffen and he quickly changed tactics. Glancing at the little girl on her lap, he asked. "Whose baby?"

Jane's eyes flooded with tears. "Mine."

"You're joking, right?" But even as he said it, he knew she wasn't. He tried to hide his own shock and resisted the impulse to wipe away the tear trailing down her cheek. "Um . . . last year—when we met on the ferry— you never said anything about a kid."

"Your fault," she managed to choke out.

As baffled by her tears as he was her baby, Jay tried to lighten the sudden and serious turn their conversation had taken. "Hey, I'd love to take the credit, but believe me, I'd remember if I was involved in anything like that." *It's been my fantasy for how long?*

Jane didn't laugh, or even smile. "Your fault," she repeated as a full-fledged sob escaped her throat. "You teased me, so I answered an ad in the personals." Her tear-filled eyes met his.

"And now, I'm a widow and a mother."

* * *

Jay shut the driver's side door of the Jeep and leaned in close to Jane. "I'm going to follow you to the airport," he said. "Just to make sure you're all right."

"You don't have to—really," she assured him.

"I'm going there myself." He reached into his coat pocket and withdrew his itinerary. "My flight doesn't leave until tonight, but I can hang out and get some studying done."

She looked up at him. "You were going to see me today and then . . . Just leave?"

He gave her a half smile. "I had hope," he confessed. "I paid more for a completely refundable ticket, so I could stick around longer if you were interested."

"I'm sorry, Jay."

He patted her shoulder. "Don't worry about it. Listen, park in long-term, but instead of taking the shuttle, I'll give you a lift to the terminal. I've got to return the rental car anyway."

"Okay. Thanks."

He stepped back from the car, giving a wave. He walked along the deck, making the way to his own vehicle, several cars behind. Reaching the car, he pulled keys from his pocket and climbed in, noticing his guitar and briefcase in the backseat. He'd need to move those to the trunk so Jane could fit her daughter's car seat in. *Her daughter.* The words stuck in his mind, blocking out everything else like an enormous boulder might block a mountain road after a landslide. Jane had a daughter—never mind that she hadn't given birth to her. She might as well have, because she was *married* too. And again, never mind that her husband was MIA in Iraq—considered dead now. Jane still loved him, was completely torn up about his death and the death of *her son* three weeks ago.

Son. Daughter. Husband. The words bounced around in Jay's head. He was stunned. It was all he could do to safely drive his car off the ferry, find Jane, and follow her.

He'd worried she might meet someone over the course of the year, but in his wildest dreams he'd never expected this. Nor had he expected her to burst into tears a minute into their reunion and proclaim the whole thing his fault—all because he'd taunted her to answer an ad from one of the poor saps in the singles section of the paper.

Jay restrained himself from banging his head against the steering wheel as he waited behind Jane at a red light. He'd been so stupid. He never should have teased her, and he should have written letters, called her—anything. Instead, he'd focused on making something of himself, becoming a man she could rely on, a man she might love.

And now, it was too late. Her heart and life weren't his to win. The passionate kiss they'd once shared no doubt paled in comparison to all she had shared with her *husband.*

Jay swore as he stepped on the gas. He was angry, hurt, disappointed—devastated. The day he'd looked forward to, lived for even, all year, had ended in disaster before even beginning.

He waited for Jane to park, then helped her load her luggage into the compact trunk of his car. It took some maneuvering.

"Sorry," she said, giving him a sheepish grin that set his heart racing. "You have to take a lot of stuff when you travel with a baby."

Baby. The word washed over him like a bucket of ice water. He walked around and opened the passenger door for Jane. She murmured a thanks, and he closed it without a word.

The short drive to the terminal was silent, except for the last seconds as they pulled up to the curb when Jane turned to him suddenly.

"Jay, you look wonderful. You *are* wonderful for helping me like this. I'm so proud of you for getting your life in order—going to school . . ."

He attempted a halfhearted smile. "Druggies aren't always stupid. Sometimes they're just temporarily mixed up by the hand dealt them." He turned the car off and hit the switch for the trunk.

"Yes, but *Harvard.*" She reached out, touching his sleeve. He looked over, and their eyes met.

"Yeah, well you started me out on the right path. After rehab, I finished up my bachelor's in two years, graduated magna cum laude, and scored 179 on the LSAT. I think it was my essay that clenched the deal, though."

"Oh?" Jane asked.

"I wrote about you," Jay said.

"Me?" her eyes widened.

He nodded. "About the difference you made in people's lives—in mine—and how I felt I could do that same thing as a lawyer." He shrugged. "Anyway, someone above was looking out for me or something, because I got in. It's been a great year. I love it." *And I still love you.*

"Your past probably will help you be a better attorney." Jane smiled. "And I hope you find an Elle Woods."

Jay's forehead wrinkled. "Who?"

"*Legally Blonde,*" Jane said, as if he should know what she was talking about. "You know, the movie about the girl who goes to Harvard Law School. At the beginning, she seems really ditzy, but by the end you see she's very nice—and intelligent too. I hope you meet someone like that."

Jay nodded. "Yeah, sure." He couldn't imagine himself with a blonde—ditzy, intelligent, or otherwise. For so long now, his heart had belonged to a beautiful brunette with captivating brown eyes and more kindness than anyone he'd ever known.

He climbed from the car and went to retrieve their luggage. Jane picked up her daughter and went to get a cart. He helped her load it and got her settled in line before he went to return the car. By the time he came back, she'd checked her luggage and was waiting just outside the security screening.

"Thanks again," she said awkwardly. The little girl struggled to get free, and Jane set her down a moment, letting her toddle the few feet her bright pink leash allowed. Leaning forward, Jane hugged him impulsively.

Unable to resist, Jay hugged her back—longer than she'd planned, probably—but it was all he was getting, so he intended to make it good. They finally broke apart, and he saw tears in her eyes again. He reached for his handkerchief.

"I'm so glad I saw you," Jane said. "Thinking about you doing so well will help me get through the next few days." She bent and scooped up her daughter, gave him a quick wave, then hurried off to the line of people wending their way through security.

As Jay returned the handkerchief to his pocket, his fingers brushed an envelope—Jane's invitation back into the graduate program. He pulled it out and stared at it, unable to believe he'd forgotten to give it to her.

"Wait," he called. "Jane, wait." He ran forward, but the uniformed guard stopped him at the entrance to the line.

"Ticket and identification?"

"I'm not flying until later," Jay said. "This is for my friend. It's important. I've got to give it to her—or you could—"

The man shook his head. "Step aside, please." He motioned to the next person in line.

Jay watched helplessly as Jane walked farther and farther from his sight.

"That's a beautiful little girl you've got there."

Surprised at the voice, Jay looked at the man standing beside him. He was an older gentleman with thinning hair, white at the temples, and a face full of wrinkles to match.

Leaning heavily on a cane, the man nodded toward Jane's retreating figure and added, "Course, with a mother like that, she's bound to be pretty. You're a lucky man."

No. I'm not, Jay thought. Out loud he said, "She isn't my daughter—that's not my wife. I wish she were, but . . ."

The elderly gentleman looked off in the direction Jane had gone, then turned back to Jay, studying him a moment.

"Could be though, couldn't they?" he said with a wink.

His suggestion struck Jay forcefully. Unable to think of a response, he watched as the man hobbled away, presumably to meet his own family.

Jane is single. Just because she didn't spend the past twelve months pining for you, like you did for her, doesn't mean this can't work out. You just had the best conversation of your life with her, and you're going to let her walk away? She needs you. And if you're here for her now—as a friend—then maybe, when she is ready to love again . . .

Jay's hand went to his coat pocket, feeling for his itinerary. His ticket *was* refundable. He had a few days until classes started again—enough time to accompany Jane on the most difficult trip of her life.

Pivoting on his heel, he grabbed his suitcase in one hand and his guitar case in the other and ran toward the check-in counter. Her flight wasn't scheduled to leave for another twenty-five minutes. Maybe there was still a seat left . . .

Maybe, just once more, fate would be on his side.

* * *

For the first time in her life, Jane was able to preboard an airplane. She'd always envied those parents traveling with small children who got to board first—not necessarily because they were first on, but because they had children—and today she was one of them. If only the occasion had been different, she might have enjoyed it. Maddie did look adorable in her smocked pink sundress and matching hat.

Feeling the chill of the airplane as soon as she sat down, Jane pulled Maddie's sweater from the diaper bag. She put it on her, then let Maddie stand beside her. Sitting for the six-hour flight was going to be long enough for a one-year-old.

Jane looked out the window, watching as the luggage was loaded on. She saw Maddie's port-a-crib on the conveyer and was glad to know that it would make it safely to Baltimore.

Be grateful for the small things, had been her mother's sage advice, and Jane kept to that counsel every day. Sometimes it was the only way to make it through without crying constantly. Everything reminded her of either Mark or Peter. She continued to look out the window, not trusting her emotions if she happened to see a baby boy or a couple traveling together.

"Good afternoon, ladies and gentlemen. We welcome you aboard flight 1260 with direct service to Baltimore. We'd like to advise you at this time that this flight has been overbooked, so it is possible you may need to check carry-on luggage with a flight attendant. Also, we are asking for volunteers at this time who might be willing to wait for a later flight. If you choose to do so, the airline will compensate you with a voucher for one round-trip ticket, good to any destination in the continental United States."

Jane picked up the diaper bag as the voice continued. She'd hoped to have the row to herself, but since that wasn't going to be the case, she might as well get what she needed ready now. Unzipping the bag, she pulled out the FAA-approved infant seatbelt attachment she'd bought and the bottle for Maddie to drink during takeoff. Every one of her sisters had advised her to make sure Madison was sucking on something when the plane took off and landed. Aside from the bottle, Jane had an arsenal of other treats in her bag—fish crackers, fruit snacks, Cheerios, and juice boxes.

Maddie had recently learned how to use a straw. *Another thing to be grateful for.* Juice boxes were cheaper and a lot easier to pack than multiple bottles.

The plane was nearly full when a woman sat beside Jane. She smiled at Madison, then took out a paperback and began reading.

Good, Jane thought. She wouldn't have to make conversation. Jane looked out the window again as people continued to move down the aisle.

"Excuse me, would it be possible to change seats? My seat is in first class, but I was hoping to sit back here and help my friend."

How nice, Jane thought. She turned to see who the lucky friend was. Jay stood in the aisle, a hopeful smile on his face.

"Jay!" she gasped. "What are you doing here?"

"Helping out a friend in need," he said. "I hope, anyway. I didn't think you should fly cross country and rent a car all by yourself with a baby in tow. I'm here to offer my services as an escort."

The woman beside Jane was eyeing Jay's first-class boarding pass. "I'll change seats, if it's all right with you." She turned to Jane.

Jane nodded. She didn't trust herself to speak. She watched through blurry eyes as the woman collected her things and got up. Jay handed his guitar case to a stewardess. Jane couldn't believe he was here, that he was doing this for her. A tear slid down her face and she struggled to think of something to keep the rest at bay. He sat down beside her.

"Hey . . . don't cry." He used his thumb to wipe away the tear trailing down her cheek.

"I'm not—I won't." She gave him a shaky smile.

"Good," he said. "Remember, if it wasn't for you I wouldn't be here or anywhere else. Your therapy group saved my life. Seems the least I can do is help you through a rough part of yours."

Chapter Seventy-Nine

Jay leaned against the sedan, his eyes traveling across the street to the edge of Arlington National Cemetery and Jane. She sat on the podium, perfectly poised, her legs together, ankles crossed, and wearing a black suit that fit her slender body like a glove. Her daughter lay asleep in her arms, her little yellow sundress a sharp contrast to the somber clothing of the adults around her.

Jay admired Jane's spunk at bringing Madison along. Everyone—from the aide sent to greet Jane at the airport to the president himself—had seemed surprised she'd brought Maddie. The television crews would eat it up—if they were allowed to get to her. A tragic story made that much more dramatic with the appearance of the now-fatherless little girl. Fortunately, the press were strictly prohibited from the ceremony. The only thing Jay had seen in the *Washington Post* was a short piece about President Bush honoring two fallen pilots whose heroic efforts had saved dozens of ground troops in Fallujah. The article focused on their important victory. Little to nothing was said about the two men who had died or the families they left behind.

It doesn't matter, Jay told himself. Jane had been very obviously touched after her meeting with President Bush this morning. Tomorrow, she'd fly home and start to put her life back together—putting the past year behind her. He intended to help her every step of the way.

If anyone knew about getting beyond a difficult past, he did.

He tried to imagine the agony Jane must be going through. Her heart had been shattered a dozen ways over the past few weeks. To her it must seem the only piece she held intact was the one belonging to her daughter, so of course she couldn't let go. More than anything, he wanted to go to Jane, to hold her in his arms and tell her it would be all right. She could cry on his shoulder, and he would kiss her tears away. He wasn't her heroic husband, but he could love her just as much.

He felt like he already did.

Jay sighed inwardly as he watched Jane stand and accept her husband's award. He had waited a year, and now it looked like it could take another for Jane to heal enough before she might be willing to look at him as more than a friend. The thought depressed him, but he knew he'd wait as many years as it took. She was worth it.

Looking over at the sedan parked behind the one he and Jane had arrived in, Jay saw the federal agents he had met earlier beside it, heads bent in earnest conversation. He smiled at them, half wondering if they'd looked him up and were discussing his criminal record. When he'd arrived with Jane, they had shown immediate concern. After all, he wasn't on the guest list.

Jane had explained he was an old friend, accompanying her for moral support, but Jay had sensed the agents didn't like his untimely appearance. Not wanting to add any stress to what was sure to be a difficult enough day for her, he'd quickly offered to stay behind and wait.

Now he watched as one of the agents finished a phone call and conferred with the other men. After a moment, two of them walked toward him.

Jay stiffened. *Great.* He was sick of his past coming back to haunt him. Were they going to ask him to leave? They had nothing on him—he'd been clean a long time, and none of his crimes had ever been violent. But where the president was concerned, the policy was likely, "Act first and, if need be, apologize later."

"Mr. Kendrich." A man Jay recognized as Agent Warrens held out his hand.

Jay shook it. "Is there a problem?"

"Yes, and no. We've just received a phone call, and we're hoping for your assistance."

Here goes, Jay thought grimly. "What can I do for you?"

The second man spoke up. "We thought it might be best—given Mrs. Bryant's fragile state—if you're the one who talks to her."

"About what?" Jay's eyes narrowed.

Agent Warrens cleared his throat.

"They've just found her husband."

Chapter Eighty

"Identifiable remains or are we talking an actual body?" Jay remembered Jane's tearful recounting of how her husband's picture and dog tags were flaunted on Iraqi television. That his body hadn't been recovered had led her to fear the worst from the militant group that likely had it. Jay didn't want to be the one to tell her that her husband had been beheaded or his body mutilated.

Agent Warrens' blue eyes pierced his. "Neither. He's alive."

Jay opened his mouth to speak but found no words. In one second his hope for a future with Jane vanished. He swallowed back bitter disappointment. "And you want *me* to tell her?"

"We thought it best . . ." Agent Warrens looked toward the podium. "After the program."

"No." Jay shook his head. Pushing aside his personal feelings, he let his protectiveness for Jane take over. "This can't wait. She needs to know right now." He turned away from the men.

Agent Warrens grabbed his arm. "I know how you feel, but it'll have to wait. There's a format and security—"

"Forget the format." Jay jerked free of his grasp. "And *you're* the security. Do you have any idea what Jane has been through in the past month?" He didn't wait for an answer. "Her son died on the operating table the *same day* her husband's helicopter was shot down. I don't want her to have one more minute of anguish. She deserves to know he's alive." *She deserves it. Jane deserves happiness,* Jay told himself. *Just keep focused on that and you can handle losing her again—for good.*

The two men looked at each other a long moment. Jay stood tense, knowing he'd risk sprinting across the lawn and screaming the news at Jane before they wrestled him to the ground if that was what it took. She would be so happy. He wanted that—wanted it more than his own happiness, he realized.

"We'd better come with you," Agent Warrens said at last.

"Let's go." Jay started across the lawn.

* * *

Jay juggled Madison awkwardly as Jane walked around the desk and sank into the chair Agent Warrens held out for her. Two other agents crowded the doorway of the small office. No longer needed as escorts, they stayed just the same, eager to witness the reunion of sorts—happy endings not being all that common in their line of work.

With shaking fingers, Jane picked up the phone. "Hello."

"Jane?" On the other end of the line, Peter's voice was hoarse.

"Oh, *Peter.*" Tears spilled from her eyes. "It's really you?"

"Yeah. You sound so good."

Her voice caught in a hiccup-sob. "You too. Are you all right? What happened? Where are you?"

"Iraq, I think—don't think I walked that far." He attempted a chuckle, but it turned into a cough that lasted nearly a minute.

"Peter," Jane said anxiously. "Are you okay?"

"Just a little banged up."

She wasn't convinced. "Tell me—"

"Nothing permanent," Pete assured her. "Just a broken foot, a couple of ribs, and my right arm and hand are messed up pretty bad. Nothing a little pampering from my wife won't take care of."

Concern etched her face. "Are you in pain? Did they give you something?"

"Little morphine," Pete drawled. "But I wouldn't let them turn it up until I talked to you. Though I'm starting to think they did anyway. Hey guys?" His words slurred.

Jane's mouth curved in a tender smile. "I love you."

"I love you too." He paused. When he spoke again, his tone had changed.

"They're going to transport me now, so I've got to go. Give Maddie a hug for me."

"I will," Jane said just before she heard the click on the other end of the line.

It wasn't until she'd handed the phone back to Agent Warrens that she realized Pete hadn't mentioned Mark.

Chapter Eighty-One

Jane waited as Jay returned from the checkout counter. "All set?"

"Yes. The flight leaves in two hours." Jay's palm felt sweaty on the envelope he held. "Can I buy you a drink or something before you go?"

She shook her head and shifted her daughter to her other hip. "No thanks. I'll need to get Maddie back for her nap soon."

"Oh. Of course. I guess life changes a bit when you have a baby."

She smiled. "Just a little."

He felt her hand brush his.

"I can't thank you enough, Jay." She had tears in her eyes.

"Well, don't cry again," he joked. "That's the last thing I want to make you do. And drink plenty of water this afternoon. You've cried at least an ocean or two the past couple of days." He squeezed her hand, then let it go.

"Humphrey Bogart," she said suddenly.

Jay's brow wrinkled. "Pardon?"

"You're Humphrey Bogart," Jane repeated as she looked at him tenderly. "In *Casablanca*. He sent the woman he loved to safety with her husband, while he stayed behind, risking imminent capture by the Nazis."

Jay looked around. "Hopefully I won't meet the same fate," he teased.

"It's my very favorite movie," Jane continued. "And what I mean is, you're a hero—kind and chivalrous. A man some woman is going to be very fortunate to find."

Jay shrugged and looked away.

"It's true," Jane said. "You'll find her, Jay. It just takes some of us a little longer than others." She leaned up on her tiptoes and gave him a kiss on the cheek. He pressed the envelope in her hand.

"Take care, Jane." He turned and walked away, not willing to let her see his own misty eyes and change her new, higher opinion of him.

Chapter Eighty-Two

"Careful," Jane advised yet again. Peter leaned on her as he hobbled down the front steps and across the yard. His leg was casted from knee to foot, and his right arm and hand were wrapped from his recent surgery. They still didn't know if it was successful—and wouldn't for several more weeks—but Peter was determined to try everything possible to avoid amputation.

Jane understood, and she encouraged him, but she didn't want either of them to get their hopes up too much. The latest limb salvage techniques, while promising, were still very new. Peter faced approximately a dozen surgeries over the next two years as internal rods would be placed in his arm, muscles would need to be transferred, and skin and vascular grafts had to be completed. That he might go through the entire process and still lose his hand, broke her heart.

But she had him home, beside her, and they were both so grateful for that.

Peter looked up at the sky doubtfully as Jane led them to the wood swing in the middle of the lawn.

"We'll never be able to see anything. Who planted all these trees?" he groused teasingly.

"I believe that was you, dear." Jane helped him sit.

"Just following my wife's orders."

"I wish you'd follow those orders a little better now that you're home." She tucked a blanket in around him.

"Stop treating me like I'm handicapped, woman." Peter lifted his good arm and pulled her close. They sat quietly a few minutes, neither daring to look up at the sky. "I've warned you," he said at last. "It might not be there—I've already seen it, you know."

She nodded. "Will you tell me now? Tell me everything that happened while you were missing."

"I'll try." He took a deep breath and released it slowly. "If you're sure you want to hear."

"Yes. I think it will help us both."

Pete took another slow breath and began. "After the crash I must have been unconscious for quite a while. When I finally woke up, I saw that Ray was dead, and the Apache was completely wrecked." Pete paused. "My head was throbbing, and there was blood all over the place. My arm had been crushed beneath the panel, and it was nearly useless, but I managed to get the emergency pack out and use the QuikClot to stop my bleeding."

He glanced at Jane.

"Go on," she urged. "I'm all right."

"After I'd patched myself up as best I could, I looked outside the Apache and could tell by all the footprints in the sand that we'd had company. I figured it couldn't have been our guys or they would have helped us. What I couldn't figure out was—assuming it was the enemy—why they hadn't finished me off." Peter shrugged his good shoulder. "But in case they were thinking of coming back, I got out of there quick. I couldn't walk, but somehow I managed to crawl along all that afternoon and most of the night until I was far away from the wreck—out in the middle of the desert—somewhere." Peter pulled his arm from around Jane, wincing as he shifted positions on the swing.

"It was freezing—more so when I finally stopped moving—so I burrowed myself in and slept all the next day. The next night I moved again. The compass I had didn't seem to work, and the pack was missing the emergency locator. I felt really out of it, even when I was awake." Peter reached up and touched the scar that ran across his hairline. "Fortunately, I've got a thick head, and something inside was still functioning. I had enough sense to ration the water and MREs from the kit, and that kept me going a few more days. The trouble was, I didn't know *where* I was going."

"But didn't you say you weren't that far from Fallujah when you crashed?" Jane asked.

"I wasn't. But I also wasn't myself. I slept a lot, and when I was awake, I think I was pretty delusional. I have no doubt I retraced my steps for at least a few of the miles I walked."

"So, you did that for *three weeks?*" Jane asked.

Peter shook his head. "No. Probably only about half that time. Then I used the last of my supplies, and I got hungry. A couple of times I thought I'd heard voices from my hiding spot during the day. I didn't dare find out who they belonged to, but one night I decided I didn't have much of a choice anymore. Instead of going away from the noises I'd heard that day, as soon as it was dark, I crept toward them. And I came across a family camping trip."

"Huh?" Jane said, turning to him.

Peter smiled. "Really. It was this Iraqi father and son. Though I don't think they were really camping—probably that was their regular living arrangement. Anyway, they helped me for a day or two—fed me and gave me some of their water. Then, despite our limited communication, I could tell they were ready to move on and my presence was endangering them. So we parted ways. I wandered around some more. When you've had a concussion and you're traveling across an unfamiliar desert in the middle of the night, it's pretty difficult to find your way."

Jane carefully lay her head against his shoulder. "Oh, Peter. We're so blessed. It's such a miracle you're home."

He nodded. "I'm living proof miracles haven't ceased. Mine happened one night—I wasn't sure how many had passed—as I lay there looking up at the stars. Out in the desert there are a million of them. They were comforting, something familiar I could hold onto. But that night the sky seemed different. I couldn't figure out what it was, and I was cold, tired, and scared. I hadn't eaten in about three days, hadn't had a drink for probably twenty-four hours. I was probably delirious, but to take my mind off of everything, I decided to count the stars." He paused, remembering the difficulty of that night. "Slowly—it must have taken an hour or more—I went through every constellation I knew, counting stars, tracing the lines in the sky as I'd memorized them. They gave me great comfort."

"And," Jane held her breath, knowing what was coming.

Peter's hand found hers. "I came to Arcturus, and then, nearly due south, Spica. Those two are so bright you can almost always see them, but that night, something was different." He looked over at Jane, who stared at him, spellbound by his story.

"Go on," she whispered.

"There was an extra star—even brighter—right between the two. For a minute, I wondered if it was mine—if it meant *I* would die soon. But then, as I lay there, I thought of you and Madison and Mark. I could see you and Maddie, but I couldn't see Mark. I couldn't find him in any picture I pulled from my mind, and then I knew . . . I was looking at Mark's star." Pete lifted his face to the sky.

"I looked at that star, and it seemed to be growing brighter and brighter—beckoning me. And I thought of your heart breaking not just once, but twice—and I knew I had to make it out of there. I got up on my knees and began praying. I prayed for a miracle, for something to guide me to safety. That was when I remembered your father's story about the Salt Lake Temple. He told me the north star is on the temple, symbolizing that the lost can always find their way by aid of the priesthood."

"I had what I needed already. I held the priesthood, and I knew that God knew about me. He was *mindful* of me—of you. I looked up at that star and said a prayer. Then I started crawling—didn't stop all night. When morning came, I stumbled into a ditch outside of town and happened upon the very troops our Apache had saved."

Jane blinked back tears. "Thank the heavens—literally."

"Look up, Jane." He pointed to the east.

She followed his gaze, and there beyond his outstretched finger, she saw them—three bright stars, all in a line.

"Only tonight," Pete whispered. "It's just for you, so you'll know Mark is okay now."

"I miss him so much. It still hurts so bad." Tears spilled from her eyes, down her cheeks.

"I know." Peter looked from the sky to Jane. "But he's not gone forever."

She turned her face to his.

He leaned closer. "Someday we'll hold him again. I promise. I know."

Chapter Eighty-Three

EIGHT MONTHS LATER . . .

Jay clapped loudly, then brought his fingers to his lips and let out a shrill whistle as he watched Jane walk across the stage and receive the diploma for her master's degree. His eyes followed her as she descended the steps. Walking toward her seat, she stopped halfway, blowing a kiss to someone in the crowd. Without turning his head, Jay knew who it was. Before the ceremony began, he'd seen her walk in with her husband and daughter.

Leaning back in his seat, he tuned out the rest of the program. He didn't know or care about any of the other graduates. He'd only come to see Jane. She'd sent him an announcement, and he'd felt that to complete the "Jane chapter" of his life, he had to see her walk. He needed to know that the pardon he'd gotten for her from the dean—allowing her back into school to finish her degree—had been successful. She was on track with her life, where she'd been before he messed it up for her.

The ceremony ended, and the crowd began to disperse. Jay lingered in his seat, knowing he was missing any opportunity he might have to see Jane once more. But it wasn't his place to be the one to give her flowers or to sweep her up in a hug and say how proud he was. His only responsibility now was to remain as she thought him to be—a kind, chivalrous, hero.

A smile broke out as he finally rose from his seat. He didn't think Jane's assessment of his character was completely on target, but he hoped she'd been right about one thing—about him finding someone . . . someday. Right now, it seemed a remote possibility, and Jay knew it would take someone special to make him forget the girl with pretty brown eyes who had saved his life and stolen his heart.

* * *

The spires of the temple rose up behind them, pointing heavenward. Peter tugged on Jane's hand to get her to stop a minute, and they turned around, looking up. Beneath the clouds, the statue of the angel Moroni glistened, and Pete wondered how he'd ever had a hard time believing. The gospel was a real, tangible thing in his life. When he thought of the emptiness of his life before, it terrified him.

"Go," Maddie said, patting his face.

"In a minute, Maddie." He couldn't stop looking at the temple.

"Everyone's waiting for pictures," Jane reminded him gently.

"I know." Pete looked down at her, a tender expression on his face. "We did a good thing here today."

She smiled. "Yes. I've caught you forever now."

He squeezed her hand. "Not just for us, but for Mark, Paul, and Tamara. My parents . . ." Pete's voice broke as he thought back to the moments he'd knelt across the altar from Jane, sealing not only their marriage, but his parents' marriage, and Paul, Tamara, and Mark. Absolute joy was the only word he could think of to describe his feelings then and now.

Maddie hung her head back, dark curls trailing down the back of her white dress. "Go, Daddy."

"All right," Pete said reluctantly. "We'll go now, Madison." He looked at Jane. "But we're coming back often. After all, that's always been number one on Mommy's list."

Next from
Michele Paige Holmes

SEPTEMBER 2005

"Pick anyone you want," Archer encouraged, nodding toward the stage where the women of the Harvard Ballet Company were rehearsing. "There's Brenda, the tall blonde in the middle, or Katy the one with—"

"I *don't* want," Jay interrupted. "So just forget it." He slouched lower in his seat.

"You must be blind." Archer waved a hand in front of Jay's face. "I'm offering you the best of Harvard right here—beautiful, talented women, and you won't even consider it."

Jay looked at his watch. "I'm going to head to the library. I'll leave the bike for you and Trish." He bent over, reaching for his backpack.

"No way," Archer grabbed the pack and set it a few seats away, out of Jay's reach. He looked at Jay. "You've hit the year mark. You've got to snap out of this. Besides, I promised Trish we'd double to Homecoming in the Yard this Friday, so you'd better pick a girl today. Otherwise all the good ones will be taken."

Jay scowled. "You shouldn't have promised Trish anything. The last thing I want to do is spend the evening riding a mechanical bull or eating pie with a bunch of freshmen. Anyway, I'm sure she'd rather have a night alone with you." The music for the ballet started and he leaned his head back, brushing his hair off his collar. He'd been letting it grow since June—when he'd attended Jane's graduation. Turning into a typical suit hadn't been enough to win her, so he saw no point in continuing the farce when, as far as he was concerned, there wasn't any other woman worth pursuing.

It wasn't that he hadn't tried. In an odd sort of way, seeing Jane with her husband had encouraged him to find someone he cared for as much as she did for Pete, someone he could build a life with. But the half dozen or so women he'd taken out over the course of the summer had completely turned him off of dating. He hadn't found one who could scratch the surface of Jane's compassionate and caring nature. And he certainly didn't think he'd find one here today—in Harvard's famed ballet company.

Archer elbowed him. "You're not even watching the rehearsal. I mean, come on, check out their legs, and—"

"No thanks," Jay said, cutting him off.

Archer grinned. "I'm telling you. You're missing out on life. If I'd have known what a stuffy old law student you are, I probably wouldn't have let you rent with us." He turned his attention back to the stage.

Jay glanced at his backpack a few seats away and decided it wasn't worth a scene or struggle to try and get it from Archer. Instead of going to the library just now, he'd close his eyes and indulge in a little nap. The music *was* soothing.

Archer elbowed him again. "Sit up and at least pretend you're interested," he ordered. Jay opened his eyes, glanced at his watch, and saw that twenty minutes had passed. The music had stopped and a break had been called. Trish waved as she left the stage and headed toward them, followed by a gaggle of tutued dancers.

Jay groaned.

"Hey Arch," Trish called, bending over the row of seats in front of them. She leaned close, giving Archer a juicy kiss.

"Hi Archibald," a girl behind her said.

Jay fought back a grin as he caught his roommate's scowl. Archer hated this slander of his name. Who wouldn't? Jay had thought on more than one occasion. But it came with the territory. Archer's dad—a comic enthusiast—had named him after his favorite character, Archie. Unfortunately or fortunately, depending on how you looked at it, when Archer was just three years old he'd developed his own enthusiasm—for the movie and stories of Robin Hood. Since then he'd been telling everyone he was an archer, and the name had stuck—mostly. Though the brunette standing beside Trish obviously thought Archi*bald* a bit more appropriate. *Poor guy,* Jay thought again. Archer *was* getting a little thin on top.

"Jay, I'd like you to meet Candice. And this is . . ." Archer looked to Trish for help.

"Melanie," Trish supplied, winking at Jay. "She's a political science major. You two might have a lot to talk about."

"Oh?" Melanie asked, raising her too-thin eyebrows.

"Jay's a third-year law student," Trish said.

"Ooh," the girls chorused.

"I'm planning to work for the government," Jay said, hoping to scare off the money seekers. "You know—a simple life of public service. Hopefully it'll be enough to pay off my thousands of dollars in student loans." *Gotcha,* he thought, noting several crestfallen faces. Archer's was one of them.

Nice, he mouthed to Jay.

Jay shrugged and shot him an innocent look.

"Well, we've got to get back," Trish said. "We've only got a few minutes for break. Wanna come with me to get a drink, Archer?" She ran her tongue over her lips seductively.

Jay looked away, disgusted. He and Jane never would have behaved like that. No sooner had the thought come, than he remembered the day so many years ago now—so why couldn't he forget—when he'd taken Jane's face in his hands and kissed her in the hall at work. She'd been fired from her internship because of that kiss, and he'd almost lost his spot in the rehab program. But at the time, that one kiss had seemed worth the risk. Jay looked at Archer and Trish as they walked away, considering for the first time that maybe they really were in love.

Rising from his seat, Jay leaned over and grabbed his backpack. He put one strap over his shoulder just as the piano started playing again—though this time it wasn't the ballet accompaniment he heard. Shrugging the strap onto his other shoulder, Jay looked toward the stage and saw that it was still empty. The entire auditorium was vacant, except for him and the unknown pianist at the front of the room.

The music continued as Jay made his way toward the aisle. The melody was haunting, unfamiliar . . . beautiful. Strangely moved by the notes, Jay hesitated at the end of the row, then removed his pack and sat down to listen. His classes were over for the day, and there really wasn't any rush to get to the library. If only Archer had brought him to a concert rehearsal instead of ballet practice, Jay probably wouldn't have balked at staying. Music had always been and continued to be the one, sure love of his life. And he would have bet money that the person on the other side of that piano felt the same way.

Jay closed his eyes, feeling the music as the piece hit a crescendo, then grew soft once more. He listened intently, noting the key change a few moments later as the music built again in fervor. He leaned into the aisle, trying to catch a glimpse of the pianist, but the instrument was angled such that he couldn't see who was behind it. He imagined it must be a woman and that she was bent over the piano, as he couldn't see the top of anyone's head.

"You're still here," Archer said, coming up behind him.

"Shh." Jay held a finger to his lips and nodded toward the front of the room.

"What?" Archer said, stepping over Jay to get to the seat next to him. "Are you deep in thought, contemplating which of those beautiful women you want to take to homecoming?"

Jay didn't reply but listened as the music trailed off into a few last, lingering notes. He heard the foot pedal release, and he jumped up. "I want to meet the pianist."

"That mousy thing?" Archer's mouth hung open. "Tell me you're not going to ask *her* out."

So it is a woman. Jay felt a stir of excitement. "Behind that piano is a very passionate female."

Archer shrugged. "Suit yourself then, but I don't think Trish will want to double with her."

"I didn't say date," Jay whispered. "I said *meet*." Though for as nervous as he suddenly felt, he might as well have been going on a date. He made his way toward the front of the auditorium, trying frantically to think of a good pickup line. Reaching the piano, he leaned forward over it, looking down on a blonde head.

"Do you take requests?"

The woman looked up, and Jay could see that he'd startled her. She held a pencil in her hand, and Jay glanced down at the clipboard resting on the keys. Penciled-in notes scrawled across staff paper that Jay could tell had been erased many times.

"I wondered if you wrote it," he said, feeling his excitement mount. "It was beautiful—you play beautifully."

"Thank you." Her voice was quiet. Behind oversized glasses, her blue eyes darted around nervously.

"My name is Jay." He held out his hand as his eyes quickly scanned the name typed at the top of the paper—*Sarah Morgan*. "I play the—" Someone tapped him on the shoulder. Thinking it was Archer, Jay turned around just as the woman gasped.

A fist met his left eye and he staggered backward. A second blow immediately followed the first, and this time Jay went down, blackness overtaking him just as the lights in the auditorium went out.

About the Author

Michele Holmes spent her childhood and youth in northern California and Arizona. After marrying her high school sweetheart in the Oakland California Temple (nearly 20 years ago!), they moved to Utah, and she now feels very blessed to enjoy a beautiful mountain view from her Provo home.

Michele graduated from Brigham Young University with a degree in elementary education—something that has come in handy with her four children, all of whom require food, transportation, or Band-Aids the moment she sits down at her computer to write.

In spite of all the interruptions, Michele is busy at work on her next novel. To learn more about her writing, please visit her website at michele paigeholmes.com or contact her via Covenant email at info@covenant-lds.com or through snail mail at Covenant Communications, Inc., P.O. Box 416, American Fork, UT 84003-0416.